THE THREAT OF A KISS

"I'm going to kill you, Dar." She grabbed Dar and pulled him close.

"But Jennifer—"

"Don't 'but' me," she growled, shaking him with her tiny hands. "Do you know you almost scared me to death? And furthermore—" Another shake. "You're scaring those little kids out there, too!"

"I admire your courage, Sprite," he told her as her hands wrapped around his wide neck. "Especially as you walked through the demons without even blinking. None of the women in Asgard—"

Her hands tightened and squeezed. Luckily, they were small and lacked the strength to do him any real harm. Dar leaned forward so she wouldn't hurt herself, but it brought him into contact with her body. He groaned as her perfume, an arousing floral scent, wafted around them.

"You don't know what you're doing Jennifer." In the blink of an eye, he had her hands at her sides.

"Let go of me, you—you Norseman!" Jennifer wiggled her body as she tried to break free of his hold. "Get off me and I'll show you what I'm *gonna* do to you. I'll get a frying pan and pound some sense into your head. Just you watch me. I'll—"

Dar leaned forward and silenced her threats with his mouth.

RAVES FOR JUDY DI CANIO'S *BELOVED WARRIOR*!

"*Beloved Warrior* is nonstop entertainment!"

—*Rendezvous*

"The creative talent of Judy Di Canio brings a stunning new voice in the time-travel genre."

—Sandra Hill, bestselling author of *The Bewitched Viking*

"Combining romance, time-travel, magic and adventure . . . Judy Di Canio's *Beloved Warrior* is sure to be a favorite for romance and fantasy readers alike."

—*CompuServe Romance Reviews*

"Judy Di Canio bursts onto the scene with a debut novel that will leave readers clamoring for more! *Beloved Warrior* is mystical, moving, and memorable. Don't miss this one!"

—Deb Stover, author of *Another Dawn*

"Judy Di Canio makes her stellar debut with this utterly delightful and exciting fantasy romance . . . *Beloved Warrior* captures Norse legend and brings it to life with an ideal blend of humor and intrigue to keep you reading from cover to cover."

—*Bookbug on the Web*

"With a sexy, powerful hero you'll want to claim as your own, *Beloved Warrior* propels you into an exciting, delightful and sensuous read from opening to end!"

—Kathleen Nance, bestselling author of *More Than Magic*

"Pick up *Beloved Warrior*, and plunge into the magic!"

—*Writers Club Romance Group* on *AOL Reviewer Board*

"An absolute delight! *Beloved Warrior* is warm, touching, funny, and a wonderful read! Judy Di Canio has arrived, and with this book, she really makes an entrance!"

—Maggie Shayne, bestselling author of *Infinity*

BELOVED WARRIOR

JUDY DI CANIO

LOVE SPELL BOOKS NEW YORK CITY

LOVE SPELL®

July 1999

Published by

Dorchester Publishing Co., Inc.
276 Fifth Avenue
New York, NY 10001

ISBN 0-505-52325-6

Printed in the United States of America.

Special thanks to my critique groups, both old and new. Also to Ron, my loving husband. Without his unswerving support, this book would not have been possible. And I can't forget my mom, Mary Anna, whose love of reading first started me on the path to writing.

BELOVED WARRIOR

Prologue

Valhalla, the Hall of the Slain

"I sense a trap," Lor whispered, leaning close to Dar so no one else could hear him.

Accustomed to his brother's predictions of doom, Dar sighed as he donned his ceremonial hat, then snapped a golden armband onto his left arm. He added another to his right.

"Don't worry. I defeated Loki once today, I can do it again," Dar replied, touching the leather cord that held the translation crystal around his neck. "I doubt the Trickster will show his face here. He knows all the spectators saw him drop his sword on the practice field and cringe like a newborn dragon."

"I disagree," Lor insisted as he helped Dar don his mantle. He secured it in place using an antique golden brooch adorned with a fire-breathing dragon, the symbol of their house. "The taunts Loki received from the other gods after the battle made him angry. Watch yourself. He does not forgive a slight, no matter how small. He's hinted several times that you cheated him, using your powers to defeat him."

Dar tightened his hand around his sword. "Loki knows 'tis against my vow to use my sorcerer's abilities in battle against any lacking in such powers. Are you sure he said this?"

"*Já.* I'm sure. I've heard it from several warriors. I wish you'd take a threat seriously for once instead of dismissing it. Knowing the Trickster, he's capable of anything."

"I'll be careful, Lor. Now hand me my bag of runes and my sword. Grandfather wishes to begin the ceremony." A flapping of wings near Dar's head announced the arrival of his pet dragon. "Ah, Firedrake. You arrive just as the food is being prepared."

Violet eyes, almost too large for the small green body, peered at him with more than a hint of anticipation. Dar pushed back his mantle and held out his arm so the baby dragon could alight.

"Soon, my fierce fire breather," he said affectionately. "Soon we shall sit at the tables and eat. Then you can have your pick of tasty oxen bones." He gestured for Firedrake to depart.

The dragon's wings spread wide and his clawed back feet pushed against Dar's arm. The newly hatched dragon flew around the large hall and settled on one of the thick wooden beams supporting the roof.

"Relax, Lor. I'll be careful. The war against the giants draws near. As head sorcerer, Odin will need me at his side, and I will not disappoint him. I vow it on the sacred caves. Now go. Take your place next to Father."

Mollified by the vow, Lor nodded.

Dar walked down the long hall past the narrow tables full of warriors. He didn't stop until he stood in front of his grandfather, Odin.

Odin stood and raised his arms into the air. His dark blue mantle parted to reveal the golden armor he wore. The ruler of Asgard commanded the attention of the warriors in the room; he immediately received it.

"Dwellers of Asgard, another day of battle practice has ended." Odin's deep voice reverberated through the hall. The shiny black patch over his left eye glittered in the light of a thousand torches. "I praise the victors for their bravery." He glanced at Dar. "You may begin, O powerful sorcerer."

Dar reached into his mantle and pulled out a crystal ball. He held it in the palm of his hand, bowed his head, and prepared to say the words of blessing over the meal. Each time he used his abilities, great power flowed through him, but Dar always sensed something greater, some piece of knowledge just out of his reach. One day, he would uncover that missing piece, and when that happened, he would be the most powerful sorcerer in Asgard.

"Wait!"

The order, given in a high-pitched voice, made Dar jerk his head around. His eyes narrowed as he surveyed Loki's thin, smiling face.

"O mighty sorcerer, I desire to show you, before Odin and the other gods, that I, Loki, harbor no ill feelings after being defeated at your hand." An innocent expression on his face, the Trickster glided closer. "To show my goodwill, I give you this priceless piece of crystalite." He took his hand from behind his back and showed Dar a multifaceted blue crystal that caught the light from the candles. "Use this to begin the ceremony."

For a long moment, Dar stared at the offering Loki held out to him. The stone reeked of untapped energy. Every fiber of his being warned Dar not to accept it. But to refuse the gift in front of so many witnesses would be viewed as a terrible insult. Dar reluctantly put his crystal ball back into the pocket in his mantle.

Loki set the palm-sized object in Dar's hand. By sheer willpower, Dar forced himself to accept the offering. It felt peculiar, as if part of it resided in another dimension. It took all his restraint not to toss the rock back into Loki's face.

How odd. The Trickster was not known for his generosity. As soon as the ceremony ended, Dar would check to see if anyone was missing such an object. It would be just like Loki to give him stolen property.

"Thank you, Loki. I accept the gift in the name of Odin."

Loki's smile grew so wide, Dar could almost count every tooth in his mouth. "*Já,* I insist. Please, begin the ceremony."

With an apologetic glance toward Odin, Dar began the incantation. "Oh, lords and maidens of Asgard." The crystal began to glow. "We sit in this hall on a glorious eve . . ."

The light brightened and pulsed in time to his heartbeat. He wanted to stop the blessing and switch stones, but to be forced to do so would be interpreted as an ill omen, one that could be taken to mean they would be defeated in the upcoming war. He wouldn't let either Odin or the warriors think such a thing, which was probably what Loki had hoped. As soon as he had finished the blessing, he would corner Loki and make him confess his prank in front of Odin.

Dar forced himself to continue, even though he wanted to hurl the crystal out of the hall. ". . . we practice daily to hone the skills of warfare so we may be sure to win the battle of Ragnarok, the Twilight of the Gods. . . ."

As if from a distance, he felt Firedrake land on his shoulder. "I, Dar, sorcerer of Asgard, do hereby condemn our enemies to a life in another time, another place. . . ."

The crystalite fell out of Dar's numb hand and crashed to the floor. Dar felt himself falling. The world exploded into a realm of heat and light. Darkness and pain. A swirling void sucked his body and that of his dragon into nothingness, shattering them into a million pieces. . . .

Chapter One

The long, winding roads of
Glenmoore, Pennsylvania

". . . another time, another place." Dar materialized slowly, limb by limb, the words of his incantation still lingering in his ears. As he became solid once more, he felt rain on his upturned face. The clasp of his mantle dug into the exposed flesh of his throat. His knee rested in a frigid puddle. It was twilight, the time when witches and demons roamed the world.

Dar leapt to his feet. He surveyed his surroundings. "I will tear Loki limb from limb and feed his liver to the dogs! To which of the nine known worlds has he sent me?"

He tried to call upon his powers, but it seemed as if a dark cloud prevented him from getting his energy from the sun. It looked as if he'd have to rely on his crystal ball and magical runes to cast his spells until he returned to Asgard.

Then he saw it: a creature unlike anything he had ever seen before. A large shadowy monster with blinding bright eyes approached him at a pace no mount he'd ever ridden could match. Ignoring the tingling pain in his arms, Dar unsheathed his sword.

"Valhalla!" His battle cry echoed off the trees and into the night. "This eve is a good time to die. Against all enemies of Asgard, I declare war!"

Jennifer Giordano kept a tight grip on the steering wheel of her Jeep and drove slowly down the narrow, unlit road. The light drizzle and fog hampered her vision. Her surroundings looked eerie, unearthly.

"This rain is a bad omen. I not only get laid off, but my boss also says I'm overqualified for a secretarial job," Jennifer muttered to herself as she negotiated a narrow curve. "It's a good thing the supermarket is on the way home. I just hope it isn't crowded, or Mom will be worried. . . ."

Jennifer bit her lip as she remembered that her mother wouldn't be waiting for her anymore. Six months later, and she still had to remind herself that her mother had died and wouldn't be coming back, ever.

A piercing pain returned in the place that had once contained her heart. She tried to think of the weather, the slick driving conditions. Anything was better than dwelling on her loss, or the fact that the bill collectors had begun to stalk her like predators, their beady little eyes glistening with anticipation.

At least the car was hers. It needed a new transmission, but that could wait until she had some extra money. Money. If she couldn't find a couple of elderly ladies to rent a few of the unused rooms in her house soon, she just might have to resort to selling her few remaining possessions. She needed to pay the more pressing bills and the mortgage.

She'd do anything to keep her mom's house from being put up for sheriff's sale, but she owed so much that it seemed even winning the state lottery wouldn't get her out of debt. What she needed was a big miracle. Sort of like Santa Claus, only not wearing a red suit. Just once, she wanted to be lucky. She wanted to be in the right place at the right time. . . .

A streak of lightning illuminated the sky and brought the scenery on either side of the road briefly into view. The long branches of the trees stretched out like the emaciated arms of an unearthly apparition. Then she heard it—the sound of a bear who had caught his foot in a wolf trap and was now looking for someone to blame. The glow, combined with the headlights, illuminated a large man standing directly in front of her Jeep.

"Oh my God!" Jennifer slammed on the brakes and swerved to the right. The wet leaves provided no traction. The last thing she saw was a massive brute with a large sword running toward her. Lightning seemed to flicker from the edge of the blade. She screamed as the Jeep slid into a ditch and her head hit the steering wheel.

"What sort of animal is this?" she heard the stranger ask moments later as he tried to open her door.

Dazed from the accident, Jennifer couldn't respond to his question. She fumbled for the door handle, but her numb fingers couldn't seem to grasp anything.

He finally got the door open. The cool breeze

helped keep her from slipping into unconsciousness.

"Are you a sprite?" His gentle fingers tipped up her chin. "You are too beautiful to be a witch, too tall to be a dwarf, and you're definitely not from Asgard."

Asgard? Where was Asgard? She tried to ask the question aloud, but no sound came out of her dry mouth.

"By the bloody jaws of Garm! No wonder you can't speak! Your animal has wrapped a tentacle around your body."

Although her vision was blurred, Jennifer saw the man slash at her seat belt. She groaned, a low tone that sounded remarkably like a sob. Her rescuer pulled her out of the car, laid her against a tree trunk, and knelt by her side.

" 'Tis the oddest clothing I've ever seen," he murmured as he checked for her pulse. "This loose tunic has strange fastenings. The rough blue leggings are surely too coarse to be worn next to your smooth skin."

Hadn't he ever seen dungarees before?

Gentle hands checked for broken bones and internal injuries. He pushed her shoulder-length brown hair out of her eyes. She could sense him staring at her face. "Such a beautiful sprite. Much too pretty to die on this miserable eve."

He had a nice voice, deep and oddly soothing. Was he a foreigner? Jennifer had once worked with a man from Sweden; this man's unusual accent seemed to indicate a similar Nordic background.

"I don't know if you understand my words, but I'm going to use my healing rune to close the wound on your forehead."

Now that he mentioned it, Jennifer could feel a

throbbing ache just above her right eye. Wetness—probably blood—covered the side of her face. Her stomach threatened to empty at the thought. She swallowed in an attempt to keep from embarrassing herself and closed her eyes as steady pain, formerly a dull throb, flooded her body.

"Energy of the gods, mighty forces of the nine known worlds, channel through me the power to heal all wounds. . . ."

Soothing warmth flowed through her as his hands touched her face. She arched her back and leaned toward his palm. Immediately she felt better.

Jennifer opened her eyes and stared into a pair of dark blue eyes with thick lashes. The eyes of a giant. A giant dressed for a pre-Halloween party. He wore a metal hat with horns, a loose cream-colored shirt decorated with golden thread, and some type of flowing purple cape that sparkled in the moonlight.

"Who are you?" she whispered, her voice wavering in spite of her attempt to sound normal.

The man touched the crystal around his neck and knelt there for a moment, as if waiting for something, before he replied, "I am Dar, warrior of Asgard, son of Tyr, grandson of Odin."

She stared at the sword at his side and the black knife in a scabbard at his waist. This guy was going to be trouble.

"Of all the people I could run into, why did it have to be a man who wears a sword?" When he didn't respond, she rubbed her hand across her eyes, wondering if he was a mirage.

"My sword's name is Glaervald. 'Tis raised only against those who would harm my world." His deep voice sent shivers up and down her spine. "Do you feel well enough to assist me, O beautiful sprite of the metallic monster?''

She tried to follow his odd speech. ''What?''

''I need of your help, mainly information about this strange land.'' His lips tightened. ''I must return to Asgard immediately and seek revenge on Loki.''

''Loki?'' Her voice rose nervously. ''Who is Loki?''

The stranger touched the crystal around his neck, as if seeking an answer in its clear depths. ''Loki, the Trickster, is the one who sent me here.'' He glanced around at his surroundings. ''By Odin's gold shield! I must know to which world I've been transported so I can locate the Bifrost Bridge, the link to my home.''

''You're in Glenmoore, Pennsylvania, not too far from Philadelphia.''

The giant frowned and touched his crystal again. ''Glenmoore. An odd name. *Nei*. That doesn't help.'' He absently rubbed the gem-studded hilt of his sword. ''It can't be Muspelheim, the home of the fire giants. As we aren't in a cave, it can't be the land of the dwarfs. And although 'tis dark enough to be Jotunheim, I don't see any witches or giants lurking about the night.''

She groaned and looked at her Jeep. ''I hit you, didn't I? That's why you're not making sense, right?''

He stared at Jennifer, pinning her to the tree with his gaze. ''Tell me more of this exotic land, O mystical sprite.''

''The name's Jennifer, and I think we should get you to a doctor immediately.'' He must have hit his head against the hood of the car. Yeah, that would explain it. He might even have a concussion. ''Do you feel faint? Nauseous?''

He rubbed his temples with big, blunt fingers. ''My

head throbs with a strange, pulsating rhythm, as if a horde of angry dwarfs used hammers on it.''

''I knew it,'' Jennifer muttered, unable to believe her bad luck. ''I *did* hit you. I'm so sorry.'' She groped in the leaves for her handbag, then realized it was probably still in the Jeep. ''Would you like to see my insurance card and driver's license?''

He tilted his head to the side. ''In-sur-ance card?''

Jennifer felt the blood drain out of her face. She had renewed her car insurance, hadn't she? Trying to recall whether the bill was still in the large stack of overdue notices sitting next to her toaster, Jennifer reassessed the situation.

''D-d-don't worry. I'll pay all your medical expenses,'' she told the giant. ''You won't have to put in a c-c-claim with my insurance company.'' How she would pay for anything, she didn't know. Her main goal right now was to convince this overdressed Viking that he shouldn't sue her.

The man pursed his lips, obviously considering her suggestion. When he didn't agree immediately, Jennifer grew anxious. If he sued her, she'd lose the house and everything she owned, including the few things she had to remind her of her mother. The thought was so awful, she almost passed out.

''I'll be reasonable with the settlement.'' Her trembling hand closed around her mom's wedding band, which rested on a chain around her neck. ''To show my goodwill, I'll even sweeten the pot. Would you like a toaster? Or h-how about a black-and-white portable TV?''

Dar leaned back on the heels of his knee-high boots. ''TV?'' he asked with more than a hint of a question in his voice.

''I would give you the color set, but I may need to

pawn it to make this month's mortgage. And I still have to get the roof repaired. It's raining and I hate to tell you what the back bedroom looks like right now—"

"*Nei*. I don't need a TV, whatever that is." He crossed his arms over his massive chest. His warm gaze traveled down her wet clothes. He smiled. It was the smile of a man who knew he could have any woman he wanted. "If you are in my debt, then there is something I would like instead. . . ."

Jennifer set her jaw. "Now wait a minute, buster. I don't mind making a fair trade, but I stop short of selling myself to people who don't have enough sense not to walk in the middle of a narrow road in the dark."

"My name is not Buster. I am Dar, son of Tyr, grandson of Odin." He sounded impatient, as if he thought her slow for not having remembered his name. "I have no need for the items you mentioned. What I do need is a place to stay until I can find my way back to Asgard. That would be possible, *já?*"

"Asgard?"

Dar nodded. "The Palace of the Gods. A great city high on top of a mountain, near the Krystal Hellir, the sacred crystal cave."

"Oh, right. Asgard."

She contemplated her situation. It would take all the emergency money she had in her cookie jar—and she wouldn't be able to buy groceries for a week or two—but if it meant she could avoid a lawsuit, it would be worth the cost.

Jennifer shifted her back against the rough tree bark and grimaced as her hand sank into thick, gooey mud. "So let me see if I've got this right. You won't sue me if I pay for a hotel room until you feel better, right?''

''What is a hotel?''

Sure that he was from a foreign country and didn't have a good grasp on the language yet, she explained, ''It's a place that rents out rooms. All the rooms contain a bed and a bath.''

He pursed his lips. ''If there are lots of rooms, there will be lots of people. If Loki follows, it could be dangerous. *Nei.* I do not think a hotel is a good choice. One person I can protect. Many people would be difficult. Your home will be fine. Hopefully, I will not be there longer than morning.''

''I'll take you to a hotel. I insist.''

''I have decided. As my hostess in this strange land, it is your duty to take me to your hall.''

Jennifer frowned. The last thing she wanted to do was to bring this strange man to her house. If there was any alternative, she would have taken it. But if she didn't think of something quick, he would call the police as soon as she left him. Jennifer sighed as she stared at the twinkling stones sewn to the lining of his cape. She didn't want to admit it, but if she wanted to keep the house, she didn't really have a choice.

The strong breeze seized Dar's shoulder-length blond tresses and whipped them into the air. He rubbed his temples with his enormous fingers.

''Does your head still hurt? Would you like to see a doctor? Both the Chester County and Pottstown Memorial hospitals are about fifteen miles from here. We could get to either one in about a half hour, barring fallen trees or another accident.''

Dar shook his head and dropped a small white stone into a black leather pouch with a bat's head clasp that hung from his waist. "Thank you for your concern, but I don't need a healer. I can take care of my own injuries."

He looked honest, but her mother had always warned her not to trust strangers. Besides, he was a man, and Jennifer didn't trust men. The ones she had known in the past had always lied to her or left her. This one, with his talk of bridges and revenge, didn't seem too safe.

"I guess I don't really have a choice. I'll have to take you home with me," she said grudgingly, pulling her hand out of the mud. She wiped the wet goo on her pants and grimaced as the material absorbed the cold, adhesive substance. "Are you sure you wouldn't rather go to a hotel? I can talk to the manager and get you a king-sized bed, or maybe a suite." She held her breath as she waited for his reply.

"I'm sure."

She touched his billowing purple cape and marveled at how the rain seemed to slide off the thick material. "Why do I feel like I'm going to regret this?" She paused, then tried to elicit an explanation for his strange garb. "Halloween is still a while away, so you must be an actor."

The crystal around Dar's neck took several seconds to translate the words. Having traveled to several worlds over the years, he was adept at several languages, all of which seemed to have a common root in a long ago forgotten tongue. His facility with new languages was one of the reasons Odin always chose him to visit new worlds. As he learned this language, it would take less time to interpret her speech. If he stayed on this world long enough, he wouldn't need the crystal at all.

"*Nei*. I'm not an actor." Relieved that the rain had

finally stopped, Dar reached out and touched the damp mahogany locks of the woman named Jennifer. They felt soft, like the silken underbelly of a newborn dragon.

"Where I come from, a woman's long hair is her shining glory," he told her. "She would use a sword and fight with her last breath to prevent someone from cutting it."

Jennifer shrugged, obviously uncomfortable with the thought of battles and swords. "Yeah, well, where I come from, women only fight if they're in the army." She glanced toward the metallic monster. "Looks like the Jeep is stuck. It's got four-wheel drive, but I don't think they were considering a foot of mud when they did the advertisements. The front bumper is buried in the ground so far, I'm afraid it'll take a tow truck to get it out."

Dar hesitated to touch the creature but knew there was no other choice. "Don't worry. I'll return it to the road."

"Yeah? You and what tow company?"

Did she doubt his word? "I won't need assistance, only my two hands."

"I think you bumped your head harder than you think."

Dar vaulted to his feet and held out a hand to Jennifer. She put a hand in his, hesitantly, as if she was afraid he would bite.

"I'm fine," she insisted. "I can get up on my own."

Dar ignored her and gently pulled until the mud released its hold on her pants. As soon as she was on her feet, Jennifer stepped back a few feet. Her wary expression, combined with the way she held her hands in front of her, told him that she didn't like being touched.

"Thank you. But as I said, I don't need any help—"

On her last word, her black, pointy shoes slid in the mud and she fell backward. With the reflexes of a trained warrior, Dar grabbed her around the waist and pulled her against his body.

She was unlike anyone he had ever held in his arms. Thin and slight, she barely came up to his chin. Nothing like the tall, blond female warriors he knew. Dar tightened his arms around her waist. She was definitely too thin. Did they have a shortage of food on this world? He could feel each of her ribs.

Jennifer licked her lips, drawing attention to her generously curved lower lip. He smiled as he watched a dusty rose color steal into her face.

"Sometimes," he told her, admiring the way her thick lashes caressed her cheeks, "one should be grateful for help and accept it without argument."

She stepped out of his arms, her back straight, her lips pinched together. "And sometimes one should know when it is best to retreat from temptation."

Dar shrugged, unexpectedly disappointed by her withdrawal. "That is true." He felt the sudden urge to taste her lips and discover if she was less reserved in her lovemaking than she seemed to be in her conversation, but stifled the yearning. It wouldn't be fair to her. If things went as he planned, he would return to Asgard by morning.

"Come. Let us take care of your metallic monster."

"It's a Jeep. A car."

The crystal failed to translate the word. That happened from time to time, more frequently than Dar liked to admit. He rolled up the sleeves of his ceremonial shirt. "To you it is a car. To me it is a creature."

Before she could protest, Dar swept her up into his arms and carried her toward the immobile dark green beast.

"Put me down." She beat on his shoulders, but he barely felt the blows. They were puny, like the protests of a fly caught in a spider's net.

"The mud is thick. You'd do best to save your strength for the battle to come." With those words of warning, Dar deposited her onto the front seat. "Now, when I nod my head, try to get this thing to obey your commands."

"You mean turn on the ignition," she said dryly.

"If that's how you order it to move, then that's what I mean." He walked to the front of the creature and nodded. Nothing prepared him for the roar it made.

Gritting his teeth and hoping the thing didn't have long, sharp teeth, he put his hands on the shiny silver lip under the bright eyes and nodded his head. Jennifer did something with her right arm and the monster squealed like a mortally wounded ox.

Dar focused his energy on pushing the creature backwards up the steep bank and onto the road. He blocked out the sucking sound of the mud pulling at his boots and pushed. The monster gave a snort and rumbled backward out of the ditch.

"You've done it!" The shout was followed by a joyful laugh.

Dar climbed up out of the mud and returned Jennifer's smile. "Did you doubt me?"

Her smile faded. "I didn't know what to believe," she whispered.

He could understand her sentiments because he didn't know what was real either. Without seeing the position of the stars, he didn't even know where he was. He also didn't know if he had been sent into the past or the future.

Jennifer leaned over and opened a door. "Well, come on. Don't just stand there. Get in."

Dar assessed the interior and gingerly eased his huge body onto the odd beige chair. He pulled his mantle close to his body. The black crystal lining crackled as he moved.

He glanced around warily. Just because the metallic monster hadn't bitten him yet didn't mean that it was completely tame.

"Did you have to cut the seat belt?" She gestured toward the severed straps next to her seat.

"It was the only way I could get you out of that thing."

"Do you know how much it's going to cost to replace it or clean the mud off these seats?" Jennifer asked, moving a long, thin stick with her hand.

He gripped the side of the door as he felt himself being pushed back in his seat. "By the sacred horn of Heimdall!"

"Calm down. I only put the car in gear." Jennifer put both hands on the wheel in front of her. "Look, if you're one of those men who worries whenever a woman does the driving, why don't you put on *your* seat belt?"

Him? Frightened? Did she actually believe the most powerful sorcerer in Asgard knew the meaning of the word *fear?* Hmph. Dar willed his knees to stop shaking.

"I am fine," he told her through gritted teeth.

Jennifer chuckled. "That's good. Then I can go faster."

The creature lurched forward, forcing a low growl from Dar's paralyzed throat.

"How's that?" she asked cheerfully.

"Fine."

She must have heard his hoarse whisper because she shrugged and focused her attention on the road.

Dar heard a familiar screech and looked into the tiny mirror on the outside of the door. There, in the distance, he saw the flapping of shiny green wings. Firedrake's exceptional sense of smell and sight were hereditary. Dar didn't worry that he would lose the dragon.

The car went over a bump and Dar found himself too busy concentrating on keeping down his breakfast to worry about anything else.

Chapter Two

At her house, Jennifer wondered if Dar would notice the threadbare carpets or the peeling wallpaper. Although the five-bedroom Victorian house needed repairs, overall it was spacious and cozy.

"Would you like something to drink?" she asked.

"*Nei.*"

Dar took off his hat, careful not to catch his cape on the sharp horns. He laid it upon the coffee table, then picked up a small porcelain figurine and touched the fragile bouquet of flowers in the statue's hands.

"It's a ballerina" Jennifer said, but Dar gave no response. Unable to bear the silence any longer, she cleared her throat. "The house—is it bigger or smaller than your home?"

" 'Tis smaller. Much smaller." He pursed his lips as he looked around. "The dining room in my hall could fit fifty warriors and they wouldn't have to take off their swords."

He put down the statue, as cautious with it as if he handled a priceless antique. She grimaced as he turned around and knocked his long scabbard against the coffee table. Luckily, nothing toppled off. She didn't know whether to frown or sigh with relief as he walked toward the dining room.

"Why don't you take off your coat and make yourself comfortable?" she called after him.

" 'Tis a mantle, one that has been in my family for many generations." His huge hand went to the golden brooch at his neck. "But you're right. 'Tis warm in here." Without stopping his scrutiny of the furnishings, he dropped his mantle onto the floor.

"There is a closet, you know."

Dar grunted.

Jennifer wondered whether she had made the right decision in giving her new boarder a room in her home. She frowned as she bent down and picked up the heavy, dark purple cloak. It still felt warm from his body. She caressed the soft material. "Let me guess: You have a bunch of servants where you come from."

"*Já*. I have several thralls. But it's the duty of the woman of the house to ensure that the guests are adequately supplied with everything they need."

Jennifer bit her lip. Was he married? Did he have any children? She chided herself for drawing hasty conclusions and tried to think of a tactful way to ask her questions. "Does your wife see to your guests' needs?"

Dar hesitated. Then, his back to her, he replied, "*Nei*. Neither I nor Lor, my brother, have wives. Several of my sisters are unmated also. My mother, Solveig, is mistress of our hall." His deep voice became husky, almost as if he had a cold. "And you—does your soul mate help you with your duties?''

''I assume you're asking if I have a husband. No, I'm not married. I don't even have a boyfriend, not since my fiancé, Ed, left me for another woman.'' Now why had she told him that? Jennifer shook her head, hoping he didn't realize she was rambling because she was nervous.

''Finding another job is my first priority right now. I'm a computer programmer. I took a job in Pottstown to be closer to my mother while she was ill. The project is finished and now I'm out of work again.''

Dar grunted again and turned toward her. This was the first time Jennifer had ever really seen him without his mantle.

Boy, he was big. Really big.

She started at the top of his blond head, moved her gaze to his powerful, wide shoulders, down his muscular arms, past the flat stomach, a jewel-studded knife, the dangerous-looking sword, and ended with his long, sturdy, Viking legs.

''Are you a body builder?''

It took him a moment to reply. ''I am a warrior.''

He could crush her with one hand. Without even trying. Her gaze traveled back up his body and centered on the golden dragon etched on his belt buckle. She shivered. Was every part of his anatomy so large?

''The answer to your question is *já.*''

Oh, God!

''*Já,* I build my body by practicing on the battlefield daily.'' His blue eyes twinkled. ''Do you have any other questions?''

''No. No. That was the only one.''

''Good. Then, if there's nothing else to discuss, I'd like you to show me the way to your outhouse.''

Before Jennifer could answer, the grandfather clock

next to the china closet chimed the hour. Dar unsheathed his knife in one swift motion.

"Valhalla!" he yelled as he threw it at the clock.

Jennifer watched his rigid muscles relax as the silver blade flew through the air and shattered the beveled glass. She could still hear the tinkle of glass hitting the polished wooden floors as the blade imbedded itself into the antique cherry wood.

"I can't believe you did that!" She pressed trembling hands to her cheeks and her mouth fell open.

"I'm sorry." Dar's body uncoiled. His square jaw visibly relaxed. "It was important to you, *já?*"

"It is—was an expensive antique." And she could have pawned it and used the money to pay the mortgage.

"I'll pay you for the item." Dar unsnapped one of the gold bracelets on his upper arms. "How many pieces of gold will you require?"

Why did she have to run over someone with a warped sense of humor? "Are you telling me that piece of jewelry you're holding is pure gold?"

"Já."

"Yeah. Right." She snorted. "And my name is Marie Antoinette."

Dar frowned at her. "I thought your name was Jennifer."

"Never mind." She took a deep breath and counted to ten. "Forget about the clock. Come on. Let me show you to your room. It has a connecting bath, so you won't have to walk through the drafty hall and catch a cold."

He put the armring back on. "As you wish."

Jennifer had just put her foot on the first stair when she heard a rustling near the living-room window. She tensed, worried about robbers. Dar didn't even hesitate. He walked over to the window, threw it open, and stuck out his head. His loud roar almost made her heart stop.

"What do you think you're doing?" Jennifer asked as he squeezed the upper half of his body through the window. She tried to peer over his back and almost bumped into him when he stood upright. She moved back so fast that she slammed into the wall.

That was when she saw it. The ugliest creature in the world. About the size of a cocker spaniel, it had scaly green skin, deformed wings, and the largest set of claws she had ever seen. Claws, that at that moment were wrapped around Dar's burly wrist.

Jennifer gasped. "I can't believe you brought that . . . thing into the house."

The muscles in his arm rippled as he brought the creature nearer to her nose. "This is Firedrake, my friend and faithful companion."

His companion reeked of something she couldn't quite identify. Taking a deep sniff, she pinned it down to a cross between a wet leather glove and a dead squirrel.

"Your friend needs a bath," she told him, gagging at the foul smell.

Dar raised his chin and looked down his aquiline nose at her. "Soap has never touched Firedrake's scales. He may become upset by your proposal. I wouldn't suggest it."

"Oh, yeah?" Jennifer stepped closer to the critter. She looked into the creature's large violet eyes and made a decision. "Either that thing gets a bath or it stays outside."

Dar's firm mouth curled at the edges, almost as if he was holding back laughter. "If you wish, try to bathe him. But don't be surprised if Firedrake objects to the bath."

"What would it do, bite me?"

"Or singe your soft, pale skin," he warned, his gaze sweeping over her body with more than a hint of interest.

"Humph. Well, if I were him, I wouldn't even try it."

Firedrake blinked but didn't try to fly away.

"If you'd be so kind as to show me to the outhouse . . ." He rubbed his stomach. "And then I would like to eat. I missed my supper because of Loki's unkind prank. When we're done, we'll discuss how I can get back to my world."

"I think you mean see about returning home."

He petted the creature's shiny skin. "You will excuse my misuse of your language, *já?* It seems that many words have more than one meaning, and I'm not always sure which one to use. It will take me some time to get used to your strange vocabulary. You'll tell me if I say or do something wrong, *já?*"

"Of course."

"Good. Please, lead the way." He grabbed his mantle and threw it over his arm.

The bathroom on the second floor needed tiles and a new shower curtain. Jennifer hoped he wouldn't notice. "Here's the bathroom, and the bedroom to the right is yours. If you need anything, just yell."

Dar set Firedrake down in the tub while Jennifer mentally contemplated the contents of her refrigerator. Since she hadn't gone shopping, it was empty.

She had one foot on the stairs when she heard him throw open the door. "Jennifer!"

"Yes?" Why did he sound so nervous?

"I'm unfamiliar with your outhouse. Will you show me how to use it?"

She rested her hand on the wooden banister and stared at her guest. "You're kidding, right?"

He shook his head. "*Nei.* I'm serious."

She must have hit him harder than she thought!

She slowly walked back to the bathroom. He took up so much space in the small area, she could barely breathe. "This is the sink. You turn the faucet like this." Cold water trickled out in a small stream. "And here's the toilet. You flush it like this."

Dar frowned as he stared at the swirling water.

"Any questions?"

"*Já,* but I'll try to do it on my own first."

The sound of someone chewing made Jennifer narrow her eyes and turn toward the bathtub. The sight of Dar's pet eating the blue-and-white towel hanging on the side of the tub made her gasp and snatch it out of his claws.

"What do you think you're doing? That was my mother's favorite towel!" She thrust the slimy towel into Dar's hand. "Make sure he doesn't eat anything else. Everything in here is an antique."

Which meant they were old, and she didn't have the money to replace anything, she added silently, touching the chain holding her mother's wedding ring. Caressing the thin piece of gold helped calm her.

Jennifer left her guest to get washed and ran down to her bedroom. She wanted to change her stained clothing as soon as possible.

Once she was dressed in a pair of fresh dungarees, she strode into the kitchen. "I must have been delirious when I agreed to bring him home with me." She checked the stack of bills near the toaster. As she'd feared, she'd just received her renewal for her car insurance. Unfortunately, right now she didn't have the money to pay the bill. "Trouble has a name and it isn't Santa Claus."

Hoping the day wouldn't get any worse, she peered into the freezer, took out a couple of boxes, and carried them to the microwave. "With any luck, he'll remember where he lives by the time dinner is over."

Dar hurried down the steps, anxious to eat a good meal. He was so hungry, his ribs were sticking to his stomach. Standing in the dining room, he sniffed the air. Where was the food? When his servants prepared a large feast, the aromas welcomed him at the door of his hall.

"Oh, there you are." Jennifer came into the room, a covered tray in her hand. "Sit down anywhere." She placed the steaming dish on the table, just out of Dar's reach. "I'll be right back with the rest of the food."

"Ah, the first course! I hope it's good." Dar eased his body into the narrow chair and reached for the black crystal dagger he always wore in his belt. He peeled back the transparent paper on top of the trencher and looked at the tiny portion of food. Realizing Jennifer would soon be back with the second course and he hadn't even finished the first dish yet, he began to eat.

"Darn!" she muttered, returning to the room. "I forgot the lemonade."

Dar watched Jennifer put another tray on the table and head back to the kitchen. "By Mimir's beard! If she keeps bringing out these small portions, she'll be serving me twenty courses."

Unsure of the eating customs of the people in this world, Dar reached for the second dish and gulped it down. Things must be the same all over, he mused, picking up a pea on the flat of his blade and bringing it to his mouth. The mistress of the house always ensured the kitchen ran smoothly, and she usually sat down at the table after everyone else had eaten their fill.

"Okay. I think I've got everything." Jennifer handed Dar a glass of yellow liquid. "I hope you like lemonade. I'm all out of mead."

Dar grunted and looked toward the kitchen, hoping that the next course was almost ready. He didn't see the strange expression on her face until he heard her muffled gasp.

"What happened to my dinner?"

Dar glanced at the empty food containers. "I finished both courses; now I'm ready for the main meal."

"That was the main meal! Both yours and mine."

Surely she was jesting? "But that wasn't enough for a dwarf! That was hardly a fragment of the portion needed to sustain a warrior."

Jennifer nervously ran her hand through her dark hair. "I guess, since my father left, I'm not used to feeding men with big appetites." She looked at the empty dishes and shrugged. "Looks like I'll have to buy more microwave meals the next time I go to the store. I have a loaf of bread in the refrigerator. Would you like a couple of peanut-butter sandwiches?"

Anything to fill his stomach. *"Já."*

Over an open jar of gummy brown paste that tasted like the underside of a muddy rock, they discussed how he would get back home. Dar willed the thick goo to travel down his throat and helped it along with a swig of the sweet lemon juice. "From the description of your world, it would seem I have been transported to Midgard, the planet you call Earth."

"Oh, no." She rolled her eyes. "Don't tell me you think you're an alien."

"*Nei.* I'm not an alien," he said haughtily. "I'm a Norse sorcerer."

"I don't know if that's better or worse." She bit her lip. "Please, continue with your story."

Dar rubbed his neck and tried to put the pieces of the puzzle together. "This isn't the Midgard I know. It would seem I've also been transported to another time." He narrowed his eyes. "What century is it?"

"The twentieth century."

Ah! That would explain it. "I wonder if Loki knew of the time difference when he sent me here?" Dar forced himself to remain calm, reasonable, not to give in to his fears. "And you've never heard of the Bifrost Bridge?"

"No." She shook her head. "Er, is it near Italy?"

The situation was worse than he had feared! "*Nei.* It's the rainbow bridge that stretches between Midgard and Asgard," he explained. "Maybe if I gave you more information, you would remember its location. The bridge, at first glance, resembles a shimmering rainbow. It looks flimsy, but it can withstand the weight of a full-grown dragon. The red in it is a glowing fire that burns the feet of jotuns and trolls."

"Sounds interesting," Jennifer said, putting her hand in front of her mouth as if to hide a smile. "What's a jotun?"

"A jotun is a giant. They live in Jotunheim, and most are enemies of the inhabitants of Asgard."

"Oh."

Dar shook his head. The trip through time and space had drained his energy. He was so tired, he could barely keep his eyes open, but he couldn't think of sleep until he settled his affairs.

"Jennifer, I must return to Asgard immediately. There will soon be a battle in which our warriors will be outnumbered. I have vowed to be at Odin's side, to protect the people I love. You'll help me find a way to return to Asgard, *já?*"

The talk about battles and war made her stomach clench. Just the thought of men and women being skewered by razor-sharp swords gave her nightmares.

"Listen, Dar, your vow sounds interesting, but I think you've had a rough day. You were probably on your way to a masquerade party and, since you can't find your wallet, you may have been clobbered on the head and robbed." She shrugged. "On top of that, I hit you with my Jeep. Why don't you go to sleep? In the morning I'll take you to the hospital and you can see a psychiatrist . . . I mean a doctor."

She didn't believe him! Dar bent his head and stared at his clenched fists. She thought him crazy, insane. Dar seriously considered gathering up his belongings and slipping away in the middle of the night.

But where would he go? He was in a strange land, in another time, and, judging from the clothes Jennifer wore, he would stand out like a golden dragon.

"There is only one thing to do," he told her, slowly getting to his feet. "I must convince you that I'm telling you the truth."

Jennifer paled and pushed herself against the back of her chair. "What are you going to do?"

He frowned. Surely a great sorcerer would be able to think of something to prove he was a warrior of Asgard. The crystals in the sacred cave were the source of his abilities. Without them nearby, he had to rely on his runes or crystal ball for his powers. He glanced around the room, looking for something, he knew not what. His gaze fell on the bag of magic runes.

"I've got it!" He searched through the small white squares until he found the one he wanted. "Watch." He put the rune in the palm of his open hand, closed his eyes, and recited an incantation. "O powerful forces, hear my plea, take this rune and set it free."

He opened his eyes and smiled at the levitating object.

"Is that it?" She snorted. "Any magician can do that. It's a common trick."

The skepticism in Jennifer's voice wiped the smug smile off his face. Dar's hand clenched around the rune. So now she considered him common, did she? There was only one way to convince her.

"Don't move from that chair. I'll be right back."

He ran up to his room, grabbed his mantle, and hurried back down to the dining room. He relaxed when he saw her sitting in the chair, her arms crossed against her ample chest.

He gripped the mantle in both hands and held it in front of himself at waist level, the black crystal material facing outward. "Tell me if this is a hoax." Before she could speak, he whipped the mantle over his head and settled it around his body.

"Oh my God! Where did you go?"

Dar chuckled and moved toward the large hearth.

"Dar?" she called, the skepticism replaced by amazement at his accomplishment.

"I'm right here, Jennifer. Can't you see me?"

"No, I can't. One minute you were standing there, the next minute you disappeared."

"I'm right in front of you."

Dar watched Jennifer put her hands out in front of

her and begin to grope in the air. He moved to the right, behind a large stuffed chair.

"Where are you?"

"Now I'm over here," he told her, keeping his voice even so as not to startle her.

She inched closer, her hands searching for him. Dar watched her walk toward him. "I can't see you."

"I know."

She was so close, he could see the dark flecks in her chestnut-colored eyes. He stepped away from the chair, right into the path of her arms.

Jennifer felt her hands touch the rough material of his cloak but could see nothing in front of her. "Dar?"

"*Já?*"

She moved her hands upward and felt the stubble on his face. "Is this a trick? Are you using mirrors?"

She heard him sigh and felt his chest move. "*Nei,* Jennifer. 'Tis no trick."

She hadn't thought so, but she had to hear the words from his own lips. Jennifer touched his thick eyebrows. "How do you do it?"

" 'Tis a secret handed down from generations of sorcerers," he told her, his breath warm on her face. "The mantle is the key to the feat."

"Oh. You must be a very powerful sorcerer."

"I'm Asgard's head sorcerer. It's a position I've had since my uncle disappeared. My brother Lor is the dragon master and my sister Dalia is my assistant."

"If you're so powerful, can't you just wish yourself back to Asgard?"

"*Nei.* There is no spell that will transport me home. I can only return by the bridge, or with another stone like the one I used during the ceremony. My powers may be great, but they are only at their fullest when I'm in Asgard. Here, in Midgard, I must rely on my crystal ball or runes for almost all of my spells."

"Do all sorcerers need to use their crystal balls?"

She felt Dar shake his head. "*Nei.* My teacher, the sorcerer Mimir, has risen above the need for the use of runes and crystals."

His breath caressed her cheek. "Will you eventually reach his level?"

"Mimir says I must first conquer that which is stopping me from rising to my maximum potential."

"And how would you do that?"

"I do not know. The answer to that question has plagued me for a long time."

Why couldn't she think? Jennifer ran her hand over his lips. They were so soft, and so close.

He cleared his throat and dropped the crystal mantle from his shoulders. It lay in a shimmering amethyst pool by his feet. "You are convinced I'm telling the truth, *já?*"

She must be crazy. She must be hallucinating. Her hands now resting on his visible wide shoulders, Jennifer stared at the giant standing in front of her and knew that her life would never be the same again.

"Yes, Dar. I believe you. I'm crazy, but I believe you." *Which doesn't bode well for the state of my mind,* Jennifer mused. She was sure her face reflected the shock she felt.

"Good. And you'll help me get back to Asgard?"

His warm breath caressed her face. She dropped her hands to her sides, away from the temptation he represented. "Yes, Dar. I'll help you."

"Good. Now, if I could ask you one more favor . . ."

What would he want? A magic carpet? A spaceship

so he could go to the moon? She looked at his mouth and wet her lips. Then she stepped backward, away from him. "Yes?"

"If it's at all possible, I would like more of those dinners." He rubbed his stomach. "I'm as hungry as a starving ox who's just plowed several fields."

Disappointed, but not sure why, Jennifer went to prepare another frozen dinner. In the kitchen, she turned on the microwave and stared at the revolving tray of food. Her life was being turned upside down by a tall, powerfully built man with a magic mantle, one who would leave at the first opportunity.

She'd wished for a miracle and she'd gotten it. Jennifer touched her mother's ring. Her mom had always warned her to be careful what she wished for. Now she knew why.

Chapter Three

"Hold still. You're going to mess up my shirt." Jennifer soaped up the washcloth. "Lift your leg. That's right." She winced as soapy water splashed her face. "Now the other leg."

She ran her hand down his firm muscles. "Okay, now turn around." A smile on her lips, she washed his wide back. "See. That wasn't so bad, was it?"

A low grunt was the only reply.

"Stay there until I get a towel." Jennifer padded over to a white cabinet next to the washing machine and took out a big, fluffy towel. "You're so cute. I can't resist kissing you." She kissed him on the nose. "Now, what would you like for breakfast? Are you hungry?"

He nodded so hard he almost knocked the towel off the table. The answer was a definite yes! Jennifer dried the thin green wings. They were shaped sort of like the wings of a bat. She dried his sharp claws. All four of them. The odd crystal around his neck drew her eyes like a magnet. Hung on a black leather cord, it was identical to the one Dar worc. She made a mental note to ask the Norseman its purpose.

"Now we'll do your head. Close your eyes." Firedrake sniffled as she put the towel over his head. He tried to usc his talons to remove it. "I'm almost done. Just a little more." She stretched out his tail and stared at the strange, triangular-shaped thing on the end. She'd wondered if she should use a hair dryer to get him completely dry, but she needn't have worried. The water slid off his green scales almost before she could soak it up with the towel.

"You're not any type of bird I've ever seen." She felt the soft, flexible skin, admired the iridescent green scales. "You must have some relatives in the lizard family. I'll have to ask Dar what type of critter you are."

Almost faster than she could move, Firedrake leaned forward and grabbed the damp towel. His sharp teeth tore the white terry cloth to shreds. Jennifer opened his mouth, stuck her hand past the rows of sharp teeth, and pulled out the tattered remnants.

"Don't do that again!" Seeing him eye the soap, she grabbed it before he could eat it, too. "Let's get out of here before you do something I'm gonna regret. We'll go make breakfast." She bent down and picked up the shiny, squeaky clean green animal. He was about as heavy as a sack of potatoes.

"You must be hungry," she said as she walked up the cellar steps, careful not to drop him. "Since you were so good, I'm going to give you some of the birdseed I keep in the shed. Yum, doesn't that sound nice?"

Jennifer filled a shallow bowl with sunflower seeds

and put it out on the front porch. "There you go. Now be a good little beastie and eat all your food."

She left the front door cracked open so she could see Firedrake. She frowned when the strange creature stood there with his head tilted at an angle, staring at the seeds, but not eating them.

"Oh, well, he'll eat when he's hungry."

Glad she had one chore out of the way, Jennifer made breakfast for herself and her guest. She'd never considered renting a room to a man. First of all, they were unpredictable. Secondly, they always left the toilet seat up. As if that wasn't bad enough, they left just when you had grown used to having them around. Thinking of her ex-fiancé made her hands clench around a wet dish towel and wring it until her hands hurt.

She had almost finished buttering the toast when she heard an alarm clock go off, followed immediately by a roar, the thump of someone falling out of bed, and then a loud crash.

Her heart in her mouth, she ran up the steps and pushed open the door of the guest room. His sword in his hand, Dar crouched next to the bed wearing the early morning rays of the sun and not much else. Her gaze traveled down his broad chest and had almost wandered lower when she realized she was staring. Averting her eyes from the hulking giant with tousled blond hair, she gazed down at the remains of her mother's clock.

"By Odin's eight-legged horse! It shrieked at me while I slept," Dar complained, his eyes scanning the room for other, more pesky foes.

"It is—*was* an alarm clock. Its function is to wake people."

Dar grunted. "It made a noise just like a demon does just before it attacks."

"That was my mother's clock." Her vision blurred as she realized she'd lost yet another of her mother's possessions, but she resolutely blinked away the tears. "You mentioned being a sorcerer. Can you fix the clock?"

"*Nei.* My powers of healing work only on live creatures, not inanimate objects. I will, of course, pay for the clock." Dar's stomach rumbled loudly. "Is it time for breakfast yet?"

Jennifer pushed back her regret at the destruction of the clock, knowing from experience that tears brought back neither people nor things. She sighed at his expectant expression. "I'm preparing breakfast now."

"I'll be down as soon as I'm dressed."

A polite hint for her to leave the room. She turned around and walked toward the door. "Well, if you need me, call."

"Jennifer?"

She kept her back to him. "Yes?"

"Are there any other creatures in the room that will make a screeching noise like that?"

"No. That was the only one and it's dead now." Well, at least in a lot of little pieces.

"You can turn around if you wish. I'm dressed."

She peeked at him over her shoulder. The pale beige pants, tied at the waist with a braided cord, hugged his body like a second skin. The strange fabric molded his long, muscular legs and emphasized the large bulge just below his tanned belly.

"Thank you for coming so quickly." The husky tone of his voice sent shivers of pleasure down her back.

"It was my pleasure." And if she didn't leave now, she'd soon be thinking of other, different kinds of pleasure.

His smile rivaled a ray of sunshine, making her want to linger and talk to him longer. Realizing that could lead to trouble, Jennifer almost ran from the room.

The image of his naked body stayed on her mind. There wasn't an ounce of fat on him. And she had seen almost all of him. From the tip of his head to his bare toes.

She opened the door of the refrigerator and took out a carton of juice. He had a long scar on the right side of his stomach, right below his belly button, right next to the light blond hair running down his abdomen toward . . .

"I'm ready for breakfast."

Startled, Jennifer almost dropped the juice carton. "Dar! I didn't hear you come in."

"*Já.* I know. I've been standing here for a while. I didn't want to disturb you."

She walked over to the table and poured him a big glass of orange juice. "How much toast would you like? Will four pieces be enough?"

Dar looked at the small charred squares on the table and grimaced. His breakfast usually consisted of oxen, salmon, a few loaves of bread, and several mugs of sweet mead. The lack of nourishing food on this world boded ill for a prolonged visit. He resigned himself to eating the same food as Jennifer.

"Four will be fine."

She pointed toward one of the narrow wooden chairs next to the small table. "Sit down. It'll be ready in a minute."

The round platter amazed Dar. It in no way resembled the long, bowl-shaped trenchers of Asgard. He tapped the object on the edge of the table to test its strength.

"Be careful. It's breakable." Jennifer handed him a glass. "Here's some juice. Drink it while it's cold."

She placed the toast on his dish. Dar waited until she sat down across from him before he began to eat.

"*Skal.*" He raised his glass in her direction and washed down the dry toast with the sweet orange liquid.

"I'm sorry I don't have any butter or jam to offer you." She nibbled at her piece of bread like a small bird. "I've been working overtime to get all my work finished. I planned on going to the grocery store last night, but ran into you instead."

"Over time?"

She nodded as she sipped her juice. "As you can probably guess, I need all the money I can get. There aren't very many computer programming jobs in this area. With my mother ill, I had to quit my job in the city and take something that paid only half the salary. And if that isn't bad enough, now that I've been laid off, I hadn't been working long enough to collect enough unemployment to pay my bills."

Dar understood the need to settle debts. He bit into another dry piece of bread.

"As soon as breakfast is over, I'll look downstairs for jam. Mom used to bottle everything from strawberries to prunes, then give them away as gifts at Christmas."

Knowing thoughts of her mother made her sad, Dar changed the subject. "Have you given any thought to how I can return home?"

Jennifer wiped up the crumbs with her hand and

put them on her napkin. "Well, we could call the headquarters for NASA."

The crystal failed to translate the word. "NASA?"

"That's the name of our country's space program."

Dar shook his head, wondering why anyone would want to go into the cold recesses among the planets. "*Nei.* Asgard isn't located in a room. They would not be able to help."

"A room?"

"Space means room or area, *já?*"

"Not exactly." She pinched the bridge of her nose as if she had a headache. "Forget it. There's got to be something else we can do."

"Like what?"

Her expression pensive, Jennifer bit her lip. "There's always the president of the United States." She stared at her hands. "But I've heard that the government doesn't believe in aliens. And in this country, sorcerers were apparently aliens until proven otherwise. The last thing we would want is for the government scientists to capture and begin experimenting on you."

A stream of lightning crackled from his fingers. "Let them try to experiment on me or Firedrake and they will feel the power at my command."

Jennifer didn't notice anything amiss.

"Maybe it would be best to wait before we announce my presence to your leader," Dar decided. "Is there anyone on your planet who is familiar with time travel or the Bifrost Bridge?"

"Not that I know of."

"Then I will have to curb my impatience and look for someone who can help me to return to Asgard."

"Good idea." Jennifer poured herself another cup

of coffee and put it down on the table. As she turned, the pot hit the cup. Dar reacted instantly, before the hot liquid could burn her. He focused on the cup and kept it hovering in the air.

Jennifer looked from Dar to the still smoking coffee.

"Thank you. That would have hurt." She reached down and tentatively grasped the cup. "And you didn't spill a drop. I'm impressed."

"I'm glad you weren't hurt." Dar nodded for her to move the cup, then reached for his orange juice.

"Oh, I forgot to tell you—I gave Firedrake a bath this morning," she said proudly.

It was a good thing Dar didn't have anything in his mouth, or he would have choked. "*Nei!* Surely you jest."

Jennifer shook her head. "No, I'm serious. He didn't give me any trouble. Actually, other than when I got some soap in his eyes, he seemed to like it."

Amazing. Simply amazing. "He didn't show his sharp little teeth? Or hit you with his tail?"

"Nope."

"I'm more impressed than you know."

"Well, thanks." She toyed with her food. "I know he's not a bird, but I'm not sure exactly what type of creature he is."

"Firedrake is a *drakna.*"

"A what?"

He touched his translation crystal for several seconds. "A dragon."

"The dragons must be different on your world, more like lizards." Jennifer shook her head, obviously surprised. "Considering he's only about the size of a medium-sized dog, he's nothing like the creatures I've seen portrayed in the movies."

Dar grunted, unsure if that was good or bad.

"While I washed him, I noticed he had a crystal identical to the one you wear around your neck." She cocked an eyebrow expectantly.

" 'Tis a translation crystal. As I travel frequently to the nine worlds, I wear it all the time. A sorcerer never knows when he'll travel or fight on Odin's behalf. Without it, I wouldn't be able to understand your speech."

Jennifer stared at the object in question. "Then I suggest you keep it on while you're here."

"I agree."

"From all the scars on your body, it looks as if you fight a lot."

"Between practicing with my sword and skirmishes between the jotuns and demons, I fight almost daily."

Dar noticed her shiver. "Are there not wars here, too?"

"More than I care to think about. Actually, I try not to think about them at all."

"Do both your men and women fight in these wars?"

"Some do. Others don't." She rubbed her arms, as if cold. "Let's change the subject. I hate talking about death or the poor children who suffer for human greed."

"In Asgard, men, women, and children talk about nothing but war."

Jennifer clenched her hands around her glass so tightly that her knuckles turned white. "Which is why I want to change the subject." She took a deep breath and wiped her hands on her pants. "Dar, there's something I want to discuss."

This sounded serious. Very serious. *"Já?"*

"I realize it may take you a while to find a way to return home." She peeked at him through the fringes of hair that curtained her eyes. "And normally I wouldn't mention it, but . . . since I was going to rent out the rooms upstairs, and since you may be staying here for a while . . ."

"You wish to receive payment for my lodging and food? *Já?*" A perfectly logical request.

"Well, yes."

"I understand." He raised his arm and unsnapped one of his armbands. "How many pieces of gold will you require?"

She stared at the thick golden object and frowned. "Don't you have anything smaller, like coins?"

Dar shook his head. "*Nei*. When I dressed, I didn't prepare for a journey; I clothed myself for a ceremony. Most Norsemen wear their currency on their person in the form of golden rings, necklaces, or armbands."

She judged the weight of the object. "I guess my first stop today will be the jeweler's to exchange this for some cash." Jennifer slipped the armband over her wrist and admired the effect. Dar smiled. The armband was so big, it emphasized her slim, shapely hands.

He looked at the calluses on his palms and the pads of his fingers, symbols of his years of training for battle. The differences in their culture could be measured by more than just the food they ate, he realized sadly.

Jennifer put the armband into the square leather pouch she called a handbag. "If you're ready, I'll just clean off the table and we can go to town."

"We?"

She put the dirty glasses in the sink and nodded. "Yes, we. Is there a problem?"

"Will this trip involve us getting into that metallic creature of yours?"

"Yes, it will." She raised her eyebrows. "You aren't scared, are you?"

A warrior of Asgard frightened? "Of course not."

"Good." She dangled a bunch of keys from her fingers. "In that case, let's go."

Dar secured his mantle with his golden brooch and followed her out the back door. "You'll tell the monster not to growl, won't you, Jennifer?"

"I've told you, it doesn't growl. That noise you hear is just the motor underneath the hood."

Dar grunted, and gingerly eased himself into the seat on the right side of the beast. He believed her, but he kept one hand on the hilt of his sword, just in case.

Jennifer paused by the bank and pretended not to notice the interested stares of the people walking down the busy streets of Glenmoore. Hadn't they ever seen a man wearing a cape before? Hating the attention, she ignored them and hoped they'd go away without asking Dar for an autograph.

"You wait here," she told the Norseman. "I'll go—" One second he was standing beside her, the next he was sprinting across the busy intersection. "Dar! Where are you going?"

Then she saw him—a young child standing in the path of a fast-moving red sports car.

"Hot damn and hallelujah!" an older woman in a flowered dress shouted. "Look at him go!"

"Valhalla!" Dar yelled at the top of his lungs, his mantle billowing out behind him.

Almost faster than the eye could follow, Jennifer watched him grab the boy and roll to safety.

"Like, wow! Did you catch that act?" A young boy with three earrings hurried toward the crowd surrounding the Norseman and the crying boy.

"I dropped my bunny wabbit," the kid sobbed.

"Are you hurt?" His amethyst cape a little the worse for wear, Dar checked for broken bones. Jennifer tried to reach Dar, but a bald man with a large nose pushed her to the back of the crowd.

"I want my bunny wabbit!" the child screamed in a loud, piercing tone that had all the women in the throng trying to reach out and hug him. Tears ran down his face and splashed onto his jacket.

Scanning the street, Jennifer spotted the stuffed animal. Dar must have seen it, too, because he whistled and pointed toward the blue object. She was just going to tell one of the bystanders to get the rabbit when she saw Firedrake swoop down from the sky and scoop it up in its mighty talons. Without any effort, the dragon flew over to Dar and dropped the rabbit into his outstretched hands.

Loud cheers rent the air as the crowd applauded.

Jason Wells couldn't believe his eyes. He craned his neck in an attempt to catch another glimpse of the small dragon flying beside the strangely dressed man. He'd tried for years to create something as unique, but so far, all his efforts had been in vain.

"Did you see what I saw, Jason?" His assistant Henry Sneed, sputtered.

"Yes, Henry, I did. Imagine getting our hands on that creature for our experiments." Jason tried to contain his excitement so as not to draw attention. He forced himself to lean back against the wall of the store as he peered across the street at the scaly creature. "There are too many people to make a move now. We'll wait until they leave, then follow them. Once we find out where they live, we can go in at night and grab the creature."

"Well, how are we gonna do that?" Henry demanded.

Jason took his time and contemplated several different scenarios before he settled on the one that would work the best.

Still a little shaken, Jennifer stopped in front of Martin's Jewelers, one of several small shops in Glenmoore, and waited for Dar to straighten his mantle before she spoke. "Now remember, let me do the talking. The jeweler rarely sees massive blond giants wearing odd clothing entering his store, and I don't want you to scare him."

Dar jerked his head toward the sky as they heard Firedrake's sharp cry. He held out his arm so the dragon could alight.

"I thought I told you to close your bedroom window so he couldn't get out of the house," she said, scowling.

Dar shrugged and urged the dragon into the air. "Firedrake doesn't like staying indoors."

"Aren't you afraid he'll escape?"

"*Nei.*" He watched as the dragon hurtled out of the sky and swooped down to catch an unsuspecting pigeon. "Firedrake would never leave me of his own free will."

"You're frowning. What's the matter?"

"All is well. Firedrake has announced Loki is not near."

"Good. Let's go."

Although the Norseman looked like he was going to argue, he just nodded and followed her into the store. A tiny bell above the door tinkled, alerting the proprietor to their presence.

Jennifer watched as Martin walked out of the back room. His starched white shirt and black bow tie made him appear older than his thirty-four years.

"Hi, Jenn. Nice of you to pay me a visit." He pushed his oval wire-frame glasses further up on his thin nose and nodded to Dar. "I'll be right with you, sir. I believe this lady came in first."

"He's with me, Martin. This is my new boarder, Dar . . . Tyrson." Son of Tyr. That sounded right. "Dar, this is Martin Wright, an old friend of mine."

"Nice to meet you, Dar." Martin held out his hand. The Norseman ignored it and continued scowling.

"Having to take in boarders to make ends meet? Gee, that's tough." Martin leaned over the counter and motioned for her to come closer. "There's a new movie starting tonight. Would you like to see it with me, Jenn?"

Did he have to look so expectant, like a puppy being shown a nice juicy bone?

"I'm sorry, Martin, but I've got a lot to do this weekend." Jennifer couldn't meet his eyes so she peered at the wedding bands in the glass display case.

"You said that the last time—and the time before that." He took off his glasses and wiped the lenses on a towel hanging next to his workbench. "It's been four months. Isn't it about time you forgot about Ed?"

"Ed? Who is Ed?" Dar asked, his voice so deep it sent shivers down Jennifer's back.

Martin cleared his throat. "He's the guy who ran off with a rich widow from Pottstown."

Dar grunted.

Humiliated by the conversation, Jennifer felt her cheeks grow warm. "I don't want to talk about it, Martin."

Martin put his glasses back on and peered at her with a sad expression. "I think you keep saying no to a date because you're afraid I'll leave—just like your father."

"What?"

Martin nodded, obviously delighted that his amateur psychology had unsettled her.

"That's the most ridiculous thing I've ever heard." Jennifer ran her hand up and down the chain holding her mother's ring.

"But it's true," Martin continued. "When was the last time you had a date? Or even went out with some girlfriends?"

It was true she'd been busy fixing the house, but she'd been out several times since her mother's death. Sure that she could put Martin's mind to rest very quickly, Jennifer frowned as her mind became a blank.

"Well?"

"It's none of your business, Martin."

"About this weekend—"

"I'm going to be busy," she said before he could ask about another time. "I want an appraisal on a piece of jewelry."

The jeweler frowned and ran a hand though his thinning sandy brown hair. "I'm sorry, Jenn. Like I said last month, I can't give you any more for your father's watch. It just isn't worth what you want for it."

"I'm not here about that, Martin," she told him, embarrassed that he had brought up another delicate subject in front of her new boarder. "I have something else."

She took the armband out of her handbag and slid it onto the counter. Martin stared but didn't pick it up.

"I think you're wasting my time." His watery blue eyes stared at her face, silently accusing her of playing a joke on him. "That thing is too big to be real gold."

Dar, who had been silent for the previous exchange, now leaned over the counter and grabbed Martin's shirt in one extremely large hand. "You are accusing Jennifer of lying, *já?"*

"N-no." Martin swallowed loudly. "Of course n-not."

Dar took his time letting go of Martin's shirt. "Good. Because the armband is mine. I would hate to have to run you through with my sword."

Jennifer groaned as Martin's face paled even further.

"Um. You can calm down now, Dar."

The hulking Norseman grunted but didn't let go of Martin.

Having Dar around did have its advantages, Jennifer mused. Like getting the attention of reluctant salesclerks. "Martin, about that piece of jewelry . . ."

"I-I'll look at it immediat-tely."

"You can let him go now, Dar."

Martin scurried over to the small worktable in the corner, out of Dar's reach. After a few minutes he returned. "I can't believe it, Jennifer. I tested it and you're right—it's almost pure gold!"

Dar crossed his arms against his wide chest and gave her an I-told-you-so look.

Martin whipped a calculator out of his pocket and

entered numbers. "I won't be able to give you all the money today," he told her, weighing the piece of jewelry on his scale. "I don't keep that much here at the store." He stared at Dar's enormous biceps. "How about a down payment and the rest in a few days?"

He named a figure that made her light-headed. It was worth that much? Jennifer couldn't speak. Her vocal cords had frozen together.

"That is a fair amount, Jennifer? *Já?*" Dar asked, his tone promising reprisals if she said no.

Realizing they were waiting for a reply, she said, "I'm not sure. I really should have checked it out before we came here."

"It's fair, Jenn. I wouldn't cheat you. Honest."

Realizing she would have to either take his word or wait several more days for the money, Jennifer bit her lip. Martin might be pushy, but he wasn't dishonest.

"I guess that will be all right, Martin."

The jeweler nodded and opened the cash register. Jennifer eased closer to the counter and watched him count out some bills. Her hands trembled as she accepted the money.

Now she could afford to pay some of the more pressing overdue notices. Her hand tightened around the bills. But the money wasn't hers. It was Dar's. As much as she would like to keep it, he needed it more.

Briskly, she counted out a week's worth of rent money and handed him the rest. If only her mother could have been here to see how well Jennifer was coping with her new boarder. But her mother would probably say Dar reminded her of Jennifer's dad. Since he'd left her all those years ago, almost every man seemed to remind her mom of him.

"Come on, Dar. Let's go."

Dar wondered why Jennifer's voice had grown husky. He stared at the tears hovering on the corners of her lashes. "You are upset. You should be happy he gave you money, not crying."

She almost ran out the door. "I'm not crying. I've got something in my eye." She ran down the steps of the store and crossed the street, with him right behind her.

Was Martin responsible for her tears?

"I will go back and beat that little man for upsetting you," Dar growled, stalking back toward the shop. He had almost reached the front door of the establishment when he felt her hand on his arm, pulling him away from the jeweler's.

"No," she whispered sadly. "I'm just thinking of my mother."

"Why does thinking about your mother make you sad?" He had seen pictures of a white-haired woman on Jennifer's table, but hadn't had time to ask her to identify them.

"My mother passed away about six months ago. I still miss her, especially when I come home to an empty house at night."

The death of a loved one was a painful experience, no matter what world you lived in. "What about your father? He still lives, *já?*"

Her lips twisted into a cynical smile. "I'm not sure. My dad came home drunk one night, packed his bags, and left us. He never came back, so I don't know if he's dead or alive."

"A true warrior would never abandon either his people or his family. Honor would not permit it." Dar clenched his fists, unable to understand the reason behind such a selfish action.

She raised her chin and walked faster. "Mom and I managed fine without him. Let's drop the subject, okay?"

Looking at her grim expression, Dar realized her father's betrayal had left deep scars. Was that why she had never chosen a mate?

"If you're ready, we'll go finish the rest of our errands. Our first priority is getting you out of those clothes and into something less noticeable. Then we'll buy groceries."

"Good. I'm hungry."

Jennifer sighed. "Is food all you can think about?"

Dar looked at her rosy cheeks and parted lips, so close and yet a world too far away. "*Nei,* but 'tis the safest thing right now."

"What's taking you so long?" Jennifer asked through the dressing-room door.

"I can't secure these clothes," Dar growled, trying to pull up the small metal tab on the stiff blue pants.

"You mean the zipper on the dungarees? Just grab it and pull. Do you want me to do it?"

Dar leaned his head against the mirror as he envisioned Jennifer's hand reaching toward his body and . . . He felt himself grow larger. Too large to fit inside the pants.

"*Nei.*" He gritted his teeth. "These are too small."

"Okay. Stay right there. I'll go get a larger size."

Dar struggled with the tight pants. Why would anyone want to wear such constricting clothes? He finally peeled them off and dropped them on the floor, right next to the huge pile of garments he had been forced to try on.

"Open the door and I'll hand you the next pair."

He stuck his hand out of the small cubicle and

grabbed at the items in Jennifer's hand. In addition to another pair of blue pants, she had given him a small white garment with several holes.

"Jennifer, what is this?"

"It's underwear."

When he remained silent, she stepped closer to the door and whispered, "You wear them under your pants. You stick your leg in each hole and . . . I'm sure you can figure out how to put them on. If not, I'll get a male salesclerk to help you."

Dar spent several minutes struggling with the undergarments. By the time he was done, sweat poured off his forehead.

"How do they fit?"

What should he tell her? If only he could show her how tight they were. Or the way they clung to his hips. But that led to temptation, and it was best to have on as many clothes as possible when he was around Jennifer. He'd found her much too alluring to be leaving so soon. He should avoid situations that intensified his attraction.

"They are fine." He pulled at the too-tight waistband. "Just fine."

Next, he tried on what she called "dress clothes." In the back of the store, at the alterations section, the tailor measured his leg, then put his hand by Dar's crotch. Dar roared and grabbed the man by his shirt collar.

"Dar! Put him down," Jennifer said with more than a hint of shock in her voice. "Slowly. That's right. Let his feet touch the ground before you let go of him."

"But Jennifer . . ."

"Dar, I'll explain later. Just let the man finish." The weary expression on her face, combined with the nervous way she kept plucking at her coat, told him she was as upset as he felt.

Hungry and tired, Dar stood immobile while the tailor poked, prodded, and stuck him with a pin—several times, in fact. He listened patiently as Jennifer explained how clothes were fitted on this world. Finally, after what seemed like an eternity, the man allowed Dar to move freely.

"Aren't you going to wear your new clothes?" Jennifer asked as she paid the salesclerk with some of the bills from the jeweler.

Dar shook his head. *"Nei.* I'll save them for another time. Let's go purchase some provisions."

Outside, Dar scowled as he watched the cars zoom down the street. If he didn't look both ways, he could be struck down in an instant. A low roar, coming from the sky, made him tense and search his surroundings, a hand on his sword.

"It's an airplane." She pointed toward a small object flying near the sun. "People travel from place to place in a matter of hours. It's sort of like my Jeep, only bigger."

"Your Jeep can fly?"

A logical question, surely not one to make her bite her lip and smile. "No. It can't fly. But it can do zero to sixty in less than fifteen seconds."

An unintelligible answer, if ever he heard one. Dar continued to stare at the sky, amazed at the things the people here took for granted.

Inside the supermarket, Jennifer tried to ignore the curious glances being cast at Dar, but it was hard. When his flowing mantle caught on yet another shopping cart, she sighed. "I should have insisted you change out of that thing," she whispered to him in the vegetable aisle.

Dar just grunted and threw bags of potatoes into the shopping cart. Jennifer wondered if he knew how much money this trip would cost them.

"You'll take me somewhere nearby where I can pick herbs, *já?* A densely wooded area near a running stream would be best."

Trying to look as if she went to the store with an overdressed Viking every day, Jennifer took him down the baking aisle to look for the herbs. "What type of stuff do you want?"

Dar peered at the rows of tiny bottles. "I need basil, bay leaves, marjoram, mint, rosemary, sage, tarragon, and thyme."

"What do you need all that for?"

"I must restock my bag of spells. It grows low."

Jennifer threw the bottles into her cart. "I asked for that one."

When Dar continued scanning the shelf, Jennifer couldn't contain her curiosity. "What are you looking for now?"

"Rats' tails, snake skins, spiderwebs, gnome's tears. The usual sorcerer's ingredients."

Seeing two people in the aisle stop and whisper, Jennifer pulled on his arm. "They're out of the basics. We'll have to try somewhere else, maybe South Street in Philadelphia."

The meat counter was next. Jennifer could almost see the drool on Dar's lips as he tossed large hunks of beef into their shopping cart. Whole chickens and pieces of salmon were next.

"Who is the person in charge of this business?" he asked, his eyes glued to the huge slabs of meat hanging behind the window.

"The butcher," she replied, mentally adding up the cost of their purchases.

''Get him,'' he ordered, his expression intent.

My, he became abrupt when he was around food.

The butcher, Orville Webster, looked like the perfect stereotype. Rotund, with a huge, bulging stomach, he carried a large cleaver in one hand and a piece of cellophane in the other.

''Yeah. Who wants the butcher?'' he growled.

Dar pounced on the man with the speed of a thundering train. ''I desire some meat.'' The tall Norseman ticked off his list of demands. ''We will buy several sides of oxen, freshly cut, without the heads. Ten savory roasts, twelve whole salmon, and three barrels of sweet mead.''

Jennifer didn't know whether to laugh at Orville's dazed expression or sneak out of the store before he called the mental hospital.

''Uh huh.'' Oliver thumbed the handle of his cleaver. ''And would ya like that wrapped with a big red bow?''

Dar frowned. *''Nei.* The bow won't be necessary.'' He turned to confirm that with Jennifer. ''Unless the bow is a custom with which I am unfamiliar. Then you may include it with the order.''

''Dar . . .'' Jennifer tried to warn him, but it was too late.

''Listen, buster, I don't know which planet you just flew in from, but they don't pay me enough to take orders from weird dudes in purple capes.'' He held up the knife. ''Now get out of here before I split you in two.''

The Norseman disarmed him in the blink of an eye.

''Dar!'' Her hands clenched around her handbag. ''Let go of Mr. Webster's neck. Now! His face is turning red!''

Slowly, Dar set the man on his feet. Jennifer picked

up the discarded cleaver by its wooden handle and gingerly moved it out of temptation's way. After this, they would never be allowed in the store again. Jennifer grabbed Dar's arm, but it was like trying to move a mountain.

"I'm so terribly sorry, Mr. Webster. Dar is the son of my mother's cousin. You know, the one in the insane asylum? You'll have to excuse him. He gets a little agitated when he's hungry."

The butcher clutched his throat and pointed a finger at her companion. "I'm gonna have you arrested for attempted murder," he gasped between breaths. "Wait and see."

Jennifer gave up trying to move Dar. She clutched her mother's ring, but for once, the cool gold failed to soothe her. She pulled so hard, the fine chain snapped. Horrified that she'd almost lost the most important thing she owned, Jennifer held the ring and chain in her clenched fist.

"Please don't call the police, Mr. Webster. We're leaving now."

"I can see that your cousin isn't the only person who should be in an asylum," the butcher yelled. "It probably runs in the family. Your mother was probably crazy, too."

Dar's roar shook the cans on the shelf. Orville reached for his cleaver.

Jennifer shrieked. "Oh, no!"

The butcher never had a chance.

Chapter Four

In the car, Jennifer tried to control her trembling. ''I can't believe you held him upside down and dunked his head in the pickle barrel!'' She put her foot on the gas and urged the Jeep to go faster. ''So what if he got you angry? It didn't justify half-drowning him.''

''It was his crude reference to your ancestors, your mother in particular, that compelled me to jump to your defense.''

Jennifer waited until she turned the corner before she continued. ''Now, where was I? Oh, yes. The pickle barrel.''

Dar clutched the door handle so hard, his knuckles turned white. ''You mentioned that several times. I've said I'm sorry and sworn I will not go near the pickles again. That is enough? *Já?*''

Maybe she was overreacting. Jennifer drove around Morgantown, helping Dar search for his Bifrost

Bridge, knowing they wouldn't find it anywhere south of Canada.

"Okay, Dar. But there are only two other supermarkets in the area. I'm not taking any chances. Next time I go in alone."

He heaved a sigh of relief and clutched the door handle as they went over another bump. "As you wish, Jennifer."

An hour and a half later, Jennifer pulled into her driveway and shut off the engine. Dar grabbed three of the bags in the backseat and carried them toward the house.

Inside, Jennifer slammed her bags on the kitchen counter. Dar hovered next to her, peering at everything she took out of the bag. His nearness unnerved her. Her hands trembled as he watched every move she made.

She put away the frozen food first. Next came the refrigerated items. When that was done, Jennifer stood on her tiptoes and tried to put a can of olives on the top shelf of the cabinet.

"Here. Let me do that."

A large masculine hand reached over her head and gently pried the can from her grasp. A warm chest brushed against her back. She heard his steady breathing. She smelled a unique masculine blend of soap and sweat. She felt his thigh muscles bunch as he put the can on the shelf. She saw his shadow, large, dependable, and oh so close.

"Thanks." Jennifer hoped he didn't notice the bright red flush that she knew stained her face.

"You are most welcome, Jennifer," he said gravely.

He stepped back, allowing her room to put away the rest of her groceries. As she moved about the kitchen, Dar's piercing blue gaze never wavered from her face. It was intimate. It was unnerving. If only she knew what he was thinking.

Jennifer became so rattled, she walked into an open drawer. She gasped at the pain in her hip. Immediately, his arms were around her, steadying her shaking knees.

"Steady. There is no blood." His breath tickled her ear. "Can you speak?"

She couldn't find her voice. Not when her head was pressed so closely to his beating heart.

"Shall I destroy that treacherous piece of wood so this won't happen again?"

Would he set fire to her cabinets? Jennifer wrapped her arms around his waist and squeezed. Anything to stop him from breaking the drawer. "I'm fine. Just a little sore."

He grunted and shifted his weight. That was when she noticed the large bulge against her stomach. And that he had dropped his hands to his sides. And that she was embracing him so tightly her arms were beginning to hurt.

Her ears burning with humiliation, Jennifer eased herself away and averted her eyes from his face. "I'm sorry." What could she have been thinking of? "I overreacted."

"There is nothing to forgive."

Did his voice sound a little stiff? And did he have to turn his back on her?

The doorbell echoed through the house, diverting Jennifer's attention away from Dar's taut shoulders. "You stay here," she told him. "I'll get the door."

Who could it be? She rarely had company, and it was the wrong time of day for the mailman. Pushing Firedrake out of her way with her foot, Jennifer opened the door and came face-to-face with Mrs. Elvira Nordstrom, her neighbor from across the street. The two of them had grown to be good friends over the years, though the woman was forever trying to set Jennifer up with her son. Jennifer knew that it was only because the older woman had an overpowering material instinct and just wanted her to be happy, though, so she quietly ignored the woman's not-so-subtle hints.

Although Elvira's son had dark brown hair, twinkling green eyes and an athletic body, Jennifer had never been attracted to him. At thirty, he still played the field; Jennifer refused to be one of his one-night stands.

"Good afternoon, dear." The older woman peered into Jennifer's house. "I really hate to bother you, but I was wondering if you've seen any squirrels running around in your backyard."

"Squirrels?"

Mrs. Nordstrom plucked at the strings to her wide red hat. "A family of squirrels made a home near my yard. I'm sure you've noticed me going out to feed the cute little creatures every morning."

Elvira's dark sunglasses made seeing her eyes impossible, but Jennifer could tell by the wide tracks in her makeup that the woman had been crying.

"Yes, I've seen them running up and down the trees in the back." Jennifer massaged her sore hip. "What about them?"

"Well, I noticed that you had some birdseed on your porch, so I thought you might be feeding them. It seems that one of the parents is missing."

The statement, delivered in a hesitant tone of voice, made Jennifer reach for her necklace. Too late, she remembered it wasn't there.

"As I was saying, I wondered if you've seen any of the cute little creatures near your house." Elvira took a step forward and peered over Jennifer's shoulder.

Jennifer flattened her palms against her dungarees. Had Elvira seen her boarder do anything out of the ordinary?

"Why would you think they'd be here?"

Mrs. Nordstrom bit her lip. "Well, dearie, I did see that huge bird that you must have bought playing with the mother squirrel right before she disappeared."

Firedrake!

"What was the bird doing?" Jennifer asked, resisting the urge to spin around and check to see if Firedrake had dragged the poor squirrel into the house.

"Well, I think they were fighting."

Jennifer took a deep, unsteady breath. "Fighting?"

"Yes. You see, I was watching my soaps and I heard a loud screech. When I looked out the window, your bird was hovering over the squirrel, and it was hissing and running toward the big tree in my yard. By the time I got to the door, the squirrel and the bird were gone."

"Gone?" Her voice squeaked like an unoiled door.

Her friend nodded her head. "Yes, dearie. Gone. And I've been wondering what happened ever since. Could you check around your house and let me know if it's in there?"

Jennifer hugged her arms around her waist. Apprehension settled around her mind like a shroud and made it hard for her to think. "Of course, Elvira. I'll do it right now." She almost pushed the old woman off the porch. "Why don't you go back and watch the rest of your stories? If I find any squirrels, I'll call you immediately."

"Oh, thank you, dear." Elvira paused. "I don't want you to think I'm lonely, but I've been thinking about getting a pet. Something I could put in my lap while I watch TV."

"Well, Firedrake isn't a lap type of animal. Maybe you should get a cat or something."

Mrs. Nordstrom shrugged. "Oh, I almost forgot. Marcus said to say hi."

"That's nice," she managed to say. She'd never been able to muster up any enthusiasm over the man.

"Oh, he also told me that if you ever need anything, just let him know. He's still working at the same place and he knows a lot of important people."

Since Jennifer didn't remember what Marcus did for a living, that didn't really help in any way. If he was anything like his mother, the man would drive her crazy within a week.

"That's kind of him to remember me," Jennifer replied. "I've got several job interviews this week. If none of them works out, I'll call him." She'd do no such thing, but it was the best way to get rid of her neighbor.

Jennifer waited until Elvira tottered off the porch before she slammed the door and leaned against it. Several squirrels were gone and Firedrake was the last one to see them. She looked around the room. Where was that critter now?

"Firedrake?"

A soft hissing noise made her stare at the large, flowered chair near the sofa. There, sitting with his claws covering his bulging stomach, was Firedrake. Jennifer felt the color leave her face. Why did he have such a pleased expression on his face, as if he were smiling? And why did he keep rubbing his stomach, as if he had just eaten a big meal?

Firedrake burped. The sound echoed throughout the room. She stared in amazement as he yawned. *My, what numerous sharp teeth he had.* Almost too many teeth for such a small, innocent dragon, who looked noticeably larger than when she'd first seen him.

"Oh, my God! Dar, where are you?"

The large Norseman immediately appeared in the kitchen doorway. "*Já?* What's wrong, Jennifer?"

"Mrs. Nordstrom's squirrel is missing."

His expression grew more serious as his crystal translated her words. "I assume this animal is important to you?"

"Yes. I mean, no." She leaned against the peeling door. "Dar, she said Firedrake was playing with the mother squirrel right before it disappeared."

"That's impossible. Firedrake would never do such a thing. He would never play with such a creature!"

Did he look wary? Jennifer was sure he knew something about the rodent's disappearance, but was hesitant to tell her. "Do you think the squirrel is somewhere in the house?"

Dar stared at Firedrake—more accurately, at his stomach. "*Já,* it's possible," he said.

"Mrs. Nordstrom wants me to take the squirrel back."

"*Nei.* I'm afraid that is impossible, Jennifer."

She closed her eyes and took deep breaths in an effort not to scream. "Why is it impossible?"

"Because, if my suspicion is correct, Firedrake ate the squirrel."

Firedrake wriggled into a more comfortable position and picked his teeth with his curved, sharp claws.

"Dar, please tell me you're joking," she pleaded, her hand to her chest.

"I'm sorry, Jennifer. But 'tis most likely the truth."

Mrs. Nordstrom was going to be devastated.

"I can't believe you brought a squirrel-eating dragon into this house," she shouted, hoping he was kidding, but knowing he wasn't.

Dar's mouth dropped open. "Fire-breathing dragons are meat-eaters. What did you expect him to eat? Berries?"

Her visions of Firedrake as a a cute little lizard-type creature burst like a balloon. A meat-eater. A carnivore, one who ate squirrels—bones and blood and tail—for dinner. Bile rose in her throat as she realized how stupid she'd been.

Dar put his hands on her shoulders, as if to prepare her for a shock. "Firedrake eats small animals. Cats, dogs, squirrels." His hands tightened around her arms. "As he grows bigger, he will devour larger mammals such as sheep and goats."

Her knees gave way. He held her as the room started spinning like a child's top.

"Jennifer, are you all right?" She felt him lift her into his arms and hold her against his warm chest. "Can you hear me?" When she didn't answer, he cursed under his breath.

How would Mrs. Nordstrom take the news that her boarder's pet had eaten the squirrels? She should go outside and check if the beast had left any remains, but the thought made her weaker.

"Jennifer!"

She was beyond speech. A few moments later, she felt cool sheets against her back and a soft pillow under her head.

"I'm sorry, Jennifer. I thought you understood."

How could she have known? she screamed silently. It wasn't as if she had studied the diets of dragons before. She'd never seen a live dragon in her entire life, fire-breathing or otherwise. They didn't exist. At least, not in her world. Which emphasized the fact that Dar wasn't from Earth.

The bed tilted at a steep angle as the sorcerer sat down next to her and rubbed her hands, "It's all right, sprite. I'm here." The rich timbre of his voice soothed her. "Nothing will harm you." She felt him take her in his arms and brush his callused hand against her face. "Sleep, Jennifer. I'll watch over you. I swear it."

She closed her eyes and listened to his husky whisper. Then, suddenly exhausted, she snuggled closer to his body and put her arms around his waist. Why couldn't he be a normal person? One without a dragon. Or a magic mantle. Or a crystal dagger. A tear slid down her cheek. His gentle fingers immediately brushed it away.

Hidden in the bushes outside of Valhalla, Lor waited until Loki drew close; then he seized him. *"Stodva!"* He tightened his grip upon Loki's shirt. "Where have you sent my brother?"

Loki paled. He clawed at Lor's hands. "O mighty Dragon Master, I am also concerned about Dar. I am at this moment going to search for him."

Lor didn't believe him, but there was naught he could do to the Trickster except threaten him. Loki was Dar's only chance to return to Asgard. "I'll give you until the next banquet. If Dar isn't sitting at his seat in the hall, you'll feel my wrath. And you won't like it." He gave Loki one more shake. "Do you understand me?"

"Já," Loki gasped. "I understand."

Unable to tolerate the Trickster so close to him, Lor shoved Loki's thin body away. "Good. Go now and find my brother. Don't return until you can tell me to which of the nine worlds you have sent him."

Lor laid a gentle hand on the neck of his dragon as he watched Loki limp into Valhalla, the Hall of the Slain. "Firestorm, I do not trust that jotun as far as I can throw him."

The dragon grunted and twitched his long brown tail.

"Excellent idea, Firestorm. I think we must watch his every move, also." Lor crept along the bushes. "Come, he's entering the hall. Let's see what he does next."

Lor stood watch and saw Loki disappear in a shimmering burst of light and thunder. Hearing the noise, a thrall lumbered out of the kitchen area and looked about, a perplexed expression on his wide face.

"I will stay here until Loki returns, no matter how long it takes." A grim smile on his face, Lor tested the sharpness of his dagger.

Jennifer awoke to the tantalizing aroma of the food being waved under her nose.

"You are awake? Good. I've prepared food."

Dinner? She heard Dar put a dish on the bedside table.

"Are you hungry, sprite? Open your eyes and eat. I have cooked oxen and roasted potatoes."

She gasped as she opened her eyes and stared at the huge man who was only inches away. He helped her sit up.

" 'Tis all right. I won't harm you. I've brought you food." He fluffed her pillow with hands that looked strong enough to bend steel.

Although he looked mighty enough to break her nightstand over his knee, his big hands were gentle and graceful. "Thank you. I didn't know you could cook."

Dar chuckled, a throaty sound that urged her to stare at his deeply tanned face. "I have many talents I have yet to mention." He handed her a napkin. "Cooking is but one of them." Dar cut the steak and speared it onto his dagger. "Here. Taste it."

She stared at the piece of meat for a few seconds, then put the morsel into her mouth. "Hmmmm. It's just the way I like it—burnt on the outside, but juicy on the inside." She opened her mouth for another bite. "Aren't you going to have some?"

Dar busied himself cutting the meat. "*Nei.* I've already eaten," he said, preoccupied with the task before him. "But I will have some to please you."

Jennifer soon realized that sharing a meal with a handsome man in a bedroom was a lot more intimate than she could have imagined. His every gaze reminded her that she was a woman. She averted her gaze to the dish and willed her heart to slow its frantic beating.

Dar made sure she ate everything on the dish but maintained a distance between them that reassured her that his intentions were honorable.

When she had eaten every last piece of meat on the plate, Jennifer sank back into the soft pillow. "Thank you for dinner. It was delicious," she said, unable to stop staring at the muscles that rippled in his arms every time he moved.

"You are most welcome, Jennifer."

"I'm amazed you learned your way around the kitchen that quickly, Dar."

Dar smiled and accepted the praise with the demeanor of a person used to compliments. "I didn't use the stove in your kitchen. I cooked the meat out back over a fire."

His words made her break out into a sweat. "But Dar, I don't have a barbecue grill."

"I did not use a grill."

The food in her stomach began to twist and turn. She put a trembling hand on her stomach in an attempt to calm her nerves.

"If you didn't use a grill, then how did you cook the food?" she asked, trying to keep a tight rein on her temper.

"I made a fire and used the pots hanging over your sink."

Jennifer closed her eyes and forced herself to ask the question. "How?" She drummed her fingers on the comforter. "I have no firewood. There aren't any small trees on my property."

"You're worried, *já?* You shouldn't be worried, Jennifer. I didn't touch your cabinets."

"Then what did you use?" she asked, not really wanting to know his answer.

He wiped off his dagger and stuck it back into the waistband of his tight beige pants. "I chopped up that kitchen chair you complained about, the one with the trick leg that collapses when you sit on it." He pushed out his chest, proud of his resourcefulness. "I remembered what you said at dinner last eve. 'The next time that chair tips me on the floor, I'm going to chop it and use it for kindling!' I saved you the trouble."

"You did what?" she bellowed, almost jumping out of bed.

"Calm down." He pushed her back against her pillows. "It is, how do you say, okay?"

"How could you do such a thing?" Her nails dug into his arms. She tried to restrain herself from strangling him.

"I did it for you," he said gently.

Jennifer sighed, her anger disappearing like dew on a sunny day.

"You are not pleased?"

What could she say? She tried to smile, but all she could manage was a grimace that threatened to turn into a sob. "Words can't describe my emotions right now. I'm speechless. Utterly speechless. Now, if you don't mind, I think I'm going to lie down again. Suddenly, I don't feel so well."

"I understand." He put the empty dishes on the tray and moved toward the door. "And please do not worry about the long bench Firedrake mauled. I will, of course, pay for the damages."

"Not the sofa, too!" Her face must have been red because he reached out to gently touch her forehead, as if checking for a fever. She batted his hand away from her face. "I'm going to make sure you don't leave before you pay for everything."

"I always pay my debts."

"Good."

Just for a moment, his guard came down and she could see his emotions. Sexual awareness burned in his gaze, followed by desire and, momentarily, by wistfulness. If she had blinked, she would have missed it. But then he turned away, and all she could see were his wide shoulders and narrow hips.

"Sleep well, Jennifer."

"Good night."

The door closed with more than a hint of a slam.

Jennifer stared at her ceiling and compelled her rapid pulse to slow down. Somehow, she knew she would have a hard time falling asleep. And when she did, she had the feeling she would dream of a tall blond man with bulging biceps and a rich voice that made her shiver every time she heard it.

Henry Sneed tried to rub some warmth into his trembling hands. The offices inside the Wells Institute were ultramodern, but they reminded him of a morgue, cold and sterile; it was a place he felt uncomfortable even thinking about. At night, the building was even creepier.

"What do you mean you can't find the dragon?" Jason's tone could strip paint off a door.

Henry nervously fiddled with the buttons on his purple shirt. "The men have searched almost every inch of the surrounding area. They haven't seen hide nor scale of anything even resembling the creature we saw."

He stared at the director of the Wells Institute and feared for his life. Several scientists had disappeared in the past few years, and they had all been people who had failed in performing a task Jason had given them.

Wells tapped his fingers on the desk, a mild reaction but one Henry knew well. Jason was furious, and he would bear the brunt of his anger.

"This is all your fault," Jason reminded him yet again. "If your car hadn't gotten a flat, we would have been able to follow those people."

Then, obviously realizing that Henry was still waiting for an order, the director clenched his fists. "Send double the amount of men out again. I want to know the whereabouts of that dragon, or I will be reading résumés for my assistant's job.'' Jason leaned forward and snarled, ''Do you understand me?''

Unable to get any sound past the huge lump in his throat, Henry nodded.

''We have to talk,'' Jennifer told Dar over breakfast.

Feeling comfortably tired after two hours of practicing with his sword, Dar grunted and reached for another piece of bread. This was his sixth, but who was counting?

''You've been here a week. How's the spell-casting coming along?'' she asked. ''Have you thought of a way to return to Asgard?''

Dar scowled. *''Nei.* I have tried every spell I know. Nothing seems to work. Without the crystal caves nearby, my spells are reduced to half their strength. Not even my crystal ball has the ability to return me to my own time.''

''I'm sorry, Dar. Do you think your mentor, Mimir, would be able to help you?''

''Mimir is extremely wise, yet ancient,'' Dar explained, leaning his head on his palm. ''He speaks in riddles that confuse most who talk to him. As soon as this war between Asgard and the Jotuns is done, I will seek him out and question him as to my seeking the next level of spiritual growth.''

''Sounds like it would be an interesting conversation.'' Jennifer tapped her fingers against her lips. ''What do you think about us trying to find another piece of crystalite?''

''A good idea, but it would not work unless I knew the exact words of the spell Loki used.''

Jennifer drew circles on the table. ''I hear you pacing in your room. I know you want to go home, but staying up all night and searching for the Bifrost

Bridge all day will only make you ill.'' She sighed. ''Since it looks like you're going to be my guest for a while, I want to go over a few rules.''

No one ever gave orders to a sorcerer except Odin. Dar crossed his arms, a small smile on his face at her bravery. ''What are your demands?''

''First of all, you must try not to destroy anything else in the house.''

Easier said than done.

''No more chopping up my kitchen chairs to make a fire. And you can't continue to sheathe your sword in that big high-back chair. It's going to take me days to sew all those holes.''

Dar glanced out the window in time to see Firedrake dive and catch another squirrel.

''. . . I don't want you to come into my room unless the house is on fire or you're dying.''

She was talking so fast, his crystal had a hard time translating all her words. At this point he would agree to almost anything but the purchase of more peanut butter. He used his tongue to scrape the thick substance off the roof of his mouth.

''And last but not least, you've got to talk to Firedrake and tell him not to eat any more of my neighbor's pets.''

He slammed his hand on the table. ''Firedrake is a dragon, Jennifer. Dragons eat living animals.'' And as they got bigger, they ate bigger live animals, a fact she seemed to despise.

''Tell him it's either frozen meat or birdseed.'' Jennifer refused to look intimidated. ''He'll get used to it.''

Dar admired her courage even as he tried to accept her requests. ''I'll talk to him.''

''Good.'' Dar watched her hand reach for the last

piece of toast. He wet his lips. Although the small squares tasted like the burnt skin of an old dragon's tail, they were better than starving to death.

"I'm so stuffed I can't eat this last piece. I guess I'll have to toss it down the disposal."

Dar leapt to his feet and grabbed the piece of bread before Jennifer could toss it away. "Norsemen hate to see food wasted. I'll force myself to eat the last piece of dry . . . I mean, toast."

"Okay, Dar." Jennifer put the dirty dishes in the sink. "Oh, and don't forget: We have to go into town tomorrow to pick up the rest of the money from your bracelet."

"And more provisions?"

"Yes, we'll need to get more food, too. I'm hoping one of those people I interviewed with yesterday will call me back for a second interview. Just in case, I have to mail a couple of résumés, so we'll stop at the post office on the way to the store."

"And don't forget fresh meat for Firedrake. He won't like being unable to catch his dinner, but he will eat other meat if it is fresh."

"I don't know, Dar. That's going to be expensive. And I don't know if I can afford anything other than ground meat. . . ."

Thunderclouds gathered outside as Dar's magic searched for an outlet for his tension. Lightning flickered from his fingertips as he snapped his fingers. It lit up the sky. "I will pay for his food."

Unaware of his actions, Jennifer smiled in approval. "Okay." She leaned her hip against the kitchen table and watched him, a pensive expression on her face. "I was thinking about making an apple pie for dessert. I haven't made one in a long time, but it isn't that hard to bake. Do you like pie?"

Did sorcerers love incantations? He unclenched his hand. The howling wind stopped rattling the shutters. "*Já!* If it is at all possible."

"Good." She took a piece of paper and jotted down notes. "I'd make a blueberry pie, but they're out of season. Only the baneberries are growing right now, and they're poisonous."

None of the women in Asgard would even think of preparing dinner. They left the cooking to the thralls. Jennifer, in old dungarees and with her hair falling naturally across her face, was more beautiful than most of the women in Asgard, a high compliment.

"My mother used to go right out back and pick the berries from the bushes near the trees," Jennifer mused, her mind obviously still on dessert. "Then she'd make the crust and put it in the oven."

Dar closed his eyes and breathed in her unique scent. On Earth, it seemed humans chose a mate when they were in love. At home, most of the women he knew chose husbands more for the man's ability to protect them than they did for love. When one lived in a world where demons and jotuns attacked on a regular basis, emotions such as love sometimes took second place to a man's ability to yield a sword.

Hearing Jennifer put the piece of paper in her pocket, Dar opened his eyes and sighed. Somehow, he knew that life with this woman would never be dull or boring.

In an effort to take his mind off the beautiful woman standing just within reach, he contemplated the jars of herbs on the counter and said, "Jennifer, you will show me how to work the fire machine?"

"You mean the stove?" She narrowed her eyes. "What do you want to make?"

He shrugged. "I must boil some rosemary so I can add it to my bag of spells."

"Why don't you do it after we come back from the store?"

"As you wish." He unscrewed the jar of bay leaves and breathed in the delightful aroma. It took him back to his early training in sorcery. He heard again his mother's voice. *"When you place a leaf in each corner of the room, it sanctifies the chamber."*

Three leaves under a pillow inspired prophetic dreams. It also made a good addition to healing incense. A good sorcerer knew the secrets of herbs and how to use them to enhance the spells he cast.

"Ready, Dar? I'll go get the Jeep. You grab Firedrake and lock him in the house."

Dar put the jar back on the counter and walked over to the back door. How did one confine a fire-breathing dragon against his will? Especially in a house with large, fragile windows?

Hoping Jennifer would be tolerant of a few indiscretions of a furious dragon, Dar hesitated, and reached out to touch the transparent window. They didn't look expensive, but he couldn't judge the price of an object he had never purchased before.

"Are you coming, Dar?" Jennifer's impatient voice dragged him out of his musings.

"*Já.* In a few moments, Jennifer." Then, lower, he added, "First I must have a few words with my faithful companion."

He opened the back door and called Firedrake. While he waited for the dragon to appear, he rehearsed his speech. "Thou shall not eat furniture. Thou shall not gnaw on doorknobs. No eating of small, live animals. And no breaking of windows."

Firedrake flew into the kitchen and landed on the

long beige countertop near the sink. Dar winced as he looked at the deep gouges left by the dragon's powerful talons and sighed. "Jennifer will not be happy about this, um, minor accident."

Seeing the dragon blow smoke out of his nostrils, a talent he'd be better able to control as he grew larger, Dar thought of another rule. "No breathing of fire while inside the house."

Built of wood instead of stone, the hall would ignite with Firedrake's first strong, fiery breath. If Jennifer even suspected that such a thing could occur, he knew the dragon would find himself tied up, gagged, and stuffed in a closet. That would make the dragon angry, and, as anyone knew, an angry dragon was a dangerous dragon.

Firedrake took the sermon better than Dar expected, and although he did not get an agreement on every issue, the dragon did assent to the most important rules.

"Hurry up, Dar, or I'm leaving without you."

"*Já.* I am coming now, Jennifer."

Dar smiled. He still wasn't used to the fact that Jennifer did not stand in awe of him. Most Norsewomen he knew went out of their way to wait on him hand and foot. They admired his fighting ability and gave him everything he desired, even their bodies, if he encouraged them.

Not Jennifer. She said what was on her mind. Dar liked her honesty.

"Dar," she called out from the driver's seat of her car, "I'm going to count to three and then I'm going to turn on the ignition and take my foot off the brake."

Well, not actually liked, he told himself as he shut

the door and locked it. But he definitely admired her courage.

He stared at the doorknob, wondering why Jennifer was so sure the flimsy object would stop someone from entering her home. He could break it off with one sweep of his hand.

They were from two different cultures, with nothing in common. Dar knew the differences between them. So why did he still have this urge to forget about them and take Jennifer in his arms and show her how a Norseman caressed his woman?

Refusing to give in to such a tempting desire, Dar strode toward the metallic creature growling at him from the safety of the shade of an old oak tree. No matter what explanation Jennifer gave him, he would not relax while riding in the thing.

"I wish you wouldn't wince every time I put the car in gear," she said as he closed the door. "Men. They're not happy unless they're in the driver's seat."

Dar didn't think that human males from Earth had anything in common with sorcerers from Asgard. Except their anatomy, of course.

As for Jennifer, someone so squeamish about the death of a few squirrels would never fit in with a culture where men battled jotuns on a daily basis. So why couldn't he remember that fact and stop staring at her lips, wondering what she would do if he leaned over and kissed her?

Chapter Five

Loki contemplated the tall, lifeless buildings and hard, black streets of the alien world. "So this is Dar's new home." He tossed the crystalite from one hand to another. "It seems quiet. Too quiet. I must remedy that."

A wicked smile on his face, Loki buried the rock under a pile of leaves. "Now, I must announce my presence to Dar. It must be something simple, distinct. Something that can be seen from a great distance."

The large black demon next to him stretched his wings. At a distance demons appeared similar to dragons, but upon closer perusal, demons were meaner, smellier, and liked nothing better than tearing their food apart. Since demons usually ate men, this one scanned the area with more than a hint of interest.

"Come on, fiend. We've got to find Dar, then kill him. No one, not even Odin's grandson, makes a fool of me in front of my peers."

Atop the demon, Loki soared over the trees. There was nothing better than a good storm to give an immoral demon an appetite. Loki's evil laughter floated away on the icy breeze.

Sweating from a long workout, Dar sat down in the yard, next to his pouting dragon. "Come, Firedrake. You must eat." Dar dragged the bowl of raw, shredded meat closer to the dragon. "You must keep up your strength."

Firedrake averted his snout and nuzzled the small, shiny red berries growing on the high bushes. Dar glanced over his shoulder toward Jennifer's house and tried again.

"Jennifer swears she eats this ground meat and that it's full of healthy things." He poked at the unappetizing red sustenance. " 'Tis for your own good you eat this. 'Tis not healthy for you to eat the neighbor's pets. The owners have weapons and you might get killed."

The dragon nibbled at a berry and grunted, obviously unimpressed. Dar leaned his back against a tree. He hoped Jennifer appreciated his efforts to curb Firedrake's appetite. This wasn't going to be easy.

The icy wind announced the coming of a storm. For a moment, Dar thought he smelled the stench of a demon, but the odor was gone as quickly as it came. Sure he'd imagined it, Dar stared at the moonless sky and tried to think how he could talk his scaly companion into trying the lifeless Midgard food. He shook his head and plucked a few of the berries.

"The meat tastes much better than it looks."

This got him an assessing glance. Ready to follow up on the positive reaction, Dar picked up a handful of ground meat and put it in his mouth. "See? 'Tis fresh and savory and"—he grimaced and forced himself to swallow the vile-tasting beef—"unfit for consumption."

Dar ate a couple of the berries to clear the taste from his mouth. "By the flaming swords of the fire giants! We have a big problem."

Firedrake grunted and used his long tongue to spear another berry.

Dar stared at the raindrops splattering his sneakers. Although dragon skin naturally repelled water, they usually flew to a nearby cave and waited out the infrequent Asgard storms. He reached into his shirt pocket and pulled out his crystal ball.

"Dark night, clouds above us, form a covering above our head that will deflect the water from touching us."

Instantly, an invisible barrier separated them from the storm. Dar put the crystal back into his pocket and stared at the foraging dragon.

"Don't worry. I'll talk to Jennifer about the meat. I'm sure there must be something else you can eat on this world."

Dar heard the screen door open. He jumped to his feet.

"Dar, dessert is ready."

"I'm coming." He gave Firedrake one last assessing glance. "Don't forget: You must not eat any nocturnal animals. *Já?* They may be someone's pet out for a walk. And do not even think about using the porch railing to sharpen your nails. It will take me days to get the deep gouges out of the soft wood."

His lecture over, Dar hurried inside the house just in time to see Jennifer cutting a steaming pie.

"I hope you like it. I couldn't find Mom's cookbook, but I'm positive I remembered all the ingredients. I used to watch her bake all the time.'' She waited until he was sitting at the table, then handed him a plate. The smile on her face rivaled the brilliance of the sun. ''This is the first pie I've made in a couple of years. I want to know what you think of it.''

Dar's hand trembled as he grabbed a fork. Slowly, savoring every moment, he slid a large piece into his mouth.

And gagged.

''What's the matter?''

He coughed and motioned for a glass of water. It felt as if he'd swallowed fire from the pits of the fire giants. Jennifer rushed to the sink and poured him a full glass.

''Can you talk?''

Dar drained the entire glass and held it out for a refill. ''More,'' he croaked.

''Does this mean you don't like the pie?''

He emptied the second glass in one gulp. Gasping for air, he glanced sideways at the rest of the pie. The golden juice had pooled on the bottom of the plate. It looked so innocent. And delicious.

Looks could be so deceiving.

''What did you put in it?'' he asked, trying to think of a tactful way of telling her how awful it tasted.

''Oh, the usual. Sugar, apples, cinnamon, butter.'' She gestured toward the cans on the counter. ''Now you've got me worried. Maybe I should check the expiration dates.''

Jennifer picked up a small red container. ''I wonder if cinnamon has an expiration date.'' She looked at the label and paled. ''Oh, my God! It's cayenne pepper. I grabbed the wrong container. And I didn't even notice. It looks enough like cinnamon, I didn't think twice before I used it."

"An honest mistake, *já?*" he said hoarsely. Dar's insides still burned, all the way down to his stomach. He didn't know if he could talk above a whisper. He wet his burning lips.

Her face crumpled and it looked like she was going to cry. "I'm so sorry, Dar. Forgive me?"

Unwilling to hurt her feelings any further, Dar swallowed the lump in his throat and smiled. His lips trembled, but it was the best he could do. "Don't worry. You're forgiven, sprite. I'm growing used to the taste of cayenne."

Words could not express how he felt. Nauseated. Thirsty. Ill. Those words seemed the closest. He drank more water. If he didn't know better, he would swear Jennifer was trying to poison him.

An hour later, crouched next to the indoor outhouse facility called a toilet, Dar learned the meaning of the word misery. He couldn't keep anything down in his stomach. He was so dizzy and nauseated, he could barely stand.

"Jennifer." The shout for assistance came out sounding like a croak. Dar staggered out of the bathroom and down the dimly lit hallway toward his room. He squinted as beads of sweat trickled down his forehead and dripped into his eyes. With the last of his strength, Dar reached for the brass doorknob.

"If I live through this, it will be because the old gods are aiding me." A brief search of his room yielded no healing runes. He needed help or he would soon lose consciousness. And the only person he could turn to was the one who might have poisoned him.

* * *

Jennifer untied the sash of her robe. "If I don't find another job soon," she murmured to herself, "I'll have to do something desperate, like rob a bank."

She draped the robe over the chair next to her bed and reached for her nightgown. She held it to her nose. It smelled of lavender and crisp air.

"I hope Dar's forgiven me and doesn't think I was trying to poison him."

Wondering what her blue-eyed boarder was doing now, Jennifer sat down on the edge of the bed. If only he wasn't so handsome. If only she had the courage to share his bed and not even think about the consequences. But despite his protests, he was probably just like all the other men she'd known in the past. He would leave her and never come back.

Unable to go through that anguish again, Jennifer pulled the warm flannel over her head. The door to her room crashed into the wall with a bang that rivaled a clap of thunder. She jumped to her feet.

Had she conjured the sorcerer with her thoughts? Wearing an unbuttoned shirt and dungarees that rode low on his hips, he appeared too masculine. Too virile. Too intimidating. His wide shoulders spanned the doorway. The air of danger surrounding him seemed twice as strong as usual.

"What are you doing in here?" She took a step backward and reached for a weapon. Her hand grasped her hairbrush. She waved it in front of her as if it was a sword. "Get out. Now."

He took a step closer. "Jennifer."

The crystal around his neck looked cloudy and glowed with a strange, eerie green light. It was nothing like the transparent white color of that afternoon.

"If you don't leave now, I'm going to scream."

She tried not to show her fear, hoping he didn't notice her hands trembling.

Dar closed his eyes and leaned his weight against the wall. "You told me not to come into your bedroom unless I was ill." He raised his eyelashes to reveal dark blue eyes that appeared unfocused and glassy. "I'm dying. Please help me."

"Oh, my God!" Jennifer hurried to his side, imagining a large wound that would require stitching. "Where does it hurt? Did you cut yourself with your sword? Do you have a fever?"

When he didn't answer, she grasped the lapels of his open shirt and dragged his face closer. "Dar, answer me! Don't stand there and die. Do something!"

His gaze trailing down her body, Dar put his hands on her shoulders. "It hurts all over. I don't know why I am ill." Then he paused. "What is a fever?"

"Never mind. You're sick," she said, reaching out to feel his forehead. He was so hot she could barely touch him. "You've definitely got a fever."

She tried to ignore the way her body responded to his nearness. He was sick and he needed her help. She didn't have time to wonder how it would feel to be in his arms right now.

"I feel ill again. I can't locate my runes. The bag isn't where I left it. Without them I cannot invoke a healing spell." Dar groaned and clutched his stomach. "I must lie down or I will lose consciousness."

"Damn it. Don't pass out on me now." She pulled on his arm and tried to drag him toward her bed. It was like trying to move a car.

With a little nudging and a lot of encouragement, she helped him walk across the room. When he reached the bed, she let go of his arm and pulled back the cream-colored comforter. "Lie down."

"I'm sorry to bother you," her boarder whispered. She had to lean her head closer to understand his slurred voice. Dar wet his lips and added, "You can trust me. I won't harm you."

Jennifer's heart lurched with tenderness. The man was dying and he used his last breath to try to comfort her. She ran to the bed to pull down the sheets so she could cover him.

"That's okay, Dar. I believe you. Now get into bed." She watched him close his eyes and begin to fall toward her. "No, Dar! Wait until I move out of the way." She hadn't even gotten the words out of her mouth when his body landed on hers. He pushed her down to the soft mattress.

"I think I am going to be sick again," he advised her, his voice a half an octave lower than normal.

Pinned underneath his massive, heavy frame, Jennifer grimaced. "Don't even think about it."

She put her hands on his half-naked chest and pushed. He was bigger than a car; more like a truck. Then he shifted a few inches, just enough so that his eyes met hers.

"Although I would prefer to die on the battlefield, I will be glad to die here, in your arms."

Jennifer ground her teeth together. "Of all the compliments I've received, that one tops them all." Then, realizing he was serious, she sighed. "Thank you, but I don't want you to die."

"Neither do I." He clenched his hands around the soft sheets. "But I fear I may not be given a choice."

Jennifer put her arms around Dar's waist and her head against his body. She sighed, relieved when she heard his heart beat steadily against her ear.

"My soul leaves my body. You will mourn me, *já?*"

"I repeat: You are not going to die. Do you hear me, Dar?"

"*Já,* Jennifer. I hear you. Now, could you be quiet so I can perish in peace?"

Swearing, Jennifer frantically tried to think of a way to save his life. She had already watched her mother die in her arms. She'd be damned if Dar would die there, too.

"Try to get up. If I can get you to a hospital, the doctors can cure you."

"I think I've been poisoned."

"Poisoned?" The word made Jennifer stop her struggles and clutch Dar's wide shoulders. "What do you mean, poisoned?"

He swallowed convulsively. "It must have been the pie."

Oh, my God! She had poisoned her boarder! Thoughts of police, courtrooms, and prisons whirled through Jennifer's mind. "You must be kidding."

"*Nei,* Jennifer. I am serious."

"Tell me exactly what you ate today."

But Dar wasn't listening to her; he was staring at the wall. "Do you see the long, slender hands of the Valkyrie maiden? She stands there in her armor, beckoning me to join her. Soon, Hela, the mistress of Death, will come for me."

He was delirious! "Dar. Pay attention." Jennifer yanked on his hair and turned his head toward her. "What did you eat?"

"Oh, sprite. If only you were an Aesir maiden. Then I could be free to love you. But I feel my life force ebbing."

Jennifer wouldn't let him die. Gathering all her strength, she slapped him on the cheek. Dar's eyes narrowed and his body tensed. Good. She had gotten his attention.

"What did you eat?"

"I ate little squares that tasted like dragon's tails. We had burnt fowl for lunch and more fowl for dinner." His head drooped and rested on her chest. "Firedrake and I ate a few berries. Then I consumed apple pie laden with pepper. I do not think I like pepper."

Toast, chicken, leftover chicken, pie, berries . . .

"Berries! Where did you get the berries?"

"Did you know that Valhalla, the Hall of the Slain, boasts five hundred and forty doors? Or that Odin will not rest until eight hundred champions pass through each door on the day we begin the war with the jotuns?"

Jennifer forced herself to remain calm and repeat the question. "Dar, what color were the berries?"

"Red. *Já.* They were red. Just like the sacred apples guarded by Iduna, one of the Aesir goddesses."

"Oh, my God! You must have eaten the baneberries out back. Mom always told me never to go near the plants or get them confused with blueberries. They'll make you real sick."

Dar nodded. "I told you I was going to die. Now you believe me. Would you ensure that my body is placed in a dragonship and lit? My ashes should be scattered to the four winds."

She refused to think about the fact that if he died, she would have to call the police and hand over his body. He didn't have any identification or a passport or birth certificate. A situation she had no intention of facing.

Jennifer shook her head. As long as he hadn't eaten

too many berries, he would live. She would make him live.

Or die trying.

"Dar, here's what I want you to do: You must move over to the side so I can get up. Do you hear me?"

Once he lurched to the side, Jennifer jumped to her feet and reached for her robe. "I'm going to see if I can find the antidote for the berries."

A lone tear made a path down her cheek as she ran downstairs and picked up the phone. She got no dial tone. "What the—"

She tugged on the phone cord. It flew up onto the table, one end showing signs where something—most probably a mischievous dragon—had eaten through the cord. She stared at the exposed wires and groaned.

There wasn't much time. The houses on her street were clustered, with two or three on the same block. Other than that, her nearest neighbor was almost a mile away.

Jennifer ran to the front window. Mrs. Nordstrom's house across the street was dark. Bingo night. Her other next-door neighbor had gone away to visit her grandchildren last week.

The nearest phone was too far away, and she didn't want Dar to wake up, call for her and not get a response.

She would have to save the warrior herself.

Jennifer sprinted toward the book shelf in the dining room and ran a trembling hand down the spine of each book until she found her mother's book of edible wild plants. If the news wasn't good, she'd drive to the nearest house or store and call an ambulance.

She dropped the book several times before she finally found the page she wanted. " 'Baneberries,' " she read. " 'The berries and roots contain a poisonous glycoside. As long as the patient vomits, he should survive. Symptoms last between thirty minutes and several hours.' "

Relief coursed through her body. She collapsed into a chair. "Since he vomited, he should be all right." Remembering something else Dar had said, she glanced toward the doorway. "Didn't Dar say Firedrake ate the berries, too?"

Slowly, reluctantly, she entered the living room. As she had feared, the little dragon lay next to the couch. He was so still. If she didn't know better, she would think him a stuffed animal or toy. His scales, usually a shiny green, were dull and brown. Beside him, the evidence that he would live stained the carpet.

"So that's where my slipper went. And my handkerchief." She stared at the slimy stain. "At least you didn't eat that many berries. This is what happens when you eat things you shouldn't," she whispered, picking him up and cradling him gently against her body. "Just remember that the next time you look sideways at another squirrel."

Firedrake didn't answer. Jennifer wasn't sure he'd heard her, but she kept talking as she carried him up the stairs, making sure to cradle his head against her arm.

"Dar told me how much you hate the ground meat. As soon as he's better, we'll go to the city and pick up something different." She tenderly laid the dragon on her mother's bed. "Would you like chicken, or maybe spare ribs?" Jennifer covered him with a blanket and tucked the edges of the striped afghan under his chin. She put a pillow beside the dragon so he wouldn't fall off the bed, then hurried back to Dar's side.

If only she had taken a first-aid class while in college. Jennifer walked back and forth between the two bedrooms, fussing over her unconscious patients.

Dar looked so young and defenseless while he slept, nothing at all like the powerful, dangerously masculine sorcerer she knew him to be when awake. She smoothed back his damp hair, then ran her fingers against his stubbled cheek. She pulled back her hand and put it behind her, embarrassed by her desire to continue touching his damp skin.

She was very attracted to Dar. The thought of lying in his arms, his mouth on hers, made her knees weak.

She checked on Firedrake and found him lying precariously close to the edge of the bed. His scales looked a little less brown. Needing to feel his warmth, Jennifer picked him up and gathered him close to her chest.

"Go to sleep and dream happy dreams." She hummed a tune her mother used to sing to her when she was a toddler.

"Jennifer?"

She tensed at the low cry, coming through the connecting door. A muffled squeal, followed by a whimper, told her that she had squeezed the small dragon too tightly.

"I'm coming, Dar."

Jennifer tucked Firedrake back into bed and walked toward her bedroom. At the door she paused and quickly turned back toward the bed. "Sleep tight, little one." She bent down and kissed his nose. "Don't let the bed bugs bite."

When she entered her bedroom, she hurried to Dar's side. "You've kicked off the covers again. If you aren't careful, you'll catch pneumonia, and then you'll really have something to moan about."

Her joke, murmured in a shaky tone of voice, elicited no response from her sleeping patient. She pulled the comforter over his sweating body and, reaching for a wet washcloth, bathed his forehead in cool water. He tossed, dislodging the covers. He muttered more words in Norse, but Jennifer couldn't translate them.

She sat down on the bed and tried to keep him from shaking off the comforter. "You've never told me about Asgard. When you feel better, I would really like to know more about the people who live there." She pushed a strand of damp, blond hair away from his closed eyes, wondering at the ease with which she touched him, worried she might want to continue the action when he awakened.

After what seemed like hours, Jennifer couldn't keep her eyes open anymore. She laid her head down on the pillow, next to Dar. "I'll just lie here for one minute. I won't fall asleep; I'll just rest before I check on Firedrake."

"Please don't die," she whispered, one hand on her stomach, the other on Dar's arm. "Don't die in my arms or I won't be able to face the morning."

Caught in the web of a vivid dream, Dar knew he was too close to the flames, but he couldn't move. "I'll fight for Asgard until I take my last breath."

He raised his sword and slashed at a red-eyed demon. "By the sacred apples of Asgard, I send you back to where you belong, you devil!" The giant black creature flew near Dar's face. Its wings beat against the smoke-filled air.

Dar turned on the bed and threw off the covers. It was so hot, he couldn't breathe. When he was on the verge of awakening, his dream changed. It melded with the present until he couldn't tell where reality ended and the dream began. . . .

The bodies of dead demons littered the path. Blood drenched the parched ground. Dar stood on the field before Asgard. He sensed someone on the edge of his consciousness. He turned and focused on her identity.

As if by magic, he entered Asgard. There, beside him, was a slim, beautiful sprite with shoulder-length brown hair and chestnut-colored eyes. He took pride in showing her his home.

"Your family is nice, Dar."

"They were on their best behavior. Never before have I taken home a woman to meet them."

"What's that?" she asked as they strode down the dirt path toward a massive oak tree.

"That is Ygdrassil, the Tree of Life. It has three roots. One grows under Midgard, the world you call Earth. Another grows under Jotunheim, the world of the giants, and a third grows above Asgard."

"Wow! And what's that big building?"

Dar smiled and put his arm around her waist. "That's Valhalla, the Hall of the Slain. 'Tis so big, you can barely see the opposite wall. The spears on the sides hold up the roof, which is shingled in round shields. Inside, the walls are hung with coats of mail and helmets."

"Somehow, I expected your home to be more . . . warlike."

"Most of the battles are fought away from Asgard."

"I'm so glad you took the time to show me some of your world. It's not as menacing as I expected."

Dar steered her behind the large hall in the center of Asgard and pulled her toward a clean pile of hay. "Would you be happy living here, sprite?"

"I'm not sure." She stared around, as if wanting to see everything before she left. "Our cultures are so different. I don't know if I could get used to the violence that seems a part of your world. Just the thought of being in the middle of a war makes me ill. Besides, I vowed that I would keep my mom's house from being put up for sheriff's sale, and I can't do that if I stay here."

Knowing how sacred vows were, Dar nodded. "I, too, have made a vow. I pledged to be at my family's side during the war."

"You may be killed."

He shrugged but didn't say any words of comfort that she was exaggerating. "If I do not keep my vow, all the men and women of Asgard could die. If you stayed, you could die, too."

"But I'm not going to stay. I'm going home. Which reminds me—we don't have much time," she said as she lay down, a seductive smile on her beautiful face. "So please, show me everything important."

"It will be an honor, sprite."

Dar gave her every opportunity to change her mind. He pulled her into his arms and lowered his face to hers. The kiss, when he finally claimed her lips, surpassed everything he had anticipated. He pulled her tighter.

"Touch me, sprite."

He groaned as she ran her hands down his bare chest.

"Now you touch me."

The flannel gown she wore was no obstacle to his exploring hands. Dar caressed her curves through the soft material. He started with her long legs and pushed the hem of her gown up. By the time he reached her nipples, her groans of pleasure had him throbbing with pent-up desire.

"I've never felt like this before."

Her admission, coming between kisses to his neck, did not help his control. "You've never kissed a Norseman before, sprite."

"It's so hot in here."

Dar groaned and pushed off the rest of the covers, freeing their bodies from the woolen confinement. If this was a dream, he never wanted to awaken.

He turned to the woman in his arms and whispered, "It would be much cooler if you did not wear this gown. Here. Let me help you." Gently, Dar removed her clothing. "What is this flexible material on your undergarment? I've never seen such fabric."

"That's elastic." She raised her hips and helped him remove the offending piece of clothing. She didn't even blink when he tossed them as far as he could throw them.

"Your skin is as soft as a newborn dragon's." He ran his hand down her body. "You're lovelier than Freya, the most beautiful of the Vanir goddesses." Reverently, he kissed her lips. He lowered his head until he touched her quivering stomach.

"Dar . . ."

The softly spoken summons made him smile as his lips caressed her body.

Jennifer wanted him to touch her. She felt her soul reach out and seemingly touch Dar's mind. She reveled in her dream. It seemed so real, as if she actually visited Asgard. She had never had a full-color dream before, nor one where her senses felt so heightened. The hay on her back smelled of horses. It felt rough against her skin.

"Do you want me to continue, sprite?" Dar eased

himself on top of her and made her fully aware of the hardness of his arousal. Dar rotated his hips against her leg. The coarse hairs of his chest rubbed against her swollen breasts.

"Kiss me again." Her answer told him of her decision to quench the fire burning in her veins and give in to the throbbing desire to join with him.

Dar didn't hesitate. His tongue darted into her mouth. Her heart began to beat faster. She reached down to his jeans. The sound of the zipper being pulled down echoed loudly in her ears. She removed his jeans and tossed them to the floor.

"Touch me, sprite."

Jennifer did as he asked. The warmth of his flesh set her on fire. He shuddered at her hesitant touch. She meant to be bolder . . .

A loud screech woke Jennifer from her dream. She stared into Dar's glazed eyes so closely that she could see her soul reflected in their depths. Jennifer wet her lips.

"I think Firedrake is having a nightmare," she whispered.

"Dragons are used to living by themselves in caves. He will be fine." Dar tensed. He moved off her body, giving her a glimpse of the rippling muscles in his back. "By the tail of a dragon!"

It took her several seconds to realize that it hadn't been entirely a dream. They were really in bed together. Naked. Her lips still tingled from his touch. She had never felt this alive, this hungry for his kiss, his gentle touch, his straining body.

"Oh, my God!" Jennifer scrambled off the bed and hurried to put on her nightgown. "I can't believe this happened! One minute I dream I'm touring Asgard and the next thing I know, all my clothes are scattered across the room and we almost . . ."

Dar's mouth thinned as he obviously tried to come to terms with reality. "In the dream you toured the Sorcerer's Den, my home, *já?*"

"That's what you called it. Hey! Wait a minute. I can't believe I made up a name like that." If only she could stop her hands from trembling. If only he would cover himself. If only she didn't feel so upset that the dream had been interrupted.

Dar raised himself on one elbow. "You met my father, *já?*"

"In the dream you introduced me to him."

Without any warning, Dar jumped to his feet and grabbed her arm. Jennifer couldn't resist a quick glance at Dar's naked body. She felt her cheeks grow warm as she remembered exactly how much of it she had caressed.

"Do you remember his name?" he asked.

He was close, so close, and yet a whole world away. "Yes."

Dar didn't seem to hear her. "What did he look like?"

"Who?"

"My father."

"Oh, you mean Tyr?" She pushed her bangs away from her face. "He was tall, had blond hair, wide shoulders, and, although he wasn't as handsome as you, he was wearing similar clothing and a long black cape."

"A mantle. He was wearing an ebony mantle."

"With little black sparkling things on the lining."

"Black crystals," Dar said tersely. "From the crystal cave."

"Whatever."

He shook her gently. "Tell me more."

Unable to see why he insisted, Jennifer tried to remember the rest of her dream. "He had only one hand. The other one ended at the wrist. He kept trying to hide it beneath his mantle, but every once in a while I saw the stump."

Dar remained silent. Too silent. Jennifer wet her lips and tried to remember the rest of the dream. "He was standing next to a massive, chained dog. One of the ugliest animals I have ever seen. The thing was almost as big as your father. He kept saying that he forgave the animal. For what, he didn't say."

Dar's fingers tightened until she was sure her circulation was cut off. "Your eyes are sharp, but that wasn't a dog. It's a wolf, and his name is Fenrir. He is one of Loki's offspring. And a more deadly animal I've yet to meet. He's the animal who bit off my father's hand."

"You mean there really is something that big in Asgard?"

His lips a thin line, Dar nodded.

"Wow! I must have a vivid imagination."

Dar massaged the cold skin of her arms. He resisted the urge to pull her closer. Now was not the time to give in to passion, he reminded himself, allowing himself one last glance at her very delectable body.

"I'm afraid it has nothing to do with your imagination. My subconscious drew upon my powers and melded our dreams together. We each experienced the same fantasy. Your pleasure became my pleasure. Everything you saw, I saw. What you felt, I felt."

Remembering where her hand had been before she woke up, the banked passion of his kisses, Jennifer blushed. "So, we had an interesting dream. It's over now, Dar. Forget about it."

"*Nei.* I can't forget about it, Jennifer. I put you in danger by my lack of control."

She swallowed the large lump in her throat. "Danger?"

"*Já.* If something had happened to either of us while we were linked, both of us would have been affected."

"Dar, what are you talking about?"

He touched his crystal. It glowed with a white-hot fire that almost seared her hand. "The experience can be both good and bad. If the poison I ingested had taken effect, both of us would have had the life force sucked from our bodies."

"We both would have died?" she asked, her voice shaking with amazement and something else she found easy to identify: fear.

"*Já.*" Dar's fingers caressed her arms. "I must ensure that it doesn't happen again. Luckily, the bonding wasn't completed."

She gazed at his narrowed lips, remembering how she had groaned when he'd kissed her. She found it hard to concentrate on the matter at hand. "How do we make sure it doesn't happen again?"

When he didn't answer, she became worried. "Well?"

One corner of his mouth twisted upward. " 'Tis not as easy as you would make it, Jennifer. The ability is called soul bonding, and it's done when two people mate."

"You mean when two people have sex."

"*Nei.* It happens when two people bond for life. They become soul mates." His voice shook, telling her exactly how much the experience had affected him.

"Oh." When people married, they trusted each

other enough to put themselves at the mercy of the other. Trusting didn't come easily to her, considering her experiences with men. "You sound so serious."

" 'Tis something that isn't taken lightly." Dar dropped his hands to his side. "As I have no intention of staying on this world, it isn't something I intend to do at this time."

"I see."

He raised her chin and stared into her eyes. This close, she could still see the passion he kept under tight control. "You are disappointed. I am sorry."

Refusing to give in to the tears hovering on her lashes, Jennifer stepped back a couple of feet. "Don't be. I'm just reminding myself that you're here for a little while longer, and then you'll leave without even looking back."

The thought caused her stomach to clench so hard that she gasped from the pain. She sat down on the bed and wrapped her arms around her waist. Dar sat down beside her. She felt his hands on her shoulders but refused to turn around.

"I would never leave without saying good-bye, Jennifer. I swear it on the sacred crystal cave."

"Sure you would. If the opportunity presented itself."

Dar sighed and removed his hands. Immediately she felt the loss of his warmth and comfort.

"I'm sorry you believe that, but there's nothing I can say or do that will change your mind except to tell you that I'll do everything in my power to let you know when I leave your world."

"I don't want to discuss it." Unable to face him right now, Jennifer stood up and walked unsteadily toward the door. This room held too many memories for her at the moment. "I'm going to sleep in the spare room." At the door, she paused. Her hand tightened on the doorknob. "I found that bag of pebbles you were looking for."

His mood seemed suddenly buoyant. "My runes?"

"Yeah."

"I'm forever in your debt." Dar smiled. "Where did you find them?"

"Underneath the sofa next to my extra set of keys, a wad of freshly nibbled newspaper, and my comb."

"I assume from the tone of your voice that you're blaming Firedrake for the deed?"

"You guessed it."

"I'll talk to him about it." He shrugged his broad shoulders.

"I hoped you would." Did he have to look so handsome when she was chastising him? She tried not to notice the way his muscles rippled as he moved. Or the way his graceful movements drew attention to his tall, beautifully proportioned, naked body.

She averted her eyes as he tugged on his jeans and boots. "How do you feel? Are you suffering any effects from the baneberries?"

"I will live."

"Good. Tomorrow, I want you to relax. No sword practice. No ten-mile walks trying to find the Bifrost Bridge."

"I will do as you wish."

At the sound of his husky voice, she lifted her head and stared into his eyes.

"I will try to forget about the way you responded to my caresses."

She closed her eyes. Images of his passion-filled expression swam before her eyelids.

"I will try to forget the sweetness of your lips," he whispered, his voice as faint as the rustle of leaves.

Jennifer let out a long, audible sigh.

"I will try to forget the feel of your body against mine as you trembled with desire." She heard him sit down on the bed. "I will try to do as you ask, for both our sakes."

Standing by the window, her face averted from his gaze, one part of Jennifer hoped he would honor her decision and stay in her room. Another portion of her mind—the one that yearned for his touch—hoped he would follow her and kiss away the tears flowing down her cheeks.

Chapter Six

Three days had passed and Dar was still thinking about how good Jennifer had felt in his arms. Sitting on the couch, he shifted in his seat, aroused by the sight of her sitting across from him, watching the thing she called a TV.

He jumped to his feet when he heard glass shattering. A loud screech told him that Firedrake had returned. "Something is wrong."

Jennifer turned toward the stairs. "It sounds like he broke a bedroom window. He's never done that before."

Dar reached for his sword, only to realize he'd left it in his room. " 'Tis unlike Firedrake to be so impatient. Normally he would go to my room and fly in through the open window."

"Yeah, well, I think he misjudged his landing by a couple of rooms."

When Firedrake emitted an even louder shriek, Dar

knew something was very wrong. "Stay here. I'll be right back."

Jennifer didn't want to be left behind. "Oh, no, you don't. If there's a problem, I have a right to know about it at the same time you do."

They found Firedrake in one of the spare bedrooms shaking broken glass off his wings. Dar could tell by the little dragon's wild eyes and trembling body that he had been right. "What is it, Firedrake?"

The crystal around his neck translated the short snorts and grunts into words.

"What's he saying?"

Dar muttered a few choice Norse oaths as he ran toward his bedroom. "Firedrake warned me that Loki is coming." He ran into his room and belted the heavy silver blade around his waist. "I don't have much time. I must catch him before he disappears."

He ran toward the stairs. When he realized the dragon was following him, Dar shouted, "Stay here, Firedrake. Protect Jennifer in case one of Loki's jotun friends sends a demon."

The dragon hissed his disappointment but stayed, flapping his wings at the top of the stairs.

"Stay here, Jennifer." Taking her silence as agreement, Dar ran outside. "Valhalla!" His roar shook the ground. "Where are you, Loki? Show yourself."

The evening stars had given way to a cool early morning dawn. Dar stalked around the yard, his breath visible in the crisp air, and reveled in the dropping temperature. It helped to keep him awake and moving. He stared up into the tree limbs. The Trickster was close. He could feel it.

"Maybe he's passed us by," a voice said from behind him.

Jennifer! She had disobeyed his orders! He spun

around and grabbed her by the arm. She was so fragile. It wouldn't take much to cause her injury. His breath caught in his throat at the thought of his sprite lying on the ground in a pool of blood.

"He's here," Dar whispered. "And he's dangerous. Go inside and don't come out until I tell you."

"But Dar, I want to see what he looks like."

" 'Tis not safe for you to be out here. Don't make me carry you inside."

Out of the corner of his eye, Dar saw movement. His seventh sense, the one that he used in battle, screamed a warning. He thrust his sword into the earth and grabbed Jennifer in his arms. Both of them fell to the icy ground. He rolled toward the house, his naked back taking most of the brunt of the fall.

"Uumph. Are you crazy? What are you doing?"

Before Dar could reply, he heard something large hit the grass. He turned his head toward the spot where they had been standing. There, a few feet to his left, was a boulder the size of an ox.

The sound of evil laughter pierced the air and caused Dar to tighten his hold on Jennifer. "Loki!"

"*Já.* 'Tis I," a devilish voice said from somewhere above him. "You are swift, my friend, but I am swifter."

Taking Jennifer with him, Dar rolled quickly to his right and avoided another massive rock by a fraction of a second. Dar searched the trees. He had to do something quickly, before Loki injured Jennifer.

"Show yourself, Trickster, and fight like a warrior." He paused. "Or are you afraid?"

Loki cackled in reply.

Still somewhat sluggish from his recent brush with death, Dar could not afford to let Loki know how weak he felt. Using his body as a shield, he scooped

Jennifer up into his arms and ran to the far side of her metallic monster.

"Lie down and don't move," he warned her.

"What's the matter, Dar?" Loki taunted. "Afraid for the woman?"

The last thing Dar wanted was for Loki to use Jennifer as a shield, or worse, as a hostage.

"The woman is under my protection and none of your concern," Dar bellowed. " 'Tis you who has roused my anger with your trickery." He curled his lip. "I could have expected nothing less from a slimy jotun."

That got a response. Above him, Loki soared from the sky, riding a black half-grown demon. The creature was fast, but Dar moved faster. Jennifer screamed as the demon's sharp claws snapped above their heads.

Sweat beading his forehead, Dar raised a trembling hand and let loose a bolt of lightning that lit up the sky and scorched the tail of the surprised demon. It also started a smoldering fire on the dry wood of a tree limb.

" 'Tis fire you want, *já?* Then fire is what you will get." Loki urged the demon toward the burning branch. One stroke of the beast's powerful tail sent the branch hurtling toward the ground. Before Dar could move, Loki dropped small round pearl crystals on the wood. Within an instant, the small fire turned into a blazing inferno that licked ever closer toward the walls of the house. Bright light lit the sky and settled on the crackling flames.

"My house!" Jennifer scrambled out from underneath the Jeep. "He's going to burn down my house!" She jumped up from her hiding place and ran toward the flames.

Dar muttered a curse and tackled her before she could get into the door. "You must calm down, Jennifer." He didn't want to hurt her and exerted only enough restraint to drag her back to safety. "I'll take care of the fire as soon as I finish with Loki."

Jennifer dragged her feet, resisting him. "Oh, my God! Let me go, Dar. Firedrake is in there. If the fire reaches the house, he'll burn to death!" she screamed.

Dar cupped his hands over his mouth. "Firedrake!"

Within seconds, the dragon responded to the bellow by crashing through another window. Firedrake emitted a high-pitched screech and circled Dar's head.

Dar pointed toward Loki. "Grab Loki and bring him to me."

But Loki had other ideas. "*Nei.* I think not, Dar. 'Tis past time I returned to Asgard. I don't wish to miss the feast Odin is preparing. But I will return."

In a blinding burst of light, Loki threw a handful of glittering dust at their heads and flew away. Dar and Firedrake closed their eyes. Jennifer, unaware of Loki's tricks, wasn't so lucky.

"Oh, my God! I'm blind. I can't see!" Jennifer raised her terror-stricken face toward Dar. "What happened?"

Dar stared into her unseeing eyes and vowed to get revenge on the jotun who had injured his woman. " 'Tis okay, sprite." He pulled her trembling body into his arms. "Loki used a blinding powder to distract us. It'll soon wear off. You'll be fine."

The sound of a loud siren in the distance warned him of approaching humans. With Jennifer unable to see, there was nothing he could do but wait for their arrival. He watched the flames lick at the bushes surrounding the front of the house. They were going to catch fire very soon. He knew a brief and profound relief that Jennifer wasn't trapped inside the building.

"It smells like the smoke is getting worse." Jennifer's nails dug into his arm.

Dar didn't want the house to burn either. He had grown used to the small hall and, more importantly, Jennifer would be upset if she lost all of her mother's belongings.

Dar took a deep breath. It would require a lot of energy, almost more than he had. He should run to his room and get his crystal ball. The sorcerer's tool would act as a conductor and amplify his abilities, but time was of the essence. He really didn't have a choice. For Jennifer's sake, he would try.

She wrapped her arms around her body and shivered from the cold. "What are you planning?"

"I'm going to make it rain." Dar rubbed the goose bumps on her exposed flesh as he made her sit down at his feet. "You look pale. Rest. Firedrake, make sure she doesn't move, *já?*"

The little dragon stood guard next to her, his claw resting lightly on Jennifer's leg, his somber violet eyes raised to the cloudless sky. Dar lifted his empty hands toward the faint stars. The sun, a promise on the horizon, cast a silver glow on the house, giving him enough light to do what he had to do.

"Oh, powers of the night, hear my plea. Wind and rain come to me . . ."

Lightning flickered from his outstretched hands and soared into the heavens. Jennifer shivered and leaned against his leg as the first crash of thunder struck and vibrated the ground beneath their feet.

". . . clouds billow and water descend, through the timeless eons of the universe . . ."

Firedrake screeched as cars skidded to a halt in front of the house and the people inside pointed in their direction.

". . . torrent thunder shower. I do hereby command it!"

Frigid rain splattered Dar's body, soaking him in seconds. He relished the icy drops. They helped to numb his exhausted body and allowed him to forget his frustration at not being able to command the elements as easily as he wished.

Mimir would only have to flick a thin, bony hand to have a deluge of water descend from the heavens. Dar had to use every ounce of energy in his body to squeeze drops of moisture from the few black clouds he was able to summon.

Ignoring the open-mouthed spectators peering at him from the next yard, Dar lifted Jennifer to her feet and tried to protect her from the worst of the squall. He didn't have enough strength left for a shielding spell.

She stood there, wringing her hands with tears running down her face.

Once the fire was out, Dar hung his head. His knees quivered and his hands trembled uncontrollably. As he had feared, he had used almost all of his energy. If Loki reappeared, Dar doubted he would have enough strength to lift his head, let alone fight. Piercing sirens and flashing red lights announced a massive red creature ridden by strangely dressed humans.

"I'm Albert Cleary, captain of the Morgantown Fire Company. Is everyone all right?" One of the firemen, a portly fellow with bushy white eyebrows, jumped down from the back of the monster. "Is anyone still in the building?"

Dar shook his head and pulled Jennifer closer. "There is no one in the hall."

"The woman looks like she could use either a hot bath or a quick trip to the emergency room. Want me to call an ambulance?"

Jennifer shook her head, then rested against Dar's shoulder, obviously exhausted.

"No ambulance," Dar told the captain.

The man glanced from the smoldering roof to the jeweled sword embedded in the front lawn. "What happened?"

A bolt of lightning as bright as the noonday sun lit up the sky and illuminated the broken windows of the house. Jennifer sneezed and threw her arms around Dar's damp neck.

"I don't think you'd believe me if I told you." Two men threw blankets over them. Dar appreciated the action more for Jennifer than for himself. "Thank you for your kindness."

The rain slid off the man's shiny red coat. "Don't mention it, buddy." He pointed to Firedrake. "What type of creature is that? I ain't never seen anything like it."

Dar smiled. " 'Tis a *drakna*. Imported from Asgard. There aren't too many of them around anymore."

The young blond man shook his head. "Yeah. Well . . . it sure is something. The rain just pours off its scales. It's almost as if it was part fish or something."

"You are more right than you know."

It seemed as if the night would never end. Dar answered so many questions, he lost count of them. Through it all, Jennifer remained silent, refusing to release her death grip on his neck.

Finally, he lost his patience with the men. He gestured for the "fire fighters," as they called themselves, to leave. "Go! The rain has put out the fire and there is nothing more for you here."

"Care to tell me one more time how the fire started?"

" 'Tis none of your business." Dar pulled the drenched blanket closer to Jennifer's face. The strain of the evening had left its mark by etching dark shadows under her haunted eyes.

"Listen, buddy, I'm the fire captain." His bulbous nose quivered with indignation. "Every fire in this area is my concern. Now—"

"Enough!" Dar roared. "I've told you the truth, now leave us!"

Captain Albert Cleary's face turned as red as the huge machine he called a fire truck. "I should have known you'd tell me some cock-and-bull story. Anyone who'd keep that ugly green bird ain't got all his marbles."

" 'Tis not a cock-and-bull story; it is a true Asgard tale. And Firedrake isn't a bird, he's a dragon!" he yelled to the man's back. "And I don't possess marbles. I own ancient magical runes that have power over matter!"

The man in the hard red hat shook his head and made strange circular motions next to his head. Dar waited until they left; then he scooped Jennifer up into his arms and carried her up the steps and into her bedroom.

"Don't worry, sprite. Your eyesight will return come the rising sun. 'Tis but a temporary blindness."

When she remained silent, he became worried. "You've gone into shock. Your skin is as cold as the bottomless pool near the crystal cave. You need a hot shower to warm your blood."

He undressed first her, then himself. Naked, he carried her limp body to the shower and turned on the water. When he judged it to be the right temperature, he stepped under the warm spray and propped Jennifer against the wall.

"Don't you want to know the extent of the damage to your house? I'm surprised you aren't complaining about the cost of the repairs."

No answer. Dar reached for the pink drying cloth near the toilet and wrapped her body in fluffy fabric. "I will of course pay for the repairs to the roof and the windows, so you can focus on getting better." He tucked her into the bed and slid in beside her. Jennifer shivered and moved closer to him. Dar dried her damp cheeks with his finger. "Do not worry, sprite. I will keep you safe. Loki will never harm you again. I swear it."

It took a long time for Jennifer to ease her tight grip around his neck. Dar spent the hours murmuring words of reassurance into her ear as she tossed and turned, in the throes of countless nightmares.

The noonday sun blazed through the window and he still hadn't closed his eyes. Dar stared at the sleeping woman in his arms and frowned. Loki now knew the location of Jennifer's house. If Dar judged the Trickster's reaction correctly, Loki would return home to Asgard and request the assistance of his odious friends, the jotuns, to aid him in his revenge.

Dar shivered as the image of hundreds of jotuns being unloosed on an unsuspecting Earth flashed through his mind. "I can't allow that to happen," he whispered. "I must find a way to return to Asgard."

Dar pulled the covers up to his chin and tucked Jennifer closer to his side. He had no other choice. He had to double his efforts to return home. Loki had to be stopped, and only Odin had the ability to do that.

He pulled Jennifer's head against his naked chest. He would do whatever it took to keep her safe—no matter what.

"Are you telling me that you can't find any record of this scientist?" Jason's shout could be heard from one end of the institute to the other.

Henry Sneed shifted uneasily from foot to foot and wondered if the scientists down the corridor enjoyed hearing him being chewed up and spit out like an undercooked french fry.

"His name's Dar Tyrson," Henry replied. "We got it from that jeweler. It seems the guy's new in town."

"I don't care where you got his name. Answer my question."

"None of our spies could find any information on any scientist named Dar Tyrson." Henry wiped the sweat from his brow.

The director of the institute slammed his fist on his blotter, causing a model of a DNA molecule to totter dangerously close to the edge of the desk. "I don't pay you to come up empty-handed. He could be using an alias."

The words, uttered in a low tone of voice, made Henry shiver in his new pair of Dexters. "There are no reports of any scientist working on genetically engineered dragons. I've checked with every university and lab, even the ones in Europe."

Jason stared out the window. Henry held his breath and waited. "He's succeeded where we have failed. If our investors learn about this before we can duplicate his work, our funding could be pulled and redirected toward his project."

Henry knew the repercussions of something like that happening. The whole institute would be in jeopardy.

"I can't allow that to happen." Jason stood up and shuffled the papers around until they formed neat little piles. Henry knew that everything Jason did had to be just so, or the man became maddened and irrational.

Henry couldn't take the suspense any longer. "So, what are you going to do?"

A thoughtful expression on his face, Jason walked over to the window and clasped his hands behind his back. "I'm going to do something I should have done the first time we saw that specimen. I'm going to use my own vast intelligence to find out more information on our competitor instead of leaving it to inferiors."

Jennifer slammed the door of the jewelry shop and almost ran across the street to where Dar was waiting with the car. She had lost count of the number of times Martin had asked her to date him. Each time she turned him down, she felt more and more anguish as he failed to accept her answer.

Until she could come to terms with both her father's and her fiancé's desertions, she couldn't allow herself to try to form another attachment.

With only part of her mind on where she was going, Jennifer didn't see the car until it was too late. The blare of a horn was drowned out by Dar's roar. His purple cape billowed behind him as he lifted her out of harm's way. Jennifer gasped as they both rolled on the hard pavement.

They stopped with Jennifer on top, her body pressing down against his.

"Are you hurt?" She felt his chest move as he

talked, felt it all the way down to her toes.

Her heart was racing, his arms squeezing the breath out of her, and her mouth had gone dry, but she believed the symptoms had nothing to do with the near accident.

"I'm fine. I think."

"Good."

He'd insisted on wearing his Norse outfit, saying he felt uncomfortable in his new clothes. At least he wasn't wearing the horned helmet, she mused. That would have been more than she could have handled.

Dar cleared his throat, reminding Jennifer of exactly where they were. She felt heat warm her face as she scrambled to her feet.

As it was, people stopped and pointed toward them. One, a young boy wearing a skull earring, actually came up to them and asked if Dar was a character advertising a restaurant or a costume shop. Needless to say, Dar told him the truth, which made the boy laugh.

"Come on, Dar," Jennifer urged, embarrassed. "Let's go home."

The flapping of wings warned Jennifer of Firedrake's approach before she saw him. She spun around and frowned at the dragon. "I thought you locked him in the house."

Dar held out his arm and urged the dragon to come to him. "He can't be confined to the house all the time, Jennifer. His wings would grow weak and he would be unable to fly."

His eyes narrowed against the sun, Dar raised his arm and watched the dragon glide into the sky. "Stay out of sight, my young *drakna.* We will leave shortly."

Dar waited until Firedrake perched on the top of

the building before he turned back to Jennifer. ''Your trip to the jeweler went well, *já?''*

''Yes! With your rent money I can finally pay some of my more pressing bills. Thank goodness most of the damage to the house was superficial. I never could have afforded to replace the roof or half the house.''

''What about the windows?''

Jennifer stopped at the street corner and waited for the light to turn green before she said, ''The men are coming today to replace them.''

''Good.'' Dar put his hand on her arm as they crossed the street, careful to ensure her safety.

On the other side of the street, Jennifer counted out what Dar owed her in rent and gave him the rest. ''Here. You can just give me what you owe me once a week.''

''Thank you. Let me know when you need some money for repairs and I will give it to you.'' Dar stuck the money in his belt. He glanced across the street. His eyebrows rose. ''Wait here. I will be right back.''

Confused and not a little angry, Jennifer watched him run across the street. The wind whipped his mantle and made him look aloof and foreign, like a Viking raider looking for a maiden to defend or ravish. He stopped at a shoe store, stared at a cardboard box on the pavement, then went inside.

Jennifer paced back and forth, reminding herself that Dar hadn't done anything to make her distrust him. He wasn't like other men, she reminded herself silently. He never told a lie. He always tried to protect her. He would never just run off. Nevertheless, she breathed a sigh of relief when he reappeared.

Holding her breath, she watched as he stooped down and picked up something in the box, which he promptly stuck under his mantle. Then, with cars zooming toward him from both directions, he crossed the street.

"Watch where you're going," she shouted as he almost got hit by a bus. She ran after him. "That was close!"

The huge Norseman shrugged. "They would not have dared to hit a sorcerer. My wrath is great when I am angry."

She rolled her eyes at the sky. "Yeah. Right."

Something moved in his jacket and Jennifer gasped. "Oh, my God! What do you have there?"

An orange-and-white paw peeked out of his mantle and clawed at the fastenings of his white tunic. "It's for your neighbor, Elvira. I'm aware nothing can make her forget about her missing squirrels, but I feel it's my duty to give her something, since Firedrake ate her pets."

"Elvira will love it." The kitten stared at her sweater with more than a hint of interest. Jennifer wiped at the moisture in the corner of her eye, sure a piece of dirt had made it tear. She couldn't think of any other man who would care about the feelings of an elderly woman he barely knew.

"Now Elvira will have someone to love other than her son," he told her.

Loving was easy; it was the feeling when the person you loved left you that was harder to bear. Jennifer knew all about the pain of loving and avoided it like a plague.

"What are you going to call the kitten?" she asked, stepping closer to peer at the small furred creature playing with his crystal.

"I will name her Solveig, after my mother."

"Your mother. That's good." Not a girlfriend or fiancée. Jennifer reached out a hand and petted the furry head. Dar glanced down at the kitten, a tender expression on his face.

"If only you'd glance at me that way," Jennifer whispered.

"What did you say?"

To tell him the truth would not change his desire to return home. Embarrassed, she shook her head. "It wasn't important."

"Did you get your chain fixed? I know how much it means to you to wear your mother's ring on it."

"No. I was so focused on the money, I forgot all about the chain." She patted her handbag. "I'll have Martin fix it the next time we're in town."

"As you wish, Jennifer."

The sun never seemed so bright. Maybe it took a brush with death to make a person realize how precious life could be. The cool breeze ruffled the leaves of the trees. After making sure the windows were cracked open, and using the spare blanket from the trunk, they left the kitten settling down to sleep in the back seat of the car, then set off to finish their errands.

An hour later, Jennifer breathed in the crisp air and smiled. "I'm so happy, Dar. Nothing can ruin such a perfect day. Not even the threat of rain. To prove my good mood, tonight, once you get back from looking for the Bifrost Bridge, I'm going to try making hamburgers. What do you think of that?"

"More burnt offerings," the Norseman teased. "I can't tell you how that makes my stomach feel."

She hit him on the shoulder and basked in the warmth of his heated gaze. Since Loki's attack, he'd been much more attentive. He saw to her every need even before she realized she needed anything.

"I've been taking lessons from Elvira," she said proudly. "I might not be a master chef, but I'm getting damn good at boiling water. Oh, and before I forget, I have a couple of bills I need to pay and your gold has—''

Jennifer never finished the sentence. One minute she was stepping onto the pavement, the next thing she knew, she had bumped into a stranger. Tall, with dark brown hair lightly sprinkled with gray at the temples, the man exuded an aura of confidence she found slightly arrogant.

''Oh, I'm terribly sorry,'' he said as his hands wrapped themselves around her jacket, preventing her from moving away. ''Are you hurt?''

Jennifer stared into ebony eyes that held something like the morning chill. ''No. I'm fine.''

The man smiled, revealing even white teeth. ''That's good. Allow me to introduce myself. My name is Jason Wells. And this is my friend, Henry Sneed.''

Common courtesy forced Jennifer to make introductions. ''It was all my fault. I wasn't watching where I was going. I'm terribly sorry, Mr. Wells. My name is Jennifer Giordano and this is . . .'' Why did she always hesitate when she introduced the Norseman? ''Dar Tyrson.''

If the man noticed her hesitation, he didn't say anything. But his gaze never left her companion's face. Jenny was sure that a less secure person would have become uncomfortable with the intense stare, but Dar just waited for the man to move out of his way.

''It is a pleasure to meet you, Mr. Tyrson.'' His small black eyes narrowed as they assessed Dar's bone structure. ''I don't believe I've seen you in town before. Are you new around here?'' He held out his hand, waiting for Dar to take it. Dar returned his stare but didn't make a move to return the gesture.

''Dar's a foreigner,'' she stated. ''He isn't aware

of the custom of handshaking.'' Better to tell a partial lie than to stay silent.

Jason lowered his hand. ''I see.''

His companion stepped forward. Short, with thinning red hair and a matching red nose, Sneed reminded her of a clown who had forgotten to take off all his makeup.

''A foreigner,'' Sneed said. ''That's great. Where ya from, Dar?''

''Norway,'' Jennifer said at the same time Dar replied, ''Asgard.''

Jason Wells raised his eyebrows, obviously amused by the discrepancy of their answer.

''I'm from Asgard,'' Dar repeated.

Jennifer jabbed him in the ribs, but Dar refused to lie.

''Asgard.'' Jason Wells rubbed his mustache. ''It sounds familiar, but I'm not exactly sure where it is.''

''It's located on top of a tall mountain, on the beautiful plain of Ida.''

''Sounds like a very remote place. Of course. Why didn't I think of that!'' Jason took out a tissue and dabbed at his runny nose. ''I hope you will excuse me; I have a cold.''

''A cold?'' Dar sounded perplexed. ''Your body is below normal temperature? Or are you lacking warmth of feeling?''

''Dar.'' She smiled sweetly and wondered if a swift kick to the shins would go unnoticed. ''Don't ask the man so many questions.''

''I don't mind explaining the term, Miss Giordano. It's obvious he's unfamiliar with English terminology.'' Jason slowly lowered the tissue to his side and stared assessingly at the Norseman. ''A cold, Mr. Tyrson, is a disease caused by germs that effects the human body. It is marked especially by its affect on the respiratory system.''

Sure his translator probably wouldn't understand the phrases, Jennifer tried to drag Dar away before he could ask another question. He refused to budge.

''Ah. A disease. I've never experienced one. It doesn't sound pleasant.''

Jason measured Dar with a cool, appraising stare that reminded Jennifer of a shark eyeing its next meal.

''I agree. Colds aren't pleasant,'' Jason finally replied. ''They drain you of energy and can linger for quite a while until your body's immune system can defeat it.''

''Jason,'' Sneed's excited voice cut into the silence, ''did you hear what he . . .''

''Not now, Henry.'' The order, delivered in a short, low tone of voice, silenced his companion. Then, as if he was pondering a serious matter, the man tapped his finger against his cheek. ''Dar—I can call you Dar, can't I?''

The sorcerer nodded.

''We don't get many foreigners around here, Dar. Especially ones who have never been ill before.''

Jennifer saw an opening and took it. ''Well, it was nice meeting you. Now if you'll excuse us, we have to go—''

''Are you staying in town long, Dar?'' Jason's voice cut through Jennifer's announcement like a battering ram through a thin wooden door.

The Norseman took a while to reply. ''My affairs are my own concern.''

''Ahem.'' Jason didn't look happy at Dar's reply. Jennifer cringed at the verbal skirmish being waged right in front of her nose. If this man, or any of the news media, found out Dar was from another world, the consequences would be devastating. "It sounds as if you like our little town."

Jennifer sensed rather than saw Dar look at her. "*Já.* I do."

"I see. If I can be a little forward . . ." Jason smiled. It was more a baring of teeth than a grin. "I just wondered what you did for a living."

Jennifer was so busy trying to think of a lie that she almost overlooked the oddity of the man's persistence. "He's a soldier on leave."

Without hesitation, Dar told the truth. "Yes, I am a warrior. Right now, since I can't return home, I will remain here."

"A warrior, eh? You strike me as very loyal, and I admire that. And I also know that very few soldiers would be trusted to keep such a very . . . important secret as you have. Taking that into consideration, I'm extremely interested in discussing your . . . qualifications for such a job." The man smiled as if he knew some secret Jennifer did not.

The smile made her nervous, but his next words were even more of a shock.

"Sounds like you're out of work. If money is a problem, you could always come to the institute." Jennifer watched Jason hand Dar a business card. "As the director there, I'm sure I could find you a job until you have enough money to go home to . . . where was that? Asgard?"

Dar handed the card to Jennifer to have her read it to him.

"The Wells Institute. Isn't that out on the old highway by the wildlife preserve?" she asked, wishing she could just excuse herself and leave. But the last thing she wanted to do was leave Dar alone with a very forward stranger.

"Yes, it is."

"Exactly what do you do at this institute?" Dar asked.

Jennifer already knew the answer, but she waited to see what Jason would say.

"We are a facility that employs a number of scientists and . . . warriors. Of course we need to protect the men who are working on so many different and important fields of study."

That told her absolutely nothing. Obviously Dar thought the same thing because he said, "A field is a piece of land. Do they farm those fields?"

"I forgot. Being from a different country, you wouldn't be familiar with the nuances of our language. No, I was referring to topics such as astrophysics, pharmacology, geology, biology, quantum physics, chemistry." Then, as if he had been saving the best for last, he said, "And bio-engineering. We're studying everything."

Standing beside Dar, Jennifer sensed him tense and focus all his attention on the man standing before him. She doubted he understood all the terms the man had used, but she could tell that Dar was interested.

"Are you studying time-travel?"

Now he's gone and done it. Jennifer felt the blood drain from her face. She put a trembling hand to her chest. If she didn't know better, she would swear that someone had stomped on her lungs and stolen all her breath. She gulped some much needed air as she waited for the institute director's answer.

But Jason didn't even blink at Dar's question.

"Yes, we do. As a matter of fact, there is a scientist in my employ who has spent most of his life dedicated to cracking the secret of that very thing." He smiled, a false, plastic smile that revealed impossibly even teeth. "If you come to visit the institute, I'll introduce you to him."

"I look forward to it," Dar replied.

"Good." Wells looked at his watch. "I'm afraid I must go. It was a pleasure meeting you both. I'll be looking for you, Dar. And you, too, of course, Miss Giordano, as I'm sure you both work as a team." He held out his hand to Dar; but then, remembering that the Norseman didn't shake hands, he let it drop to his side. "Come, Henry. We mustn't be late for our meeting."

"But, Jason—"

"We'll discuss it in the car, Henry. Now let's go."

Jennifer watched the two men walk down the street. Gone was the feeling of rapture she had experienced just a few short minutes earlier. She shivered.

"I have this sinking suspicion that meeting wasn't an accident," she told her companion.

"*Já.* You may be right."

The way he said it—as if his mind was somewhere else—made Jennifer turn her head sharply to look at him. "You aren't actually thinking of going out to the institute, are you?"

Dar's body was as tense as a coiled whip. "You heard what the man said—he knows someone working on time-travel."

The implied reason behind his words made Jennifer close her eyes. She wanted to scream and beat on his chest. She wanted to beg him to forget he'd ever heard about the institute. She wanted to beg him to stay. But she didn't.

"Dar, I've heard rumors that the institute does strange experiments. Employees who have worked there have quit, saying they do cruel research on stray animals." Her voice rose in intensity. "And since it was built, countless pets have disappeared out of people's backyards."

"Jennifer, do these people have any proof that the scientists from this institute have stolen their animals?"

"No."

"Has there ever been an investigation on the matter?"

Did he have to sound so logical? "No."

"Then I'm afraid I have no choice. I must visit this place and speak to the human who is experimenting with time-travel."

Jennifer took an abrupt step away from him and stared at the blinking candy store sign across the street. "Do you have to do it today?"

She felt his dark blue gaze search her face and knew an emptiness she couldn't or didn't want to name.

"*Nei*. But I must do it soon. I can't put it off too long. Much rests on my returning home."

"I'd like to come with you, if you don't mind," she said, relieved that she would have him for at least one more day. And night.

Dar took a long time to reply. "Are you sure 'tis wise?"

"Yes. I feel I have a right to know firsthand if that scientist can send you home."

He held her arm as they crossed yet another street.

"I have decided. Tomorrow we will visit the institute and ask the scientists about possibilities of time-travel."

His tone brooked no argument. Jennifer pulled her coat closer to her body as an icy wind whipped her hair into her eyes.

"You're determined to return to Asgard." She sighed. "I only saw a little bit of it in our dream. Tell me more about your home," Jennifer demanded, obsessed with the place after her brief visit, even if only in a dream.

They turned the corner onto a deserted street. Another few blocks and they would be at her car.

"What would you like to know?"

"Everything."

The temperature dropped again, making Jennifer huddle even closer to Dar. Since they had parked closer to the grocery, they still had a bit of a hike before they got back to the car. Taking a short cut she knew, Jennifer turned the corner onto a street filled with boarded-up stores, a pawn shop, and a tattoo parlor. Another few blocks and they would be at her car. "I wish you hadn't been so insistent on walking," she said.

"Telling you everything about Asgard would take days," Dar said, apparently choosing to ignore her last comment.

"Well, it looks like we'll have time on this walk."

Jennifer opened her bulging handbag. "Now, where are my keys? I know they're in here somewhere."

A frown on his face, Dar peered into her cluttered handbag.

Jennifer shoved aside a half-eaten candy bar and burrowed under a stack of old it-wasn't-my-fault parking tickets. Her mother's wedding ring glistened at the bottom of her handbag. She made a mental note to try to find another chain when she got home. Of all her mother's possessions, this meant more to her than anything else.

Busy searching through her handbag, Jennifer frowned when Dar squeezed her elbow and hauled her to a stop.

"What's the matter?" Confused, she glanced from Dar's solemn expression to the four young men who had just stepped out of the alley in front of them. "Uh-oh."

A scruffier bunch she had yet to see. The torn dungarees, high-priced sneakers, and black leather jackets proclaimed the name of their gang, the Tecks. The way the men stared at Dar, with a cold glare that dared the Norseman to say something, warned her that they planned something more than simply asking directions.

"Let's turn around and walk away," she whispered urgently.

When Dar didn't respond, she tried pulling on his arm. "Come on, Dar. They can't do anything if we get back on a main street."

The pack, like a bunch of hungry rats who had just found a cache of expensive cheese, had no intention of letting their victims leave. "Hey, dude," a tall, lanky blond with a shaggy beard said. "Going somewhere?"

Jennifer stepped back a pace and leaned against Dar's solid shoulder. "Whoops. Wrong street. I think we'd better go back the way we came and ask directions."

"Don't leave on our account, babe," said a burly bodybuilder with a tattoo on the back of his hand that declared I EAT NAILS FOR BREAKFAST.

Dar pushed Jennifer behind him and took up a relaxed stance, his legs apart, his hands at his side. "Leave now, before it's too late."

Was he crazy? "What do you think you're doing?" Jennifer hissed at his wide back.

"I am trying to send these men home."

Maybe he didn't understand the situation. "Dar, there are four of them and only one of you."

"I can count, Jennifer."

She tried again. "They may be armed."

"So am I. I have my dagger."

Jennifer glanced at the black crystal knife in the sheath hanging from his belt. That might work if there was only one of them, but four?

If they were going to run, now would be the best time to do it. "You'll be killed."

Dar ignored the hands yanking on his arm and kept his gaze on the restless pack of jackals in front of him. " 'Tis possible, but not probable." He was worried more for her safety than his own. "Go to the jewelry store. I will meet you there. Leave now, Jennifer, and don't look back."

"I won't leave you alone. If you stay, we both stay."

Suppressing a frustrated sigh, Dar blocked her from the hoodlums. "Promise me you will not interfere."

"Okay. I promise not to do anything—as long as you're winning."

Dar didn't have time to argue with her. Out of the corner of his eye he saw the leader of the pack nod his head and advance. Dar flexed his muscles and pivoted to face them.

Although he didn't change his impassive expression, he was really relishing the thought of being able to break some bones and grind their grinning faces into the sidewalk. He missed the danger and excitement of the daily battles fought in Asgard.

"Advance at your peril," he growled as he prepared himself for the confrontation.

"This dude thinks he's tough," stated the leader, a mean-looking fellow with hollow cheeks and dark, brooding eyes. He caressed the baseball bat in his hand and glared at Dar. "But we're gonna show him who's the boss around here. Right, guys?"

"Right!"

Accustomed to the technique of spurring on the troops, Dar waited patiently for them to finish with their threats and make the first move.

"And we're gonna kick his butt. 'Cause we're the Tecks. Right?"

The four gang members nodded in unison. "Snake's right. We're gonna kick his butt!"

Snake pushed his stringy, dirty blond hair out of his eyes and slapped the baseball bat against his right hand. "Let's get him, dudes."

Didn't they know it was both poor battle tactics and detrimental to one's health to announce the beginning of an attack? Dar didn't have time to contemplate anything as the leader raised his arm and swung his bat at Dar's head.

Accustomed to fighting three or more opponents at a time, Dar spun out of the way of the weapon and used the side of his hand to break the man's nose. Two more punches to the ribs and the leader went down like a shattered crystal.

"Aw, geez!" the one known as Snake cried. "I'm bleeding!"

"Dar! Look out. Behind you."

He didn't need Jennifer's warning to tell him that the others had gotten over their initial surprise and joined the fray.

Chapter Seven

"By the hind leg of Garm! I'll teach you not to assault women." On his last word, Dar reached out and grabbed one of the charging men by his long, greasy hair. Before the man could guess his intention, Dar used his momentum to bash the gang member's head against a nearby Dumpster

"Two down. Three more to go," Jennifer called out, her face pale.

A short, swarthy teenager backed up several paces. "This here dude knows karate or something. He's knocked out Kareem. And look at Snake. His nose is busted." He glanced at the body builder beside him. "C'mon, Killer. Let's split."

His tattoo rippling as he gripped his large knife tighter, Killer shook his head. "You run if ya want to, Zombua. I'm gonna show this here dude just who he's dealing with."

Dar knew this man was the most experienced and

the most deadly member of the gang. From the way he held his knife, low in front of him, it was obvious he was an expert.

"Flee now, while you still live," Dar suggested.

The man called Killer ignored the warning and smiled. "Not on your life."

"Then prepare to meet your destiny." Dar pulled out his dagger. The dark crystal caught the light and seemed to shine with its own brilliance. Although it did not possess magical powers, it was made of a material that could slice through bone and sinew, a task it had accomplished more times than Dar could count.

His opponent made the first move. An upward slash toward Dar's face was just a ploy to throw him off balance, but the Norseman knew it. His attention on his opponent, Dar countered each thrust with a parry and riposte of his own.

"Let go of my handbag!" Jennifer's shout, unlike the threat of death, sent trickles of icy fear running down Dar's spine. The thought of Jennifer being in danger made him realize just how much he cared for her. Why did revelations come at such inconvenient times?

Pivoting to the right, he cast a quick glance behind him. Greed obviously outweighed good sense. Zombua fought with Jennifer for possession of her cumbersome bag.

"Give it to him, Jennifer," Dar shouted. "Do not risk your life over something so insignificant."

"No," she yelled back as she beat on her attacker's shoulders. "My mother's wedding ring is in there!"

Dar gritted his teeth. "I'll buy you another ring. Give it to them."

"Never!"

Killer maneuvred so that Dar had no choice but to turn his back on Jennifer. "Your chick don't stand a chance. Zombua's gonna break her arms and bust her teeth."

Didn't she realize the danger? Dar tried again. "Jennifer, I'll replace the ring. Give him the bag. Now."

"Some things can't be replaced, Dar."

He had to save her before she was injured or killed. Realizing he didn't have much time, Dar feinted to the left and created an opening. Killer never saw the punch coming. Dar put all his strength behind his blow and slammed his fist into his opponent's chin. Then, for insurance, he followed that with two more blows to the man's stomach. Killer grunted, reeled backward under the impact, and slammed into the wall. The knife slid out of his senseless fingers and the man collapsed to the street.

Jennifer's cry recaptured Dar's attention. Without pause, he spun around and ran toward her.

"Give me the bag or I'll break some bones," Zombua was snarling. The thug grabbed Jennifer around the waist and pushed her to the ground. Dar could see her head slam against the sidewalk.

Dar's hand tightened around his dagger. "Get your hands off her and prepare to die."

His furious growl must have scared Zombua, because the gang member staggered backward and let go of the handbag. Without a backward glance, the man took off like a rabbit that had just seen the shadow of a circling dragon.

Dar slid his dagger into its leather sheath and knelt down beside her. "Where does it hurt, sprite?"

The precious handbag clutched to her chest, Jennifer touched the back of her head and winced. "I'm more scared than hurt, I think. Let me get up and see if anything is broken.''

Dar reached out and grasped her hand. ''Let me help you.'' He stood up.

''Dar! Behind you!''

As he tried to turn, the searing white pain in his left shoulder took Dar completely by surprise. He collapsed to his knees as his opponent drove the knife deeper.

Jennifer's scream echoed in Dar's head.

''Thought ya could best the Killer Teck Beast, did ya?''

Dar took deep agonized breaths, glanced at the ground, and watched Killer's shadow. With a detachment that cost him a lot of energy, he saw the man behind him withdraw the blade from his shoulder as he felt it leave his body.

Killer raised the knife toward the sky. ''Well, now you know that I always get my prey. No one messes with the Killer Teck Beast and lives to tell about it. Dude, you're history.'' Killer liked to gloat. A dangerous habit that had cost many a mortal his life.

Behind them, Snake was rising and cursing. The leader of the gang staggered to his feet, then knelt down, gasping as he held his side.

An evil laugh on his lips, Killer sent the dripping blade plunging toward Dar's unprotected back.

Dar ignored the searing pain of the knife wound in his shoulder and concentrated instead on the man's voice. He would have only one chance to deflect the blade as it arched a death path.

Dar waited until the absolute last second—when the breeze from the blade caressed his skin—before he moved. With reflexes honed from thousands of fights, Dar turned his body and caught the man's wrist, the blade only inches from his face.

Killer had aimed the knife toward Dar's heart. Another second and he would have been dead. Even his extraordinary powers would not have saved his life this time. He lived, but he still had to win the battle.

"Hey. What happened?" Killer glanced into Dar's eyes. He must have seen his doom there because he paled and tried to bury the blade in Dar's chest. Dar felt the strength in the gang member's arm and knew it was no match for his own, even in his weakened state. It would be a pleasure to tell Killer the bone-chilling news.

"You have roused the wrath of Odin's sorcerer," Dar snarled, "Now reap the consequences of your deeds."

The bones in Killer's hand snapped like dry twigs. Dar watched the expression on the gang member's face change from triumph to shock. Dar moved the knife toward Killer's chest. Inch by inch, he brought it closer to the man's black heart.

"Don't do it, Dar!" Jennifer screamed. "Don't kill him! People on this planet are sent to prison for murder. The police will come looking for you and they'll find you. Let him go. He isn't worth it."

"Whatcha mean, from this planet? Ain't he from Earth?" Snake asked as he staggered drunkenly to his feet, one hand pressed against the wall of the building. "What is he? Some kind of Martian or something?"

The blood lust drained from Dar's mind. Jennifer was injured and should be his first priority. He squeezed harder. The knife fell out of Killer's crushed hand.

Dar lifted the man off his feet and brought him

close to his face. He could feel Killer tremble. Good; he should be terrified.

"It would be very easy to kill you, human." Dar kept his tone low and menacing as he bent Killer's arm backward. The criminal screamed in pain. "There are many more things I could break, but I will not if I have your pledge you'll never bother anyone again."

It took a few seconds for Killer to respond, but when he did, he couldn't speak fast enough. "I'll never mess with anyone again."

Dar contemplated the response. Not good enough. At this point, Killer needed incentive to turn his life around. "Do you swear this on your soul? Or would you prefer more persuasion?"

Beads of terror-and pain-induced sweat dripped down the man's face onto Dar's arm. "Yeah. On my soul. I swear."

Dar nodded. He judged the distance toward a gray trash canister. "The fates must be kind to you. Today is not the day you die, or at least not by my hands. Remember your vow, or I'll show no mercy the next time we meet."

It took hardly any of his strength to hurl the man the ten feet. Killer landed in a large pile of restaurant refuse. Dar waited a few seconds, and when the man didn't move, he hurried back to Jennifer. Putting his arm around her, he looked to where his other opponents had fallen. The one called Snake was just getting to his feet again.

"Aw, geez!" The goon shook his fist at Dar. "You ain't seen the last of me, alien. I'll find you, and when I do, you'll wish you were dead."

Dar watched the Teck gang leader stagger toward the street. He could stop him, but Jennifer took precedence over his desire for revenge. He looked into her eyes.

"Whew!" She let out her breath. "For a minute there I thought you were really gonna kill him."

"I was." Ignoring the pain in his own back, he bent down, picked her up, and held her against his rapidly beating heart.

"Dar! What do you think you're doing?"

He thought it was obvious. "Your hand is bleeding. I'm taking you home. Find the keys to your creature and urge it to get us home immediately. You must be treated as soon as possible. You may have a head injury." The thought made his stomach twist with grief. He found that her safety and well-being had become a bigger priority to him than ever.

If he'd been in Asgard, all he would have had to do was utter an incantation and she would have been healed. Since he was on Midgard, he had to rely on his healing rune, which at this moment rested next to his sword in his room.

If only she hadn't fought to keep her handbag. Dar scowled at the offending object, clasped tightly against her dirty shirt.

With her arms thrown about him, Jennifer must have felt the stickiness of the blood trickling down his back; she shivered. "You're bleeding."

"'Tis a small cut. As soon as I go to my room I will close the wound."

"That 'small cut' is gushing blood." She struggled against him. "Put me down. You'll just hurt yourself more by carrying me."

Dar refused to argue. "*Nei.* Find the keys. Now."

Jennifer reached into her handbag. "They're in here somewhere." After a few seconds she dangled the clump of long, strangely shaped metal objects in front of his nose. "I found them."

"Good. Now use them to get us home." As Dar carried her to the car, his anger at her senseless actions grew until he could think of nothing but how close she had come to being seriously injured—or worse.

A few minutes later, the two of them were headed home. Jennifer tightened her hands around the steering wheel. The scowl on Dar's face and the tense silence during the drive told her more eloquently than words exactly how angry he was. That and the fact that he radiated negative energy. She could feel the air around her crackle and vibrate like the charged air of an approaching thunderstorm. The temperature in the Jeep plummeted. Jennifer shivered.

"What would you like for lunch, Dar?"

He shifted in his seat and stared out the side window. "I'm not hungry."

Uh-oh. It was even worse than she'd thought. Jennifer drove faster, worried about his wound.

"Are you sure you're all right?" she asked anxiously as the kitten in the back mewled loudly.

"I'm fine."

A typical macho response if ever she'd heard one. Jennifer bit her lip as vivid streaks of indigo neon lightning flashed across the cloudless sky. She shivered and glanced out the window of the Jeep. Was it her imagination, or did the lightning seem to emanate from Dar's rigid body? Two more bolts in the shape of a Viking's hat blazed in front of a nearby tree, confirming its origin.

"Are you angry because I didn't let that punk take my mother's ring, Dar?"

More lightning, followed by dark clouds hovering over the Jeep, were her only answer. Jennifer smashed her foot down on the gas pedal and floored it. She wanted to be well away from the Norse sorcerer when he lost his temper, preferably behind a locked door.

She almost wept with relief when she pulled into her driveway. If there were two things she didn't relish, they were being zapped by a stray bolt of lightning and sitting next to an angry Norseman with sorcerons powers.

"Do you need help with your wound?"

"*Nei.* I'll be fine."

She slammed the driver's side door and walked toward the house. "Are you sure?"

"*Jà.* I'm sure."

"Then I think I'll go lie down for a little while." *Until you cool off.*

Dar picked up the kitten and held it against his chest.

Jennifer quickened her pace. She opened the front door and hurried up the steps toward the second floor and safety, the vexed Norseman only inches behind her. She glanced over her shoulder. "I suggest you lie down, too, Dar. You look a little pale." And very grim. Too grim.

Jennifer reached her bedroom and sighed with relief as Dar walked past her and opened the door to his room.

"See you in a couple of hours, Dar. If you need any help, just yell."

Jennifer stepped inside and closed and locked her door. Now she could wash the blood off her hands. Getting away from Dar was easier than she had expected. The smell of dampness and the faint odor of smoke still lingered from the fire, but Dar had put out the flames before anything inside the house had gotten ruined.

I feel like I've been run over by a truck. She slid her skirt off and tossed it to the floor. She fixed the straps of her black lace bra, then bent down to remove her sneakers. *Ooh, my back hurts. I hope I didn't pull anything. It feels like someone's hammering inside my head.*

She couldn't stop her hands from trembling. Nor could she get over the realization that Dar could have been killed. Although she hated to admit it, she'd fallen in love with her boarder! Of all the foolish things for her to do, loving a man who would leave her seemed the most foolish. And this man *would* leave. He had to.

A tree branch bumped against the window and she jumped. Nightmares had plagued her from the time she was a child. She had always run to her mother's room to throw herself into her mom's welcoming embrace. Now that her mother was dead, there was no one to turn to.

Jennifer sank onto the bed and rested her head in her hands. She felt so alone, overwhelmed by all that was happening to her. Unwilling to sink into despair, she unbuttoned her shirt. She winced as she moved her arm.

A sudden pounding on the door startled her so badly that she toppled backward onto the bed.

"Jennifer. Open this door," he boomed.

Did he have to be so loud? And did he have to sound so angry? Jennifer hesitated. When the banging continued, she contemplated her options. There weren't many. Either she opened the door or he would break it down. And she'd have to buy another one.

She tried a different tactic. "Listen, Dar, I'm not

dressed. Why don't we talk another time?''

''I do not care about what you're wearing. I'm concerned about your injuries. I've brought my runes with me.''

Jennifer rubbed her temples as she walked over and opened her door. ''It's nice of you to offer to help, but all I really need is a few hours' sleep. Then I'll be fine.''

''*Nei*. I'm not leaving until I am sure you are well.''

Stubborn Norseman! Jennifer leaned her head against the door frame and sighed. ''Will it take long?''

''Nei.''

If it was the only way she could get rid of him . . . ''Okay. Then you can come in.''

The huge Norseman invaded her room. Jennifer stepped backward. Had her bedroom suddenly gotten smaller? He looked too large and too handsome for his own good.

He had changed clothes, sort of. She stared at the huge expanse of naked chest and his tight jeans. He was so close she could touch him with no effort at all. The long black cord holding his crystal pendent beckoned to her. She put her hands behind her back.

''Where's your shirt?'' she whispered.

''On my bed.''

''Let me see your wound.''

He turned. Jennifer stared at the almost entirely healed gash on his back. ''Oh my god! That's amazing! How did you do that?''

''With my magical runes.''

''Oh.'' A delicious shudder heated her body. ''Why did you take your shirt off?''

Dar reached into the waistband of his jeans—and

pulled out his leather pouch. He removed one of the stones and held it in the palm of his giant hand. "I used my powers to heal the knife wound on my back. The runes work better if they are held against bare skin."

"Oh." Jennifer took a deep breath and held it. She had to control her reaction to him. She couldn't keep hyperventilating every time he got close to her.

"Come here," he whispered.

Jennifer's eyes widened. "What?"

"I said, come closer."

A vivid picture of a naked Dar lying in bed flashed through her mind. This was going to be harder than she thought. "Why?"

Dar's voice grew softer. "Because I must check your injuries."

Oh, yeah. Her injuries. "Okay." Jennifer stepped forward.

"Closer."

Without taking her gaze from his face, Jennifer stopped only inches from his chest. Dar reached out and, with a gentle hand, touched her chin. "This won't hurt, sprite. Relax."

How could she relax when a seminaked man who had the power to melt her insides stood right in front of her?

Dar put one hand—the one with the white stone—behind her back. He ran his other hand slowly down her neck. Jennifer bit back a moan. His hands felt feverish, too hot for those of a normal human. She could feel the little white stone pulsating as if with a life of its own.

He muttered a few words in a language she didn't understand, then chanted the healing spell. "Energy of the gods, mighty forces of the nine known worlds, channel through me the power to heal all wounds. . . .''

His touch melted her resistance. She stepped closer to him. She put her palm against his warm chest to keep her balance. He flinched but didn't move away.

''How does this feel?'' he whispered.

It was as if someone caressed her body with a soothing massager that got under her skin and touched her bones. Hot. Stimulating. Calming. She smiled dreamily and closed her eyes. ''Delicious.''

''Good.''

His palm trailed a fiery path down her back. Massaging. Caressing. Arousing. ''Oooh. Harder. Right there.'' She licked her lips. ''That's the spot.''

This close to him, she could almost taste him. He smelled of sweat and blatant masculinity, a dangerous combination. One she found impossible to resist. She could sense his anger and something else, something more elemental and intimate. Desire.

Jennifer swayed and leaned against Dar's shoulder. Only a few inches more and her face would be resting against the golden hair tickling her nose. She gave in to her longing.

Dar caught his breath but didn't stop the exquisite ministrations. Was it her imagination, or did she feel a bulge growing against her stomach? Jennifer pressed her body closer to his and grinned. It wasn't her imagination.

She knew she should move away from him, but his hands on her body felt so good. Jennifer groaned at the heated sensations coursing through her.

''You can turn around now.'' He cleared his throat nervously.

''Mmmmmm.''

With her eyes closed and her shirt off, she could

feel almost every part of him, only her bra lay between their heated flesh. Jennifer turned in his arms and leaned back against his chest. His translation crystal bumped into her head and she nudged it aside.

Dar cleared his throat and moved back a few paces. Seeking his warmth and the comfort of his arms, Jennifer followed. His chest reminded her of a big pillow. She could stay there forever.

"Jennifer." Dar gripped her arms and moved her away from him. "How do you feel?"

How did she feel? "Tingly, warm, alive, and aroused."

"I have apparently used too much energy on you." His voice, a mere whisper, sounded strained.

"I don't think so. Don't stop. It feels good."

Dar turned her around again. Jennifer rested her head against his arm and opened her eyes. The massage had obviously affected Dar also. Gone was the remote expression he normally wore. In its place was a tension-filled look that told her that he was as aroused by her nearness as she was by his.

He gazed down at her bra, intently studying its shape and size. He shook his head, as if to clear it. "Maybe you should put on your shirt before we continue. 'Tis obvious my mind wanders, and the spell is being affected by my thoughts."

Jennifer stared at the drops of sweat forming on his forehead. "I thought you said the runes work best against naked flesh."

"That's true, but if a spell is not cast correctly, there could be side effects."

"What type?"

Dar's eyes deepened as his gaze wandered over her body. "Anything from heightened senses to thoughts that involve things other than healing."

She quivered as he stared at her lips.

"You shiver. I'm concerned that you may catch a coolness dressed as you are."

"You mean catch a chill—and no, I'm not cold at all. Actually, I'm hot. Too hot. But if my lack of clothing bothers you . . ."

Dar took a long time to reply. Would he admit she affected him? Jennifer held her breath.

"Fine. If you're not cold, we'll continue."

His husky voice sent shivers down to her toes.

"I'm ready when you are. What should I do next?" Jennifer turned and put her hands on his waist. He flinched as if burned.

"You do nothing," he replied, his voice a mere whisper. "I will make sure your ribs are healed properly."

"Your hands are trembling. Are you tired?"

Dar's gaze traveled over her face and searched her eyes as if gauging her sincerity. Then he looked at the bed. His mouth tightened. "*Nei.* I am fine."

Dar put his hand on her rib cage, just above the waistband of her jeans, and moved his fingers upward. Even though she was expecting his touch, Jennifer wasn't ready for the way her body reacted. The quickening of her pulse and her surprised gasp of pleasure drowned out the uneven rhythm of her breathing.

"Does this hurt?"

It felt so good, she couldn't answer, so she just shook her head.

His hand continued its upward journey. "How about here?"

She stared into his eyes, eyes so intense she could drown in them and never regret it for a moment. "It's a little sore."

His hand brushed against her breast and Jennifer's

knees buckled. He caught her and held her tight.

"I'm sorry. That was an accident." He loosened his hold just a little. "Maybe we should continue this another time, *já?*"

But she didn't want him to stop. Not now. Not ever. "That's okay, Dar. You might as well continue. You're almost done, aren't you?"

He closed his eyes and she could see the tightness of his throat as he swallowed. The tension in his jaw. "*Já.* I'm almost done."

His hand trembled as he touched her chest, right above her heart. His palm, so warm and gentle, moved in circular motions as he continued to repeat his strange words.

"Are you still mad at me, Dar?"

Dar stopped chanting. "*Já.* You should have listened to me. You could have been killed."

The gentle rebuke, coupled with his pain-filled expression, was her undoing. Unlike the other men in her life, he cared what happened to her.

Love blossomed from a bud to a flower, one needing sunlight to live. Dar was like the sun, a man who shone above all others. She needed him. She wanted him, more than she'd ever wanted anyone in her life. It was so simple, she wondered why she hadn't realized that revelation before.

Only the knowledge that he couldn't stay kept her from telling him how she felt.

Unable to resist touching him, Jennifer put her arms around his neck. "You saved my life. And I haven't even thanked you yet." She reached up and briefly kissed his lips. "Thank you, for everything."

"You're welcome." His lips parted, as if he would continue speaking, but he shook his head and remained standing stiffly.

"I was so scared that I didn't really think. I'm glad you weren't killed because of me."

Dar's hand was trapped between their bodies, right next to her heart. She could almost feel the need in him to touch her. She wanted him to give in to his urge. She ached to feel his arms around her. Remembering their near brush with death, Jennifer shivered and hugged him tighter. Now that he was here, she didn't want to be left alone.

"Dar, I'm exhausted, but after that fight, I'm afraid my nightmares will come back. Would you stay with me?" His low growl made her realize how her words sounded. She quickly added, "That wasn't a proposition. I just don't want to be alone."

She sensed his indecision.

"Please?"

"I should not."

"I want you to."

"It would not be right."

"I need you."

His tortured sigh echoed in the silent room. "As you wish."

He would stay. Jennifer smiled and reluctantly moved away from him. "Thanks, Dar. You won't regret it. Oh . . . can you do me one favor?"

Dar looked warily from the bed to Jennifer. "What is it?"

"Remind me later to call the number by the phone and reschedule my job interview? I don't think I'll feel up to going out tomorrow."

"It will be done."

"Thanks." She laid down on the bed. She closed her eyes.

Dar stared at Jennifer, wanting to get into bed with her and hold her, but resisting the urge. If those scientists could actually send him home, then it was best that he and Jennifer remain just friends.

He waited until she was asleep before he gave in to the desire to touch her face. Her skin felt smooth, and very tempting. He finally admitted the truth: When he returned to Asgard, he would not only be leaving Jennifer, he would also leave a good portion of his heart behind.

Although he knew they were from different worlds, he would love her for the rest of eternity and beyond. The thought made his hands tremble. His parents had a love that was just as powerful, and having seen the passion in their eyes on more than one occasion, Dar knew that his physical desire for Jennifer could weaken his resolve to keep his distance from her.

He ran his fingers down her arm. His trip to the institute would have to wait until Jennifer felt better. No matter what, he could not leave her weak and alone. He hoped she regained her strength soon, before he lost his resolve to keep his distance, before he gave in to this desire to sweep her up into his arms and make mad, passionate love to her.

"It's been two days and he still hasn't come like you said," Henry whined, tossing a ball of paper in his hand.

"Haven't you been listening to anything I've said? Let me explain it to you this way, Henry. We've planted the seed. He'll show up when he's ready and not a minute before." Jason enunciated each word and grimaced when Henry scratched his head. "Dar Tyrson is a very powerful man who isn't going to give away his plans to just anyone he meets on the street."

When his assistant frowned and scratched his head

yet again, Jason made a mental note to have the institute doctor check him for lice.

"You heard what the young lady said," he continued. "Tyrson has gold, lots of it. And he's a soldier. It's obvious that his country—and he's keeping it a secret exactly which one it is—has made a huge break-through that can only be used for one purpose: War."

Jason pulled down one of the rare books he kept in his office and ran his finger down the expensive leather spine. "If I had to guess—and I'm never wrong—they are going to use the genetically engineered dragons as a secret weapon. Tyrson must have brought one to show his contact. It's obvious that he had to bring a young one. He never would have been able to transport a full-grown dragon." He rested his chin against the book. "I wonder exactly how large they grow?"

"Probably as big as elephants," Sneed avowed.

Jason curled his lip and glared at his assistant. "If I've told you once, I've told you hundreds of times, never assume! A scientist must check and double check his research and then *know* a fact before he can breathe a word of a result to anyone."

"But, Jason, you yourself are assuming that he's a scient—"

One glare stopped Henry's speech. "Do you think they would send a mere soldier to do this type of job? No, Henry, Tyson is much more than he appears."

Forcing himself to take long, calm breaths, Jason slid the book back on the shelf and gave it one last caress.

"But how do you know he's actually gonna come here? If he's already got a contact, he ain't got no reason to talk to us."

Jason closed his eyes and counted to twenty.

"Please use proper English, Henry. And don't worry, Tyrson will come." He'd seen the interest in the man's eyes when they'd discussed time-travel. Was this Dar Tyrson's country close to inventing a time-travel device as well as the incredible bio-engineering feat of creating a dragon?

He gripped his desk until his knuckles turned white. "But he must be handled with finesse." The man would never tell him his country's secrets—would he? What could he offer the man? Fame, fortune, a Nobel prize? Like Jason, he probably coveted them all. "And I must have them all! No matter what the cost."

"All of what, Jason?"

Realizing how close he had just come to disclosing his aspirations, Jason folded his hands on the table and smiled at his assistant. "Why, all of Tyrson's secrets, of course."

"Oh. Yeah. Of course."

Jason glanced at his watch. "Don't you have something else to do? I don't pay you to sit in my office and socialize."

Henry jumped to his feet. "Yeah. I have lots to do. I'm so busy, I never have time to do anything else." He couldn't get out of the office fast enough. "I'll see ya around, Jason."

"It's 'see you around,' Henry."

"Yeah. See ya. That's what I said."

Allowing himself a small smile, Jason waited for the imbecile to leave. "The question is—how can I persuade Tyrson to turn his back on his country and give us his secrets? Should I tell him about our secret genetic projects and promise to include him as one of the creators?" Jason tapped his finger on his mustache. "No. That wouldn't work. All he would have to do is point to his dragon. Our experiments don't even come close to duplicating what he's created.''

Jason walked over to the window and clasped his hands behind his back. ''I could always offer him more money, but he doesn't look like the type to be swayed by wealth.''

A howling wind blew the limbs of the trees. The leaves on the east lawn needed to be raked. He would have to fire the gardener for his negligence. Jason walked over to his desk and made a note on his people-to-be-reprimanded list. The intercom buzzer interrupted him and made him frown.

''Yes? What is it?''

''Excuse me, Dr. Wells, but the guard at the front gate said to inform you that you have two visitors.''

Jason's frown turned into a full-fledged scowl. ''Miss Wingfield, you know that I do not allow visitors on the institute grounds. Tell the guard to send them away.''

He took his hand off the intercom button. But before he could pick up his pen, his secretary knocked on the door. Sighing, Jason made a mental note to contact the Human Resources director and ask for another secretary.

''Yes? What is it now?''

Miss Wingfield opened the door and peered inside. ''I know you dislike interruptions, but Lenny said this was an emergency.''

''Yes? I'm waiting.''

The elderly blonde straightened her plaid skirt. ''It seems that the visitors wouldn't take no for an answer. Lenny said to tell you that a huge blond giant has lifted him off the ground and won't let him go until you let him through the gates.''

Tyrson! And he had almost sent him away without asking his identity. ''Why didn't you tell me this immediately? I've been expecting these visitors." Jason shook his head at the incompetence of his underlings. "Tell the guard to admit them. And warn him that under no circumstances is he to hurt our guests."

"I don't think you have to worry about that, Dr. Wells. It seems that your guest disarmed Lenny and bent the barrel of his rifle with his bare hands. Lenny couldn't fire the thing even if he tried."

The white halls of the Wells Institute had made the building seem stark, sterile, somber. It reminded Jennifer of the hospital where her mother had died. She hated hospitals.

A chill crept down her back and enveloped her heart. She shivered and stepped closer to Dar. Next to his large body she felt secure, safe from any harm. He was her defender, her protector against all things evil.

For the past two days, he'd slept in the chair by her side at night and chased away the demons that hovered on the edge of her dreams.

She wanted him, she needed him, and if she wasn't careful, she knew that he would devour her and then disappear forever. Like a moth, she would be burnt in the flame of her own desire, and like ashes she would be blown away on the first strong wind. What she needed was a miracle. What she needed was someone or something that could protect her from herself.

From the reception lounge window, Jennifer stared out at the early morning sun rising above the horizon. "It doesn't look like anyone's going to come meet us. Why don't we go home? I'll fix you another nice big breakfast."

"*Nei.* I'm staying until I get the information I need."

His determined expression told her he wouldn't budge in his decision. She'd been afraid of that.

"You look well, but you can go home if you still don't feel well," he told her.

After two days of not being allowed out of bed, Jennifer had begun to feel a bit stifled by his protectiveness. Still, she'd enjoyed the undivided attention of the handsome Norseman and wouldn't have missed it for anything.

Jennifer shivered as she glanced around the lounge where they waited. Dar wanted her to leave him in this sterile prison? Not likely. The only way they could move her from his side would be if they carried her out on a stretcher. "No. That's okay. I'll stay, too."

Dar shrugged and sat down on one of the hard white chairs. Although he hadn't said anything, the dark rings under his eyes and the deep lines around his mouth told their own story.

She sat down beside him. He reached over and put his hand over hers. "Are you feeling okay?" he asked. "You had another restless night."

She'd had nightmares full of big black birds and demons with glowing red eyes. But if she said she didn't feel well, he'd probably order her to go home. "I'm fine. What about you?"

"I'll be fine once I speak to the scientists."

She squeezed his hand. It was twice the size of her own and powerful enough to rip her arm from her body, but she didn't feel the least bit afraid.

The door swung open and banged against the wall. Jennifer leapt out of her seat and spun around to face the door. Dar, who had also stood, grabbed her by the shoulders and thrust her behind him.

"Stay there and don't move until I tell you it's safe."

Through the open door, Jennifer could see the guard from the front gate staring warily in their direction. The hand on the butt of his rifle didn't reassure her one little bit, especially since it was a new weapon, one without a bent barrel.

The guard nodded and a white-coated, high-heeled woman breezed past him and sauntered in their direction. Jennifer scooted over to Dar's side. Dar put his arm around her and held her close to his body.

"It's okay, sprite. No one will harm you while I am here."

"I'm okay, Dar. I wasn't frightened."

Dar raised his eyebrows but didn't refute her lie.

"Hi. My name's Dr. Monroe. Margie Monroe." The woman strolled past Jennifer and held out her hand toward Dar. "You must be Dr. Tyrson."

Dar looked at her hand but didn't take it. Monroe put her arm down to her side. Her sickeningly sweet smile didn't waver. Jennifer waited for the woman to notice her. When the doctor's eyes continued to be glued to Dar's powerful body, Jennifer crossed her arms over her chest. Now she knew the meaning of the term "hate at first sight."

She cleared her throat. "Hi. My name's Jennifer Giordano."

The woman barely glanced in her direction. "Nice to meet you." She turned back toward Dar. "Jason mentioned that you are going to be working with us. So, what's your specialty?" she asked, flicking her waist-long hair over her shoulder. "I'm in the genetics section, myself."

"I have no specialty."

"Oh. That's interesting. You've worked in several different fields, then? That's impressive." A calculating gleam in her eye, she tried a different tack. "So, at which institutes have you worked?"

"I have not worked at any institutes."

The woman couldn't seem to take her gaze off Dar. If Jennifer didn't know better, she would have sworn the woman thought he was a piece of candy that should be eaten in little nibbles.

The skinny brunette laughed. The sound—which Jennifer thought resembled a cross between the bray of a hyena and the pants of an asthmatic person in the last throes of a violent attack—irritated her. She stepped closer to Dar and glared daggers at the woman, who was now inspecting him like he was a specimen under a microscope.

"We don't get many visitors here," the woman stated, "especially with such big biceps."

The Norseman didn't seem to notice her admiration. He had obviously grown bored with her questions and was now staring at a diagram of the building displayed on the wall. Jennifer narrowed her eyes. What was this, an interrogation? The woman continued asking questions. Her expression didn't change as Dar continued to answer the questions truthfully, if somewhat vaguely.

Aware that this could go on for hours if someone didn't do something, Jennifer stepped in front of Dar and stared into the doctor's ice-gray eyes. "We're here to see *Dr. Wells*."

She could tell by the way Monroe's coral lips tightened that the woman hadn't liked her interrupting her questions. "But of course. Dr. Wells said to tell you that he will be here shortly."

"And when were you going to tell us this little piece of information?"

"As soon as I was finished talking to Mr. Tyrson," Monroe said sweetly. Too sweetly. The brunette glanced at her watch. "Oh, look at the time. I'm going to be late for my meeting." She gave Dar a look that was so hot, the ivory wallpaper almost burst into flames. "If you need anything here, anything at all, just ask for Margie Monroe. I'm sure I can get you whatever you want."

Jennifer raised her eyebrows at the suggestive comment and found herself quietly grateful that Dar didn't even acknowledge the woman as she left the room.

"All the rooms of this building would be on this map, *já?*" he asked Jennifer.

"I guess. I'm not really sure."

Dar grunted and began pacing up and down the dark gray carpet.

"Dar, why don't we—"

The door slammed open again and in walked Jason Wells.

"Ah. Dr. Tyrson." Jason Wells extended his hand toward Dar. "I'm so glad you could visit our humble little institute."

Didn't she exist? Jennifer ground her teeth as she found herself ignored for the second time in less than ten minutes.

" 'Tis my pleasure," Dar said. "You remember Jennifer, *já?*"

Jason's gaze settled on Jennifer's face as if he had just seen her. "But of course. It is a pleasure to meet you again." His smile, more a widening of the mouth than a true smile, didn't fool Jennifer one little bit. The man didn't want *her* there.

"I promised you a tour of the institute," Jason said,

gesturing toward the hallway where the guard, Lenny, stood glaring at them. "Come. Let me introduce you to some other scientists."

The director of the institute nodded to the guard. "It's okay, Lenny. You can go back to your station now."

The short, squat man ambled off down the corridor. But every few seconds he would glance over his shoulder and touch the butt of his weapon.

"You will have to tell me if your facilities are as advanced," Jason said as he walked briskly toward the elevator.

The tour covered most of the second and third floors. Jennifer grimaced and tried holding her breath. Everything stunk of antiseptic and chemicals. They traveled through most of the building and finished with the basement.

". . . and this is the research section." Jason glanced over his shoulder to see Dar's expression. "Allow me to introduce you to a few of the employees."

He gestured toward a short man with thick black glasses. "This is Dr. Hershall Furrari."

Jennifer nodded to the gentleman and watched the expression on his face. He seemed introverted, not at all used to meeting new people. Hershall kept peering at her, then bending his head. He appeared to find the shoelaces of his beat-up sneakers fascinating.

"And this distinguished-looking man is Norman K. Rockville. He wields a mean microscope."

The lanky, gray-haired scientist chuckled on cue and leaned back on his stool. "Jolly good that you could visit, Tyrson. I say there, you look familiar. Didn't you once work at the Orlando Foundation?"

Dar shook his head. "*Nei.* I did not."

Jason forced a smile and pointed to the third person in the room. "I'd like you to meet Professor Snorri Sturluson. Snorri is a genius. He's an expert on just about every subject you can mention. Isn't that right, Snorri?"

Was he kidding? Jennifer couldn't tell. She supposed that if one went by looks, Snorri could be the perfect absentminded professor. His thinning white hair stuck out at all angles on his head and his round, owlish glasses were balanced precariously on his wide nose and threatened to fall off at any moment.

"What? Oh, yes, yes." Snorri's hands fluttered in front of his rotund body. "You could say that." His twinkling blue eyes stared at first Dar, then Jennifer. "Oh my, my. We very rarely have visitors here. This must be a special occasion. What did you say their names were, John?"

The director of the institute grimaced. "As I've told you countless times before, my name is Jason. And their names are Dr. Dar Tyrson and Jennifer Giordano. Please try to remember that, Snorri."

"Oh yes, yes. I rarely forget a face or a good meal." His smock had enough food stains on it to divulge everything he had eaten for the last two years.

"I'm pleased to meet all of you," Jennifer said. Her smile included everyone, even Snorri, who was at that moment wiping his smudged glasses on his pink and purple polka dot tie. "I haven't been in a lab since I was in college. I remember we had a poster of the elements on the wall near the door—"

"Now where was I?" Snorri muttered. "Oh, yes—elements. The chemical elements in alphabetical order are: actinium, aluminum, americium, antimony, argon—"

Jason cleared his throat. "That will be all, Snorri."

"—arsenic, astatine, barium—"

Dar squeezed the old scientist's arm. "You'll tell me the rest of the list later, *já?* After I have finished my tour of the facilities."

"Oh my, my. You're really serious? You're asking me to finish the list later?"

"Já."

If the excited gleam in Snorri's eyes meant anything, Jennifer thought it was safe to assume that very few people ever asked him to continue talking.

"Would you also like to know the different parts of a leaf? Or possibly the phases of the moon?" He trembled visibly, like a starving puppy who had just been shown a juicy bone. "I could even give you a speech on the structure and process of the human digestive system."

"*Já.* That would be fine, when I've finished my tour."

Snorri's pudgy fingers worried the hem of his white jacket. "Of course, of course. Please, don't hurry on my account. Take your time. I'll be here when you're done." The scientist hopped from one foot to the other. "You won't forget, will you?"

"*Nei.* I will not forget."

"That's good, good."

A hand on Dar's arm, Jason steered the Norseman toward the door with more than a hint of impatience. "I hope you noticed our new—"

Before Jason could finish, Snorri interrupted him. "Oh, Dar?"

Dar turned around so quickly, and Jason's hold on him was so tight that the man bumped hard into the wall behind him and slid to the floor. Apologetically, Dar helped the dazed institute director to his feet.

"*Já,* Snorri?"

"I've also got a collection of slides you might like to see."

He nodded. "I would like that."

Jennifer was sure Dar had no idea what a slide was, but she applauded his tact.

The wide smile on the short scientist's face grew even wider. "Good. Good."

Glancing at Jason and seeing the fierce expression on his face, Jennifer frowned and stepped closer to Dar. But the look disappeared quickly as the man set about straightening the lapels of his charcoal gray suit. "Don't you have any work to do, Snorri?" he asked.

That got quick results. "Plenty. Plenty. Lots of work."

"Then get to it! And don't expect Mr. Tyrson to visit you later. You've got too much work to finish before you leave tonight."

Snorri blushed and scurried over to one of the white marble tables lining the walls of the room.

"Come this way." Jason stalked out of the room.

Her lower lip caught between her teeth, Jennifer couldn't help but give Snorri another glance. She couldn't swear to it, but she thought that she saw narrow wet trails running down the pink cheeks of the elderly scientist.

"And that concludes our tour." Jason guided Dar down the corridor. Jennifer ran down the hall and caught up with them just as the elevator arrived. "Tyrson, I would like to make you a proposition that I am sure you won't be able to refuse."

"To be propositioned is good, *já?*"

"In this case, yes. I'd like you to work for me—and I do not want to hear the word *no.*"

Dar glanced at Jennifer, a worried frown on his

face. "You must offer a job to us both or we will not accept."

A job! Still, as much as Jennifer needed money, she hated the thought of working in this place even more. "Thank you, but I've got an interview this afternoon—"

"Jennifer accepts, also."

Was he crazy? "I'm sorry, Dar, but—"

Dar put his hand on her arm and interrupted her refusal. "She accepts."

Sighing, Jennifer said nothing. She did need this job—and work in an institute would look good on her resumé. Especially if she planned to continue her career in programming.

"Well, in that case, I'm pleased. There is a secretarial position which I'm sure you'll fill nicely." Jason's teeth as he smiled reminded her of a steel trap, one that had just closed on her lower leg. "We're having our weekly Friday staff party tomorrow night. Why don't you join us?"

"*Nei.* I have prior commitments."

The director of the institute shrugged. "Too bad. I could have introduced you to your coworkers. But you will meet them soon enough. You can start right away?"

Jennifer didn't like the idea of Dar working for Jason and tried to stall for more time. "Tomorrow is bad. We'll start on Monday."

Dar shook his head. "Tomorrow will be fine. I will be here."

Jason smiled. "Ahem. Good. We'll talk more about the special project you've been working on then."

What exactly did the scientist know about Dar? Unable to stop a shiver of foreboding, Jennifer dragged Dar toward the exit. She glanced over her shoulder, saw the calculating look in Jason's eye, and walked faster.

"Dar, I really don't want to work here," she whispered, dragging the massive Norseman behind her.

"But, Jennifer. I need you."

His words, said in such a passionate voice, sent shivers of desire down her back. Then he continued and the shiver turned to one of fear.

"I know nothing about scientists or this institute. You are the only person who can help me understand my new job."

Jennifer sighed with resignation as she drew up the collar of her coat and strode quickly toward the car. Dar needed her, but it wasn't in the same way she needed him.

Chapter Eight

Jennifer put her dirty lunch dishes in the sink. Tomorrow, Dar would start working at the institute. She had a bad feeling about it but couldn't put her doubts into words.

The front door slammed. Jennifer frowned as Dar walked into the kitchen, his shoulders sagging and his expression sad.

"What happened, Dar?"

"I do not understand yon Midgarders." His voice lacked its normal vibrancy. "I showed her Solveig, praised the creature's abilities to keep her safe, and then I handed the kitten to her. Then all Elvira did was weep and tell me she would tell her son Marcus about it."

Jennifer knew the Norseman was upset when, instead of dropping his mantle onto the floor as he usually did, he folded the purple cape neatly and put it on the back of a chair.

"I made her cry," Dar explained sadly, "and I don't know how to make her happy again."

Jennifer led him into the living room and tried to think of a way of explaining about women and tears. "She *was* happy, Dar." When he threw himself on the sofa and put his head in his hands, she tried again. "Earth women cry when they're happy. It's stupid, I agree. But it's a fact of life."

"Thanks, Jennifer, for trying to raise my spirits, but you need not lie."

Suppressing a sigh, Jennifer sat down beside him and put her hand on his knee. "It's the truth. You have to believe me. Elvira loved it-him-her—I mean, Solveig."

He raised his head and stared at her, a hopeful expression coming over his pale face. "Really?"

"Undoubtedly." Well, she had a *few* doubts, but she wasn't going to mention them now, not when she had almost talked Dar out of his sulks. She shivered as a draft came around the warped front door. "I'm just glad you got the kitten out of the house before Firedrake ate it."

"You are cold." He reached for her chapped, icy hand and enclosed it between his massive warm ones.

She did feel a little chilly. It could be because Dar had set the heat at don't-go-on-until-icicles-are-hanging-off-my-nose. Jennifer closed her eyes and sighed as he rubbed some warmth into her fingers. He made her feel as if he really cared about what happened to her.

"There. That is much better, *já?*"

Indeed. Who needed central heating when Dar was around? Jennifer closed her eyes and relaxed. She could get used to this. Warmth, companionship, amusing conversations, and gentle hands caressing her.

Dar looked down and assessed her long legs, shown off in her sheer stockings. "Why are you dressed so oddly?"

"I've got to go on a job interview, remember? I know we took jobs at the institute, but I want to keep my options open. And this company's looking for computer programmers. Will you be okay while I'm gone?"

Sad that he would soon have to let her go, Dar concentrated on her question. "*Já.* You have nothing to worry about. Firedrake and I will be fine."

"I'll be back around dinnertime." Jennifer adjusted her jacket, pulling the hem so it fit snugly against her sides.

"What type of clothing is that?" Dar eyed the striped blue material warily.

"It's called a suit. People wear them in offices."

Dar frowned at the crystal's translation. "Suit means to conform. What are you conforming to, Jennifer?"

"It's also the term for a skirt and jacket," she told him, her brows furrowed in thought.

Dar grunted. The only thing nice about the garment was the fact that it displayed her long, shapely legs. "And the foot coverings?" They emphasized the muscles in her legs.

"High heels. Impractical, but just another part of office attire."

Dar pursed his lips and leaned back in his chair. "They look uncomfortable."

"Only because they are."

He grunted, unable to understand the logic of her statement.

"Wish me luck."

Dar frowned and fingered the hilt of his dagger. "You are uncertain about this venture?"

"Of course," Jennifer said, her voice containing more than a hint of desperation. "There are probably lots of people interviewing for the position. I'll be lucky if I get a second interview."

"If you wish, I could cast a spell over you that would ensure that you are held in the highest esteem by anyone you meet."

Jennifer snorted. "Yeah. Right."

Didn't she believe him? "I'm serious."

"That's okay, Dar. I appreciate all your help, but I'd like to think I can get the job on my own merits rather than on the enchantment of a couple of pebbles from your bag."

She apparently didn't think highly of his sorcery skills. "At least let me lend you the use of my crystal." He drew the leather cord over his head. Holding it in the palm of his hand, he murmured a quick incantation and then placed it around her neck. The crystal hung tantalizingly in the valley between her breasts and briefly shimmered with an ivory glow that he'd found few things in this world could match. "With it around your neck, you will be safe and aware of danger."

Obviously hesitant about wearing the object, she fingered the cord. "What about you?"

He shrugged. "I wear it more from habit than need. I can translate your language without it now."

"Okay. If you insist."

Dar waited until she had her car keys in her hand before he gave her his final blessing. "May luck go with you, sprite."

Her smile rivaled the most magnificent sunrise on

Asgard. "Thanks, Dar. When I get back, I'll let you know how it went."

Jennifer folded her hands on her lap and listened to her interviewer explain the company's benefits package. "And you also get three weeks' vacation."

That was very generous for a new employee, she thought. She wanted this job with a desperation unmatched by that which any of her other interviews had inspired. She would do anything to get this job. Anything.

"And you're entitled to three personal days to use at your discretion."

Jennifer hoped her uneven breathing didn't betray her nervousness. "It sounds wonderful," she told the computer programming manager.

"Only because it is, Miss Giordano." He peered at her over his wide black frames. "It is *miss*, is it not?"

She nodded. "Yes, it is."

He cleared his throat and peered at her application. His pudgy fingers tapped an expensive pen on a spotless blotter. "Now, where were we? Oh, yes. There's a little overtime every once in a while. Would that pose a problem at home?"

She'd work all the overtime required, as long as she got paid for it. "No. I don't mind."

"That's good." He smiled widely, revealing a large gap in his front teeth.

When he cleared his throat and patted his protruding stomach, Jennifer nervously rubbed Dar's crystal. When she got home she would thank the Norseman for lending her the object. The slight weight around her neck reassured her and kept her from getting down on her knees and begging the manager to hire her.

She's got a great pair of legs.

The thought, coming into her mind out of nowhere, made Jennifer blink and grip the arms of her chair. Oh, my God! Now she was hearing things.

He cleared his throat again and smiled before he resumed his perusal of her résumé.

"I see you used to work for the Morak Corporation."

Jennifer pulled herself together and forced herself to speak. "Yes. For three years." She put her hand on the crystal.

Morak. Ha! A lousy company. They let their employees get away with murder.

The truth hit her like a heavy frying pan. Dar had given her his crystal, something rarely worn by humans. Who knew what sort of energy it emitted? She let it fall back against her neck.

As she sat there, she fondled the crystal again and another thought popped into her mind. *Wait until she finds out she has to work every weekend and holiday. She'll complain for a while, but only the men quit. Women will work twice as hard for half the pay.*

Not only was Dar making her lose her focus at this interview, he was making her go crazy! She couldn't be reading Mr. Johnson's thoughts. Her hand trembled on the crystal.

"We often work on weekends. Can you manage that?"

Then again, maybe the crystal enhanced her own natural abilities. She couldn't be reading his thoughts. It was impossible. Or was it? Jennifer's hand trembled around the crystal. "Yes. As long as it isn't every weekend."

He just smiled and reached for another folder.

Can't wait to get this one to the Dallas convention. We'll have two adjoining rooms. It will be just her and me.

"Did I mention that this job will involve some travel?" He licked his lips.

Jennifer cleared her suddenly dry throat. "No. I don't believe you did."

"There's a convention in Texas coming up. If you get the position, I would need you to accompany me."

Just how badly did she want this job? Jennifer wondered. "I see," she answered neutrally.

"Good. That's good."

Jennifer's hand tightened on the crystal with enough force to break the cord. On second thought, she could always get another bank loan. Her vision of paying her overdue mortgage popped like an iridescent soap bubble.

The man put a finger to his lips and cleared his throat. *I wonder if I can teach this one to fetch my coffee?*

"Would you like a cup of coffee, Miss Giordano?"

How dare he! The crafty expression on his face warned her to think carefully about her answer. "Um. Yes. I would," she said through gritted teeth, wishing she had taken martial arts training when she was younger.

"A coffee drinker. That's good." He smiled. "The coffeepot is in the other room right next to my secretary's desk." His nasal voice grew noticeably brighter. "Maybe while you're there you could get me a cup, too."

He waited until she stood up before he added, "One sugar and just a drop of milk. I'm on a diet." He patted his belly. "Oh, and while you're there, maybe you could get me one of those small sugar doughnuts, in the box next to the coffee. I didn't have any breakfast this morning."

Jennifer flung open the door and had one foot on the outer office rug when she put her hand on the crystal.

This one will do anything I tell her. Anything!

The jerk! She spun around and faced the interviewer. "Sir?" He frowned, obviously surprised she was still there—and without his coffee.

"Yes?"

"I just wanted you to know"—she spaced her words evenly—"that I wouldn't work for you if you were the last company on Earth. And furthermore, the Morak Company doesn't let their employees get away with murder. They are a caring company with honest managers. Which is more than I can say for this lousy outfit."

The shocked expression on his face was worth the loss of ten jobs. Jennifer slammed the door behind her and stalked toward the elevators.

"Of all the no-good, dirty, ignorant, chauvinistic rats." She pushed the DOWN button. "He has to be the biggest, fattest one I've ever met."

One of the secretaries behind her laughed and talked loudly into the telephone. "I know, Jeffrey. Just be patient. Mommy will be home in a little while and then we'll dress you in your nice Halloween outfit and take you trick-or-treating."

"Trick-or-treating?" Jennifer tried to remember the date.

"Yes. I bought the candy you like, but you can't eat any until after dinner. Now you be a good boy and watch TV until I get home."

"Candy? Costume? *Halloween!*" Jennifer stabbed

the DOWN button again. Oh, God! Dar was home all alone on Halloween. She had to get some candy and get home quickly. If Loki was going to return, wouldn't he do it on a night such as this? And if he did, Jennifer thought, she would be by Dar's side. The elevator door opened and she leapt inside. *Halloween.* How could she have forgotten?

The doorbell rang. Dar turned from the refrigerator and reached for his dagger. His belt was empty.

"By the throne of Odin's lofty watch tower! We have a visitor." He stared out the window. Twilight. The time when wicked inhabitants of the other worlds walked the night. "I hope Jennifer comes home soon. One never knows what will happen at twilight."

Dar dried his hands on a dish towel and walked toward the front door. "Don't make any noise, Firedrake, until I see who it is."

Expecting Elvira, Dar opened the door—and came face-to-face with a demon. A short demon to be sure, but a demon nonetheless. It had deep, inset eyes, a hooked nose, black horns, and an evil smile. Even its attire seemed sinister. Its long black cape swung in a wide arc as it moved.

"Trick or treat." The high voice was terribly bizarre on such a hideous demon.

"By the sacred branches of Ygdrassil, be gone from my door." The exhortation, growled in his most lethal tone, had no effect on the creature.

"Trick or treat." The scowling face bobbed as it shoved a bag with handles toward Dar's face. "Gimme some candy or I'll turn you into an ugly toad," it growled.

The threat hung in the air like a sword aimed at his heart. If they exchanged spells, there could be some damage to Jennifer's house. Bolts of lightning disfigured wood and carpets. Jennifer had already mentioned that—several times. What could he do?

Since Dar's sword was in his bedroom, and he didn't know the strength of his opponent, he waited for the demon to make the first move. To his surprise, the monster shrugged and turned around. "Gee. If ya don't have any candy, just say so."

Dar loosened his grip on the door and forced himself to take calming breaths. What sort of demon demanded sweets? He heard a noise, like the sound of children's laughter. Dar peered down the street. There, past a massive elm tree, were a witch and a dwarf. It was an evil combination that boded no good. Dar slammed the door and ran up the stairs to get his sword.

As soon as Jennifer turned her car onto her street, she knew there was something wrong. The entire neighborhood, the kids and parents from the local school, and a busload of people from a local church, stood outside her house. They had probably been on the way to the school's annual Halloween party. She looked at all the costumed children and their parents and groaned. *What had Dar done now?*

There were so many people in the street, she had to leave her car at the bend in the road. A plastic carry bag of miniature Milky Way and Nestlé Crunch bars in her hand, Jennifer pushed her way through the crowd and got her first good look at her house. Nothing prepared her for the sight that met her eyes. Floating above her house was a diaphanous, fire-breathing dragon. Its snarling mouth opened, revealing long rows of pearly whites inside.

When I get that darn Norseman, I'm gonna strangle him!

Then she saw what caused everyone to shake their head in amazement. A solid wall of energy formed a circle around her house; every few seconds a rainbow of colors would travel around the circle. "Oh, my God!"

A blonde, possibly in her early thirties, nodded at Jennifer's side. "Isn't that awesome! It's been like that since dusk. If you get close to the house, the hair on your head stands on end. Do you think it's a hologram?"

Her temper escalating almost as high as the dark clouds above, Jennifer replied, "I'm not sure, but whatever it is, I'm going to get it shut off."

Immediately!

"Strangling is too good for him," she muttered as she elbowed her way through the crowd. "I'm gonna hang him by his toes on the porch."

When she got to the edge of the barrier, Jennifer stopped. She could feel the eyes of the crowd on her as they waited to see what she would do next, but she refused to let it bother her.

"Dar," she shouted. "Shut this thing off immediately!"

Silence.

"Dar! I'm going to count to three and then I'm going to walk forward." She took a deep, trembling breath. "One!" No response. "Two!" Did she see the door open a crack? "Three!"

"Jennifer. You're wearing my crystal. You can enter the force field without fear of being nullified."

"Nullified?" she repeated incredulously. "You mean I could have been fried alive?"

Unsure whether the crystal would protect her, she

tightened her grip on her handbag and her candy and cautiously inched forward. So far, so good. A few millimeters away from the throbbing energy, Jennifer felt the hair on the back of her neck rise. She was sure she was going to be struck by lightning any second.

"Dar, I'm coming in." Talking to keep her mind off the threat of impending "nullification," she walked into the light. "Whatever you're doing, knock it off!" There. She had one foot through the weird barrier. "I'm getting angry. Very angry!" Half of her body crossed over the divider. Was that something burning she smelled? Hoping it wasn't her clothing, Jennifer closed her eyes, screamed, and rushed blindly toward her porch. "If I live through this, I'm going to strangle you."

Almost tripping over the uneven ground, Jennifer steadied herself and ran up the porch steps. She had barely taken another breath when she felt herself slam into something big, something that wrapped its arms around her and lifted her off her feet.

Dar carried Jennifer into the house. "By the winged tips of a full-grown dragon's wings! The crowd of demons grows larger with each passing second. There are creatures out there so hideous, I have only imagined them in nightmares And you Earthlings associate with them! I must reevaluate my opinion of this world."

"What do you think you're doing?" Jennifer said, her voice a mere whisper.

Dar slammed the door shut with his foot. How could he maintain the energy field and explain the situation to Jennifer at the same time? In the kitchen, the muffled grunts of the bound dragon caught his attention. *Firedrake*! He was the solution.

Setting Jennifer on the sofa, Dar ran upstairs to release the dragon. Dar waited until Firedrake took up the position of watch dragon by the window before he concentrated his attention on the pale woman sitting stiffly on the sofa.

"Dar! Are you crazy?" Jennifer shrieked.

"Jennifer." He sat down next to her and grasped her hand. "We're in grave danger. Hordes of witches, dwarfs, and demons surround us as I speak. I do not know how you made it through, but—"

"I'm going to kill you, Dar." She grabbed the front of his shirt and pulled him so close, he imagined he could see smoke curling out of her nostrils.

"But, Jennifer—"

"Don't 'but' me," she growled, shaking him with her tiny hands. "Do you know you almost scared me to death? And furthermore"—another shake—"you're scaring those little kids out there, too!"

"I admire your courage, sprite," he told her as her hands wrapped around his wide neck. "Especially as you walked through the demons without even blinking. None of the women in Asgard—"

Her hands tightened and squeezed. Luckily, they were small and lacked the strength to do him any real harm. Dar leaned forward so she wouldn't hurt herself. This brought him into contact with her body. He groaned as her perfume, an arousing floral scent, wafted around them. She shifted, and her leg rubbed against his arousal. He gritted his teeth and leaned closer as one of her long nails dug into the skin of his neck.

"I realize you don't know what you're doing, sprite." In the blink of an eye, he had her hands at her sides. The intimate position also made him well aware that her skirt had ridden up her thighs and she wore tantalizingly little underneath. His body reacted to her closeness in a throbbing manner that made him yearn to kiss the lips so close to his own.

"Let go of me, you—you Norseman!" Jennifer wiggled her body as she tried to break free of his hold. The movements didn't help Dar's condition. They made it worse.

"Stop struggling, sprite. You know not what demon you awake with your frantic movements."

"Get off me and I'll show you what I'm gonna do to you. I'll get a frying pan and pound some sense into your head. Just you watch me. I'll . . ."

Dar leaned forward and silenced her threats with his mouth. This brought him into even closer contact with her soft breasts. She smelled of the sweet flowers that grew in his mother's garden, a scent that made him hunger to taste more of her skin. Only when he was sure she would no longer fight him did he loosen his grip on her arms.

"Will you listen to me now, O furious sprite?"

Her only response was a shudder he felt in every fiber of his being. He rested his head next to hers. "We're in danger. You must do as I say or we won't last through the night." When she remained silent, he continued. "The house is surrounded by creatures bent upon our destruction."

"Your belt buckle is digging into my stomach."

Dar groaned and tried to get into a more comfortable position. "That is not my belt buckle," he told her, his voice husky despite his attempt to sound normal.

"Oh."

"What do you suggest we do?"

Jennifer put her hand on his cheek. "I suggest you get off me so I can think."

A logical suggestion, one Dar found hard to accept at this time. But given their current situation, it was the only thing he could do. He stood and helped her to her feet.

"Turn off the force field," Jennifer said as she pulled her skirt down and straightened her clothes. Red underwear. It was very scanty red underwear underneath the silky clear stockings she wore. Dar averted his gaze and concentrated on her words.

"Turn off the force field? You jest with me!"

"No, I'm not kidding." She pulled determinedly on his arm. He allowed her to drag him back to the sofa and sit him down on the still warm cushions.

"Listen very closely." Jennifer held his hand. "There are no such thing as demons."

"But, Jennifer . . ."

"Listen to me. What you have been seeing are just cute little children dressed in costumes. Each year, on the same day, we celebrate a holiday known as Halloween. Don't you have anything like this in Asgard?"

"Nei."

"Believe me, Dar." Jennifer patted his arm. "There is nothing outside the door that could harm us. No witches, goblins, or demons. Just adorable kids wearing cute costumes." She glanced toward the window. "The kids' parents are probably calling all their friends to come and see the laser show we're putting on for the neighborhood—that is, if none of them have fried themselves trying to get through."

Dare he believe her? The explanation sounded too outrageous to be the truth. "You'll swear those creatures are not dangerous, *já?"*

She nodded. "Absolutely."

If she was wrong, it would cost them their lives. He pulled her against his chest and decided to put his faith in the woman in his arms. "Okay. I will shut off the force field."

"A wise decision, Dar."

How could he think when she stared at his chest with such hunger in her eyes? "I will do it now."

"That's good."

Dar closed his eyes and mumbled the words that would obliterate the spell. " 'Tis done."

He almost groaned out loud when he felt her fingers touch his chest. His eyes opened. "Sprite, you are stirring up things that are hard to control."

"Dar, I . . ."

Firedrake screeched and flapped his wings. Dar sprang out of the chair and pulled his sword free of the scabbard. "By the mighty walls of Valhalla, someone's at the door!"

"Put that sword down and tell that dragon to shut up."

Dar watched Jennifer stalk over to the door and fling it open, which showed him the reason for Firedrake's distress. While he had been busy dreaming of Jennifer, the demons had walked up to the porch. There was now a large crowd of monsters of varying shapes and sizes at her door. He stared at the sprite, standing in the doorway as if she would face down the creatures alone.

It was amazing. None of the Asgard women affected him the way she did. None had the ability to seduce him and make him forget about everything else but the thought of taking them to his bed. Jennifer's powers must be strong indeed to make a sorcerer forget about the danger outside.

Her power over the demons was another matter; one that would command the respect of almost every inhabitant of Asgard.

"Oh, how cute." Jennifer bent down to eye level and stared into the face of a jotun covered with blood. "And what are you supposed to be?"

The small creature lifted an orange and white bag and thrust it into Jennifer's face. "I'm a witch. Can I cast an evil spell on you?"

Dar growled and moved closer to Jennifer's unprotected back.

"Oh, how adorable. Don't you think she's adorable, Dar?" Jennifer cooed.

"Beyond words," he growled, ready to strike if any of the diminutive beings tried to harm the woman before him.

"Dar, hand me some candy from the bag over there, please."

Candy? Jennifer thought about candy at a time like this? He grabbed the entire bag and dropped it at her feet. She opened the bag of gaily wrapped small squares and gave one to the jotun.

"There. Now, who's next?"

A tiny monster in a white sheet floated forward. "Trick or treat."

"Oh my, I'm so scared!" Jennifer's laughter belied her words, but it didn't put Dar at ease one little bit. She sought to appease these creatures of the night!

"Look, Dar, a ghost. Have you ever seen anything so scary?"

Actually, he had. The fire giants of Musepelheim were reputed to curdle the blood of even the stoutest warrior of Asgard. "He's very scary," he conceded.

That earned him one of her rare smiles. "See, you've scared both me and Dar."

The little head turned in his direction and edged closer to the door. "Your husband's big! He could be a giant."

Jennifer bit her lip and turned to look at Dar. "He's not my husband. He just rents a room here."

Did her voice sound sad? Dar wasn't sure. His nerves stretched taut, he watched as every form of creature paraded up to the house, to be met by Jennifer's smile and an offer of sweets.

"How did you do that light show? That was neat."

Jennifer looked from the little monster who had spoken to Dar. "See that big man over there? He's a Viking." Dar scowled at her insolent tone. "He's also a magician. He can do lots of tricks and even pull cars out of ditches."

"Wow! Can he do that at my birthday party? It's next week."

A smile on her face, Jennifer bit her lip as if seriously contemplating the matter. "I'm sorry, but Dar is going to be busy next week."

The little monster shrugged and seemed genuinely disappointed. "Oh, well, I just thought . . ."

One little being, dressed all in white, with feathery wings and a halo, seemed younger than the others. In her arms, she carried a small animal.

"Look, Dar. A teddy bear. What's your name, dear?" Jennifer asked the girl.

The child spoke in a soft whisper. "Ba-ba."

Until this moment, Firedrake had stayed immobile, his powerful talons resting on the back of the winged chair. But as soon as he saw the animal, he leaned forward and flicked out his forked tongue.

His movements deliberately casual, Dar crept toward the chair. "Jennifer, I think the angel has been here long enough. Let the next demon enter the house."

"But Dar, she's so cute. I just have to hug her."

Dar knew he had only seconds to act.

"Oooh. Pretty birdie."

Dar froze as the little angel began walking toward Firedrake.

"Hi, birdie." She reached out to pet the dragon.

Jennifer smiled.

At the same time, Dar shook his head in dismay. "*Nei.* Firedrake doesn't like to be touched."

But the little girl didn't listen. The bear tucked in the crook of her arm, she climbed on the chair and stood face to face with the fire-breathing dragon.

"Hi there, birdie. Candy?" In her tiny fingers, she held out a small brown square. Drops of sweat trickled down Dar's back. If Firedrake ripped off her arm, Jennifer would never forgive either of them.

Firedrake seemed to smile. The rows of his sharp teeth glistened like mini-daggers.

"Go ahead, Firedrake. Take it," Jennifer said.

Dar held his breath as the dragon leaned forward so far that his nose almost touched that of the angel. Dar's eyes bulged out of his head as Firedrake gently took the tiny piece of candy out of the angel's hand.

"Oooh. Tickles." The angel laughed and patted the dragon on the head. "Nice birdie."

Dar slumped down onto the chair and put his head in his hands. By the sacred well of Mimir! If he hadn't seen it with his own eyes, he would never have believed it could be possible. She had succeeded in taming a wild, furious dragon. What would she do next?

"Look, Dar. Isn't this two-headed monster fierce?"

Jennifer leaned forward and kissed the demon on

one of his many cheeks. Dar just sat there and shook his head. Alas, he thought, it was a feat beyond that of many sorcerers—the taming of demons. The only problem was, he realized as he watched her invite another witch into the house—she had also cast a spell on him. There was no other way to explain how quickly he'd fallen in love.

Loki peered into Dar's woman's hall and grimaced as yet another demon stepped on his foot. As long as the creatures did not attack him, he would ignore their rude behavior.

Seeing the young woman at Dar's side give a piece of food to a smiling devil, he narrowed his eyes and turned his back on the scene. To attack now would be foolhardy, especially when the woman had just gained so many powerful allies by feeding them. He would wait until Dar was alone, and preferably unarmed.

Amazed at the powerful abilities displayed by the woman with Dar, Loki walked toward the small glade that hid his demon and the hoard of magical devices stolen from this world.

He would need assistance to defeat the sorcerer; then he would destroy all of Asgard and the warriors who had dared to laugh at him.

Chapter Nine

"Here's your crystal back."

Jennifer placed the necklace on the kitchen table. The early morning rays of the sun, coming through the kitchen window, reflected on the numerous facets of the crystal. Dar moved aside his empty cereal bowl, picked up the necklace, and put it around his neck. With all the excitement the night before, and in preparing for their jobs at the institute, he had forgotten to ask about her interview, a serious mistake, to judge by the scowl on her face.

"Was your interview successful?"

Jennifer snorted. "It was one of the worst experiences of my life."

"I see." Actually, he didn't see, but as he didn't know what an interview entailed, he couldn't ask the right questions.

"Let me put it another way, Dar. I would have died to get that job. But the interviewer was a major jerk."

When he would have consoled her, Jennifer jumped up and slammed her empty coffee cup on the counter. "And it's all your fault."

His fault? What had he done that would cause her to have the worst day of her life?

"If it wasn't for your crystal, I would have been ignorant of the problems until I collected several pay-checks, by which time I would never have quit!"

Dar fingered the leather cord. "I see."

"No, you don't see." Jennifer flung her arms up in exasperation. "Every time I touched that darn crys-tal, I heard the interviewer's thoughts."

"An unexpected side effect. One that even I don't experience." Dar contemplated the matter as they ex-ited and locked up the house. "It's a very rare gift. Your powers must be very strong."

"I don't have any powers!"

"Everyone has powers, but most don't know how to use them. If some of the people of Asgard knew about your abilities, they would be envious."

"What type of powers does Loki have?"

"No one knows the extent of Loki's magic. He is neither wholly man nor wholly god, but he *is* wholly dangerous."

Jennifer waited until Dar got into the car before she turned on the ignition. They pulled out of the driveway. "He's definitely got to be stopped. I just wish there was some other way to earn money and get you home than having to work at the institute."

"If you do not want to work with the scientists, I will give you my other armband," Dar decided, want-ing her to be happy.

"But I hate to think you'll be broke if you give me all your gold."

"I will be without funds for only a short time, Jennifer. I can always create more as I need it."

Jennifer gasped. "Are you telling me that you can make gold out of thin air?"

"*Nei.* I make gold out of lead, not air." Dar spoke without a hint of boastfulness.

Jennifer pulled over to the side of the road, leaned over, and grabbed Dar's shirt collar. "You can make gold out of lead and you didn't think it important enough to tell me?"

Dar couldn't believe how upset she looked. He dabbed at a tear running down her cheek. "The subject never came up before."

She leaned forward until he could almost taste her lips. "Never came up before?"

He didn't blink as he met her stare. "*Já.*"

"If I could make gold," she stated, "I'd *find* an opening in a conversation and stick it in." She let go of him and buried her head against the steering wheel to hide her tears. "I can't believe you never mentioned this."

"Why are you crying?" He pulled her onto his lap—it was crowded in the jeep, but he relished her nearness. "I do not have the necessary ingredients to make the gold with me. I'm sorry, sprite. I didn't know you'd react so strongly." He rocked her back and forth against his warm body. "Please, don't cry."

If he could have made time stand still, Jennifer would never move from his arms. Tenderly, Dar kissed the tears from her cheeks. Then time did stand still. Her back rested against the dashboard. Gently, he kissed her lips. His hands caressed her and he deepened the kiss.

Wherever he touched, Jennifer's body burned. Her hands trembling, she caressed his broad shoulders. It seemed as if she had waited an eternity for this kiss.

Dar's lips seared a path down her neck, to her shoulders. He didn't stop until her shirt was unbuttoned and he touched her swollen breasts.

When Dar lifted his head, Jennifer almost screamed with frustration. "Don't stop," she pleaded.

"I do not wish to stop, but the people in the passing cars can see us." He buttoned her shirt.

Her trembling fingers could never have accomplished the task, but Dar seemed unaffected by this encounter.

"If it were possible, would you return with me to Asgard?"

Leave Earth to go to a world where she would be caught in the middle of a bloody war? Go to a place where she didn't know the language, culture, or people? Dar said even the women there were prepared to fight. She shuddered when simply putting down mousetraps.

Though that wouldn't matter as much if he loved her, she mused. Lord, but he was a handsome warrior.

Still, she had to think. What would she do if he decided at a later date that he was ashamed of a wife who didn't fit into his society? It was bad enough that the men in her life left whenever the going got tough. She didn't think she could live if Dar was attracted to a beautiful, powerful Asgard maiden and regretted his impetuous offer to take her—someone who would never be good in the middle of a battle—to be his woman.

"I'm sorry, Dar"—she looked down at her hands—"but I can't."

"That means you *won't.*" He stared out the window as the passing of a huge truck rocked the Jeep. "I understand."

His steady hands and calm voice grated on her nerves. "How can you just sit there looking as if nothing happened? As if you don't want me as much as I want you?

Dar turned to face her, revealing passion-filled eyes that burned a path to her soul. "As a warrior, I learned to control my emotions. That doesn't mean I don't feel any desire, sprite. My body throbs to join with you, but as much as I want to continue, the time isn't suitable." He gestured toward the cars passing by with increasing frequency. "I would like a bed when we consummate our desire."

Realizing how emotional she sounded, Jennifer took a deep breath and tucked her shirt into her jeans. She wriggled back into the driver's seat.

"You will accept my gift of gold?" he asked, staring at her with an intensity that made her blush.

"Yes, I'll take it. Thank you."

"You are welcome, sprite." Dar's smile rivaled the sun on the horizon. "This weekend, go to the jewelers and give him my remaining armband so that you will have money for the mortgage."

She joined the flow of traffic, and tried to take her mind off his arms wrapped about her—her body pressed so intimately against his. "While I'm driving, tell me a little more about how you go about making gold. Then we'll discuss our new jobs . . ."

Dr. Margie Monroe leaned so close that her breasts pressed against Dar's arm. Dar moved back a pace. The doctor followed.

". . . and this picture shows the growth after just two days. What do you think of the success of our project so far?" she asked, her voice low and full of sensual promise.

Having spent most of the day being asked questions about something called genetics, which had nothing to do with time-travel, Dar shrugged. "I am not sure."

He heard her teeth snap together. Her mouth thinned. "If you'll excuse me, Dr. Tyrson, I'll be late for my meeting with the director of the institute."

She was going to talk to the man named Jason, Dar thought. Everyone had been questioning him about some vague project that they hinted about, but no one actually explained. He thought it had something to do with his dragon.

He waited until Monroe left, then went down the hall to get Jennifer. She was sitting at a desk, answering the phone. At his signal, she finished the conversation, got up, glanced around, then joined him.

Even with a frown on her face, Jennifer had never looked more beautiful to him. She drew him as no other woman ever had. Dar wished things could be different between them. He understood her hesitation to leave the world she knew but wished she had chosen differently. Maybe, just maybe, he could change her mind before he left.

"How did it go?" she asked as they tiptoed down the hallway.

"It went poorly. They think I am a scientist from a foreign country with knowledge of 'genetics.' " Dar sighed. "I know not where they got such an idea, but it could not be further from the truth. It seems we must find out about time-travel another way."

They hurried down the flight of stairs toward the basement.

"Why would that man be so interested in you working here? Do you think he knows about your ability to make gold?" she asked as Dar peered around another corner to ensure that no one saw them.

His hand hovering over his crystal dagger, Dar frowned. "I'm confident I will learn what he wants soon. Jason doesn't seem like the type to beat around a tree."

"You mean beat around a bush."

Dar grunted, sure he'd never learn the nuances of the English language.

"Are you sure Snorri is the best person to talk to about time-travel?"

"He may be my only hope." His last hope.

They entered the end laboratory and studied the man sitting on a stool by a long light gray table.

Although Dar knew he hadn't made a sound, the scientist stood up and waddled over to a table. "Oh my, oh my. Now, where did I put my glasses? They were here a moment ago."

"You are looking for these, *já?*" Dar bent down and picked the glasses up off the floor.

Snorri squinted in his direction. "Is that you, John?"

"*Nei.* 'Tis Jennifer Giordano and I, Dar, son of Tyr, head sorcerer of Asgard." He handed the spectacles to the scientist.

"Thank you. You don't know how glad I am that you found them. I lose them at least once a—" He stopped in mid-ramble. "Did you say *sorcerer?*"

"*Já.*"

"From Asgard?"

"*Já.*"

Jennifer groaned. Snorri collapsed onto his chair. "Asgard is the 'Palace of the Gods.' It was populated by the Vanir and Aesir."

Dar couldn't believe his ears. "You have knowledge of my world?"

"But of course. I'm familiar with all nine Norse worlds. I have studied the folklore extensively. Do you know Odin or Thor?"

"*Já.* Odin is my grandfather. And I have caressed the handle of Miolnir, Thor's hammer."

"That's wonderful! To think that I've finally met someone from Asgard—" Snorri blinked, then blinked again. "But that's impossible. You can't be from Asgard. You must think it amusing to make fun of me."

Dar frowned. "I am not mocking you. I am who I say I am, and I can prove it." He glanced around the room, searching for something that would convince the scientist.

"My mantle is at home, so I can not use that, but I can do basic levitation without runes." His gaze settled on a row of glass tubes on the table to his left. "Watch this." He raised his hands toward the ceiling. "By the sacred crystal cave, I command you to rise and do my bidding."

"Be careful, Dar," Jennifer warned. "They're very breakable."

"I will be careful, Jennifer."

The objects lifted as if on a current of air. Dar narrowed his eyes. The tubes swirled and danced near the ceiling. Only when he knew the scientist was convinced did he put them back on the table in their little slots, one at a time.

"Oh dear, oh dear. I think I'm going to faint."

Jennifer leapt forward and helped the pale scientist to sit down. "Put your head between your knees. It'll help you recover."

Snorri's wheezing and occasional snorts worried Dar, but there was nothing he could do. The scientist had to believe or all would be lost. Every few moments Dar glanced at the door to ensure that they were still alone.

"But how can that be?" Snorri muttered as he stared at the floor. "An Asgard sorcerer. Here. In my lab. It's beyond comprehension!"

" 'Tis true." Dar helped the scientist to sit up again.

"But how . . ."

"Loki." The one word said it all.

"Aaah. The Trickster." He clapped his hands. "I should have guessed!"

Jennifer strolled slowly around the lab, lifting up a bottle here, glancing in a glass tube there. At the sound of Loki's name, she shivered and rubbed her arms.

"When I get my hands on that slimy jotun, I'm going to feed him to the wolves," Dar vowed.

"Well, well. That explains it. And of course you are looking for a way home. But why did you come here? I'm sure there are other, much larger institutes you could have chosen."

"Jason Wells."

"Who?"

"The director of the institute," Dar said patiently.

"I should have guessed." Snorri grimaced. "That man has a keen eye, I think. Or was that someone else . . ." He paused. "Did you use your powers in front of him?"

Dar thought back to their first meeting. "I did not use my powers that day, did I, Jennifer?"

"No, Dar. You didn't."

Snorri played with a pen in his pocket. "Did you speak Norse?"

"Nei."

"Tell me a little bit about yourself."

Where should he start? "I arrived on Earth at twilight and met the most beautiful sprite on the planet. She lay there with a cut above her eye. Jennifer is proud, courageous, and very—"

Snorri cleared his throat, blushing as he glanced at the girl at Dar's side. "Maybe we should skip the next part and start with what you are doing here at the institute."

"Wells offered us both jobs with the intent of helping me to master the secrets of time-travel. Since I arrived this morning, I've been subjected to strange questions from his minions."

"Interesting, interesting. Such as?"

"They ask if I have heard of oddly named people, where I have worked, what I know, to whom I have talked. With each negative answer, they become more and more exasperated, as do I."

Snorri wiped his glasses on a stained crimson and yellow tie. "My, my. It sounds as if Jason is after something. I wonder what he wants? Has he asked you about your sorcerer's abilities?"

"*Nei.* Always questions concerning scientific matters."

"Who are you working with?"

"Dr. Monroe."

"Aaah. Genetics."

Jennifer paused by a large blackboard. She glanced from the equations on the board to Snorri. "Is Dr. Monroe working on a secret project concerning time-travel?"

"No, no." Snorri shook his head and dislodged his glasses, which fell into his lap. "Genetics is a branch of biology that deals with heredity and the chromosomal make-up of an organism.

"They deal with genetic drift, which is the changes

of gene frequency in small populations due to chance preservation or the preservation of particular genes. They also have been experimenting with genetic engineering, which is the direct alteration of genetic material by intervention in the genetic process, most usually by gene splicing."

Dar understood little of what Snorri said. "That is involved in time-travel, *já?*"

"No, no. That has nothing to do with time-travel."

It sounded as if the director of the institute had lied to him. Dar's lips tightened. "The last time we met, you offered to discuss some topics, *já?*"

Snorri nodded.

"I wondered if you'd be willing to teach me more about the culture of this planet. I also want to discuss whether it is possible for me to return home."

"Why, I would love to do that!" Snorri exclaimed, and his plump little body twitched so hard, he almost fell off the chair. "We can discuss anything you like. Pick a subject. History? Geography? Chemistry?"

"History. I'd like to learn more about what happened in Asgard after I left."

"Ah, mythology. A good choice." Snorri must have finally noticed that his glasses were missing because he felt around in his pocket. "Now, where did I put those things? I had them a moment ago."

Jennifer smiled as she came back to Dar's side. "In your lap."

"Oh, yes, yes. Thank you." He put them on, then proceeded to take them off and clean them. "If I'm not mistaken, you probably departed just before the war between the giants and the gods."

"Before I left, we were preparing for war with the jotuns." He forced himself to ask the question that weighed heaviest on his mind. ''You can tell me about the outcome, *já?''*

''Of course, of course. Now, let me see. Where should I start? Oh, yes. Not much is known of Loki's origins, so no one was surprised to learn that he and his corrupt children by the evil witch Angerboda betrayed Asgard and joined the side of the fire giants.''

That was an unholy union! Dar reeled at the thought of Odin's blood brother turning against his own kin. ''Go on.''

''Yes, yes. After a very bloody battle where many Aesir and Vanir were killed, the Bifrost Bridge was destroyed and Asgard was ravaged.''

Dar closed his eyes and wept for his friends and homeland. He felt Jennifer put a consoling hand on his arm. ''I must find a way to return to warn Odin of Loki's intent.''

''Yes, yes. But in order to do that, you'd have to travel through time and space back to Asgard.'' Snorri tapped his pudgy fingers against his lips. ''Well how did you get here?''

''Loki presented me with a piece of crystalite. You are familiar with this substance, *já?''*

''Yes, yes. I have a degree in geology.'' The scientist closed his eyes and frowned. ''It is possible. If we can learn the composition of the rock Loki used to send you to another time and place, then you'd be able to return home.''

''I'll tell you as much as I know.''

Snorri waddled over to the blackboard and picked up a thick piece of chalk. ''All right. Let's start at the beginning.'' He peered over his glasses. ''Jason won't notice you're both missing and come looking for you, will he?''

Dar looked at Jennifer. She nodded encouragingly.

Dar made a decision. "We will risk it." Then Dar proceeded to tell Snorri everything he knew about the crystalite.

"Good. Good." Snorri pushed his glasses up on the bridge of his nose. "Now. If I put this here and add this here . . ." His arm moved at a furious pace. "And we calculate the time element factor . . . it might just work!"

Dar watched as his new friend continued to make notes. It seemed that his only hope of warning Odin of what lay ahead rested in this human's brain.

"Oh, my; oh, my. That isn't right. Let's try this . . ."

Jennifer sniffed loudly. "What's that smell?"

Dar scanned the room and spotted a cloud of black smoke rising from a nearby counter. The odor made him cough, and he put his hand in front of his nose. He ran to the sink, filled up a container, and doused the flames.

Snorri didn't even notice.

". . . and of course that would mean we would have to add . . ."

Dar wondered how the man had survived this long without killing himself. "You had something on the stove, *já?*"

The scientist didn't even turn around. "That's my lunch. You can have some if you like. I know Jason doesn't condone eating in the lab, but I see no reason for such a stupid rule, don't you agree?"

Should he tell Snorri about his lunch? Jennifer and Dar peered at the congealed mess at the bottom of the container. "It's no longer edible."

"What? Oh. I guess I forgot about it and it burned. That's the second time this week. I've lost count of how many times this month." Snorri picked up an eraser and used it on a section of the board. "I've got some more soup in the fridge, behind the specimens. Would you like some?"

Specimens? Although he was starving, Dar shook his head and answered for both of them. "*Nei.* Neither of us is hungry."

"You'll let us know if you discover the secret of time-travel, won't you, Snorri?" Jennifer asked, disposing of the burned food and cleaning the pan at the sink.

"What? Oh, yes, yes. Immediately, but it may take some time. Lots of time. Maybe years." Snorri put his glasses in his smock pocket. "You'll come back tomorrow, won't you, Dar? You, too, Jennifer. There is so much I'd like to learn about the people of Asgard. And if you're going to stay on Earth for a while, you really should have a crash course on the basic subjects such as reading, writing, and arithmetic."

Dar would give anything to learn how to read Jennifer's newspaper. The written language he knew, the Fupark, consisted of only sixteen symbols and was used mainly to indicate the ownership of objects. "Thank you. I would like to learn how to read."

"Good. Good. Oh, Dar?"

Dar's hand paused on the doorknob. "*Já*"

"If you see Jason, don't mention the episode with the soup. He tends to get upset at the first sign of smoke."

"I won't say a word."

"Neither will I," Jennifer promised.

Snorri squinted at the wall. "Now, where did I put those glasses? I just had them a moment ago . . ."

Dar slipped out the door. Once he confirmed that no one was in the corridor, he nodded to Jennifer. She strode ahead of him. This afforded Dar a leisurely

A
Special
Offer
For
Love
Spell
Romance
Readers
Only!

Get Two
Free
Romance
Novels
An $11.48 Value!
Travel to exotic worlds
filled with passion and adventure—
without leaving your home!
Plus, you'll save $5.00
every time you buy!

view of the black stockings hugging her long legs. Who would have thought that the thin material could make her look so erotic?

Dar cursed as he responded to her nearness with a severity that made him groan and take deep breaths to cool the fiery blood singing through his veins. He seemed so powerless to prevent his attraction to her.

Sorcerers should have better control over their bodies, he told himself as he followed her. But in Jennifer's case, his body reacted before his mind could control it.

With a little effort, he resisted the urge to throw her on a desk and kiss her until she moaned with desire.

He thought of other, less pleasant things. The icy wind whipping through the trees of the Iron Woods. A rampaging fire giant on a massive black steed. His breathing became normal.

"How long do you think it will take for Snorri to figure out the secrets of time?" he asked when they reached the main floor of the institute.

"It could be days, months, or even years," she informed him. "Inventors had been trying for centuries to crack the barrier between time and matter."

Centuries. Dar resigned himself to the fact that he might never find a way to go home. Surprising himself, Dar couldn't help but be little glad that he might be staying here, as long as it meant spending the rest of his life with Jennifer.

He'd given her enough time to become used to him, he decided. And perhaps he would stay. It was now or never. *Ja*, it was time to explore the attraction he felt for her, see if it was strong enough for a lifetime. For once a man in his family fell in love, it was forever.

"Tonight I wish to give you a present," he told her, aware that he couldn't always be near her to protect her.

"What type of present?"

"A *drakna.*"

"Another dragon? Are you crazy?"

"This is a special type of dragon, one that dwells on both the physical and astral planes."

Jennifer smiled. "Oh. In that case, I accept. I think."

She'd accepted his gift. That meant a commitment on her part. Pleased with her answer, Dar smiled. Soon, he would bind her to him with more than just his words. When he returned to Asgard, he wanted her to go with him.

Careful not to crush her hand, Dar entwined his fingers with hers. Tonight, if the opportunity arose, he would seduce her. It was time.

Later that night, Jennifer followed Dar down to the basement. Dressed in the garb he'd arrived in, complete with sword, Dar laid his mantle down on the cold cement floor and set everything else he was carrying on top of it. Neither the darkness nor the damp bothered him. He was used to the musty odor of underground caves.

A cobweb brushed against his cheek. "Ah, silken strands of spiders. My supply of these is low." He tucked the silvery threads into one of the vials in his spell pouch and made sure he secured the demon head flap tightly.

"The sun has finally set. What do we do next?" she asked. "I've never helped cast a spell before."

"You do nothing. I will cast the spell."

Firedrake flew down the steps and landed on a pile

of dirty towels next to the contraption Jennifer called a washing machine.

Dar put several gold coins in a dish embellished with spells and runes. He knelt down and cleared his mind of all things until he could see the emptiness of his soul. Now came the hard part.

Dar held up a small cobalt blue bottle sealed with a black cork. Jennifer stared at the cloudy liquid showing through the sides of the glass.

"Is that stuff important?"

"It's vital to the transformation. I have only enough for one spell."

Jennifer cleared her throat. "Can you make some more of the liquid?"

"*Nei.* Not without the proper ingredients."

"Well, why didn't you say so? We'll go to the store and pick up whatever you need."

Dar shook his head and slid the bottle into a small pocket by his belt. "That isn't possible. I don't believe your world contains all the items I need."

Nervous, she gripped her hands together to stop their trembling. "What would you need?"

"Viper's bugloss, bilberry plants, eye of newt, fur of a wolf, the toenails of a witch, hair of a jotun, a crystal from the sacred crystal cave, to name but a few.

"I grind them up, put them under the root of an ash tree and wait until a full moon. Once the potion begins to expand, I cast my transformation spell." Dar's eyes twinkled as he told her the secret recipe. " 'Tis a simple spell. One that most experienced sorcerers can cast. Do you know where we could get the items?"

Jennifer bit her lip. "What is viper's bugloss? And where in the world would I find a jotun?"

"I thought as much. The only world that has all I need is Asgard." Dar rolled up his sleeves, exposing his lightly tanned arms. "I'm ready to begin. Remember what I told you: Don't come between my body and the coins."

"Got it."

"And don't touch me while I'm casting the spell."

"Okay."

"Lastly, under no condition are you to touch the gold until I say it's safe."

"No problem."

Dar nodded, obviously satisfied with her answers. "Then I can begin."

He needed absolute silence and peace. If anything or anyone interrupted him during the casting of the spell, his mind could be irreparably damaged. This was the main reason the meager number of Asgard sorcerers who hadn't been killed by the fire giants refused to cast powerful spells outside the crystal cave in Asgard. But he had neither the luxury nor the availability of a cave full of crystals, so he would have to make do with the basement and his black crystal mantle.

Dar lit two white candles and took off the brooch from his mantle. The sweet smell of vanilla wafted toward his nose and helped him to relax his tense muscles.

"I got the candles on sale, so if you need more let me know."

"These candles will be fine." He stared at his brooch. The fire-breathing dragon adorning it had been in his family for eons. The two ruby eyes glowed with a radiant light that took no brilliance from the crystal ball. He laid the brooch between him and the saucer.

Jennifer watched as Dar uncorked the small vial

and carefully poured several drops of the liquid onto the gold. Was it her imagination, or had the temperature in the room dropped several degrees?

A keening wind, like that of an approaching storm, battered at the windows from outside.

Dar reached into his mantle and extracted a round crystal ball that shimmered with the radiance of a cup full of twinkling stars.

Had the Norse sorcerer cast a spell on her? Enchanted by the man before her, Jennifer had a hard time keeping her eyes off his muscular body and on his strong, gentle hands. She tried hard not to let her imagination run wild and think of how good his hands had felt on her body or the way his eyes seemed to glow when he became aroused.

Breathless, she watched Dar kneel down on his mantle. He looked so powerful and majestic, Jennifer believed he could do just about anything.

"Light and air. Sun and stars." Dar raised the crystal toward the roof and closed his eyes. "With the power of the universe, I do hereby begin the transformation of matter."

Jennifer tried to memorize every word, every movement. Mesmerized, she watched the way he raised his face upward, his expression intent, inward, as if he could see things in other dimensions. Bright light filled the room as the crystal glowed first white, then went though all the colors in the rainbow.

The shutters on the basement windows rattled.

A whimper, barely noticeable, made her look down. There, next to her leg, stood Firedrake. And a more miserable dragon she had yet to see. "Didn't I feed you not too long ago?"

Firedrake whimpered again and leaned against her leg.

"Not now. I'm busy."

The violet eyes filled with tears and his head quivered. "It won't work." Small yet extremely strong paws wrapped themselves around her leg and squeezed. Jennifer tried to shake him off. "You just ate a couple of hours ago. Your next meal is breakfast tomorrow morning."

Whining, like a cat with his tail caught in a door, Firedrake clutched her leg harder and wriggled his wings. Her heart melted at the surprisingly expressive dejected look on the dragon's face.

"All right. All right. You can let go now. I'll go get you some chicken bones."

The squeaking grew louder.

"Okay, already. You can have the spareribs. But tomorrow you eat ground beef." She sighed loudly, a sucker for his hungry squeaking. "Is it a deal?"

Firedrake grunted softly and snuggled his little green head against her leg. She tenderly caressed his head as she listened to Dar chant. His soft, melodic voice hypnotized her. If only Firedrake would wait another few minutes so she could listen to his sexy voice. His nudge told her he wouldn't. Sad that she would miss part of the ritual, Jennifer tried to pry the sharp claws from her jeans.

"Ow! Stop squeezing my leg so hard, you little *drakna.* Clinging isn't going to get your food any faster." Firedrake refused to let go. "As a matter of fact, it'll probably take me longer to defrost it with you hanging on to me."

She watched as Dar opened his bag of spells and withdrew a container of gems. Emeralds and diamonds, common but strong trinkets, winked at her from behind their prison of glass. Dar extracted four round rubies, identical in their appearance and added those to the saucer.

"Are they real?" she asked, stunned at the brilliance of the stones.

"They are real."

Dar held his hands over his head. "With the eyes of jewels and the form of a *drakna,* I do hereby command you to appear, two in number and except for size, indistinguishable from the other."

Light, brighter than the sun and more powerful than lightning, emerged from his fingers. The ensuing crack of energy rocked the house. Jennifer bent down to hug Firedrake tightly against her. The tiny dragon clung to her. He buried his pointy head against her shirt.

Through the billows of smoke and the crackle of flames, she could see the gold move from the saucer and hover in the air. With movement faster than her eye could perceive, the pair spun until they appeared as nothing more than blurred globes.

"O mystical dragon of the universe, I call upon you to come to me now." Dar raised his hands toward the wooden ceiling. "I, Dar, son of Tyr, sorcerer of Asgard, do hereby command your presence in this transformation of matter."

The gold shimmered with light.

"Circles of gold, spun with threads of magic into the head of a *drakna,* the tail of the Midgard Serpent. I do hereby command you to form."

He kept up a steady stream of energy until she heard the sound of metal hitting metal. The noise broke the silence like the cracking of ice on a sunny day. He closed his eyes. " 'Tis done and nothing can reverse the spell except the death of the wearer. You may touch the jewelry now."

A thick white mist swirled about her legs. The wind, having grown in strength, beat at the house. The noise echoed through the cellar like the roar of an angry dragon.

With hands that trembled, Jennifer leaned forward and scooped up the items in the saucer. There, before her eyes, were two golden rings, one large and one small. Each was curled into the shape of a fire-breathing dragon with two ruby eyes that glowed with a life of their own.

"They're beautiful."

His arms tightened around her shaking form. "Not as beautiful as you. You are so beautiful, I could bury myself within you and never let you go."

His passion-filled words melted the reserve around her heart. Jennifer stared up into his concerned blue eyes. How could she bear to live here when he returned home? Everything in the house, even the berry bushes out back, would remind her of him.

His hands gentle, he peeled Firedrake off her leg. Dar drew the sniffling dragon up to eye level.

"Firedrake, cease your whimpering and grow used to waiting for your food. You can't always eat when your stomach is hollow." He shook the little green body to emphasize his words.

Would wonders never cease? Firedrake actually listened to him. Jennifer shook her head, amazed at his control over the dragon's actions.

Although it suddenly seemed late, Jennifer hated the idea of leaving Dar alone. She sat on a large wooden box filled with clothes and watched silently as Dar removed all traces of his spell. Finally, he leaned down next to her. He put the two rings in the palm of his hand and closed his fingers over the warm metal.

"I have fashioned rings bearing the crest of my family." He knelt down in front of her and took her cold, trembling hand in his. "This smaller one is yours. The matching one is mine."

As Dar slid the ring over her finger, Jennifer shivered; she could have sworn that part of his soul had entered hers. She stared in fascination at the perfectly sculptured dragon head. The red eyes returned her stare.

"It's beautiful. I can't thank you enough," she told him, vowing never to take the ring from her finger.

"You'll put this one on me, *já?*"

Jennifer accepted the ring. It was heavier than she expected, and the heat radiating from it almost burned her fingers. And then he kissed her. She drank of the sweetness as she would a fine wine, but it ended too quickly.

"If you're ever in trouble," Dar was suddenly saying, "say these words: 'O, spirit of the dragon, hear my plea, spirit, spirit, come to me.' You'll remember this, *já.*"

"What exactly will happen?"

"A fire-breathing dragon will appear."

Jennifer didn't know whether or not he was kidding. Just in case he was serious, she decided not to say the words unless she really, really needed help.

"The ring is warm. Do you want me to wait until it cools?"

"*Nei.* Do it now, while the spell is at its height of power."

She took a deep breath. "Okay. Here goes." It slid on his wide finger easily, as if it had belonged there since the beginning of time.

"From the frozen fog to the high heavens, I beckon the powers of light to hear me. Come, O dragon spirit that is the protector of darkness. Enter these rings.'' Dar's expression grew intense as he raised his head toward the ceiling.

A white vapor rose about Jennifer's legs, climbing up her body to swirl around the ring on her finger. Her hand trembled.

''Separately the rings unleash the specter within; together they harness the energy of the universe.'' Dar clenched his hand. ''I, Dar, son of Tyr, grandson of Odin, do command it.''

Outside, a streak of lightning, brighter than the sun, lit up the cellar.

Dar's tenderness and generosity brought tears to her eyes.

''I've got a present for you, too,'' she told him, wiping at the tears in her eyes. ''I was saving it till Christmas, but I want you to have it now.''

She dragged him up the stairs and padded to the hallway closet.

He looked at her for a brief moment. ''I have all I want or desire right here.''

He pulled her into his arms and pressed feather-light kisses to her neck. The delicious sensations flooding her body almost made her forget the gift. She pulled out of his embrace and put her hand against his lips. The ring glittered with an unearthly light. It felt heavy on her finger. ''Stay here.''

She put the red-and-silver-wrapped package in his hands and waited, a smile on her face. ''Well, aren't you gonna open it?''

Dar sat down on the couch. The springs squeaked a protest. It took Dar several tries before he finally figured out how to untie the bow. He put the box on the coffee table and opened the lid. She watched his expression, anxious to see his reaction.

"Well? Do you like it?"

He lifted the heavy book out of the box and stared at the openmouthed dragon with the shiny golden wings on the cover. She pointed to the silver letters on the dark brown leather. "It says *DRAGONS AND OTHER MYTHICAL CREATURES*."

Dar traced the raised lettering. " 'Tis beautiful, but is surely too expensive. You have expressed great pain at having little wealth. I can't accept it."

It would be just like him to try to save her money. "Don't worry about the cost."

She could sense his yearning to keep the book and it pleased her. His fingers caressed the golden spine. Dar's blue gaze searched her face and reached into her thoughts. "Return it. You need the money to pay the bank."

Her stubborn Norseman wouldn't give up until she told him the truth. "It didn't cost a lot. I passed a flea market on the way to my interview. This book was on one of the clearance tables."

"There is a market with tiny, leaping, bloodsucking insects?"

Did he have to take everything so literally? "No. It's a place where people bring things they don't want anymore and sell it for a song."

"You sang for this book?" He held it out to her.

"No. I gave them cash." She pushed it back into his arms. "I want you to keep it. Please. It isn't half as beautiful as my ring, but it is the best I could do with my limited funds." She narrowed her eyes. "I would be very angry if you continued to argue. I might think you didn't like your present."

That got a reaction. He put the book on the table and pulled her into his arms. The cushion dipped beneath their combined weight. " 'Tis a good present.

The rarest I have ever received. Thank you."

Her ear against his chest, she listened to his steady heartbeat. "You're welcome." She kissed the golden skin at his throat. "It's late, but I know how your stomach is. Would you like something to eat?"

She looked up, and her heart lurched madly as his gaze dropped from her eyes to her shoulders to her breasts. "*Nei.* I'm hungry, but not for food."

Her knees weakened as his mouth descended toward hers. The kiss ignited her blood. She felt a tingling within her body, making her cling to his neck for support. His warm hand moved under her shirt and seared a path toward her spine.

Dar sighed. "After talking with Snorri, I realize it is possible that I may never return home. You may be glued with me forever."

She licked her lips. "You mean stuck, not glued."

He gave her a quiet, sensual look that made her toes curl. "How do you feel about me being here, with you forever, Jennifer?"

"I-I'm not sure."

Dar reached out his hand and ran it down her cheek. He dropped his hand to his side. "Then 'tis best you go to your room now, sprite, until you are sure."

Even though he denied it, she feared he would leave her the first chance he got. She should go back to her room now, before she became physically involved, but somehow, she knew it was already too late. Her heart pulsed with a slow, steady throb, a need for satisfaction. "Do you want me to leave, Dar?"

His answer sounded as if it had been torn from his lips. "*Nei.* But 'tis what's best for you that matters.

I can't ask you to stay with me, sprite, unless you are sure."

Did he have to keep reminding her of that? "I can't ask you to stay either, Dar. But maybe, for just a little while, we can forget about your leaving and concentrate on right now."

He drew her into his embrace. "You are sure?"

It was now or never. "Yes, I'm sure."

"Good, because I desire to hold your body, naked, next to mine." His hands warm on her arm, his body rigid, he waited for her to make the first move, to prove her trust.

She leaned forward and kissed his bared chest. The shudder that passed through him made her smile and run her tongue along his taut muscles. He tasted delicious. Like a person hungering for warmth, she moved closer to his heated body.

"You've awakened something that has been dormant for a long time, sprite."

"Good." She put her arms around his neck and arched her body against his. He pulled her onto his lap. His smile was brighter than the sun and melted her bones.

The bulge against her thighs grew even bigger. She wanted to get closer to his warmth and reach for the flame of his passion, but she wanted him to want her, too. "So, Dar, are we going to sit here all night, or are you going to show me what you can do?"

"I have many abilities I have yet to show you. Do you want to learn my secrets?"

Jennifer reveled in his ragged breathing. She felt drugged by his closeness and made no effort to hide her trembling. "I want to know everything about you."

Her pulse beating out of control, Jennifer sighed as

he showed her with his kiss just how much he desired her. Unable to stop herself, she rotated her hips, grinding against him.

"Go slowly, sprite."

"I don't think I can."

Dar kissed her. Jennifer put her arms around his neck and allowed her mouth to tell him what she could not find the words to say.

A seeking hand searched for and found her breast. It cupped and molded and caressed, until she couldn't stand the sensations anymore. Restless with unfulfilled desire, Jennifer ran her hands down his strong back curving around to where she sat upon the tense muscles of his thighs.

"Do you think it's safe? Will we be interrupted?" she asked, worried that Loki might take this time to return. It would figure.

"I am not sure."

She could feel the hesitation, hear the apology, feel him mentally withdraw from her embrace.

"You're thinking about Loki, aren't you?" Jennifer could see indecision warring with desire in his eyes. She sighed as she removed her arms from around his neck.

"The Trickster could strike at any time," he told her gently, the mood breaking somewhat. "I couldn't bear to see you harmed."

Although he didn't continue, Jennifer could read his mind. Loki might use her as bait to get to Dar, and her chances of escape would be very slim indeed.

Jennifer believed Dar would do anything in his ability to keep her safe. "I trust you with my life, Dar. Do you think he'll ever return?" she asked as he eased a few inches closer.

"Loki will return, but he won't risk Odin tracking

him here. He'll spend as little time in this world as he can. Knowing the Trickster, he'll find a way to lead me to him. And when he does, the moon will weep tears of silver as she witnesses our battle."

This close, she could hear the beat of his heart. "You have a beautiful way with words," she whispered.

"You inspire me to poetic thoughts."

Jennifer kissed his beard-stubbled jaw. "Does Loki have the same powers as you?"

Dar raised his hand, as if to touch her face, but he never completed the caress. "*Nei.* Loki is no match for a trained sorcerer, but he can call upon others who feed on the blood of the innocent."

"Sounds like a jerk. I'm surprised nobody has flattened his face for him."

Dar chuckled. "Loki is my grandfather Odin's blood brother. Few can touch him without feeling the wrath of Asgard."

Dar's sensual mouth tightened. Jennifer ran her fingers along his full lower lip.

"But the Trickster is more dangerous than we realized. No one knows of the future except me. 'Tis up to me to warn Odin of his trickery before he can cause more harm to your people or mine."

His throbbing arousal pushed against her, making her blatantly aware of his need. She arched toward him, giving him freer access to her body.

Without saying another word, he picked her up in his arms and carried her toward the steps. Then he paused and walked back to the coffee table. He bent down with her and urged her to take the book. "You will read it to me, *já?*"

She pressed the heavy tome against her chest and nodded. "Of course."

He kissed her until a moan of ecstasy escaped her lips.

"Good. It will give us something to do when we need to regain our strength."

"What about Loki?" she asked as he lifted her up into his arms and carried her up the steps to his bed.

"I will protect you with my life," he replied, his voice hoarse with desire. Slowly, their bodies pressed intimately together, he lowered her to the mattress.

Chapter Ten

The sheets felt cold to the touch, but the sight of Jennifer lying beneath him, her gaze full of longing, warmed Dar all the way to his toes. He hurriedly stripped off his shirt and tossed it across the room.

Jennifer gasped for air as Dar put his arms around her and drew her against him. Her hair brushed against his naked chest. His body instantly responded with a throbbing insistence that made him grit his teeth. His dragon ring tingled on his finger, a reminder of the power stored inside. The scent of Jennifer filled his senses, and it was impossible for him to think of anything but the woman in his arms.

He couldn't hold back a low groan of anguish as she pressed her body closer against his. Caught in this trap of his own making, he hesitated one last time. "Are you sure this is what you wish, sprite?"

"More sure than of anything else in my life, my talented sorcerer."

She kissed his neck. Dar closed his eyes and rested his head against her shoulder. She had him so aroused, he could barely speak. "You're right, Jennifer. Now is an excellent time to show you my abilities. Let the first lesson begin."

Jennifer closed her eyes and buried her face in his throat. The stubble of his beard tickled her face, but she reveled in the feeling.

He removed her shirt. His hands lingered on the straps of her bra. "How do you remove this garment?"

Jennifer showed him the tiny catch in the front. "You unsnap this and the whole thing comes off."

"Amazing." He slid the lacy object off her body and stared at the flesh he revealed. "But what's underneath it is even more fascinating." He rubbed his finger across her raised nipples. She whimpered at the intense sensations that spread from her fingers to her toes.

Dar moved slowly. By the time his exploring hands reached her stomach, the woman was grinding her teeth with frantic need.

"Dar, if you don't hurry I'm going to scream."

The huge Norseman just chuckled and captured her hands, creeping down toward his pants. "You must learn patience, sprite. There are rewards to being held in my arms."

"Hurry. I'm having a hard time breathing."

Dar rubbed his lower body against her leg and continued with his exploration. When he urged her to remove her clothes, Jennifer didn't hesitate. Dar leaned back on his elbows and admired her body.

"You are beautiful, sprite." Dar didn't give her time to respond. A moan of ecstasy slipped through

Jennifer's lips, and he proceeded to worship her body with his tongue and mouth.

"Dar." She forced the words out through lips gone dry with desire, addressing the man who stoked her flame hotter than it had ever been. "I want you."

"I'm here, sprite."

Was the man dense? "No, Dar. I mean I need you, and I need you *now!*"

A sigh on his lips, Dar rolled off the bed. Her gaze on his face, Jennifer held her breath. Was his conscience forcing him to stop? Long agonizing seconds passed in which she could hear each beat of her pounding heart. Then, slowly, knowing she watched his every movement, Dar removed his pants. He folded them and put them neatly on the chair by the window. The moonlight cast a silver glow on his naked body.

"You don't wear any underwear?"

Dar eased himself onto the bed and took her in his arms. "*Nei.* They restrict my movements."

Jennifer ran her hands down his back, reveling in the hard muscles that flexed under her fingertips. "You have a lot of scars on your body, Dar. Have you been in many fights?"

"*Já* In Asgard, I participated in battles on a daily basis," he told her as she caressed him much more intimately. "We must always be prepared for the day of reckoning, when the jotuns attack." His body moved to partially cover hers. "Come with me, sprite, and I will take you to places you have never imagined."

"I'm almost there."

"You're not there yet, sprite. You've only begun your sensual journey."

He moved toward her, and she pushed against his chest. "No. Wait!"

"Sprite, if you've changed your mind, now is not a good time to tell me."

"I haven't changed my mind, just come to my senses."

Jennifer reached out her hand toward the table beside the bed, but she couldn't reach it. "Dar, can you open the drawer and pull out that little blue box?"

For the space of a moment, she didn't think he would answer. Then he sighed and did as she asked. "Is this what you want?"

She nodded and broke the seal on the box. "I think you should wear one. You wouldn't want me to get pregnant, would you?"

Dar looked from the small foil package in her hand to the open box. "This small item will prevent you from having a child?"

"Yes." She held her breath and waited.

"How does it work?"

Somehow she knew he was going to ask that question. And she had no idea how she would explain the process. "Well, you see . . ."

"Já?"

She tore open the packet and put the slick item in the palm of her hand. "You unroll the condom and put it . . ." Unable to continue, she thrust the box into his hand. "Here. Read the directions."

"You forget—my crystal does not translate your written language, only verbal speech. You'll have to read it to me."

Jennifer felt the heat rush up her face and reach the roots of her hair. "I'm only going to do this once, so listen carefully."

When she finished, Dar shook his head. "Are you sure this will work?"

"I think so."

Dar shrugged and tried to unroll the condom. The first one broke in his large hands. Jennifer groaned and pulled out another one. There were eleven left. She handed it to him and held her breath. It had taken all her courage to get this box.

After much cursing Dar finally succeeded. He rolled over and pulled her into his arms. "We have no such things in Asgard. For that I am glad." Then, giving her ample opportunity to move away, Dar raised his body over hers. "Put your arms around me, sprite, and together we will reach for the stars and catch a comet by its tail."

Jennifer's breath caught in her throat as he lifted her hips and moved his hard body on top of her. Then she didn't even think about breathing as he gently filled her with his desire.

Her impatience grew to explosive proportions. "Hurry, Dar."

" 'Tis not wise to rush. You must relax and enjoy my caresses."

Jennifer had grown tired of waiting. "Dar, if you don't—"

His lips captured hers in a soul-searching kiss that promised ecstasy beyond her wildest imagination. She raked her nails down his back, urging him to give her what she desired. He began a moderate pace that was mind-numbingly delicious.

The kiss ended and Jennifer breathed in much-needed air.

"Dar. Please?"

His expert touch urged her to even more desperate levels of yearning. Jennifer cried out for release. Dar slowed his rhythm. She wrapped her legs around his body, pulling him nearer, and heard his grunt of approval.

Dar had been right. It was wonderful to go slow. Shimmering lights burst behind her closed eyelids. The comet approached at a speed too fast for her to comprehend.

Just when it seemed as if she would pass out from the overwhelming sensations, Jennifer felt him begin to move faster. Light, brighter than she could endure, washed over her body and made her shudder with wonder. She tightened her hold on his broad shoulders as waves of ecstasy flooded her body. It seemed to go on and on. A few seconds later, she heard his groan of release.

Content, Jennifer almost purred when Dar drew her against his damp body and kissed her brow. The hazy veil of sleep had almost claimed her when she felt the covers being drawn up and a strong hand clasp her waist.

Dar had shown her the stars and handed her the moon on a golden sword.

Jason stared at the moon. He wouldn't wait a day longer. Tomorrow he would have that dragon or someone's head would roll down the drive of the institute. He paged his assistant and waited impatiently for Henry to return the call.

"Yeah, Jason. What is it?"

"Tyrson isn't going to reveal any secrets." Jason sat down in his brown leather chair. "As soon as they leave for work, I want you to send two men for the dragon. Make sure no one is watching. I'll keep them busy all day working with Dr. Monroe."

"But, boss—what if the creature decides to bite them?"

The disembodied whine made Jason grimace. "Get them nets, tranquilizer guns, and whatever else they'll need. But under no circumstances is that dragon to be seriously harmed. Do you understand me?"

"Yeah, boss. Don't kill it."

Did he have to do everything himself? Jason closed his eyes. "If that dragon is harmed, you're fired. Do you understand that equation, Henry?"

"Gee, Jason, I'd better go with them, just to make sure they don't hurt the dragon."

"I thought you might say that." Jason lowered his voice. "Henry, come closer to the phone."

"Yeah, boss?"

Jason slammed down the receiver and smiled wickedly as he strolled toward his office.

Unable to sleep, Dar pulled Jennifer closer. The sun would soon rise. As much as he would like to remain in bed with Jennifer all day, he sensed danger in the chill morning air.

Dar threw back the cover, and his gaze traveled down her body and lingered on her long legs, those same legs that had been so passionately wrapped around his waist. Memories of how she had responded to his caresses had him shifting on the bed. He re-covered them with the blanket. No other woman had made his blood sing and his body taut with such throbbing desire. It was almost as if a part of his soul had fallen into her possession. He knew of only one other instance similar to this. He remembered his father's words. . . .

Son, you will know the woman to whom you give your heart by your body's reaction. Your soul will soar whenever she enters the hall. When you are together, the rest of the world will cease to exist.

The sound of a truck backfiring woke Jennifer. "Did you hear that? Was it Loki?"

Dar pulled her soft body closer and she snuggled sleepily against him. "Don't worry, sprite. You're safe. I'll protect you with my life."

Even before the words left his mouth, Dar knew them to be true. He would throw himself in the path of a berserker if it would keep Jennifer safe. If someone took her captive, he would search until his last breath to find her.

Dar inhaled much-needed air into his barely functioning lungs. The veil had been torn from his soul. He now knew the identity of the protector of his heart, and she was a human. A woman from another time, another world. Dar tightened his grip around the girl resting upon him and tried to ignore the tears falling freely down his cheeks.

Within a few minutes, her even breathing filled the room. He listened to the comforting sound until the alarm clock shrieked.

"Come, sprite. It grows late and we must leave soon for work."

This time, when she woke, her response was much warmer, and, to his dismay, extremely arousing.

Jennifer stretched and put her arms around his neck. "Let's call in sick. It's freezing outside and the bed's much warmer."

Dar resisted the temptation she offered. He bent down and kissed her soft lips. "*Já.* 'Tis not what I wish to do. 'Tis what I must do. I promised Snorri."

She leaned forward until her lips were a fraction of an inch from his mouth. "Dar, what would you do if you couldn't find a way to return to Asgard?"

His arms still around her, Dar tensed. He couldn't admit the realization he'd come to. "I would have no choice but to stay on your world."

"Would you be very upset if that happened?"

"My first loyalty is to Asgard. The only thing that would take precedence over that would be if I took a soul mate. And I can't do that while there's still a chance of returning home."

"From what Snorri said, you could die if you return."

"I'm a warrior. Death is something I face on a daily basis. I'm not afraid of it. A warrior would welcome death if it was in the defense of his land and of those he loves."

She looked crushed, and a tear ran down her cheek toward her quivering mouth. "But I don't want to see you die," she finally managed.

Dar caught the small drop of warm liquid on his callused finger and held it in his closed fist, touched by her concern for him. He searched her face. Then, without saying another word, he sat up and lifted her onto his lap as if she weighed nothing.

"We will call and tell them we will be late," he whispered against her lips. "Kiss me again, sprite. I need to hear you groan my name one more time."

As soon as her lips touched his, Dar forgot all about his father, his brother, and his dreams of returning. Instead, he set about showing the woman in his arms exactly how much he loved her.

Crouched in the bushes behind the hall of Valhalla, Lor peered through the leaves toward the entrance to the massive building. Loki kept appearing and disappearing near the hall at odd times. Lor had yet to learn where the Trickster traveled.

He didn't know how it could have happened, but everything had gone wrong. First his father had summoned him to look at a sick dragon, and then Odin had requested that he settle a dispute between two warring gnomes.

Although the task hadn't taken long, he'd missed confronting Loki. Now he was forced to leave his surveillance yet again to attend a banquet in honor of Odin.

"Lor? Are you near?"

The sound came from his left. Lor had no choice but to answer. "*Já.* I am over here, father."

After much thrashing through the bush, Tyr walked to his side. "Still following the Trickster?"

"He is the only link to Dar."

Tyr sighed. "Come, my son. I am worried, too, but Odin wishes to depart. As Dragon Master, 'tis your duty to ride by my father's side."

"Is it really necessary that I go?"

Tyr nodded and rubbed the stump of his right hand. "*Já.* 'Tis necessary."

"I need to stay here and wait for Dar," Lor said, infuriated that the task would take him away from his vigil.

Tyr's lined face grew sad as he stared at the doorway of the Hall of the Slain. "As much as I want to see your brother once again at our side, I also know that if it happens, it will only occur because the old gods have willed it. "There is naught we can do."

"I can sense danger on the wind and evil on the tide."

"I sense it, too, my son." Tyr's eyes grew bright

with unshed tears. "The future is vague and shadowy."

Tyr drew himself to his full height and tried to shake off his foreboding. "Come. You will be pleasantly surprised by our host's hall. 'Tis surrounded by a fence of white sea foam and its roof is hidden by clouds of screaming sea birds."

When Lor sighed, Tyr added, "Aegir has nine red-headed daughters. They are wild and graceful maidens who adore the roaring squalls that strike their home unceasingly. Let me tell you about the time I fought with the crafty old jotun. This was before I had met your mother, of course . . ."

Lor knew his father was trying to help him forget the fact that he may never see his brother again. Of the several warriors over the years, none had ever returned.

With one last regretful glance toward Valhalla, Lor followed his father toward Odin's palace.

Chapter Eleven

Henry peered into the back window of the house. Silence. Nothing moved. Dar and Jennifer had left for work slightly late, but it was no problem. As long as one of the neighbors didn't get too nosy, the team would be in and out before anyone even knew they were in the neighborhood.

He glanced back at the two gang members. "Now remember, I don't want the creature harmed."

The huge guy with the skull-head tattoo curled his lip. "Hey, man. What's so important about this bird that you're willing to pay so much? Is it rare?"

A smile on his lips, Henry replied, "Yeah. Very rare. You might even say it's a one-of-a-kind."

"What say you we split once we got it, Killer?" the short one asked.

Never having used these particular ruffians before, Henry felt the blood leave his face. Jason would draw and quarter him if he didn't bring him the dragon.

"Nah," Killer shrugged. "We do what we're paid to do. Just don't screw this up, Zombua, or I'll kick your ass so hard you'll end up in China, got it?"

Henry's sigh of relief was lost in a gasp of dismay. Would they really end up fighting each other? He touched the soft skin of his neck. That large knife hanging at the larger thug's side took on a new significance. Even though the man's one hand was twisted at an unnatural angle, Henry knew he didn't stand a chance against the massive murderer. His heart beat so loudly, he was sure that it drowned out the sound of his knocking knees.

"Come on," Killer growled. "Let's get this kidnapping over with. I got me a real looker hanging out at the bar waiting for me."

Henry frowned. "Grab the b-bird but don't kill anyone."

"What do you think we are, stupid?" Killer growled.

"Of c-course not."

Using his good hand, Killer whipped out his knife and held the business end toward Henry's heart. Unable to scream for help because of the lump blocking his throat, Henry watched Killer walk toward him, a deadly expression on his face.

"Will ya move out of the way? What's the matter with you, ya wanna get cut or something?"

"Umm. No." Henry moved so fast, he didn't even feel his feet touch the ground.

The old wood around the window groaned in protest and split with the first thrust of the knife. Within seconds, icy cold air breezed in through the damaged window.

"Okay, Zombua. Get in there and open the back door."

Dressed in dirty jeans, old sneakers, and a green Eagles jacket, the youth hesitated. "I don't know, bro. What if the bird bites me?"

Killer's lip curled. "Then bite it back, stupid."

Shivering in his down-filled coat, Henry wondered how Killer could stand there and look so warm. The man looked so—he searched for a word to adequately describe him and found it—so lethal, almost as if his black sneakers, dungarees, and Grateful Dead T-shirt matched his black heart. The dart gun slung on his back just reinforced the perception.

"Come on, dudes. We ain't got all day." Zombua's voice shook Henry out of his musings. Allowing Killer to go first, Henry entered the back door and quietly shut it behind him.

As soon as Dar stepped out of the Jeep, he sensed a wrongness with the house.

"Jason seemed so nice to me today," Jennifer said as she shut the car door. "He talked highly of your knowledge about lizards and horses."

" 'Tis because I grew up with both dragons and steeds."

"He said your information was invaluable. He's looking forward to you writing a paper on the subject."

Dar paused by the side of the car, his every sense directed toward the house.

"I talked to Snorri again today." Jennifer grabbed her handbag and locked the car. "He's flaky but brilliant. Do you think he will ever discover the secret to time-travel?"

"I don't know."

The odd tone of his voice must have alerted her to

his mood, because she said, "You look angry. What's the matter?"

"The protective spell on your hall has been broken."

She came to stand at his side. "What does that mean?"

"It means someone has entered the hall without our permission," he explained as his gaze scanned the front of the house for signs of forced entry.

"Oh, my God! My money. And your gold!"

Before he reacted, he needed to know exactly who or what he faced. Had Loki returned with an army of jotuns to finish him off? Or had Mrs. Nordstrom dropped by for another visit and left something behind the door?

He turned toward Jennifer. "Wait here. I'll go see what is wrong."

Her mouth set in a straight line, Jennifer shook her head. "No way! I'm coming with you."

Did all humans not listen to orders? " 'Tis for your own good."

"I'd die of curiosity out here."

She could die of something more dangerous inside. Dar weighed his choices. He could order her to stay here and wonder if she obeyed him, or he could take her with him and protect her with his life. "You'll do everything I say, *já?*"

"Of course."

Why didn't he believe her? Dar sighed and walked up the steps to the porch. With one powerful kick, he snapped the lock on the door.

"My door!" Jennifer shrieked. "Haven't you ever heard of the advantage of surprise?"

Intent upon locating the source of the intrusion, Dar continued walking toward the dining room. He circled toward the steps and put one foot on the stair. He closed his eyes and listened. Silence greeted him, a thick lack of sound that screamed of danger.

"I don't see anything. If Loki was here we'd know about it by now, wouldn't we?" Jennifer asked. "I think your imagination has run amok."

The hint of a breeze pulled Dar toward the kitchen. He stood in the doorway and scrutinized the broken window. The screen door banged against the door frame, like the touch of death on a warrior's shoulder.

"Maybe we left a window open and a squirrel got in—" Jennifer peered around Dar's body. "Oh, my God! Is someone still in the house?"

"*Nei.* It feels empty. Someone was here but left." He ran his fingers over the twisted frame of the window, then stuck his head outside.

"What are you doing?"

"I am searching for footprints," he told her, staring at the ground, his mind assessing the almost invisible clues left by the unknown entrants. He counted only three intruders. According to the tracks in the yard, they had already left.

"What did you find?"

He turned and faced her. "They're gone."

"Who were they?"

"I don't know." He touched the split wood, then shut his eyes as impressions swirled in his mind. A knife. A large knife. That was of no help to him.

"My money. I've got to see if they've ransacked the house."

Dar watched Jennifer run out of the kitchen and up the steps. Even though he was sure that no one remained in the hall, he had to ensure that they had left nothing that could harm Jennifer. "*Stodva!* Wait for me."

But Jennifer either didn't hear him or didn't listen.

Dar sprinted toward the bedroom. His scowl deepened as he saw the signs of a fight. With each step he took, the rising tide of anger in his heart grew higher. The scorched walls could be repaired he knew. But if anyone had harmed Firedrake, they would pay with their lives.

"My money hasn't been touched," Jennifer told him as she clutched her money pouch to her chest. "What about the gold?"

Dar knew without looking that they hadn't been after the gold. "I haven't checked yet."

The stress lines around Jennifer's mouth didn't disappear. "I don't see anything missing. What do you think they wanted? Do you think we scared them away? I'm surprised Firedrake didn't attack them. He must have been out all day foraging for food."

By the sacred well of Mimir! If only they were so lucky.

"Oh, my god!" Her face paled as she glanced at the beige rug. "That looks like blood."

"It is."

"But—"

"They have what they wanted." He saw her hands start to tremble and told her the truth. "They have Firedrake."

She gasped and dropped the bag. "No! Not my baby. Anything but Firedrake."

He caught her as she crumpled to the floor. Dar held her tightly as she sobbed against his chest, the money pouch forgotten on the floor.

"Well, what are we going to do to find him?" she asked, her voice rising with each word.

Dar took a deep breath before he answered. "I'll cast a spell to discover the identity of the intruders."

With Jennifer watching his every move, Dar set

about preparing for the trance. "You understand that I must have complete silence, *já?*"

"I won't say a word."

"You won't interrupt me?"

She shook her head. "I'll be as quiet as a corpse."

An unpleasant picture, one he preferred to forget. "I'll need a piece of the burnt paper on the wall and whatever Firedrake last ate."

Jennifer got him the things while he put his mantle on the floor. Finally, everything was ready. Dar cut off a piece of Jennifer's old boot and put it in the golden dish resting on his mantle then lit a candle. He held up his hands toward the ceiling.

"O powerful gods of the universe, hear my plea, show the identity of the intruders to me. . . ."

Dar didn't flinch as a flash of lighting rocked the hall. Time as he knew it ceased. He closed his eyes and let his mind wander, down the stairs, toward the rear door. He stood there, a ghostly observer as three humans entered Jennifer's house. Finally, the white candle before him sputtered and died. The smoke wafted toward his nose, vying with the burnt walls for his attention.

He knew their identity.

"If they harm one scale on that hatchling's tail, they will suffer the fury of an angry warrior," he vowed. "I, Dar, son of Tyr, sorcerer of Asgard, do swear it."

Dar sensed Jennifer's curiosity and silently applauded her self control. Slowly, as if waking from sleep, he returned to normal consciousness. He opened his eyes and stared at her pinched face.

"Do you know who did this?" she asked.

"Já."

She leaned forward and ran her fingers down her semi-gnawed boot. "Well?"

"Henry."

Only one word, but it held a wealth of meaning.

"Oh, my God! Those scientists have got my poor baby!"

Dar began to gather up his possessions and waited for her to fully understand the meaning of the kidnapping.

"Somehow, they must have realized he's a dragon," she stated. "They're going to experiment on him."

"*Já.*"

Her glare would have sent a fire demon scurrying for cover.

"Well, they're not going to get away with it." She jumped to her feet. "I won't let them."

He admired her courage even as he tried to think of some way to keep her safe. "Save your anger for later, when you will need it."

"When are we leaving?" Her fists clenched by her side.

"*We* are not going anywhere. *You* are staying here to ensure that they do not return for the gold."

"No way."

"Don't argue. On this I will be firm. You will stay here, where 'tis safe."

"Not a chance."

He clenched his jaw, knowing she didn't understand the danger. "There could be a battle to get Firedrake back."

"Then you'll need me to be your backup.

"You will do as I say, *já?*"

"On one condition."

Dar groaned. Her smile, a combination of grim determination and willful stubbornness, boded ill for his digestion.

"What is your condition?"

"That you don't get mad when I disobey your politely worded order."

If she stayed home, she would be safe. But she was determined to go with him, a fact that worried him more and more with each passing second.

He took Jennifer in his arms and held her next to his heart. "Fine. It is time, sprite. We will go now to get our *drakna.*"

Jennifer would never forget the tension of the long drive to the institute, or the way Dar kept clutching the crystals on the inside of his mantle. They parked the car a few blocks away and walked along the narrow dark roads to the institute.

Only a few overhead lights illuminated the parking lot. Jason was a miser, and it was evidenced by all sorts of company policies. In the distance, near the front of the building, Jennifer could see several cars parked near the door of the institute.

Her back to the road, Jennifer watched Dar slice through the chain-link fence with his black crystal dagger. "Why don't we just go in through the front gate?"

"And have the guard warn Jason of our arrival? *Nei.* 'Tis better this way."

The bare limbs of the trees reflected the pale light of the moon, giving them the appearance of bony arms reaching toward them with every gust of wind. Jennifer buried herself deeper in her coat and blew on her numb fingers.

"You're cold. Come here and I'll warm you." Dar draped his mantle over his arm and pulled her into his embrace. Warmth flowed through her body, so that Jennifer could have sworn it was the middle of the summer and she was lying on a beach in Wildwood, New Jersey.

But his warmth wasn't enough. She needed more. Much more. Before he could protest, Jennifer raised her head and searched for his mouth. Her lips swallowed his groan as she tightened her grip around his waist. Her breasts strained against her shirt as he brought her more closely against his body.

Waves of heat washed over her with the force of a tidal wave. Jennifer rode the waves and ran her fingers through his hair.

Dar broke the kiss before she went under for the third time. She shivered with delight. Norse gods, she thought dreamily, should have a label on them that said: *Warning! Too hot to handle.*

Dar's voice interrupted her thoughts.

"We'll continue this later, once we have rescued Firedrake, *já?*"

Jennifer placed her hand against his shirt so she could hear the steady beat of his heart. "I'm holding you to that promise," she said as she reluctantly stepped away from the warmth of his arms. "See, there are advantages to having a Norseman as a soul mate."

"I still have many abilities I have not yet shown you. But now is neither the time nor the place."

She looked into his intense blue gaze. Then, before she could blink, he whirled the mantle—crystals facing outward—around his shoulders and disappeared. She could hear him moving through. The eeriness of being alone yet knowing someone stood right in front of her made Jennifer tremble.

"Do you have to do that when we're in the middle of a conversation?"

A gentle but invisible hand caressed her lips. "I'm still here, sprite. I wouldn't leave you without first telling you good-bye." He pulled her against his side and put part of his mantle over her shoulders.

Jennifer buried her face in his shirt and breathed in his masculinity. He gave her strength even as he kept her safe.

"You are ready?"

"As ready as I'll ever be." Jennifer looked down and couldn't see her body. She felt dizzy as her mind struggled to grasp the impossible.

His hand on her shoulder calmed her and brought her back to the present. "Stay close, Sprite. Don't make any noise, not even a whisper, all right?"

This close to his invisible body, Jennifer didn't think she could even speak. She nodded; then realizing he wouldn't be able to see her response, she put her arm around his waist and said, "I'll be as quiet as a mouse being stalked by a cat."

He shook with laughter. "Good. Now follow me and don't mention cats around Firedrake. I doubt he's eaten tonight."

Please let her little hatchling be all right, Jennifer prayed as they jogged toward the institute building. She didn't think she could bear it if anything had happened to him.

"If we get him out of here safe, he can have as many spareribs as he wants," she promised.

Dar grunted and continued walking toward the rear of the building. They entered through the maintenance door.

Inside, they took off the cape.

Knowing the layout of the institute helped with

their search. Jennifer trailed behind Dar as they peered into each room in the genetics section. His cape billowing out behind him, purple side out, Dar held his knife to his chest as he silently crept down the maze of halls.

Another door. Another empty room. Dar put on his mantle again, becoming invisible. Jennifer was just about to ask him if they should try another floor when he hissed for her to remain silent.

One minute they were alone, and the next thing she knew someone had turned the corner of the corridor right in front of where Dar had stood.

"Hey!" The short, pudgy man clasped a clipboard tighter to his chest. "Whatcha doing here, lady? This area's restricted."

Jennifer didn't even see the punch that sent the man sprawling against the wall. Dar dragged the unconscious body toward her.

"You are okay, *já?*"

Jennifer admired the fact that her hands didn't tremble as she opened a closet door and took out the gray bucket and mop. How could Dar be so calm?

"I'm fine," she replied.

"Good. This way."

The sound of voices echoed in the hallway as they edged their way toward the front of the building.

"But, Jason . . ."

"Not now, Henry. I'm too busy. This is the most important night of my life."

"Okay. But I gotta tell you about the creature's fire. It almost burned me to a crisp. If they hadn't gotten it with that tranquilizer gun, I'd have been a goner."

"Why didn't you tell me this earlier? He is receiving only a mild dose of sedative. I'll have to have it increased immediately!''

''But, Jason, you just told me that it might kill him if you give him too much. . . .''

The voices faded as a door slammed shut.

Jennifer's stomach lurched. She put her hand on Dar's chest to keep the terror at bay. ''Oh, my God! They're going to kill him.''

''Calm down, sprite. We'll save him.''

Or die trying. The thought popped into her mind. Jennifer gasped as she noticed the way her fingers were wrapped around his translation crystal.

''I hate when that happens,'' she muttered.

''What?''

''When I can read people's thoughts,'' she explained.

Dar raised his eyebrows. ''I'm sure it would come in handy at times. I wish I had the ability you experience with such ease.''

Of course! Why hadn't she thought of that before? ''Dar, give me your crystal.''

''Why? It has no magical powers. It would be of no use against an enemy, especially one who carried a weapon.''

''I'd like to wear it, please.''

He didn't even hesitate. He removed it and put it around her neck. ''All right, just don't rely on it to work on everyone, *já?''*

''No problem.'' Even through her clothes, she felt the warmth of the stone.

''When we find Firedrake, you'll stay out of the way, *já?''*

''Sure. Now let's go. Give me a kiss for luck.''

''I will kiss you, but I will kiss you for myself.''

The touch of his lips was tender and too brief. She

resisted the urge to throw herself in his arms and never let go.

"I will lead, you follow."

"Anywhere you go," she whispered.

"What?"

"Er—nothing."

Dar looked like he wanted to pursue the matter, but time was against them. He unsheathed his dagger and motioned for her to be silent as they crept toward the door at the end of the hall.

Jennifer put her ear against the cool wood. "Can you hear anything?"

"Nei."

"Neither can I."

Dar didn't let a little thing like a door deter him. "Stand back." He lifted his leg and kicked. "Valhalla!"

The wood splintered as it slammed against the wall. It sounded like a gunshot. The men inside the room spun toward them. Jennifer recognized Jason, Henry, and five of the six men. Two were scientists, and the third was a skinny black kid who looked familiar. The fourth was the Teck gang leader, Snake.

"Aw, geez. Well, if it ain't the dude who broke my nose. I owe you one, man."

Jason Wells recovered his voice next. "Ah, Tyrson. What a pleasant surprise. I'm so glad you could join us."

"But, Jason . . ."

The director shot his assistant a menacing glare. "Not now, Henry." *Later, you nitwit.* Jennifer frowned as Jason's thoughts leapt into her mind.

Dar advanced toward Jason; the two other scientists flattened themselves against the far wall.

"Where is Firedrake?" Dar growled.

"Oh, you mean the dragon?" Jason looked around the room, as if unsure where they had put him. "I believe he's here on the table, right next to the row of scalpels."

Had they already killed him? Jennifer yearned to go to Firedrake, but Dar's orders to stay where she was safe kept her from moving away from the door.

"But, Jason—"

"Not now, Henry. Can't you see I'm busy?" Jason smiled. The action froze Jennifer's blood until she felt as if she were standing on an iceberg.

Everyone was taking this too easily. No one tried to stop Dar as he bent down to hear Firedrake's heart-beat. Jennifer's mouth opened to warn him. She shut it again. What could she say?

"He is alive."

Jennifer's knees buckled with relief. She leaned against the wall. A tear ran down her cheek, but she was too happy to brush it away.

"Leaving so soon?" Jason put his hands in the pockets of his white smock. He bounced on his heels. "I hoped you would stay a while longer and tell us how you came by such a rare specimen."

"Firedrake is not a specimen. He is my friend and faithful companion."

"I see," Jason replied. "Tell me more." *Tell me all your secrets.*

The scientists edged away from the wall and whipped out their pens. Jason glanced toward Jenni-fer. She put her hand on Dar's crystal, more out of a sense of security than actual need.

"There is nothing else to say," Dar stated. "You will rue the day you kidnapped him. I swear this on my crystal ball."

Just keep him talking. . . .

Although the thought could have come from anyone in the room, Jennifer knew it came from the institute director.

"Oh, my God! He's stalling. Dar, let's get out of here, now!"

"Not so fast, dudes." A hand wrapped around Jennifer's waist and dragged her back against a huge, smelly body. She felt something being shoved against her temple. "What's the rush? The party's only just begun."

Dar experienced a thousand deaths when he saw Killer shove his weapon against Jennifer's head.

"Way to go, Killer!" Snake shouted. "Right on time, big guy."

Dar ignored the gang leader as he gently lowered Firedrake's unconscious body to the table. He raised his dagger. The light caught the ebony blade and made it glow with a sinister shine.

"One false move and the chick gets it." Killer smiled, an evil smile that revealed spaces where his teeth used to be. "Lose the weapon, dude. Now. Or I blow a hole in her face so big that you'll be able to see her tonsils."

Dar put the blade on the table, next to Firedrake's folded wing. It didn't matter if he himself lived or died; he could not allow Jennifer to be harmed.

"I'm unarmed."

Jason glanced at Snake. "Take one of the scientists and get those samples to the lab immediately."

The tall fellow uttered a low curse. "Aw, geez. It was just getting interesting in here. Okay four-eyes." He pushed a short scientist wearing glasses toward the door. "We ain't got all day here. Let's get going."

Jason waited until Snake left, then picked up the telephone and punched some numbers on the keypad. "Get one of the security guards down here. Now." He turned back toward Dar and smiled. "You've lead us a merry chase, Tyrson. More than once I've been tempted to compliment you on your cunning. At first I thought you were a scientist, but now I know differently. Exactly why did you accept the job?"

"For information," Dar said truthfully.

Jennifer struggled against the man holding her. "Don't answer him. Just keep quiet and let him do the talking."

Dar watched Killer's expression. It had changed from gleeful satisfaction to irritation. Concern for Jennifer's life became his first priority. "Don't struggle, *já?* I will do anything to keep you safe."

That was obviously the wrong thing to say if Jason's wide grin meant anything. "He loves her. So touching, don't you agree, Henry?"

"Yeah, boss. Real touching."

A gaunt, gray-haired guard limped into the room. Jason motioned toward Dar. "Handcuff his hands behind his back. We've got plans for him."

Dar gestured toward his mantle. "You will let me take this off, *já?"*

"Go ahead." The impatience in Jason's voice would have made Dar smile at any other time. He folded the mantle, amethyst side in, and put it on the table next to the unmoving dragon.

The guard obviously didn't know anything about being gentle. Although Dar could have killed the man at any time, he allowed himself to be put in manacles that restricted his movement. To do otherwise might have meant Jennifer's death.

Killer caressed the butt of his weapon and aimed

it at Dar's heart. "Don't think the score is even, dude. I still owe ya for the last time."

It was obvious from the way his hand, which was around Jennifer's waist, was twisted that the bones hadn't set properly. Dar's mouth tightened. "You promised to give up hurting innocent victims."

"Yeah, well, I lied."

Rage, so intense it could barely be controlled, flowed through Dar's body. "You have sealed your fate. You shall suffer in the pit of flames for your lies."

"My, such intensity." Jason shook his head. "And such grand emotions. It must be your upbringing. Where did you say you were from again?"

Jennifer paled. "Don't tell him, Dar!"

"Asgard."

The scientists scribbled furiously.

"Asgard." The director of the institute tapped his finger against his lip. "I believe you mentioned that when we met. Exactly where is it?"

"Asgard is located on the beautiful plane of Ida, between Muspelheim and Jotunheim."

"Interesting. I've never heard of any of those places."

Killer laughed, a harsh sound that grated on Dar's nerves. "Ain't that just grand. The great scientist don't know something. Open your eyes and see why he's so different. He ain't human. He's an alien."

"I am not an alien," Dar said. "I am a sorcerer."

Henry laughed and slapped his knee. "Did ya hear that, Jason? He thinks he's a magician. Next he'll say you're the devil."

"Shut up, Henry." Jason walked around Dar. "It is possible. . . ."

"It ain't just possible, it's the truth." Killer

grunted. "I messed with this dude before and believe you me, he's stronger than ten sumo wrestlers."

The director of the institute touched a vein on Dar's arm. "If this is true, the possibilities are endless." He nodded toward one of the scientists. "Get me a syringe."

"Do something, Dar!" Jennifer shouted. The tears running down her cheeks cut him deeper than any blade he'd seen.

Jason uncapped a long needle. "If he does anything threatening, Killer, pull the trigger."

Dar felt the needle slide into his arm. He ignored the piercing ache and continued to stare at Jennifer.

"You wouldn't want her to be killed, would you?" Jason extracted a large quantity of blood. "Remember, if anything happens to Jennifer, it would be all your fault."

"Don't listen to him, Dar. Use your powers and get us out of here."

He couldn't take the chance, not with Killer holding a gun to her head. Dar remained impassive as Jason inserted another needle into his arm.

"Please, Dar!" Jennifer strove to free herself.

An irritated expression on his face, Jason nodded to Killer's associate. "Get her out of here, Zombua. Lock her in the storeroom. Henry, give him your keys."

His assistant grimaced. "Don't make me give this kid my keys. I'll never get them back. Can't I go with him?"

"Okay, but hurry back. I need you here."

Henry reached into his pocket and extracted a silver ring with a large number of keys on them. He tossed them in the air. "Ya ready? We gotta hurry."

"No problemo, bro."

When Killer turned toward the door, Jason stopped what he was doing and shook his head. "I want you to stay here to look after him."

"Here, Zombua." Killer thrust Jennifer into his cohort's arms. "Don't hurt her unless she asks for it. Got it?"

"I ain't deaf, man."

Jennifer glanced back at Dar. The fear in her eyes hurt worse than a razor-sharp sword. "Dar! Don't let them do this!"

He made himself meet her gaze. "I'm sorry, sprite. It is best this way."

Although Jennifer knew the reason for his refusal, it still hurt to hear him say no. The tears on Dar's cheeks told her it hurt him to say the words, too. A rough hand on her arm warned her not to dally. Jennifer was half-dragged down the hallway.

"This way," Henry said, glancing back toward them. "The storeroom is too far. We'll put her in one of the unused labs. They don't have windows."

"That's cool by me," Zombua replied. "All I want is my money, and then I am outta here."

Jennifer had to do something fast. If they locked her in a room, it would be next to impossible to escape. The sharp blade at her back warned her of the danger of making a move for freedom. If only Dar was here, he'd take care of these two. But Dar hadn't even lifted a hand in his own defense.

Because of her.

What she needed was a plan. What she needed was a miracle. All she had was her cunning.

"Ya got any money, babe?"

He'd stolen her dragon and now he wanted to steal her money, too? "No. I left my handbag at home."

"Too bad."

The disappointment in the kid's voice made her want to smile. "What about jewelry? I'll take whatever ya got."

No way! Thank goodness she had taken off the chain with her mother's ring. Now all she wore was the dragon ring Dar had given her . . . the ring! Hadn't he said that it had special powers? That he had cast a spell on it?

"Oh, my God! I can't remember the words."

His red hair looking like he had been running his hands through it, Henry turned around. "You talking to me?"

She tried to clear her mind and remember Dar's voice. She trembled from the strain of getting the words right. There would only be one chance; if she messed up, she was history.

Jennifer let herself trip on a loose piece of tile and collapse onto the cool linoleum. "Ooh. I think I sprained my ankle."

"You fool! What did you do to her?" Henry screamed.

"I didn't do nothin', man. She just fell."

"Jason is gonna be upset that you didn't watch her better. He might just decide not to pay you."

The black youth stuck out his chin. "Hey, wait a minute, man. It wasn't my fault."

It was now or never. Jennifer took a deep breath and held the ring near her face. She stared at the dragon's red eyes and whispered, "Oh spirit of the dragon, hear my plea, spirit, spirit, come to me."

Both men looked at her like she was nuts.

"What did she say?"

Jennifer felt the power flow through her body. It began at her toes, coursed through her abdomen, and poured out of her fingers. Although it didn't hurt, she shivered with revulsion as the force, a living entity, used her body as a vessel upon which to develop.

The air seemed to solidify and swirl faster than the eye could see. It slowly took form. Jennifer gasped as a larger, meaner, angrier version of Firedrake appeared before her. Its two red eyes glowed like the fires of hell. Without any warning, the massive head reared back from its scaly body and it roared. The sound shook the building and hurt her eardrums.

"Oh, crap! She's got her own personal demon." A wet stain appeared on the front of Zombua's pants. "I'm outta here." His complexion gray, the kidnapper ran down the hallway, screaming at the top of his lungs.

Jennifer felt the energy swirl through the air, a living presence that seemed to become more solid with each second. She saw the dragon's gaze focus on Henry, remembered Firedrake's love for fresh meat, and gasped.

"Don't even think about touching him." She called out. She *wouldn't* be a murderer. Her command must have had some effect, because the dragon roared, but it continued to just hover in the air.

Henry was trembling so hard, Jennifer thought he was having a fit. His scream joined that of Zombua, then stopped abruptly as he slid to the floor, passed out.

The dragon seemed to guffaw, a deep echo that rumbled in the narrow corridor. The air around it began to swirl with white mist as the huge wings flapped. Jennifer watched as it began to fade, a little at a time.

Soon, it disappeared, and she wondered if she had imagined the entire thing. Only the puddle near her foot and Henry's comatose body told her it had really happened.

Jennifer didn't waste any time. She picked up Zombua's discarded knife and ran as fast as she could down the hallway. She hid in a broom closet, the knife held close by her chest, and waited until her teeth stopped chattering.

"In another few hours employees will start arriving," she encouraged herself softly. She pushed her bangs out of her eyes with a trembling hand. "I've got to calm down and think of a way to get back into the lab and save both Dar and Firedrake."

Since she couldn't risk being discovered, Jennifer stared into the darkness and allowed it to soothe her frayed nerves.

She couldn't lose either of them now. She loved them too much. She reached out her hand and touched the items on the shelves in front of her. A mop and a uniform. Not much, but it was a start.

Jennifer closed her eyes and fought back sobs. Crying was a luxury she couldn't afford right now.

Chapter Twelve

Lor gestured for a passing thrall to refill his tankard. Although he desired information about the whereabouts of his brother, Loki had yet to return from Odin's errand. Displeased, Lor raised the mead to his lips and drank deeply of the tangy brew.

"So this is where Asgard's dragon master spends his time, brooding in the back of the Hall of the Slain," Dalia drawled.

Lor looked up at the golden shield hanging over the entrance of Valhalla, then back down at his mead. " 'Tis where I wish to be."

His sister laughed and slid onto the bench across from him. " 'Tis where you've spent almost all your time since Dar vanished."

Did she have to remind him of Dar's disappearance? "Have you no chores to complete that you must badger me?"

Taking a moment to smoothe the folds of her

golden frock, Dalia smiled and tossed back her long blond hair. "*Já.* I have several things that need my attention. I don't know why I wasted my time trying to find you."

"And why would you wish to find me?"

The golden slipper on her foot became of great interest to her. " 'Tis possible that I have some news you would like to hear."

Lor knew from past experience that getting information from his fickle youngest sister was like trying to wash a full-grown dragon; one became frustrated and needed to use treats as enticement before the task was completed.

"What is it you wish? A new necklace?"

Dalia took a moment to contemplate the offer. "*Nei.* I have several necklaces to match my gowns."

His fingers tightened on the handle of his tankard. "More fabric for gowns?"

"*Nei.* That doesn't interest me in the least."

Several thralls shuffled toward the tables, empty bowls in their hands.

What did she wish? "A purse full of crystals?"

Dark blue eyes, surrounded by long golden lashes, narrowed assessingly. "I wish a hatchling. A golden one."

"A what?" Lor jumped to his feet. The bench behind him tipped over. "What would you do with a newly born dragon?"

"I wish to become a dragon master."

If he wasn't so drunk, Lor could have explained the complexities and difficulties of becoming a dragon master. As it was, he merely threw back his head and laughed.

" 'Tis not a jest." She raised her chin. "I'm serious. One day I will be head sorceress of Asgard. Then all will treat me with respect rather than patronize me."

Lor's mouth twitched, but he controlled the laughter bubbling in his throat at the thought of his sister ever being head sorceress of Asgard. "How did you know about the birth of the rare golden hatchling? Did Father tell you?"

Dalia shook her head. "*Nei.* I saw it for myself."

He was so shocked, he knocked over his tankard. "Surely you jest."

"*Nei.* I visit the dragon caves regularly and know of the two batches of hatchlings that father visits. I have seen the golden one and have held her in my hands."

"Does Father know about this?" he asked, his voice harsher than he had intended.

"*Nei.*"

A thrall darted over and wiped up the dripping mess. The man's big, hairy arms scrubbed with more fervor than accuracy.

"The news you have would have to be exceptional for me to even contemplate such a thing," Lor told her, sure she would never acquire the dragon.

Dalia met his gaze without flinching. "Odin spoke with Father earlier this morning. It seems that Loki has returned to Asgard."

"What!" It was now sunset. "It took you this long to tell me?"

She shrugged. "As you pointed out, I had to do my chores."

Lor resisted the impulse to strangle her. He ran toward the massive oak door. "Tell Father that I go to find Loki. And tell Odin that I'm going to miss tonight's feast. He'll need someone else to say the blessing before the meal."

"Lor, wait! Loki is no longer here."

"Where is he?"

A smug expression on her face, Dalia said, "He was seen traveling toward Jarnvid."

"The land of the witches?"

"Ja."

Lor clenched his teeth to hold back an oath. He touched the jeweled hilt of his sword and ran toward the gates of Asgard as fast as his feet would take him.

"Lor! What about the hatchling?"

He didn't even slow down. "He is yours on the morrow."

Her loud scream, followed by a gleeful laugh, did justice to a fierce wolf. " 'Tis not a he. 'Tis a she. And Firestar is all mine."

His sister was now the proud owner of a rare golden fire-breathing dragon. Somehow, Lor knew that Asgard would never be the same again.

If there was one thing Jennifer knew for certain, it was that no one at the institute ever looked at the maintenance crew. The janitors and cleaning ladies didn't exist; at least, not to the scientists or secretaries.

Jennifer pushed a dirty yellow bucket down the hallway. She gripped the wooden handle of the mop so hard that her palms hurt. Vile-smelling brown water sloshed over her sneakers, but she ignored it.

A few rooms down the corridor, she stepped in front of a closed door, checked to make sure no one noticed her, then opened the door and went inside.

"Snorri?" No one answered. Jennifer frowned. "Now where is he? He should have been here an hour ago."

Realizing she didn't have much time before they

found her, Jennifer tried to think of where the scientist could have gone.

"Now where did I put my pen?"

The voice seemingly came out of nowhere. Jennifer walked around a big black table. "Hello?"

"Aaah. I found it."

She stared at the floor. There, underneath a table, was Snorri. At least she thought it was Snorri. She found it hard to be sure, when all she saw was a pair of legs.

"Snorri? Is that you?"

The sound of a head banging against a table made her wince and hurry forward to help him.

"Oh, my; oh, my." The scientist rubbed his head and sat on the floor. "That hurt."

"I'm so sorry. Here. Let me help you."

"Thank you, dear."

Snorri squinted toward the door. "Where's Dar? I wanted to show him the new formula I created. I'm close to cracking the time-travel riddle."

The simple question opened up a flood of feelings. Anger. Determination. And most powerful of them all, love for the Norseman who had turned her life upside down from the moment he'd landed in this world.

"Dar's a prisoner," she said stiffly.

"What!" Gone was the usual vague expression. In its place was a look of shock.

"Jason is running tests on both Dar and Firedrake. By now he probably knows that neither of them are from this planet."

"Oh, my; oh, my." Snorri patted her on the hand. "Don't worry, Jennifer. I'll think of something. We'll get them out if it's the last thing we do."

"Snorri . . ."

"I've got it!" He padded over to the board and picked up a bright orange marker. "We'll buy guns and storm the place. No, no. That won't work. I don't know how to use a gun."

"Snorri." She grabbed his arm and tried again to get his attention. "I've already got a plan. Listen carefully. Here's what we're going to do. . . ."

The sharp peal of the fire alarm rent the silence of the building. Scientists, secretaries, and assistants from every area scrambled toward the fire escapes. Everyone, that is, except the people in the same room as Dar:

"Nobody is to move," Jason ordered. "Continue with what you're doing."

Facedown on an examination table with his hands cuffed behind his back, Dar wasn't in any position to see the men's reactions.

"Of all the times for the alarm to go off," Jason said. "Henry, go and see if it's a false alarm."

"But Jason, what if I see that big—"

"Not in front of the sorcerer, Henry. Oh, all right. I'll go with you. If it's a real fire, I'll need to find out exactly where it is, so I can advise the fire department."

"Oh, thank you, Jason. You don't know how glad I am that you're coming with me. I've got something important to tell you! Jennifer—"

"Shut up, Henry."

Dar closed his eyes and tried to sense whether he felt an increase in the temperature of the room. Even with his powers, he wouldn't stand a chance if he didn't free his hands.

"Snake, go to the front entrance and make sure nothing weird is going on. Killer, stay with our guest.

I'll be right back. The rest of you, stay where you are and continue working. Under no circumstances are you to stop what you are doing. I'm sure this is a false alarm and can be resolved in a few minutes."

Killer grunted and turned the page of a piece of literature called a comic book, another thing to add to Dar's long list of erroneously named items. Since Killer was sitting with his feet up on the table, Dar could see the man squint as he tried to decipher the colored pictures in the thin book.

The scientists mumbled among themselves, but no one questioned Jason's orders.

The director tapped Dar's shoulder. "Remember: One wrong move and Jennifer suffers a painful death."

"But Jason, don't you remember, Jennifer—"

"Not now, Henry."

The two men argued even as they slammed the door behind them.

Dar fought back waves of fury. If they'd harmed Jennifer in any way, they would die for their actions. He would hunt them until his last breath.

A loud grunt followed by snorting told Dar that Firedrake was slowly regaining consciousness. The scientists gasped and babbled among themselves. The fire alarm echoed its shrill warning. Every once in a while, one of the men would peer out the door.

Time seemed to stand still. Were they holding Jennifer close to the fire? Was she being treated kindly? Dar had faced death so many times, he had lost count. Death to him meant simply another plane of existence. But Jennifer was different; he was sure that she feared death.

Dar closed his eyes and rested his head on the cool table. He tried to clear his mind and concentrate on

Jennifer. His powers must have been deceiving him, for she felt close, so very close.

"By the sacred horn of Heimdall, I wish I could ensure that my sprite is not near the fire."

"You say something, dude?" Killer poked him in the side and laughed. "What's the matter? Dragon got your tongue? You ain't thinking about escaping are ya, because I'd hate to have to scar up that pretty face of yours if ya tried to get up from that there table."

If I try to escape, Jennifer will be killed. "*Nei.* I won't move."

"Good." Killer sat back down on his chair and picked up his comic book again.

The door flew open, but Dar kept his eyes closed. He needed to rest to save his strength. He hadn't slept in almost two days. The pain in his bound arms, held in such an awkward position, increased with each passing moment. But it was the pain in his heart that made him ache. If he found a chance to knock out Killer before the gang member could sound an alarm, he would take it.

"Oh, my; oh, my. I'm sorry I'm late."

Dar tensed. That voice! He would know it anywhere.

"Whatcha doin' here?" Killer asked in a deadly voice.

"I work here. Would you like to see my identification?"

It seemed to take an eon before Killer spoke. Dar clenched his eyes so tight, he could see a million stars on his eyelids.

"Nah. Just get to work and don't disturb the specimens."

"Of course, of course."

"Just a minute." Killer stood up.

"Y-y-es?"

Dar held his breath.

"You know anything about that there fire?"

The scientist cleared his throat. "I might be mistaken, but I believe someone may have left a pot of soup on a burner that set off the fire alarm."

Killer grunted and sat back down.

Dar breathed deeply of the sweet-smelling air. He turned his head and glanced at Snorri. Dar almost didn't recognize him. It looked like someone had groomed him. His white hair was combed back from his brow, and there wasn't a food stain to be seen on his new white smock. Only the slightly addled expression in Snorri's eyes told him it was the same person.

Glancing furtively over his shoulder, Dar watched as Snorri crept toward the stretcher containing Firedrake. Dar frowned. What was he up to? As soon as he saw Snorri's hand touch his mantle, he knew what he had to do.

"I have a need to use the outhouse again, immediately," Dar said loudly, remembering his humiliation at having the other man take down his pants and assist him with the toilet.

"You'll have to wait until the boss returns."

"*Nei.* I can't. 'Tis an emergency."

Snorri put the mantle behind his back. He inched toward the door.

Dar tried to sit up. "Take me there, now."

Killer threw the comic book down on the floor and whipped out his knife. "Listen, dude, you ain't going nowhere until the boss gives me the okay. You know there has to be two of us here to take you to the bathroom."

Snorri opened the door. Killer glared at him. ''Where do you think you're going?''

''I have a w-w-weak bladder, myself. I'll be right back.''

Killer stared at the open door. ''Wimp.'' He ran the blade down Dar's cheek. The cold metal grated across his unshaven jaw. Dar stared into Killer's eyes. They were soulless eyes, the eyes of a man who would not hesitate to dispatch a victim who could not defend himself.

''When I get my hands on you, I will show you no mercy,'' Dar told him as he dared the man to stick the blade in his throat.

''Big talk for a man with his hands handcuffed behind his back.''

Dar moved closer to the blade until he felt it prick his skin. Warm blood ran down his neck and dripped on the table.

''You had best hope no one removes them, *já?''*

The confident expression on Killer's face wavered. ''Just you lie back down and wait for Jason. I ain't putting up with your nonsense. If you give me any more trouble, I'll hit you over the head with my chair.''

Dar laid his head on the table and closed his eyes. He heard Killer walk over to the scientists and ask about breakfast. His own stomach growled from lack of nourishment. ''I am so hungry, I'd even devour Jennifer's peanut butter.''

''Gee, you must really be hungry.''

Jennifer! His eyes sprang open and he scanned the room. His sprite wasn't there. Had he really heard the whisper? Or was he losing his mind?

''Oh, my God! You've been tugging on the handcuffs. Look at your poor wrists. They're soaked with blood.'' Gentle fingers touched his skin. They trembled as they passed over the hard, cold metal.

'' 'Tis not my imagination. You're really here?''

The sound of material being dragged on the floor near his side told him her location. ''Did you have to struggle with these things? They're not very easy to break.''

''Sprite.'' She was wearing his robe. She had to be.

''It's me, big guy. Now, where did they put the keys to this darn thing?''

Happiness flooded Dar's body as he heard her voice. It hadn't been his imagination. She really was standing next to him, and she sounded irritated, a sure sign that her spirit hadn't been broken. He chuckled as he realized that she had come to rescue him and Firedrake.

''You don't need keys. I will take care of these metal restrainers.'' With a low grunt, Dar focused his energy and pulled. His bonds snapped. The sound echoed in the room, drawing the attention of his captor.

''Whatcha doing?''

Dar sat up and rubbed feeling back into his numb arms. The metal bracelets shifted up and down as he moved, reminding him of their hated existence.

''I told ya to lie down,'' Killer snarled, obviously unaware that Dar's hands weren't band behind his back. ''Now I'm gonna have to hurt you.''

Dar watched the angry gang member advance toward him. Although Killer could not see Jennifer, he could still run into her.

''Stand back, sprite.''

''Who are ya talking to? When I get you, I'm gonna bash in your brains.''

''Dar, be careful!'' Jennifer shouted.

Anxious to keep Killer's attention on him and not on the invisible woman behind him, Dar smiled. "To hit me would be to seal your fate, human."

"Oh, yeah? Take this!" Killer raised his fist and aimed it at Dar's face. The Norseman blocked the punch. He didn't know who was more surprised, Killer or the scientists.

"How did you get free?" Killer gasped. "You know what's gonna happen to your girlfriend, don't ya? She's dogmeat."

"So that's why you didn't escape earlier!" Jennifer said from behind him. "And I think you're exaggerating, Killer. No one is gonna make dogmeat out of me!"

"Huh? What? Who said that?"

Dar had grown tired of sitting. Now he would act. And his first action would be to take care of Killer. "Prepare to die."

Killer obviously didn't know when he was beaten. He pulled out his knife and waved it in front of Dar's face. "Come and get me, alien, unless you're going to use your powers to kill me."

"It is against my vows to use my sorcerer's abilities in battle against one lacking in such powers. I will kill you with my bare hands."

A smile on his face, Dar easily managed to avoid Killer's knife while he landed several powerful blows up on the man's stomach and face. The bloody man grinned at him.

"I'm gonna kill ya now, alien. 'Cause I'm a Teck and I eat nails for breakfast."

Dar looked at the yellow teeth on the floor and shook his head. "I think you will now have to change your diet, *já?"*

The enraged bellow that followed his statement

sent blood and spittle flying through the air. "I ain't gonna show no mercy now, dude."

"That's good. Neither am I."

Since he couldn't be sure of Jennifer's location, Dar tried to keep the fight near the open door and away from the scientists, quaking on the other side of the room.

"Oh, my; oh, my. I see you've done it, Jennifer."

Snorri!

"Yup. I told you my plan would work."

Both Jennifer and Snorri were right behind him, probably within touching distance. They were close. Too close for comfort. "Get back," Dar shouted.

"What? What did you say, Dar?" Snorri asked.

Too late. Dar watched Killer lunge for a rack of bubbling liquid and hurl it through the air. The sorcerer only had a moment to react. Concentrating on the objects, he mentally thrust them in another direction. They crashed against the wall. The sound of glass breaking vied with the roar of Firedrake.

"Look out, Dar!" Jennifer shouted, her voice full of fear for his life.

Killer took advantage of the distraction to hurl himself at Dar. The weight sent Dar sprawling into a wooden table full of clicking machines.

"Now you're history," Killer said as he brought his knife down toward Dar's chest. "And your chick is next."

Dar blocked the strike and looked into Killer's eyes, amused. The blade inched closer to Dar's body. He waited until he felt blood wet his shirt before he said, "You don't fight fair. For that you will pay the consequences."

"Oh, my; oh, my. He's going to kill him."

The scientists ran out the door as if their tails were

on fire. The peal of the fire alarm's siren drowned out their nervous whispers. Dar tightened his grip on Killer's good arm. The snap of a bone and a blood-curdling scream echoed through the room. Dar gathered all his strength and shoved. Killer flew through the air and landed on one of the tables. Glass and metal shattered and flew in every direction.

"Now you will feel the wrath of an Asgard sorcerer."

Killer's eyes widened and he held his twisted hand in front of his face.

Dar picked up the tattooed human by his shirt and smiled. His hand connected with Killer's chin. The bone shattered. Killer's eyes rolled back in his head and he crumpled to the ground.

"Is he dead?" Snorri asked.

"*Nei.* But he'll be unconscious for a while," Dar replied as he rubbed his blood-soaked wrists.

A very warm bundle hurled herself into his arms. "Oh, my God! Are you all right? Is anything broken?" Small hands touched his chest, running down its surface, causing him to shiver with pleasure.

"I'm fine now that you're here," he told her as he caught her hand and kissed it. Dar now knew why Jennifer had been dismayed when he was invisible. One was at a disadvantage when one could not see the other person's expression.

"By Odin's eye!" Dar closed his eyes and wrapped his hands around the invisible feminine body wearing his mantle. With the unerring instinct of a man who hungered for his woman, he lowered his head and kissed her passionately on her mouth.

Snorri cleared his throat. "Oh, dear; oh, dear. This is embarrassing."

Dar couldn't get enough of her sweetness. He

crushed her to his chest and caressed her body. Jennifer groaned and rotated her hips against him.

"And you must be Firedrake. Allow me to introduce myself. My name is Snorri Sturluson. I'm a friend of Dar's."

His name on her lips, Jennifer's mantle slid to the floor. Dar looked into her heavy-lidded eyes and wished they had some privacy.

"We must go," he said sadly.

"Must we?" She rested her head against his shoulder.

Dar fought down the urge to bury himself inside her and never let her go. "Jason could return at any moment."

"Too late. Jason has returned . . . and with a gun," the director of the institute said from his position by the door. "And he is very angry at the moment."

Chapter Thirteen

"Oh, my God!" Jennifer inched closer to Dar.

Firedrake jumped to his feet. The dragon's claws dug into the stainless-steel table. His narrowed eyes on Jason, he roared and spread his wings.

"One move from the dragon and the girl is dead."

This was the first time Dar had ever seen Jason less than perfectly groomed. He had a dirt smudge on his face and his usually pristine lab coat bore signs of being singed in several places. Even his black shoes were dirty.

Dar put Jennifer behind him and stared into the barrel of Jason's gun. Henry Sneed also strutted into the room and crossed his arms. "Ya gonna let him have it, Jason? Aim for his alien heart, if he has one."

"It isn't wise to make a sorcerer angry," Dar growled.

"You're not still trying to make us think you're a

sorcerer, are you?'' Jason asked, a disbelieving smile on his face.

''But, Jason, what if he's telling ya the truth?''

''Shut up, Henry.''

''But, Jason . . .''

''Shut up, Henry,'' Jennifer stated, peering out from behind Dar. ''I'd run, Jason, if I were you. Dar never lies.''

''You'll excuse me if I don't believe you, won't you, Miss Giordano?''

''Listen to him, Jason. He's serious.''

The director looked ready to strangle Snorri. ''I won't forget that the fire started in *your* lab, buddy. When I'm done with you, you won't be able to get a job cleaning out mouse cages.''

The scientist's lower lip trembled. He looked down at his worn black shoes.

''Don't listen to him, Snorri,'' Jennifer said. ''I'll tell everyone the truth. You'll be working in no time.''

Jason looked at his gun, then at Dar. ''If you leave now, Tyrson, I won't say a word about this incident.''

Jennifer touched the crystal around her neck. ''He's lying, Dar. He's going to kill us all as soon as you turn your back.''

''He can try, but he won't succeed,'' Dar told her, confident that he could easily stop the director.

Jason snarled, a feral growl that made the hair on Dar's neck stand up. Jason aimed at Dar's stomach and pulled the trigger.

Dar held up his hand and narrowed his eyes. *''Stodva!''* The sound of a tiny object hitting the floor made the other occupants of the room gasp.

Resisting the urge to lift the director up and throw

him against the wall, Dar leaned forward and bent the end of his pistol. His handcuffs jangled, reminding him of their presence and his recent captivity at this man's hands.

"Get out while you can," he shouted to everyone in the room. "I'm going to destroy this building and everything in it. I cannot allow you to use the samples you collected to make more *drakna* that would be used for evil purposes. I will do it. I swear it by the sacred crystal cave."

Jason still stared at his gun, a puzzled expression on his face. Dar knew shock when he saw it. He pitied the man. It was hard to admit defeat, and the director had obviously never experienced such an emotion before.

"Why aren't you dead? I shot you. You should be lying on the floor." Jason's hands trembled even as he raised his chin and glared at Dar. "You tricked me, but you won't get away with it. You don't dare touch the institute."

"You are wrong. I do dare, so leave now and make sure everyone is out of the building."

A long curl of flame, originating from the table behind them, singed the air and licked at Henry's behind. Jason's assistant screamed and ran down the hall as if a dozen fire demons were after him. Dar smiled. The smell of burnt clothing grew stronger than the odor of spilled chemicals.

"It had to have been some type of trick. No one can stop a bullet," Jason told him. "No Norseman or his dragon will ever beat me. I've got more degrees behind my name than you can read."

"I can't read your English," Dar stated. "But I will do as I say."

Jason turned so red that Dar was sure he would

grow sick from fury. "I'm going to call the police and have you arrested as a raving lunatic. If you touch anything in here, I'll have you behind bars so fast, you won't have time to blink." The director glanced around the room one last time—taking in the flaming table—before he spun around and left, too.

"Great bluff," Jennifer stated, her voice muffled as she rested her head against his back.

"It was not a bluff. I'm serious."

Snorri patted his perspiring brow. "Oh, my; oh, my. I think Dar's really telling us the truth."

"I suggest you hurry." Dar gestured for them to go ahead of him. "This building will be rubble in a few short minutes."

"Wait! What about Killer?" Jennifer knelt down and felt for the gang member's pulse. "He's still alive."

As much as Dar would have liked to see the man pay for his crimes, he didn't have a choice. "I'll carry him. Jennifer, you will ensure that Firedrake keeps up with us, *já?*"

"Okay. You go first."

Dar threw his mantle over Jennifer's arm, then lifted the Tech gang member onto his shoulder. "Valhalla!"

On the last syllable, Dar sprinted toward the exit. He did not need to turn around. He could hear Snorri's labored breathing and Jennifer's encouraging murmurs to the groggy dragon.

Icy winds pelted Dar as he exited the Wells Institute. Thunder rumbled in the distance, a warning of a violent storm approaching. He dropped Killer to the grass and draped his mantle over Jennifer's shoulders, purple side out.

"Is everyone out of the building?" she asked, her long bangs obscuring her eyes.

Snorri nodded his head. "We've had fire drills in the past. Everyone knows when they hear the bell, they go to the parking lot on the other side of the building."

Dar reached into the pocket of his mantle and took out his crystal ball. He stared into its depths and muttered a quick incantation. "Powers of light, powers of the sun, tell me now if any humans are in yon building."

The ball did not glow. No humans remained in the institute. It was time. "Stand back."

"You never told me about that," Snorri said, his eyes glazed with wonder as he stared at the crystal ball.

"I'll show it to you another time, but first I must destroy any evidence of both Firedrake's and my existence. I can't risk anyone finding our blood samples."

Dar raised his arms toward the sky. A flash of lightning arched from the crystal and rose toward the boiling clouds. "Powers of the universe, light from the sun, shine on this crystal and join as one."

The sizzling and crackling focused into a solid beam of energy. Dar waited until the power was at full force before he aimed it at the building. The energy bolt shook the ground. Dar watched the flickering of the fire grow larger and larger.

"Oh, my; oh, my." Snorri wrung his hands, as if to rid himself of invisible blood. "I forgot all about the animals."

"What animals?" Jennifer asked.

"Lab specimens.

Dar stared at the flames shooting out of the roof of

the building. "There are animals trapped inside?"

"Yes, yes, I believe so."

"Where?"

"On the basement level, near the elevators."

"Oh, my God!" Jennifer grabbed Dar's arm. "You aren't thinking of going inside, are you?"

Dar looked at her ashen face and closed his eyes. "I can't let them die without trying to save them."

Large tears ran down her cheeks. "Please don't go. I have a bad feeling about this fire."

How could he soothe her? "I promise I will return alive. You know I always keep my promises, *já?*" He gave her his crystal ball, something very sacred to him, as a sign of trust. "You will keep this safe until I return?"

Jennifer hugged the ball to her chest. She shivered from the cold. He could tell that she wanted to beg him again to stay, but she remained silent. He leaned forward and kissed her one last time. Then he looked at Snorri. "Keep her away from the building."

"Of course, of course."

Without another word, Dar picked up his mantle and put it on so that the crystals touched his skin. He ran toward the institute and shouted his battle cry. "Valhalla!"

Jennifer couldn't breathe. The air in her lungs turned to ice and refused to circulate. By now the flames seemed to engulf the entire building. The cold air did nothing to dampen the intense heat. Tears continued to run down her cheeks, forming a liquid path of anguish and pain. Seconds turned into minutes. Minutes felt like hours. She crumpled to the ground, unable to watch the flames.

"He promised he'd come back. He promised me." Finally, when she had all but given up hope, she saw a dog run across the grass toward them. She felt like cheering as more animals escaped.

"Oh dear, oh dear. Each of the animals is locked in a separate cage. He'll never unlock them all in time." Snorri bit his fingernails. "He should have gotten out by now. I hope he's not trapped inside."

"No!" Jennifer put an icy-cold hand to her mouth to stop the screams building in her throat. How could she bear to live if he died? She felt so cold without him to keep her warm in his arms.

The loud blare of a siren heralded the arrival of a fire engine. She and Snorri rushed to the parking lot to see what was happening. Firemen jumped off the truck and began unrolling hoses.

"Okay, everybody, stand back. This isn't a picnic. We need room to work." The stocky captain made a path through the crowd . His words were transformed into crystal gusts of breath in the icy air. "Come on, here. Let me see what we're up against."

When he whistled with amazement, Jennifer shut her eyes.

"Looks like we got us a red-hot-five-alarmer on our hands," he stated. "Rich, go call in the backups. Looks like we're going to need some help. Tell them to bring the foam trucks."

His assistant nodded and ran off toward the massive red truck ruining the perfectly groomed institute lawn.

"Oh, my; oh, my." Snorri saw Firedrake headed toward the building and tackled him to the ground. He tried to hold the struggling dragon. "You can't go in there. It's too dangerous." Snorri grunted as Firedrake broke loose.

Jennifer jumped to her feet. She grabbed Firedrake's tail and struggled with the determined dragon.

Firedrake's roar shook the ground. The crystal ball fell to the ground, but Jennifer didn't notice; she was too busy trying to keep Firedrake alive.

Finally, she remembered the Norse word that Dar had used back in the institute. Maybe, just maybe, it would work here, too. "Firedrake, *stodva!*"

The dragon snarled, but he finally stopped struggling and settled for pacing back and forth. His razor-sharp talons clicked against the hard earth.

The fire chief stared warily at Firedrake. "At least everyone got out before it collapsed."

Dar! "There's still someone in there." Sobs made Jennifer's words almost indecipherable.

"What! Why didn't you tell us sooner?" the fire chief roared, glaring down at her. "From the looks of it, I don't think it's safe enough to send anyone in after him." *The poor guy is doomed*, the crystal seemed to sear the man's thoughts into Jennifer's mind.

"No! Dar gave me his word," she cried, moving to stand in front of the fire chief.

Snorri hated confrontations. Hoping they wouldn't notice him, he went after the crystal ball. He picked it up, studied it carefully, then put it in his pocket. Jennifer was too upset at the moment, too worried about Dar. Snorri didn't want to disturb her. He reminded himself to give it to Dar when the sorcerer returned.

Jennifer scowled at the fire chief. "Dar never lies. I expect him to keep his word this time, too. He isn't dead!" she screamed. "He promised he'd return, and he will."

The chief looked at her as if he doubted her sanity. "Listen, lady, I know this is hard to accept, but I doubt anyone could survive that heat."

She shook her head. "He's alive. I'd bet my life on it."

"I don't think—"

"Jennifer, look!" Snorri jumped up and down as he pointed toward the building.

Jennifer scanned the building, hoping, wishing, praying. She grasped Dar's translation crystal. Snorri spoke the truth! Desperate to see for herself, she battled her way toward the front of the crowd and shouldered past the fire fighters.

A lone figure, silhouetted against tongues of flames, walked away from the burning building.

"Wait! Where do you think you're going?" the fire chief shouted.

Jennifer ignored his bellow. She ignored the danger and ran straight toward the man who she loved with all her heart. She laughed when he lifted her up in his arms and spun her over his head.

"You're happy to see me, *já?*"

She waited until he put her down and wrapped his arms around her waist before she pulled back her arm and punched him in the stomach.

Dar grunted. "I had to save them all."

"Don't ever do that to me again! Do you know how many years you took off my life? I can't take that kind of stress."

Unclasping his smoking mantle, Dar let it fall to the ground then swept Jennifer up in his powerful arms and kissed her until she couldn't think. Stars exploded behind her closed eyelids and she kissed him back with all the pent-up anger and fear within her. Warmth flooded her body and ran from her numb fingers to her deadened toes.

"Er, excuse me, but I've got to ask you to move. We want to get more hoses on the fire."

Jennifer whimpered as Dar raised his head and glared at the short fire captain. "By the tail of a dragon!"

"Hey, you, cape man. You look familiar. Didn't I see you watching another fire not too long ago?"

Did he think Dar was an arsonist? "That was my house you're referring to, and he saved it from burning down."

"Yeah? Well, we're going to have an investigation as to how this fire started and so far you two are my prime suspects.

That was the last thing they wanted, Jennifer realized. If the man did an investigation, he might find out about Dar's past. She had to stop him any way she could.

"There he is, officer! Arrest that man." Jason Wells ran toward them. He pointed his finger toward Dar. Two policemen followed, their expressions grim, their bodies tense.

"Why can't people stand back," the fire captain growled as he glared at the two policemen.

"Sorry, buddy." The taller officer shrugged. "Officers Gaines and Willis, here at the director's request."

Jennifer tightened her grip around Dar's arm.

"He's the one who started the fire," Jason continued, gesturing wildly. "He's a sorcerer from another world. He muttered a curse and the institute caught on fire."

The fire captain stared at the two police officers, who just shrugged and looked as if they wished they were anywhere but here. Behind them, the flames billowed smoke as they licked toward the cloud-covered sky.

"I've told you the facts. Now I order you to arrest

him!'' Jason urged them. ''He's an alien. Possibly a Martian, though he says he's from Asgard, the Palace of the Gods.''

The fire chief cleared his throat and looked apologetically at Dar. ''Er, buddy, you're free to go whenever you want.

One of the policemen—the shorter one with a black mustache—took out a set of handcuffs. Jennifer tensed, worried that they would believe Jason anyway. She breathed a sigh of relief as the officer pulled Jason's hands behind his back.

''What are you doing? You're arresting the wrong person. Just look at his wrists. I had a pair of handcuffs on him earlier and he broke them with his bare hands.''

''Come on, buddy. Let's go. We'll take you somewhere nice and safe where you can tell it to the judge. You have the right to remain silent. . . .''

Jason struggled to free himself before the policeman could snap the cuffs shut. He threw himself on the ground. ''You're making a mistake! Shoot him! Where's my gun? I'd do it myself, but I know the bullet will just bounce off him. I've shot him once already and he's still standing there with no bullet holes in him.''

Officer Gaines nodded to Dar. ''Is that the truth?''

Holding up his hands to show the remains of the handcuffs, Dar nodded. ''*Já.* 'Tis the truth.''

''Add attempted murder to the list, Willis.''

''Got it.''

''But he's responsible for the fire!'' Jason shouted as the officer read him his rights. ''If you don't believe me, just ask any of my employees. They'll tell you the truth.''

The fireman stopped a rotund man in a clean white

lab coat. "Excuse me, sir. Are you a scientist from the institute?"

Jennifer tensed and turned to see who had joined them.

"Oh, my; oh, my. Are you talking to me?"

"Yes, I am. Can you tell me how the fire started?"

Snorri bit his lip and shifted Firedrake on his hip. "I heard someone left some soup on the gas stove and it set off some lab chemicals. Simple negligence."

The fire chief nodded. "Thank you. That will be all."

But Jason refused to give up. "Of course it started with the soup. It was after the lab caught fire that he used his crystal to burn it down."

"Sure," the fire captain drawled, "and my name is Elvis."

"Hello, Elvis." Dar said.

The fire caption gave him a dirty look. "The name's Cleary."

Dar frowned. "But I thought you said—"

"I'll explain it to you later," Jennifer told him.

"Hey, that bird sure gained some weight," the fireman said with a laugh. "I suggest you put him on a diet before he has a hard time fitting in the house."

"*Nei.* That's not possible. Firedrake is a—"

Jennifer stepped on his boot and silenced the talkative Norseman. "Thanks for the suggestion, captain, but Firedrake is from Asgard and Norse birds grow to be very large. A lot bigger than birds in the United States."

The officers dragged Jason's struggling form toward their van. The director didn't make it easy. He kept digging his heels into the icy ground and straining with all his might.

"You have the right to an attorney . . ." Gaines droned on in a monotone.

"Henry! Where are you?"

His assistant ran out of the crowd. "Yeah, Jason. You called?"

"You imbecile. Where have you been? Can't you see there has been a huge misunderstanding? Tell these gentlemen who I am."

"Sure, boss. He's the person in charge here."

Officer Gaines hesitated. Jennifer pulled out of Dar's arms and ran over to the policemen.

She watched Willis take out a pad and pen. "Can you tell us everything that happened?"

A smug smile on his face, Henry nodded. "Sure. It all started when Jason asked me to kidnap this guy's dragon. Who would have guessed that the little bugger would be able to shoot fire out of his nose?"

Jennifer looked over the officer's shoulder and read his notes.

"Go on."

"Well, after we dragged the dragon back to the lab, the sorcerer somehow found us, and Jason had one of the gang members who usually does his stealing and dirty work handcuff Tyrson and . . ."

"Shut up, Henry," Jason roared, his face so red, Jennifer thought he might have a heart attack.

"But, Jason, you asked me to explain—"

"Don't say another word." The director raised his chin and looked at the officer. "I would like to speak to my lawyer now."

"You'll get your phone call when we get back to the station."

"See that man staggering to his feet?" Jennifer said, pointing to Killer. "He's one of the men who kidnapped Dar's drag—er, bird."

Willis reached for his gun. "You take Wells to the car. I'll go get the big guy."

Killer tried to run away when he realized he was being arrested. He glared at Jennifer and tried to struggle out of the officer's grasp. "We'll find you, no matter where you go or what you do. Just you wait; Snake will take care of you."

Snake! She had forgotten all about the Tech gang leader. Where was he when all this was happening? Jennifer looked around the crowd but didn't see the man.

"You mark my words, Snake will get you," Killer bellowed.

"If he tries, Dar will stop him," she yelled, breathing a sigh of relief when the officer dragged him toward the police van. Satisfied that justice would prevail, at least in this instance, Jennifer returned to Dar's side.

"But how did you manage to avoid being burnt?" Snorri asked.

"My mantle."

"Oh, my; oh, my." Snorri put Firedrake down on the ground and fingered the purple material. "Can you tell me about its chemical composition?"

"*Nei.* 'Tis a Norse secret passed down to each warrior." Dar reached out and pulled Jennifer against his side. " 'Tis used during battle to protect us from the flames of the fire demons."

"My, my. Would you tell me a little more about your battles with the demons?"

Dar looked at Jennifer, a passionate light in his eyes. Heat flooded her body and scorched her soul. She wet her lips and wished they were anywhere but in a crowd of people standing in front of a burning building.

"I'll tell you about the battles another time," Dar said as he walked toward the institute gates. "Right now I want to get Jennifer home, where 'tis warm."

Snorri cleared his throat and jogged along beside them. "Of course, of course. You have my home number. Call me anytime."

Glancing behind her to make sure Firedrake followed them, Jennifer gasped as Dar swept her up into his arms. "What are you doing?" He smelled of smoke and sweat, but none of that mattered. She wanted to stay in his embrace forever. She wrapped her arms around his neck and shivered.

Loki used his most persuasive tone to get the witch to agree to his plan. ". . . magical devices beyond your imagination. More than you will ever use in a lifetime."

The wart on her nose twitching, Angerboda quivered with excitement. "You tell the truth, eh?"

"*Já.* Would I tell you a lie?"

She thought about it before she answered, "*Nei.* You know better than to lie to a powerful witch of Jarnvid, eh, Loki?"

The black leaves of the bent trees shivered in the perpetual twilight. Loki found his eyes drawn to the rat's tail visible in the cauldron atop the fire. "*Nei.* I would not lie to you, Angerboda. Have I not taken you as my second wife?"

Her black, ankle-length robe billowing in the breeze, the witch threw back her head and cackled. This drew his gaze to her toothless mouth and black gums.

She wouldn't try to back out of their vow to destroy Asgard, would she? Loki couldn't take that chance. "You are more beautiful than an Asgard maiden. I am captivated by your wisdom and charm.''

Smoothing her white hair with a gnarled hand, Angerboda preened under his practiced charm. ''Fear not, Loki. I will do as you ask and go with you to Midgard. But first let us retire to my humble abode and enjoy a warm cup of mead. I will continue brewing my spells anon.''

The small hut reeked of the remains of creatures long since deceased, but Loki didn't so much as wrinkle his nose as he stepped over the threshold. He glanced toward the musty straw pallet in the corner and forced himself to smile. She would demand that he attend to her before they left for Midgard. And he would do it, because he wanted so very much to destroy the arrogant sorcerer who had dared to humiliate him in front of all the inhabitants of Asgard.

Angerboda caressed her skull necklace and sat down near the crackling fire. ''Tell me again about this world. You are not exaggerating about the witless humans, eh?''

''*Nei.* I would never lie to you,'' he said, lying even as he spoke. ''You will like the place. There are lots of trees and shady groves where you can cast your spells.''

''You know me so well, Loki.''

He would tell her anything so long as she did as he asked. ''You will like Midgard. 'Tis a thief's haven. And you, my darling witch, are a magnificent thief.''

An evil light in her midnight eyes, Angerboda nodded. '' 'Tis true, Loki. 'Tis true. And when we have gathered all the devices we can carry, what will you expect in return, eh?''

''Then, my dear Angerboda, we will slay Dar and

his pesky dragon, Firedrake. Once that is done, we will return to destroy Asgard."

"I've seen enough fires to last me a lifetime," Jennifer said as she poured two cups of hot cocoa.

"*Já.* I agree."

The soot on Dar's chiseled face and powerful arms enhanced rather than detracted from his attractiveness. Jennifer's gaze lowered to the muscles outlined by his tight jeans. How she love him in modern clothes—they emphasized his size and drew attention to his lean hips and flat stomach.

Jennifer's face grew hot as she imagined him naked and aroused by her touch. She handed him his cup and busied herself straightening the already spotless kitchen. The last thing he needed right now was to have her thinking about sex, when he had such dark circles under his eyes. The lines on his unshaven face were twice as deep as usual.

"Looks like you need a shower." She sat down on the chair next to him.

Dar reached out his hand and caressed her cheek. "You will join me, *já?*"

"I would love to, but you look tired."

He chuckled and stood up. He drew her into his powerful embrace. "I need you with me. Your presence helps to keep the demons away."

How could she resist such a nicely worded request? Especially when his hands were caressing her? "I don't want you to overexert yourself. After the shower you go right to sleep. Okay?"

"If you insist."

Dar swept her up in his arms and jogged toward the steps.

"Hey, I thought I told you not to overexert yourself."

"You're as light as a newly born dragon. I'll be fine."

She knew he flattered her about her weight, but it felt good to hear him liken her to a hatchling. As they passed through the living room she noticed his sword sticking out of a cushion on the couch.

"I just finished sewing up all the holes in that couch."

"Resting my sword there is a habit I find hard to break."

She shrugged, not really caring if he made holes in every chair she owned. As long as he stayed by her side, she was happy.

Curled up on the recliner, Firedrake grunted and made as if to stop gnawing her umbrella.

"*Stodva!* Don't move from this room," Dar ordered.

"Do you think he'll get sick from eating metal?" she asked.

Dar shook his head, a movement that caressed the top of her head. "*Nei.* He'll be fine. Just last week he ate the silver writing utensils from your desk and he suffered no ill effects."

"So that's where my pen and pencil set went!"

"I will, of course, replace it."

Somehow, she didn't really care about her possessions in the same way she had before her boarder had arrived. "Don't bother. I have another set."

Dar paused on the landing outside her room. "You're sure?"

Why did his voice have that strange tone? "Of course I'm sure. Why do you ask?"

He paused, shook his head, then smiled. "No reason.'' He nudged open the door and walked over to the bed. ''You know that Firedrake also nibbled on the corner of your sofa. It has a large hole in it near the pillow.'' He put her down on the bed and stepped back to look at her.

''I saw it. It matches the hole on the other side.''

When Dar just shook his head again, Jennifer held out her arms and urged him to join her. The sorcerer chuckled, lay down beside her, and pulled her into his embrace.

It felt so good to be in his arms, again. Jennifer couldn't think of any other place she'd rather be. She winced as she noticed the the broken handcuffs and the dried blood on his powerful arms.

''Aren't you going to take them off?''

His mouth tightened as he looked at them. ''If they bother you, I'll remove them now.''

A sharp twist of the metal and the handcuffs slid to the floor. Dar stared at the objects, then dismissed them and turned into her embrace. He peeled off her clothes, one piece at a time, and kissed her exposed flesh. By the time he finished, Jennifer trembled with a need so deep, only one thing could quench it.

''Now it's my turn,'' she told him. She started with the buttons of his shirt. Her hands shook so badly, it took her three tries before she could get them unbuttoned.

When he was naked and ready, Dar opened the drawer of her nightstand and reached inside. He frowned. '' 'Tis empty. There are no more protection packages.''

Jennifer gritted her teeth. What a time to run out of condoms! He pulled back, his eyes sad. ''We should stop, *já?''*

For a while now she'd wanted to tell Dar exactly

how much she loved him. Maybe, just maybe, she could show him how she felt instead.

“No. I don't want to stop,” she told him, putting her arms back around his neck. “I don't want you to stop, ever. I would love to have your children, O mighty sorcerer.”

Were those tears in his eyes? Jennifer couldn't be sure. He slid alongside her and kissed her mouth lingeringly. With each kiss, her passion grew, until she writhed beneath him, and she silently urged him on with her hands.

As she strained against him, he grew more demanding. She reached down and, emboldened by his husky murmurs, took him in her hand. Dar gasped as she continued her caresses. Jennifer closed her eyes and let herself explore to her heart's content. He felt as soft as velvet and as hard as marble, a combination that made her breathing shallow.

“If you don't stop, I won't be responsible for what will happen, sprite.”

“I don't want to stop,” she replied, planting tiny little kisses on his sweat-covered chest. She bit his shoulder, then kissed the bruise. “I want you. All of you.”

Dar chuckled. “As you wish, my little dragon.”

One moment Jennifer was yearning for his possession, the next she found herself swept up in a whirlwind of pleasure as he filled her with his love. Each thrust seemed to reveal new meanings of the word *ecstasy*.

Just when she thought she would surely die, Dar's pace grew faster and deeper. Jennifer gasped in his embrace as wave after wave of pleasure erupted through her body.

Her ears echoing from her own cries of passion,

Jennifer held him tightly as he trembled with his release. Dar closed his eyes and laid his head against her shoulder.

"You have exhausted me. I can't move."

"Does that mean you can't give a repeat performance?"

Dar raised his head and opened one eye. "You cast doubt on the virility of an Asgard sorcerer?"

"Yup."

He kissed her until she moaned deep in her throat. "Prepare yourself for another bout of sexual pleasure."

She almost regretted her dare when her fingers traced the dark circles under his eyes. He looked like he could barely keep his eyes open. "Are you sure you're up to it?"

"I'll be fine."

He didn't look it. "When was the last time you slept?"

"It doesn't matter."

A vague answer. Too vague. "I know you didn't sleep the other night. Did they let you sleep while you were in the institute last night?"

His mouth tightened into a grim line. *"Nei."*

He had gone through so much to protect her. She was so glad he'd landed on her world. Now she could show him exactly how much he meant to her. "I love you."

"I love you, too, sprite. And I will prove it again."

She tried to think of some way to let him get some rest. As tired as he looked, sleep was more important than sex. "You never took that shower," she reminded him as she touched a smudge of dirt on his face.

He captured her hand and kissed her palm. "You're

dirty, too. We'll take a shower together, *já?*"

The invitation proved too tempting to resist. "That sounds like fun."

Dar dragged her willingly to the bathroom and turned on the shower. He checked the temperature of the water, then stepped into the stall. Jennifer watched the tiny water droplets turn the hair on his chest to a shiny brown color. Standing there, naked and proud, he looked every inch a powerful Norseman. He held out his hand and silently beckoned her to join him.

Jennifer put her hand in his and stepped into the wet, frosted glass enclosure. Dar picked up a bar of soap and a washcloth. His blue gaze caressed her with such intimacy, she instinctively stepped closer to him.

"I will wash you first, *já?*"

She gasped as he ran the soapy material across her breasts and down her stomach. The water enhanced her sensations and made her yearn for his possession. Jennifer held on to the railing on the wall and threw back her head as Dar touched every inch of her skin. When she could stand it no longer, she grabbed the slippery washcloth from his grasp and ran it down his chest.

"Now it's your turn."

As she scrubbed, she alternated between feathery kisses on his damp arms and more intimate explorations with her hand. Soon Dar was breathing heavily and standing with white knuckles, waiting for her to finish her ministrations.

"You're done." He grabbed the washcloth and tossed it into the soap dish. The warm water cascaded over their bodies.

"But Dar, I still have to do your back!"

He stepped out of the shower and stood on the pink-flowered rug. "You'll wash it another time."

Dar dragged her against his chest. He smelled of roses. He tasted delicious, like ambrosia. He felt warm beneath her fingers. And best of all, he throbbed with need. For her.

Jennifer stood on her tiptoes and silently asked for his kiss. Dar growled deep in his throat and swept her up in his arms.

"Are you going to carry me to the bedroom?"

"*Nei.* We will stay here."

She looked around the tiny bathroom and frowned. "I don't think there's enough room for us to lie down."

"Then we will stand," he said as he slowly lowered her onto his jutting arousal.

Swept up in a world of sensation, Jennifer could only cling to his shoulders as he raised and lowered her body. His lips paid special attention to her swollen breasts.

"Oooh. That feels so good," she whispered hoarsely.

"Did you expect differently, sprite?"

"With you as a lover, I wouldn't settle for less."

Soon they were both swept away by passion. It seemed to last forever, yet she could have sworn it was only moments later when she tensed in his arms. Lights exploded behind her closed eyelids as he moved even faster.

He cried out, and his powerful voice echoed in the small bathroom. Jennifer smiled and collapsed against him. She made a mental note to take showers with her sorcerer more often.

Dar kissed her head and carried her to his bedroom. "You look sated but tired. 'Tis time to sleep, sprite."

He lowered her onto the bed and, lying down beside her, gathered her into his arms. She felt safe, warm, and loved. It was a nice sensation, one she hadn't experienced in a long time.

The door opened and Firedrake padded in, his long talons pulling at the carpet. Dar tried to sit up. She smiled as he groaned and fell back on the bed.

"I will, of course, replace whatever he is about to eat."

Jennifer didn't respond. She couldn't keep her eyes open any longer. With the sound of enthusiastic munching lulling her toward unconsciousness, she began to fall asleep with Dar's arm wrapped around her stomach.

A window shattered in the next room. Jennifer jumped out of bed. "Oh, my God! What was that?"

Dar reached for his sword only to find himself grasping air. "By the fiery tail of the Midgard serpent! 'Tis not the time to be unarmed."

Firedrake spread his wings and flew out the door. His roar shook the house.

"Dar, it is I!"

"Loki!" Dar shouted as he reached for his clothes. "You have finally returned. Now you shall meet your destiny!"

Chapter Fourteen

Dar got dressed so fast that Jennifer thought he must have used magic. He ran out the door and headed for the steps, and she still hadn't found her shirt.

"Where is it?" She tossed aside Dar's bag of runes and looked underneath the bed. "Wait for me," she shouted as she grabbed her shoe. "I don't want you to go out there alone."

Busy putting on her jeans, she didn't notice the half-eaten slipper or the large pile of drool until it was too late.

With a shriek, she slid to the floor and landed with one leg beneath her. Searing pain raced through her body, causing her to break out into a sweat.

Dar must have heard her scream because he sprinted up the steps and knelt at her side. " 'Tis all right, sprite. I'm here."

Tears trickled down Jennifer's cheeks as, his face grim, he gently moved her until he could look at her foot. She gasped as he touched her swollen ankle. " 'Tis sprained but not broken."

She could tell by the way he kept glancing toward the window that he was torn between helping her and facing Loki.

"Go ahead, Dar. I'll be all right."

"You are sure?"

She wasn't sure, but she wouldn't let him know the truth. Not if it meant he'd be worrying about her and not paying attention to the Trickster. "I'm sure."

A bolt of lightning, as black as midnight, streaked across his bedroom window. Dar's mouth tightened.

"The lightning has the stench of witches. It must be Angerboda, Loki's second wife. She is daring me to face her."

"Is she powerful?"

Dar helped her to the bed. His hands felt warm, comforting. "*Já*. But she's no match for a sorcerer with a crystal ball and the forces of nature behind him."

He sat down on the bed. Her face was at eye level with his jeweled sword. And a more deadly weapon she had yet to see. "I'll be fine. You go ahead." She squeezed his hand. "Be careful."

"Don't worry. I'll return to your side. I promise." A wry grin on his face, he stood up slowly. "You know I always keep my promises. I'll tell Firedrake to stay with you in case Angerboda sends a demon to attack you while I'm busy fighting."

Jennifer bit her lip as she watched him turn around. His mantle billowed out behind him as he walked down the steps as if every movement hurt. Gone was the warrior who usually took the stairs two at a time. In his place was a man who had almost used up all his strength.

But Dar always kept his promises. Then why did she feel this immeasurable fear that squeezed her heart and made it hard for her to breathe? "Some things are beyond the powers of a sorcerer. Even one as powerful as Dar," she whispered aloud.

The shrill ring of the phone scared her almost as much as the thought of Loki waiting for Dar out on her lawn. Jennifer hopped toward the small table in the hallway, making sure that she didn't put any weight on her swollen ankle.

She leaned against the wall and made a grab for the phone. "Hello?"

No reply.

"Hello? Who is it?" She was just ready to slam down the receiver when she heard a voice.

"Oh, my; oh, my. I think I may have finally dialed the right number."

"Snorri!"

"Yes, yes. It's me. How did you guess?"

"Snorri, listen to me. Dar is—"

"Yes, I know. That's why I called. Though I did call before—several times as a matter of fact. But then again, I might have dialed the wrong number. You wouldn't believe how irate some people get when you call their house three or four times in a row. They actually yell and scream and hang up on you."

Jennifer tried again. "Snorri! You've got to listen to me. Dar is—"

"Yes, yes. Say hello to him for me, won't you? Oh. Hold on a minute. I seem to have misplaced my glasses. . . ."

A scream clawed at Jennifer's throat as she tried to get her hand to stop shaking long enough so she could explain the problem. "Snorri, are you there?"

"Why, yes, Jennifer, I'm here. Am I supposed to be somewhere else?"

"No!" She took a deep breath to calm herself. "Now, listen. Loki has returned, and he has an evil witch with him."

"Hmmm. That must be Angerboda. She bore him three children: a serpent, a wolf, and a hag who guards the gates of the dead. And a more deadly family you have never seen. I shudder every time I think of it."

Jennifer leaned against the wall to take some weight off her good leg. "Angerboda. That's the name Dar used, too."

"Oooh. I would give my right arm and a leg to actually meet Loki. Do you think, when Dar has subdued them, he might actually let me talk to the Trickster and Angerboda?"

The thought made Jennifer's stomach clench as bile rose in her throat. "Trust me, you don't want to meet either of them."

"Oh, but I do. I've devoted my entire life to researching Norse mythology. I could tell you all the details of Ragnarok—the last battle of Asgard."

"I would love to hear the tale another time, but right now I've got to go see how Dar's doing. Maybe you could tell me about the battle later."

"Of course. Oh, I almost forgot the reason I called. Could you let Dar know that I still have his crystal ball?"

Jennifer felt the blood drain from her face. "Oh, my God! You mean Dar's out there fighting Loki and he doesn't have his crystal ball?"

"Well, yes. I guess that's what I'm saying."

"I've got to go find Dar and warn him!" Jennifer

shouted. ''Hold on to the crystal, and whatever you do, don't lose it!''

''Oh dear, oh dear. Certainly. I'll guard it with my life. You don't have to worry. I won't lose it.'' He paused. ''Oh, my, I just had the crystal ball a few seconds ago; now where did I put it . . .''

Jennifer heard the click as Snorri hung up the phone. She stared at the bedroom window. It seemed so far away. She had to warn Dar before it was too late.

It took a combination of crawling and hopping, but she finally dragged herself to the window sill. Inky darkness and silvery moonlight were the only things that greeted her. The lawn was empty, and she didn't hear any sounds other than the rattling of her window and Firedrake's growls as the dragon paced the hallway.

''Where are they?''

Knowing she wouldn't be of any help to Dar in her current condition, Jennifer contemplated her options. ''I can sit here and worry, I can hobble outside and become a prime target for a witch, or I can do something about the situation.''

A few weeks ago she probably would have whined about everything. Now, with Dar's life at stake, she realized she was more courageous than she had ever imagined.

Jennifer sat down on the bed and raised her chin. ''I'm not going to let a skinny jotun and an evil witch kill my sorcerer without putting up a fight. Where did I put those runes?'' She searched underneath the covers until she found the bag. ''Casting a healing spell shouldn't be hard. I've seen Dar do it so many times, I should be able to do it with my eyes closed.''

The healing rune in the palm of her hand, Jennifer

took a deep breath. "Here goes. Powers of the moon, strength from the sea, healing powers, harken to me . . ."

Pure energy flowed from the rune and into her body. The intensity of the tingling sensation running down her arm and spine frightened her. She dropped the rune as if it was a hot coal. After several seconds she found enough courage to try again. The rune didn't work as well for her as it did for Dar, but once she started she didn't stop reciting the spell until she could put her foot down on the floor without wincing.

She stood up, trembling from the aftermath of the experience. The healing had used up most of her energy, but she refused to allow sleep to overcome her. She tested her weight on her foot. Her ankle still hurt, but she could walk on it.

"I have to warn Dar." She looked out at the lawn again and saw only darkness. Dar hadn't returned.

"Where could they have gone?" She tossed the runes onto the bed, limped down the stairs, made a wide path around Firedrake's pacing body, and searched the living room for her keys.

How did one defeat a witch and an evil jotun? By beating them at their own game.

"Okay, Firedrake, here's the plan. I'm going to put together a costume. I'm going to be the most hideous, dangerous witch this side of Asgard."

The dragon stopped pacing. He cocked his head to the side, contemplating Jennifer's words.

"You heard me right. I'm going down to the basement to look for a flashlight." She mentally envisioned everything they would need to pull this off. "I'll get Dar's bag of magic runes and his book."

Firedrake snorted, obviously not impressed with her idea.

"I know it sounds stupid, but the book is special. It has a dragon on it. I'm going to use it to cast my spell."

As she gathered together everything she needed, Jennifer paused to stare out the front window. She was scared to death, but she would do anything, even face Loki, to save Dar's life.

A half hour later, Jennifer backed her Jeep out of the driveway. Firedrake peered at her from the hood of her Jeep. "Find Dar," she commanded.

The dragon nodded; then with a powerful flapping of wings, he soared toward the sky. Her tires squealing, Jennifer zoomed down the dark lane toward an unknown destination.

She passed the Eagle Tavern, Griffith Hall, and Ludwig's Corner Fire Company, and still saw no sign of Dar. One minute Firedrake was flying over a tree, the next she lost him.

Jennifer stifled the urge to scream. She couldn't have lost the dragon! That would mean she would never find Dar.

Then she saw the flapping of green wings up ahead as Firedrake passed under a street light. The night was so silent, the gurgling stream underneath the bridge the car was on sounded like a waterfall. Only the hum of the nearby traffic broke the silence.

Jennifer stopped the car at the entrance to the local park and shut off the ignition. She stood in a large, sloped area. In the distance she could see lights shining in the windows of a white house. To her right was a farm with a quaint wooden fence and a horse trailer sitting in the driveway.

She took a deep breath. If only she owned a gun, or if only she had taken karate lessons when she'd had the chance. A sense of unease settled over her like a heavy fog. She could almost feel Dar's life force slipping away.

Putting it down to an overactive imagination, Jennifer put her keys in her pocket, shut the car door, and set off to find the man she loved. Her Norseman would be furious that she hadn't stayed at home, but she'd rather have him furious and alive than calm and dead.

Dar narrowed his eyes as he followed the witch's trail. Although both Loki and Angerboda rode brooms, thereby conserving their energy, they still left enough bent leaves and twigs for Dar to locate them easily.

Where was Loki leading him? Dar increased his stride as he crashed through the bushes. His legs shook with exhaustion, but to give in to his weakness now could cost him his life.

He stopped running as he entered a large field ringed by trees. Witches preferred wooded areas for spell casting. He knew, without being told, that this park would be the location of their battle. He unsheathed his sword and raised it over his head.

"Valhalla!"

The night echoed with his battle cry. Lightning rolled off the blade of his sword and made a jagged path though the frigid night sky.

"We meet again on a battlefield, *já?*" Loki said, stepping out from behind a nearby tree trunk. "Only this time it will be you who will be destroyed."

"'Twas a fair fight," Dar reminded him. "One which I won honestly."

"Do you know of all the taunts I received because of your victory?" the Trickster shouted.

"If you were taunted, 'twas because you cringed from my sword."

Loki raised his hand and sneered. "Nothing will save you from your destiny. You and Asgard will feel the full measure of my wrath."

Remembering what Snorri had told him about Loki's betrayal of Asgard, Dar curled his lips. "You are a curse to the nine worlds and a betrayer of your people."

Loki threw back his head and laughed, a shrill sound that chafed on Dar's nerves like a curved talon scratching against a stone cave wall. "That is true. And as you know the truth, you must die. I shall laugh when you are begging for mercy, sorcerer." The Trickster drew out his sword, a black blade with the head of a demon on the hilt.

"Never," Dar vowed.

"We shall see. We shall see."

Loki thrust his blade toward his opponent's stomach. Dar parried. Metal struck metal. Bolts of energy leapt into the air, causing swirling white clouds to form around them.

Dar wondered where Angerboda was hiding. Although etiquette dictated that he could not use sorcery while battling unless his opponents showed themselves to be magic-users, there was nothing to stop Loki's ally from attacking while his back was turned—except decency, of course. And Angerboda did not know the meaning of the word.

With a glancing blow, Loki slashed Dar's arm. Blood welled up from the wound and dripped down his mantle.

"Victory will be mine!" his opponent crowed, his thin frame dodging yet another of Dar's powerful blows.

Dar wiped at the sweat beading his brow. His blade felt so heavy, as unwieldy as a serpent's tail and as dull as a broken dagger. Exhausted, he could barely deflect Loki's thrusts.

The night seemed so silent now, like a tomb or a crypt. Loki thrust toward the right and drew another wound, deeper than the first, on Dar's thigh. The searing pain sapped his little remaining strength.

Dar struggled against the darkness at the edge of his consciousness. If only he hadn't used so much of his energy to destroy the institute. If only Loki had chosen another night to challenge him. If only he had rested before entering into battle.

Dar fell to his knees and raised his sword over his head to barely prevent Loki from slicing off an ear. Only one thought gave him strength. Jennifer was safe. She would live even if he passed on to the next world.

Relief that she would be safe outweighed his grief at never seeing her again. Raised as a warrior, death itself did not frighten him. He would welcome oblivion with open arms if it meant he would die having defended his world from Loki's betrayal. He would be able to rest in peace knowing that the protector of his heart lived even after his flesh rejoined the ground.

His attention on the jotun before him, Dar wasn't aware of another's presence until a bolt of black lightning struck his back. His crystal mantle absorbed some of the impact, but most of it hit his body. The stench of black magic filled the air. The attack quickly depleted Dar's remaining energy. He gasped and collapsed to the ground.

"You did well, my wife," Loki praised as he bent down to stare into Dar's pain-filled eyes. "I am pleased by your timing. My arm had tired of fending off his powerful blows. I wouldn't have been able to hold him off much longer if you hadn't intervened."

Dar watched the witch hobble out of the trees in front of him. Even from this distance he could smell the rotten odor that surrounded her. He closed his eyes, his thoughts focused on taking shallow breaths to ease the growing pain in his chest.

"He is dead, eh?"

"*Nei.* But he is almost unconscious. Soon we will have the honor of sending him to our daughter, Hela, and his final resting place in Hell. Once he is in the land of the dead, we can then proceed with our plan to obliterate Asgard."

The pain in his back was so great that Dar couldn't even move his little finger. His muscles quivered with exhaustion. Although he struggled against it with all his will, he sensed his life force slowly slipping away into the atmosphere.

His thoughts turned to Jennifer. She would know of his passing. She would sense his death just as if he stood in front of her. He tried to clench his fist and only succeeded in twitching a finger.

Loki continued to gloat and he crowed to the small field. "All those who tittered with amusement at my humiliation shall die at the hands of the fire demons. Asgard will be nothing but rubble. I will even level the crystal caves and kill the dragons that dwell there!"

"Oh? You and what army?"

Dar's hand trembled as the owner of the voice strode into the clearing. Jennifer! Although he couldn't see her, he could hear the anger in her voice and perceive her fear. He hoped Loki could not.

He longed to scream, but the words came out in a whisper. Tears of frustration ran down his cheeks and onto the grass. ''Go back, sprite. Run. Before it is too late!''

''She is the one you mentioned, the sorcerer's woman, eh, Loki?''

''*Já*. 'Tis her.''

''Jennifer.'' Dar's hand twitched. She had come to help him, and in doing so, she was walking toward her own death. Dar closed his eyes and used up the last of his energy in calling to her. ''Jennifer! Do not come any closer!''

''Don't worry, Dar. I'll save you.''

She didn't know the extent of Angerboda's powers, he realized sadly. His breath coming in gasps, Dar used every ounce of his strength to move his hand toward the secret pocket inside his mantle.

If he cast the right spell, his crystal ball would channel the energy from his surroundings and might give him enough power to render his opponents unconscious. It would also use up the last of his life force, but it would be worth it to save Jennifer.

Each movement sent searing pain through his body, but he didn't stop, even though he felt himself floating on the edge of consciousness. Like a comet caught in the gravity of a planet, he spiraled closer to his own destruction, for he knew without a doubt that Loki would not hesitate to kill him when he passed out.

Dar reached into his pocket but felt only air. Where was his crystal ball? Had it fallen during the battle? Not having enough strength to search the ground for it, Dar cursed the fates and vowed to give up his own life if he could save that of his woman.

Jennifer shuddered as she felt her soul mate grow weaker. *Hold on, Dar!* If she could distract them for just a little while longer, he might be able to cast some spell to stop them. She pulled the embroidered bedspread closer around her body. "Okay, Firedrake. Let's do it."

She left the safety of the line of trees and walked toward Loki. Firedrake hovered over her head, a hatchling, but nonetheless, one with razor-sharp talons and long, sharp teeth.

It was now or never. Jennifer took a deep breath and pointed a finger at Loki. "Leave this world immediately or I will make the blood curdle in your veins and your teeth fall to the ground," she stated confidently.

Angerboda stepped closer to Loki. "The sorcerer's woman is powerful, eh?"

Loki took his time in replying. "*Já.* I have seen her charm demons to eat out of her hand. But don't worry. I'm sure you have enough evil in your spell bag to overcome anything she hurls at us. Conjure a demon and eliminate her."

"Eh. As you wish, husband." Angerboda reached into her spell bag and withdrew a black vial. "O, winged creatures, loathsome toads, form before me now and do as you are told."

A small black cloud swirled in front of the witch. Jennifer watched in trepidation as a hideous creature with bat's wings, glowing red eyes, and the head of a monster, took shape.

"Oh, my God! It's a demon. Where's a baseball bat when you need one?"

The creature was about the size of a bat, and it snarled and flew toward Jennifer. Its pointed teeth glistened with thick saliva. The smell rivaled that of a refuse dump.

Jennifer pulled the book she had given Dar for

Christmas out from under the comforter and used it as a shield. She stood up and swatted at the demon. Tiny teeth snapped mere inches from her face.

An enraged roar echoed through the park and reminded Jennifer of the dragon's presence. Firedrake plummeted from the sky like an avenging angel. His teeth bared, he attacked the demon and slashed at its wings with his deadly talons.

Smaller than the dragon, the demon was no match for their combined forces. A blow to the head and a deep wound to the neck sent it crashing to the ground, gasping for air.

Jennifer watched it die a quick death, then used her boot to push the smelly black body away from her.

"You leave me no choice," she told Loki, her voice full of foreboding. "I now must use the magical salve formulated to defeat the race of elves, goblins, and those women who consort with demons."

Jennifer took out the jar of petroleum jelly, opened it, and held it up to the full moon. She let out a deep sigh and tried to look deadly and mysterious, as if she knew what she was doing.

"Take the female hop plant, woodworm, betony, lupin, henbane, viper's bugloss, baneberries, cropleek, garlic, and fennel," Jennifer muttered as she waved her hand over the plastic container. "Put these in a vat, place under a roof, cover it, boil it in rosewater and sheep's grease, add much holy salt, strain through a cloth, throw the herbs into running water, and place in a magical vessel."

A hand to her wrinkled throat, Abergoda moved closer to Loki. Good; her plan was working.

"Take the magical vessel and rub it onto a picture of that which you wish to conjure." Jennifer rubbed jelly onto the cover, then held Dar's book up to the stars. She made sure Loki could see the golden dragon on the cover. "O spirit of the dragon, hear my plea, spirit, spirit, come to me. . . ."

A flash of golden lightning arched through the night sky. Pure energy flowed through Dar's body to the ring on his finger. It rippled along his spine and crackled through his veins, pulling his life force back from the nether region into his body.

Jennifer had invoked the dragon ring spell! Forged as one, her ring was bound forever to his. While separately they could conjure the spirit of a dragon, together they held the power of the universe in their golden depths. Together, using the rings as a conduit, he could draw on her life force to survive. Without realizing it, Jennifer had cast the only spell that could have saved his life.

Dar sat up and looked at the sky. Two separate translucent dragons rippled on the clouds. Their transparent and shimmering scales rivaled the brightness of the stars and their crimson eyes promised death to all who encountered them.

"Wow!" Dar heard Jennifer whisper to herself, obviously amazed at the result of her actions.

Angerboda gasped with horror. Her spell bag dropped near Dar's hand. "Her powers are mightier than mine. We should leave now, while we still live."

"Nei," Loki stated, his gaze on Jennifer. "We will stay and kill them. Create ten more demons. They can't possibly destroy them all before one drinks the blood from their throats."

Dar looked at the white light emitted from his glowing ring and thanked the gods that he had thought to create such a powerful safeguard.

Rejuvenated, Dar waited until Angerboda unstoppered the vial and began to mutter the long, complex words of her incantation before he leapt to his feet. "You've tried to kill one I hold above all others, Loki. Now you will feel the wrath of Odin's sorcerer."

Too late, Loki realized what had happened. The jotun tried to escape, but Dar raised his hands. Bands of binding energy flew from his fingertips and encircled the witch and the Trickster. The white light pulsed as it tightened around its struggling victims.

"Midgard is now safe from your pranks," Dar growled as he tried to control his anger and not simply kill the two responsible for all his grief. "No more will you come to me in the middle of the night and frighten my woman."

He looked at Jennifer. Never had she looked so stunning, so untamed. With her dark hair blowing wildly around her face, her eyes painted to make her look like a powerful sorceress, and her makeshift mantle billowing in the turbulence he created, she was more beautiful than the loveliest of Aesir maidens.

"Dar! You're bleeding."

" 'Tis only a flesh wound," he reassured her, knowing her aversion for the sight of blood.

The twin dragons roared, filling the night with the sound of raw power. Dar unhooked the bag at Loki's waist. He made sure the Trickster's hands were pressed against his body so the jotun couldn't stop him or reach for the fairy dust in his pocket. The witch continued with her spell, oblivious to all around her.

Taking a deep breath, Dar searched Loki. With a grunt of satisfaction, Dar pulled a palm-sized quartz object from Loki's pocket, put it in the Trickster's hand, and held it there with the power of his ring.

"From Asgard you have arrived, and to Asgard you will return. It is my hope that those who are in the Hall of the Slain shall know of your treachery and punish you for your crimes and betrayal."

Jennifer ran over to his side. "I'll protect you while you cast the spell to send them back."

"I'll be fine."

She shook out her mantle behind her with a snap of her wrist. "I insist."

He admired her bravery even as he frowned at her impulsiveness. Very few would voluntarily face a demon to keep him safe. "Stand back, sprite. Demons may appear at any time."

Her mouth set in a thin, determined line, Jennifer bent to pick up a tree branch. Fearful for her safety, Dar grasped her arm. "You're too close to them. Stand back. The bands holding them won't last forever. I must send them back now, before the demons can materialize and set them free."

"Go ahead. I'm ready."

A swirling black form appeared to the side of Jennifer. Dar had no choice. He started the incantation. "We sit in this field, the full moon shining above us . . ."

Loki tried to drop the quartz, but Dar held it firmly in place with the power of his mind.

The light brightened and began to pulse in time to his words. ". . . thousands of brave warriors from Midgard, the world of Earth, at the tables of Valhalla . . ."

A ball of deadly teeth, the fully formed demon went for Jennifer's throat. She kept it busy while Dar chanted.

The witch started to glow.

Dar didn't dare cease his chant. ". . . we warriors

practice daily to hone the skills of warfare so we may be sure to win the battle of Ragnarok, the Twilight of the Gods . . .''

Dar watched, helpless, as fighting a demon with the branch, Jennifer fell backward, allowing the demon an opportunity to strike. At the last second, though she batted it away with her hands.

The quartz turned a dark red, but Dar didn't allow Loki to drop it. Loki sneered and spat in Dar's direction. ''You think you have seen the last of me, *já?* 'Tis not so. I will seek my revenge, sorcerer. My allies, the fire demons and the giants, will tear down your hall and kill your family. I, Loki, do swear it.''

Using all his concentration to keep Loki and Angerboda immobile, Dar watched as Jennifer continued to struggle with the newly forming demons, keeping them away from him so he could finish the incantation.

Blood dripped from the wounds on her hands, but still she fought as bravely as any Asgard warrior.

Above their heads, Dar saw that Firedrake was caught in a battle of his own, fighting several demons at a time. One bit into his wing, another pulled at his tail, but within moments he had dispatched both.

Dar groaned as Jennifer jumped to her feet and moved dangerously close to Loki. The energy from the crystal touched her, causing her body to ripple with the same light surrounding Loki and Angerboda. Jennifer had saved Dar's life, but in doing so she'd risked her own.

Only one more line and the spell would be complete. Dar held out his hand. ''Move away now, sprite. Firedrake will take care of the demon.'' When she didn't immediately do as he said, he grew desperate. "Sprite! If you love me, you will try to come to me now."

Jennifer turned around. Thousands of points of light sparkled around her body and that of the slow-moving demon in front of her. She gazed at him, a questioning look in her eyes.

"Take my hand. Although I cannot promise you wealth beyond your dreams, I swear I will protect you the rest of your life. I, Dar, warrior of Asgard, son of Tyr, grandson of Odin, do hereby swear it."

In slow motion, Jennifer let go of the branch and reached toward him. Firedrake challenged the demon, she'd been fighting, moving him away from both Dar and Jennifer, and a fierce battle ensued.

Dar pulled Jennifer against his mantle and glanced at Loki. The bands of energy holding his prisoners began to break apart. As he watched, five more newly-hatched demons materialized in front of Loki, their beady eyes narrowed as they looked for sustenance. Their gaze settled on Jennifer.

Dar couldn't wait any longer. He shoved Jennifer behind him and watched as she rolled to lay beside a fallen tree. He waited until she scrambled behind the log before he spoke the final words of the spell. "I, Dar, sorcerer of Asgard, do hereby condemn all Giants, our enemies, to a life of eternal damnation, in another time, another place . . ."

Angerboda screamed and dematerialized. Two of the demons followed her. Taking a dangerous risk, Dar reached forward and knocked the piece of quartz crystal out of Loki's hand. The crystal fell on a sharp rock and broke into two uneven pieces. The Trickster gasped as he felt the rock torn from his grasp.

"I will be back—" The scream echoed for several moments in the chill night air, and Dar threw himself down to lie next to Jennifer. He held her close as lightning and thunder exploded around them. The three remaining demons, having no orders to follow, screeched and flew toward the trees.

"Firedrake." Dar dragged himself to his knees. "Destroy them."

The dragon screamed triumphantly and flew after the black-winged creatures.

Dar helped Jennifer to her feet and embraced her trembling body. Fear at almost having lost her left him weak and grateful to be holding her in his arms. He buried his face in her hair and hugged her tightly.

After what seemed like an eternity, Jennifer struggled to push herself out of his embrace. Dar let her move back a few inches but didn't release her.

"Another minute and I would have had that demon!"

"Já?"

"Yes! Now he got away."

"Forget about the demon. I'll take care of him later." He pulled her closer and lowered his head until he could feel her breath on his lips. "Thank you for saving my life, my courageous sorceress."

Dar captured her lips and pulled her against his exhausted body. Her presence rejuvenated him. His tongue delved into her mouth and plundered her sweetness. After what seemed like an eternity, Jennifer put her arms around his neck. He deepened the kiss and silently told her exactly how much he loved her with his heart and soul.

Dar raised his head and watched Firedrake land on a felled tree. The dragon burped and patted his distended stomach.

A smile was on Dar's face, and he put his arm

around Jennifer's waist and urged her toward the jeep. Firedrake flew behind them.

As Dar watched, the two dragons spirits above faded from the night sky. Jennifer snuggled closer to Dar and put her arms around his waist. "I'm looking forward to going to bed," she whispered in a voice that promised a heaven beyond his wildest imagination.

By Thor's hammer, a place to lie down sounded like paradise, Dar mused. Sleeping would not be on the agenda, of course, but to undress Jennifer and hold her through the night, to ensure that when he reached out, she would be at his side, that would be a far greater joy.

Dar looked one last time at the trees surrounding them for a glimpse of the demons, then frowned and took her hand. "Firedrake, search for the demons. Meet us at home." The dragon soared into the night sky. "Come, sprite. We go now."

"Ooh. I almost forgot your book. I'll be right back."

Dar bent down and picked up the two pieces of crystalite. He cupped them in his hands and reveled in their coolness. They felt just like any other piece of crystal. He slid the rocks into the pocket of his mantle. As he stood up, his foot struck Angerboda's forgotten spell bag.

"What have we here?"

He opened the pouch and spilled the contents into his palm. Herbs, animal parts, and vials shimmered in the moonlight. He would examine them later, after he had rested. He slid the vials back into the pouch and put it in his pocket, next to the crystalite.

"I'm ready when you are, Dar."

As he followed Jennifer back to the Jeep, her bedspread over her arm, he watched her swaying hips in the pale light of dawn and decided sleep could wait for an indefinite period of time.

Dar slid into the passenger seat of the silent creature and let the quiet wash over him like a calming wave. He relaxed for a whole two seconds until Jennifer stomped on the gas.

"Hold on tight! We're going home." Jennifer looked into the rearview mirror as they sped toward her house. "To celebrate our victory, we'll have a party. I'll make peanut butter sandwiches."

Dar grunted. Although he had at first hated peanut butter, now he found himself looking forward to eating the thick goo.

"Dar, what will happen to the demons that escaped? Will they die on their own?" Jennifer asked.

If only it were that easy. "*Nei.* They will be fruitful and multiply, fill the Earth, and devour anything that moves."

"Sounds disgusting."

Not only disgusting, but deadly, too. Dar knew exactly how large the demons would grow. If allowed to reach their full potential, they would be as big as full-grown dragons.

The crystalite and spell bag banged against Dar's chest as Jennifer took a curve. He rested his hand against the bulge in his mantle.

Unless stopped, Loki would still carry out his threat to destroy Asgard. If only it was possible to use the crystalite to warn Odin of Loki's plans. Dar frowned. Could Snorri fix or create a new crystal that could transport him back to Asgard? As soon as he could, he'd ask the scientist.

Exhausted, Dar reached for Jennifer's hand, then closed his eyes. After his latest defeat, Loki would not hesitate to take out his wrath on Dar's family. Dar vowed to save Asgard from being destroyed or die trying.

Later the next day, the light from the late morning sun warmed Jennifer as she watched Dar get dressed. He didn't know she was awake, and that made it all the more intimate. The Norseman tiptoed around the bed and pulled out a pair of freshly washed jeans. Without bothering to put on underwear, he tugged the stiff material over his firm thighs and narrow hips.

"Where are you going?" she asked finally, pushing off the covers and reveling in his intimate perusal of her body. Even after making love for the remainder of the night, she still yearned for his touch, his gentle but insistent caress.

Her voice startled him. He spun around and reached for his sword, but he hadn't put it on yet. "You're awake."

Dar walked over to the bed and raised her chin with his hand. A light of desire illuminated his dark blue eyes. Her pulse leapt with excitement. He wanted her; she could see it in the tightening of his pants, in the way his gaze made a slow but thorough path up her naked body.

"Why aren't you in bed?" She patted the mattress beside her.

"I couldn't sleep," he whispered. "I kept thinking of the way you risked yourself last night. You could have been killed, or worse, torn from this time and sent back to Asgard." His callused fingers stroked her bottom lip. "I would not have been able to follow."

The ragged tone of his voice told her how that would have affected him. She swallowed the lump in her throat.

Dar bent down and kissed her lips. His translation crystal bumped into her collarbone. ''I would spend an eternity trying to find a way to come to you.''

''Dar, if you had a choice between staying here and returning to Asgard, which would you choose?''

He hesitated. ''Without you there I would only be half alive.''

Touched by his deep love, Jennifer tried again. ''But if you had to choose—''

''I wish I could see Asgard and my family again,'' he stated, his voice low and full of sadness. ''But since you do not wish to go, I will remain here, with you.''

Although she had no desire to leave her world for one that held a questionable future, Jennifer wished there was some way to fulfill Dar's wish. If it were possible, she would help him see his family, then help him return to Earth. As soon as she finished the thought, it was as if a heavy burden lifted from her shoulders.

''I have another interview today,'' she reminded him, wishing he would stay and hold her a while longer. ''They called and left a message yesterday.''

''I am pleased for you. Good luck.''

''Thanks. I can feel it in my bones that I'm going to get the job this time.'' The company's computer programmer had left two weeks ago; they had an immediate opening.

''I have faith in you, sprite. You can do anything if you but put your mind to it.''

Grateful for Dar's support, Jennifer smiled and watched him cross the room. Thoughts of the upcoming interview flew from her mind as Dar reached for a shirt; her favorite, a long-sleeved beige garment with buttons that opened easily to the touch. ''Where are you going?'' She wished again that he would come back to bed for a little longer.

''I must watch an errand.''

''You mean 'see to' an errand.''

''Já.'' Dar nodded, obviously pleased he was learning Earth slang. ''I promised Snorri that I would lend him some money. Until he finds another job, he needs gold to buy food and equipment to run tests on the broken crystalite.''

Remembering the small, rough-edged stones, Jennifer frowned. ''Do you think he's found a way to fix the crystal and send matter to Asgard?''

Dar buckled his sword around his waist. He shrugged. ''He's only had the crystalite for a few hours. 'Tis unlikely that he has fixed it so quickly. It would take a dwarf smithy several days to choose the right degree of heat in which to repair it.''

''We've never discussed what you'll do once the crystalite has been fixed.''

He met her gaze. ''What would you like me to do?''

Dar was leaving the choice up to her. She worded her answer carefully. ''If possible, I think you should warn your grandfather about Loki. Then come back to me.''

The relieved smile that lit his face told her that she had made the right decision. ''I will see what I can do. I will discuss it with Snorri.''

She wanted to go with him, but knowing Snorri, Dar probably wouldn't be able to leave the scientist's house until he'd told the entire story of the battle with Loki and Angerboda again and again. Jennifer couldn't afford to be late for her interview.

''Do you want me to drive you?'' she asked as he

slid his mantle around his shoulders and clasped it with his dragon brooch.

"*Nei.* I'll trot to Snorri's house."

"You mean jog. And it's a couple of miles."

Dar flashed her a dazzling smile. "Distance is nothing to a Norse warrior. Besides, I'm taking Firedrake with me. He'll keep me company while I run."

The Norseman gave her a long, lingering kiss. His heat warmed her to her toes. She put her arms around his neck and tried to pull him back into bed.

"Thank you for healing my wounds."

"Flesh wounds are easy. For more deadly wounds, I must rely on the power of the sacred caves."

"Why don't you go to Snorri's later. I—"

The jingle of the telephone interrupted her intended indecent proposal. "I'll get it," she told him. "It's probably Snorri asking if we can help him find his glasses."

Dar frowned. "*Nei.* I will get it."

Jennifer reached the phone first. "Don't worry. I can handle an absentminded professor." She put the receiver to her ear. "Hello?"

"Jennifer Giordano?"

Cold fear filled her as a harsh male spit her name. Was it another collection agency? "Yes?"

"Killer sends his regards." The cocky voice sounded familiar, but she couldn't place it. "He said to tell you he wishes to repay you for all you've done for him."

Shivers of fear shot through her body. Jennifer sat there, a lump caught in her throat as the caller described exactly how he would kill her.

"It is Snorri, *já?*"

Jennifer silently shook her head. Dar grabbed the phone and put it to his ear. He listened for a few seconds, then his lip curled in disgust. "Have I not told you never to call here again? If I ever find you within a dragon's length of Jennifer, I will kill you with my bare hands."

He slammed down the phone and pulled her into his embrace. "I'm sorry. I thought I could save you from that again."

She buried her face into Dar's shoulder, remembering the man's hate-filled voice.

"Don't worry, sprite. I'll protect you."

Jennifer pulled away from him far enough to see the frown creasing his lips. "You said *again.* Has that man called before?"

He hesitated. Then, as if fighting a battle within himself, he nodded. "*Já.* Snake has called several times. Each time I took the call. He said he plans to avenge his friend Killer."

"Oh, my God! Why didn't you tell me?" she shrieked, horrified at the thought of those deadly gang members bursting into her house and catching Dar when he wasn't prepared to defend himself.

He pushed her bangs out of her eyes. "I didn't want to scare you. Don't worry. I've taken steps to shield you. I've cast a powerful protective spell over the house. No one will be able to cross the barrier without you being aware of their presence."

Now she understood the reason he'd kept getting up in the middle of the night and prowling by the window. Then she came to a terrible conclusion. Dar thought her a coward, a woman who cowered beneath her bed, one who needed a man to keep her safe. That might have been true before she met him, but it wasn't the case now.

Jennifer raised her chin, grateful for his protectiveness, even as she frowned at the thought of him treating her like a frightened child. "So that's why you want to stay. You want to protect me."

"I don't want to leave you alone." He pulled away and began to take off his mantle. "You're pale. I'll go to Snorri's another time."

For a split second, Jennifer almost agreed. Then she realized what she was doing. Dar couldn't protect her twenty-four hours a day. Besides, she refused to live like a frightened mouse, never venturing from the safety of her house. Jennifer gathered her courage around her like a mantle. "No, you go. I'll be all right."

He hesitated, obviously worried about her. "You're sure?"

If Snake had called before and hadn't done anything, why would this time be different? "Yes, I'm sure."

"As long as you don't leave the house, the spell should protect you."

"I'll go to my interview and come right home. Will that satisfy you?"

Still he hesitated; then, as if making a decision, he slid his dagger out of its scabbard. The black crystal absorbed the light in the room and glowed with an eerie radiance that fascinated yet repulsed her. "I'll leave you this as a precaution, in case you need it."

He put the dagger in the palm of her hand. The blade felt warm, like freshly spilled blood. Jennifer's first instinct was to drop it onto the carpet and get as far away from it as she could. Then common sense returned. If anyone attacked her or her house, she'd be ready.

"Remember," he warned, " 'tis sharp enough to cut through sinew and bone. Also, the runes on the handle help protect the user."

"I'll remember." She hoped she'd never have to use it.

He stepped back and put on his helmet—the metal one with the horns. Why was he wearing it now? He hadn't worn it since the day he arrived.

As if he could read her mind, Dar said, "Snorri asked if he could see it. He has never touched real Norse headgear before."

The scientist was obsessed with anything Norse. He would live, eat, and breathe Norse if given the opportunity.

"I will be back. I would never go to Asgard without first telling you," Dar vowed.

"I know."

With another concerned glance in her direction, Dar spun around and headed toward the steps. Jennifer heard Firedrake snort; then the front door slammed.

The blade gripped tightly in her hand, Jennifer slowly got out of bed. She placed the knife on the night table beside the bed and padded to her closet, deciding what she would wear to her interview.

She would get the job. She could feel it. Jennifer smiled as she contemplated the happy expression on Dar's face when she told him the good news. Today was going to be a good day.

A cloud crossed the sun, throwing the bedroom into shadow. Jennifer shivered at the sudden chill in the air, then hurried into the bathroom to shower and get ready for her interview.

Chapter Fifteen

Jennifer drove the Jeep around a pile of leaves as she pulled into her driveway.

She hoped Dar was home already because she couldn't wait to tell him the good news. She started her new job at an insurance company the next day! The benefits were great, the pay was higher than she'd expected, and her co-workers seemed very friendly. She was so happy, she could cry. The only thing that could make her happier was to have Dar's arms around her.

After parking the Jeep, she got out, remembered her handbag and was reaching for it when someone grabbed her from behind. She screamed Dar's name. A man put his hand over her mouth, cutting off the sound.

"About time you got back. I've been freezing my butt off out here all day," Snake's voice snarled. He was pressing a gun to her temple. "Now I want you to call your lover. Tell that alien to get out here.''

Dar's knife was in her handbag on the front passenger seat, out of her reach. ''Dar's not here.''

''Aw geez. That means I'll have to do him separately.'' He glanced back at the house. ''No way am I going in there to look for him. I get the creeps just looking at the place.'' He gestured for her to get into the back seat of her car. ''Sit there, and don't do anything funny. If your lover ain't back here soon, you're dead.''

''Tell me again about Loki,'' Snorri begged, getting up from the kitchen table and ushering Dar into the parlor.

''I've told you that story six times already,'' Dar said, stepping over a pile of clothing.

''Ignore the mess. The cleaning lady only comes in once a month, and she was just here yesterday.''

Although Dar had been in Snorri's house all day, he was still amazed at the clutter. It in no way resembled the spacious rooms of Asgard or Jennifer's neat if somewhat tattered furniture. Books, tablets of paper, dirty plates, and clothing covered every flat surface of the house, including the steps going up to the second floor.

Firedrake landed on the desk. A pile of books slid to the floor. The dragon bellowed and scrambled to regain his balance. Snorri didn't even bat an eyelid.

''I like hearing the story, especially the part where Jennifer was almost sucked to Asgard. I must remember to take into account the powerful vacuum of the currents when we leave.''

In the process of climbing over a tray containing a bowl of half-eaten soup, Dar paused. ''You can fix the crystal?''

"I forgot to tell you? Oh dear, oh dear!" Snorri led the way down the cellar steps. "Yes, yes. I know how. I've put the crystal back together."

"You are sure, *já?*"

"Well, I haven't run any tests on it yet, but I think it should work!" Snorri walked around a pile of clothing and headed toward the rear of the cellar.

Dar couldn't believe it! He now had a way to return home and to get revenge on Loki. He smiled widely and contemplated what he would do when he returned. The crystal caves—he could visit them and enjoy the smell of unwashed dragons. Or he could go to Valhalla and order casks of mead and sides of roasted oxen. There was nothing like carving a large hunk of meat and watching the juice drip into one's trencher. Dar's mouth watered at the thought. He would eat a meal fit for a sorcerer and not leave the table until he couldn't consume another morsel. He hadn't realized how much he had missed his home until now.

". . . so as you can see, we definitely have a problem."

The tone of Snorri's voice told Dar that he had missed something important.

"What is the problem?"

"We have to leave now, before the glue separates." Snorri pushed his glasses up on the bridge of his nose. "As I told you, I don't know if the crystal will work once the contact has been broken again. And since I don't know how long the glue will hold . . ."

Dar's first thought was to grab the stone and repeat the incantation immediately, before the glue separated. Then he closed his eyes as he realized what he would be leaving behind.

"Jennifer."

"Oh, don't worry about her," Snorri announced. "You could go to Asgard, warn Odin of Loki's treachery, and return before she'd even noticed you were missing. As you know, time passes differently between the two worlds."

Dar closed his eyes and tried to control his rapidly beating heart. He had thought it impossible to return home. But now he had been offered a miracle. If he could prevent the destruction of Asgard, save the lives of his people, it would be worth the hour or so it would take to return to this world.

Praying to the old gods that Snorri was right and Jennifer would understand, Dar opened his eyes. "You're sure we can return tonight?"

"According to my calculations, we should be gone for only five minutes in Earth time."

Dar took a deep breath. "If that's the truth, then I'll leave now. Immediately."

"I thought you might say that," Snorri exclaimed. "So I packed my trunk." He walked toward the wall and began dragging a massive rectangular object with a handle toward the center of the room. "I thought that, maybe, you, um, wouldn't mind if I came with you."

Seeing the effort Snorri exerted to move the trunk, Dar reached over and helped him carry it to the center of the room. The large brown object was taller and wider than the scientist, but Dar lifted it easily.

"Oh dear, oh dear. I didn't realize it would be so heavy."

"What's in it?" Dar asked.

"Oh, not much. Just several changes of clothing, my allergy medication, a complete set of encyclopedias, a notebook computer, several batteries for it, all my notes on Norse mythology, an extra set of glasses, an alarm clock, a . . ."

The list seemed endless. Dar was amazed that all the items fit into the one trunk.

". . . a copy of the Heimskringla and the Younger Edda. You've heard of them, haven't you?"

"*Nei.* What are they?"

Snorri pounced on the question like a dragon who had just been thrown a nice, juicy bone. "The Heimskringla is a prose history of the kings of Norway. The Edda is a handbook for poets containing a treasury of mythological lore. Snorri Sturluson, the ancestor I was named for, wrote them both back in the thirteenth century."

They might be of some use in the upcoming battle with the fire giants, Dar realized. "I would like to read them."

"Of course, of course. I promised to teach you how to read, and I will. Once we return from Asgard I am sure I'll have plenty of time to go over the alphabet."

Once they returned from Asgard.

"We'll go, but we'll return as soon as possible." Dar stared at Snorri's trunk. "I don't think you'll need to bring that. We won't be staying there long enough to need a change of clothes."

Snorri bit his lip. "I'd rather take it just in case I decide to stay a day or two. You know how much I've always wanted to visit Asgard. It's been my dream, my goal ever since you mentioned the world. Besides, a day here could be a year there. . . ."

His pleading gaze beseeched Dar to understand. Dar couldn't disappoint him. "As you wish."

Snorri ran forward and hugged him. "Thank you, Dar. I knew you would understand."

Dar suffered the embrace as long as he could; then

he cleared his throat. Snorri stepped back and wiped a tear from his eye.

Firedrake flew down the cellar steps, a piece of paper dangling from the side of his mouth.

The scientist retrieved the palm-sized piece of quartz from his workbench and handed it to Dar. "Everyone's here. We can leave whenever you're ready."

Dar tipped back his horned hat. He took a deep breath and motioned for Firedrake to land on his shoulder. "Hold on to the trunk with one hand and my mantle with the other, or one of you may not make it to Asgard."

He felt Snorri's hand tremble as the scientist gripped his mantle and pulled on it with the strength of a half-grown dragon.

"Don't pull so tightly," Dar warned the scientist. "You're choking me."

"Oh dear. I wonder if we should have left a note for Jennifer."

Jennifer! As his soul mate she would sense his leaving. He hoped she would believe his promise to come back to her.

Dar took a deep breath and rolled the crystalite in the palm of his hand. "From Asgard I have arrived, and to Asgard I will return. It is my hope that those in the Hall of the Slain shall see me rematerialize."

He paused as a cloud of foreboding descended upon him. Was Jennifer in trouble? Or was she sensing his returning to Asgard?

"Oh dear, oh dear. Nothing happened. I hope we can get there and back before it breaks again." He peered up at Dar through his thick lenses. "Do you think I could hold the crystal? It would mean a lot to me to be part of the time-traveling process."

Firedrake shifted his weight, bringing Dar back to the present. "If you wish." He handed the stone to the scientist. "I'm going to finish the incantation so hold on tight," Dar said, his voice huskier than normal. "We stand in this house, shining sun shining above us . . ."

The lights around them brightened and began to pulse in time to his words. ". . . thousands of brave warriors from Midgard, the world of Earth, at the tables of Valhalla . . ."

She would know he had left her world. She would feel him depart just as he would sense her despair as he vanished.

". . . we warriors practice daily to hone the skills of warfare so we may be sure to win the battle of Ragnarok, the Twilight of the Gods . . ."

Snorri winced. "Ouch. The crystal is burning my hand. Oh dear, oh dear. I forgot about the heat. I hope the glue holds. If it doesn't, we may not be able to return to Earth. I should have packed a tube of it so we could put the crystal back together again if it separates. Do they have Quick Seal there?"

"*Nei.* There is nothing by that name in Asgard."

What would happen if the crystal could only transport them in one direction? He would be trapped in Asgard, and Jennifer would be here, on Midgard.

He'd made a vow to tell her if he went to Asgard. He had also promised to protect her for the rest of his days. He, Dar, son of Tyr, had sworn it. Yet he had also sworn to save his world from destruction. That vow had been made first. Thousands of people could die if he did not keep his word.

"Are you ready, Dar?"

He nodded, caught in a dilemma of his own making. "In case we are separated you will find Lor, my brother, and warn him of Loki's treachery?"

"Of course, of course. I'll tell Lor everything I know about what will happen in the future."

"Good." He took a deep breath. "You're ready?"

Snorri tightened his grip on Dar's cape. "As ready as I'll ever be."

Ignoring the mantle pressing against his windpipe, Dar raised his arms toward the low ceiling. Thunder shook the ground. A streak of lightning lit up the small windows. Dar began the final words of the spell. "I, Dar, sorcerer of Asgard, do hereby condemn the Giants, our enemies . . ."

Memories of Jennifer's courage as she faced both Loki and Angerboda to save his life made Dar squeeze his eyes closed. No matter how much he wanted to save his family, he couldn't take the chance of leaving Jennifer behind forever, not without telling her of his plans. No, he'd pray that the glue held until he could return to Snorri's house.

His mind made up, Dar dropped his hands by his side. The action caused Snorri to let go of Dar's mantle. The short scientist held the crystal with both hands. "Hurry up, Dar. You've told me the words to the spell a thousand times. I'll finish it."

"Snorri, no!" Dar reached for the crystal, but it was too late. Snorri took a step backward and rested against his trunk.

"Don't worry, Dar, I believe with all my soul that your magical spell will work." Taking a deep breath, the scientist closed his eyes. "I, Snorri, do hereby condemn the Giants, our enemies, to a life of eternal damnation, in another time, another place . . ."

Lightning flickered across the small basement. The crystalite emitted sparks that burned all they touched. Dar could sense Jennifer's despair.

"Oh my . . ." Snorri gasped and arched his back, as if a thousand demons nipped at his body. He dropped the glowing crystalite. His scream, a wail louder than the sound of an enraged witch, echoed through the chamber.

Through the veil of time, Dar could see the rolling green fields of Asgard. In the distance, beyond the river, was the sacred crystal caves. The world exploded into a realm of heat and light. Darkness and pain. Dar felt himself falling away from Snorri.

A swirling void sucked Dar's body and that of his dragon toward a black abyss with no beginning and no end. He gasped as his helmet was torn from his head. Firedrake's talons dug into his shoulder, drawing blood. The void filled with nothingness; then he knew no more as the basement exploded into a million pieces. . . .

Dar had left her! That wrenching pain in her chest, a cross between a collapsed lung and a broken heart, told her that he had used the crystal. She had sensed his life force calling out to her, and then there had been an eruption of immense magical power being invoked.

A tear ran down her cheek, but she didn't bother to brush it away. He was gone! She was on her own. Jennifer knew she had to think of something now or she would soon be buried in an unmarked grave. Once her time was up, it would be too late for her to act.

The gun beneath his Phillies jacket, Snake's eyes narrowed as she moved restlessly. "You do anything funny and I'll kill you right here and now."

To be snide, Jennifer contemplated telling a joke, but she knew from the deadly expression in the Teck leader's eyes that he was serious.

"So where is your friend? How come he ain't here by your side?"

"Dar went home," she said, glad her voice didn't waver. "He left earlier this morning."

"I don't believe you."

What did the man want, copies of Dar's plane tickets? "I don't care if you believe me or not: it's the truth."

Snake must have glimpsed the anguish in her expression because his lips tightened into a thin line that emphasized his gaunt face.

"Aw geez. Of all the times to run home to Mommy."

Of all the times to leave her without even saying good-bye.

"Aw, gee. Do you have to cry?" He looked uncomfortable with the idea and glared at her with hatred shining out of his dark, crazed eyes.

"I miss him," she explained, tears forming on her lashes.

"You're lying, but if your boyfriend doesn't come soon, I'll track him down and waste him after I'm through with you."

Several plans flitted through her mind, but all of them involved using Dar's knife, which was in her handbag on the front passenger side of the car.

Jennifer frowned. Dar had vowed not to leave her without first saying good-bye. He'd never broken a promise, and he probably never would.

Her heart pounded against her chest as she finally admitted her belief. Dar loved her. She would bet anything—even her mother's wedding ring—that he would be coming back to her.

Confident in the knowledge that he loved her as much as she loved him, Jennifer searched her consciousness for some sense of his presence. He was her soul mate. Wouldn't she feel something if he was near?

Then she felt it! A tiny waver, as gentle as the breeze of a butterfly's wing. As soft as a baby's tear. Dar's presence. He would come for her. She believed it with all her heart and soul!

Jennifer's nails dug into the palm of her hand as she tried to think of a plan. She couldn't let Dar walk into a trap. She had to find some way to warn him about Snake.

Dar awoke and knew something was wrong. His surroundings looked nothing like the rolling countryside of Asgard. He was still in Snorri's house, lying at a strange angle with a piece of clothing on his stomach. Reaching down, he removed the square-legged purple-striped underwear and tossed it to the floor.

He couldn't believe Snorri would wear such clothing.

Snorri! Now he remembered. Snorri had separated himself, and when the portal had opened, Dar had been caught in the backlash.

How long had he been unconscious? He had no idea. But one thing was certain: as his soul mate, Jennifer had surely felt the power of the spell he'd cast. She would think he had returned to Asgard and be devastated to think he had broken his vow.

His first instinct was to travel to Asgard to ensure that Snorri had found Odin. But something on the edge of his conscience, a mental plea for help, urged him to find Jennifer as quickly as he could. He could travel to Asgard after he talked to Jennifer.

The phone by the work bench didn't work. Dar

listened in vain for a dial tone but heard only silence. Compelled to find Jennifer so he could explain what had happened, Dar searched for the crystallite that Snorri had dropped. Finding it, he called to his dragon. ''Firedrake! Where are you?''

A pile of papers in front of him grunted, and moved as if shaken by an earthquake. As he watched, a green wing burst through the stack. It was soon followed by long ears and a pointy head. Firedrake chewed a mouthful of paper and looked groggily over at Dar.

''Come, my fine winged friend. Wc must leave.'' Dar bent down and picked up the crystal, now cool to the touch. He searched for signs of separation but found nothing. Relieved, he slid it into his pocket.

The dragon spit out the unchewed portion of notes, which floated to the floor and rested by Dar's foot. Dar picked up the paper and stared at the writing. Snorri had promised to teach him how to read. He would hold him to that promise when they met again in Asgard.

''Let's go,'' he said, checking his pocket and ensuring that both his crystal ball and crystalite were still there.

Firedrake padded over to the workbench and grasped an old brown slipper with his talon. Dar shook his head. ''*Nei!* You don't have time to eat. I must talk to Jennifer. We don't want her to do anything impulsive, like get angry and try to stab me with my own dagger, *já?*''

''Your time's up.'' Snake gestured with his gun. ''Come on. Let's go.''

Jennifer reached over the seat for her handbag. It was starting to get dark and Dar still wasn't back. Now was her last chance to save herself.

"What are you doing?" Snake jabbed her with the barrel of his gun. Jennifer shivered as the wintry wind touched her with its frigid fingers and turned her blood to ice.

"I'm getting my keys," she told him, careful to keep her voice neutral. Her fingers tightened on the soft leather.

"Leave them. We're going in my car." Snake's voice, as deadly as a rattler and just as unforgiving, broke the silence and startled her. "Get over by the red Mustang. It's parked down the street near that big tree. Remember, you do anything funny and you're dead." He stared at her hand. "Killer said you got a secret weapon. Give me your ring. Now."

Anything but her ring! "I can't get it off my finger. It's too tight."

"Don't mess with me. I have a knife in my pocket. If you can't get the ring off, I'll cut off the whole finger."

The thought made her knees so weak, she had to lean on the car. She looked into his eyes . . . eyes so deadly she could see her own casket reflected in them.

"I'll take it off myself." *Then get the knife in her handbag.*

He grinned, an arrogant smirk that made her want to spit in his eye. Jennifer tugged on the dragon's-head ring. She had been telling the truth. It wouldn't budge. After several attempts, it started to move. Finally, she twisted it off her finger and handed it to her kidnapper.

"Good." He put it into the pocket of his jacket. "Now let's go. I'm tired of freezing out here because of you." He lowered his head as he fumbled with the large ring of keys dangling at his belt. "Aw geez! Which one is it?"

While his attention was elsewhere, she opened her handbag wide and grasped the handle of Dar's crystal dagger. It felt warm to the touch, almost as if it were alive.

Jennifer slipped the blade into the palm of her hand. She shut her handbag and hoped she would live long enough to see Dar again. She wanted to tell him how much she loved him. It was something she should have told him a long time ago, but her pride had gotten in the way. This time, when she saw him, she'd tell him that nothing else mattered as long as he held her in his arms.

"Okay. Get in the passenger side and don't try anything unless you like bleeding all over your expensive dress."

Jennifer raised the knife and slashed at his arm.

The gun exploded. Glass shattered.

Jennifer screamed.

Dar slammed the front door of Jennifer's house, relieved that the protective spell hadn't been broken. Still, he sensed a wrongness in the air.

"Jennifer?"

Silence greeted his question. Slowly, ignoring the tap of dragon claws behind him, Dar took out his crystal ball and searched for Jennifer.

In the sparkling depths, he saw her. He also saw the man beside her slap her with his open hand.

Snake! Rage, as hot as a boiling cauldron, bubbled through Dar's veins. Dar unsheathed his sword and gripped the jewel-studded hilt. "Valhalla!"

He ran toward the back door. It slammed against the wall with a force that knocked it off its hinges. It bounced on the ground like a wounded ox with a sword in its throat.

The silence of the evening taunted Dar. Which way had they gone? Dar had no idea. It would take a miracle to find Jennifer, something inhuman, something that could see in the dark and hear a blade of grass hitting the dirt. He glanced upward.

It would take a dragon.

"Firedrake!"

Out of the night soared a green body with a long, pointy tail. Firedrake roared his presence.

Dar waved his sword in the air. "Jennifer. Find Jennifer."

Without blinking an eye, the dragon curled his mighty talons beneath him and flew toward the street. Dar followed, his heart beating wildly at the thought that he might be too late.

In the driveway, he saw the shattered glass from the Jeep windows and knew Snake was responsible. Firedrake circled the car, then screeched. Dar bounded after the dragon, hoping he wasn't too late.

Once Dar turned the corner of the street, he saw them. Jennifer was lying next to a small red metallic "car", a tall man behind her. Even from this distance, he could see the redness of her cheek, as if someone had slapped her. Anger boiled in his veins. It exploded in a roar. "Jennifer!"

"Dar!" Jennifer pushed against the door of the car and stood up. The man standing behind her muttered a curse and pinned her to his side as he aimed his gun at Dar. Jennifer struggled in his embrace and tried to deflect the weapon. Snake's arm weaved as he tried to make her let go of the gun.

She screamed.

Dar saw a flash of light erupt from the tip of the weapon. Jennifer stopped struggling and slid to the ground, her mouth open in a soundless scream, her eyes glazed with shock. Her hands came away, awash with blood.

"Noooo!" Dar's shout of denial echoed through the air. Lightning flashed from his raised sword. Thunder shook the ground.

Snake raised his gun and pointed it at Dar. "Killer sends his regards."

His entire concentration on Jennifer's still form, Dar didn't worry about himself. He ran to her side, hurled himself to his knees, and felt for a pulse. It was weak, but still there. Snake stood by, obviously awestruck by Dar's lack of concern for himself.

"If she dies, you'll rue the day you were born." Dar pulled her into his arms. His hands grew damp as he touched her shoulder.

Standing behind Jennifer's body, his gun pointed at Dar's head, Snake threw back his head and laughed. "I hate to mention this, man, but I'm the one with the weapon. If you believe in God, now's a good time to say your prayers."

Dar ignored him.

"Later, dude—"

Dar had only minutes to save Jennifer's life. Since Snake didn't have any powers, Dar couldn't use his abilities, but that didn't stop him from using his fists.

A snarl on his lips, Dar laid Jennifer aside, sprang to his feet, and stood in front of the gun. Snake grinned evilly and pulled the trigger. *"Stodva."* The bullet fell harmlessly to the ground.

"What the—" Snake emptied the chamber, a bullet at a time.

Dar waited until the gun was empty before he drew back his arm and punched the gang leader in the jaw. Snake went flying through the air. He landed on the hood of his car, gasping for breath.

Worried about Jennifer losing so much blood, Dar ignored the gang leader and knelt at her side. He felt in his mantle for his runes.

"This time I'll cut your throat," Snake promised as he advanced, a long knife in his hands.

Dar reached for his dagger. His scabbard was empty. He'd given the blade to Jennifer. Even though he was willing to battle Snake with his bare hands, Dar realized he might have only seconds to save Jennifer's life. Besides, he had a more deadly weapon at his disposal.

"Firedrake!"

An earth-shaking roar shattered the silence. Snake looked up just in time to see a form plummet from the sky and sink its talons into his shoulder.

The knife clattered to the ground. Firedrake exposed his razor-sharp teeth. Snake screamed, a high-pitched wail that rivaled that of a witch's screech. Dar held Jennifer to him as he watched the furious dragon chase the evil gang leader.

Dar took deep breaths, his whole attention returned to the still woman in his arms. With trembling hands, he searched for his healing rune.

"Stay calm," he told himself. "You've healed countless wounded warriors on a daily basis. 'Tis nothing different. Just do as you've done thousands of times before."

True, he screamed silently, *but I have never healed anyone that I loved as much as I love the Protector of my Heart.* He dropped the rune and had to search frantically under the car, but he couldn't find the small bone object.

He felt Jennifer's life ebbing as clearly as if he saw her blood draining down a deep hole. Life and death. Light and darkness. He could see death as she came to claim Jennifer. Dressed in black robes, the hag carried a staff made of the bones of those long buried. One-half of the wraith was living flesh, the other half a corpse.

"Hela." It was Loki's third child, the spawn of Angerboda. Hela guarded the gates of the dead, her trusty hound, Garm, at her side. She welcomed all who passed through her domain and never let them walk back to the land of the living.

Dar stared death in the face and willed her to leave before she claimed a life. He saw her approach and hurried to stop the skeletal hand from touching the woman in his arms.

He didn't have time to take out his crystal ball. This time, he would break through the Midgard wall of energy blocking his abilities and save her life, no matter what might happen. He had to.

"Powers of the moon, strength from the sea . . ." He concentrated on the energy surrounding him. Oblivious to everything else, he dug deep inside himself. There, he found his hatred for his enemies took up almost his entire consciousness. If he wished to save Jennifer, he would have to push it aside, focus on the present and not the future.

Changing his focus from warrior to seeker of knowledge took almost all his effort, but he finally did it. The absence of his hatred for the jotuns—an emotion he'd carried since birth—left a large hole that was soon filled with peace, and it was something that allowed him to see things clearly for the first time in his life. As he saw the layers and layers of destiny woven into the universe, something inside him snapped. Power, like that he experienced near the sacred crystal caves, flowed through his body.

He harnessed it and focused it.

He commanded it.

The wind, a mere whisper of air, blew with the strength of a gale. Clouds flitted across the sky and swirled with the power of his thoughts.

"Healing powers, harken to me . . ."

Hela shielded her eyes in the face of his blinding strength. Her hand, bones bleached a startling white, returned to her side.

"I, Dar, sorcerer of Asgard, do command it!"

At first, nothing happened. The wind died a slow death. Then, as Dar watched, Hela began to fade into nothingness until only the stench of decaying flesh remained.

Jennifer groaned and stirred in his arms. "Ouch! It feels like I've been run over by a truck."

Dar removed his hand from the wound. Even without his rune, the bleeding had stopped and her wound had started to heal. "It's okay, sprite. You'll live." He looked up; Hela was gone.

"I never doubted it, not with you around to save me." She winced as she tried to sit up.

He sat back on his heels, relieved that she did not understand how close she had come to dying. She had not seen Hela. Glad he had healed her before she lost too much blood, Dar blinked away tears.

"I've got something really important to tell you." She leaned closer into his embrace and whispered happily to him. "I got the job today!"

The icy wind tugged at Dar's hair.

"You know what, Dar? I'm glad about the job, but none of that matters as long as I'm with you." Catching sight of his face, she reached out her hand and touched his damp cheek. "Why are you crying?"

"Because I'm happy." His voice was gruff, but it was the best he could manage.

"You're happy because I got the job?" She wrapped her arms around his neck and pulled him closer.

"I am happy that you are alive."

"Of course I'm alive! You have a strange sense of humor. But then again, what can one expect from a Norseman? Especially one who doesn't wear underwear."

How could she joke now? How could he make her understand the depth of his love? He tried to think of the cultural differences between his worlds. Although they were joined according to his customs, they still had not spoken their vows in front of witnesses.

"Will you marry me, sprite?" Glistening tears bathed her cheeks. Dar wiped them away. "Why do you cry? Are you not happy I asked for your hand in marriage?"

"I've never been happier in my life," she whispered huskily. "I'd be thrilled to marry you."

"Good. Then I'm happy also." Dar tightened his arms around her. If he moved his head forward just a little bit, his lips would be touching hers. He contemplated kissing her, then changed his mind. He didn't want her to exert herself. If she wasn't careful, her wound could open again.

But she obviously had other things on her mind besides her health. Dar groaned as Jennifer kissed him. Unable to resist the temptation, he put his hand inside her clothing and ran his hand down her back.

"By the tail of Garm, you are not—"

"Wearing anything underneath my pants. I know. I wanted to surprise you," she whispered against his neck. "I figured if you could go around without underwear, so could I."

A car zoomed by, its lights illuminating Jennifer's

handbag, lying against the curb, and a set of keys covered with blood. Snake's blood.

Dar pulled Jennifer closer to the warmth of his body. His body responded to her nearness, something he had never experienced with other women. Jennifer aroused him so much, he couldn't keep his hands off her, but now was neither the time nor the place to act upon his desires. Careful to keep his back to the street, Dar gave her one more lingering kiss; then he vaulted to his feet and lifted her into his arms.

"Dar! What are you doing? I'm fine. I can walk. Put me down."

"*Nei.* You're still weak." He jogged toward her house. "How do you feel?"

"My shoulder is a little sore, but otherwise I feel fine." A contented sigh on her lips, she rested her head against his shoulder and closed her eyes. "Have I told you I love you?"

Dar stopped running long enough to kiss the top of her head. "I love you more than life itself. Sleep, sprite. You'll heal faster." He'd tell her about the crystalite another time.

". . . another time, another place." Lor had barely uttered the last word of the incantation when he saw that Loki was returning to the Hall of the Slain. This was the first time the jotun had appeared before witnesses. Now, Loki would have to explain his actions.

"Stand back," he shouted to the warriors around him. " 'Tis Loki."

Odin jumped to his feet. He hurried to stand at Lor's side. " 'Tis as you said, Dragon Master. The Trickster does return from another world."

"*Já.* But Dar is not among those materializing."

"You're right, Lor. But don't give up. One day we

will find my missing grandson. Then we will rejoice at his homecoming.''

The bands of energy broke as Loki and Angerboda collapsed at their feet. Three demons, newly created and hungry for flesh, formed in front of the witch. With a loud screech that rivaled Angerboda's terrified scream, the demons flew toward the round shields that made up the roof of the hall.

Lor muttered a curse as dragons of all sizes and colors ranging from brown to blue to green roared as the rancid odor of the vile creatures reached their keen noses. Even Firestorm, Lor's well-trained dragon, sprang to his feet and unfolded his wings. His nose quivered with anticipation.

With a wave of Lor's hands, the dragons responded. They attacked the demons without mercy. Soon, only scraps of black, rancid skin littered Valhalla's floor. And that was eaten by the dogs sprawled at the feet of the Vanir and Aesir.

Odin took one look at Loki's disheveled appearance and curled his lip in disgust. ''You've gone too far this time, blood brother. I will not lift a hand in your defense.'' The leader of Asgard turned toward Lor. ''He is yours, Dragon Master. I leave it to you to choose his punishment.''

With those words, Lor's grandfather spun on his heel and returned to the dais and his untouched dinner.

Lor raised his hands toward the rafters and tried to transcend time and space to send a message to his brother. ''Dar! Heed my words. I will not rest until I have found you and returned you to your rightful place as Sorcerer of Asgard. I, Lor, son of Tyr, Dragon Master of Asgard, do hereby swear this on my sword. . . .''

* * *

Startled by the realness of the dream and the intensity of Lor's voice, Jennifer moved closer to Dar's naked body.

"'Tis all right, sprite. I'm here. Nothing will harm you. I swear it."

She rested her head on his shoulder and smiled. It had been over a week since her encounter with Snake. In that time, Dar had spent almost every moment she was home showing her how much he loved her. Now they had all the weekend to make love, something she'd been looking forward to ever since she'd started her new job, work she loved almost as much as the man beside her.

The late morning sun promised another beautiful day. Jennifer rubbed her thigh against his hairy leg and reveled in his body's response.

"Be careful, sprite. You don't know what you awaken. I won't be responsible if you continue your actions."

She kissed the golden hair covering his chest. His low groan encouraged her to become bolder, more daring.

"I'm so glad Jason, Henry, and Killer are behind bars I feel much safer knowing they're locked up and will be in prison for a long time to come. I think I'll cut out that article with their picture in the courtroom and tape it to the refrigerator."

"Snorri hasn't called in over a week." She continued her explorations, running her hands down his flat stomach. "I've had so much on my mind since I started work, I forgot to ask you about your visit with Snorri. How did it go? Did you warn your people about Loki?"

Dar sat up and stilled her hand. "As you have

probably guessed, Snorri has fixed the crystalite."

"Oh, my God! That's wonderful! Where is it? You didn't leave it with him, did you?" she asked nervously. "You know how he has a habit of losing things."

Dar squeezed her hand. "*Nei.* I didn't leave it with him. I have it in the pocket of my mantle." He paused. "While we are discussing the crystal . . ."

Somehow, she knew whatever he was going to say would affect the rest of her life. "Yes?"

"I thought I could use it, today, to return to Asgard."

Asgard. The palace of the Gods.

"I see," she said, fearing her whole world was falling apart right before her eyes.

"I was wondering if you would like to go with me."

Jennifer's hands tightened into fists. "I get ill at the first sign of blood. Someone like me wouldn't fit into your world, Dar."

"On the contrary. When everyone in Asgard hears about the way you helped stop Loki and saved my life, they will cheer and add your deeds to the songs sung around the campfires."

Could he be telling the truth? Jennifer wanted to believe him but needed more reassurance.

"You think differently than those in my land," he continued. "Unlike some warriors I know, you do not allow your anger to overcome your common sense, and you have the wealth of another world's knowledge at your fingertips. Asgard has need of someone like you."

Interested in spite of herself, Jennifer raised her eyebrows. "Really?"

Dar drew her into his arms and pressed her against

his naked chest. "With you at my side, we would have the power of both worlds at our command. No one has ever bested Loki as you did."

"It was nothing," she whispered, embarrassed at his praise.

"I do not agree. Very few people would dare to stand up against the Trickster. You were very brave. When the warriors hear how many times you've saved my life, everyone will wish to talk to you about ways to trick the jotuns."

The temptation to go with him grew stronger, but still Jennifer hesitated.

As if sensing her resolve weakening, Dar whispered in her ear. "Songs will be sung praising your beauty. You don't even need to pack. Everything you need would be provided for you in Asgard. You can choose from the softest, finest material in the kingdom." He moved back and looked into her eyes. "Will you come with me, sprite? I love you and will abide by whatever decision you make."

Jennifer saw the hopeful expression he tried to hide. Dar missed his world. He was also afraid that if he left her behind, he might not be able to come back for her.

She thought about her job, her new friends, and knew that Dar's love was more important than any earthly possession. Besides, Dar believed in her ability to conquer this new challenge.

Emboldened by the thought that she might help to ensure that his whole world wasn't destroyed by Loki's treachery, Jennifer threw her arms around Dar's neck.

"I look forward to meeting your family," she told him, "and seeing Asgard."

Dar gave her a lingering kiss on the lips. Jennifer

groaned when he broke away. "You will like my home, sprite. There are many treasures I have yet to mention to you."

"I don't need treasures when I have you, Dar." She leaned forward to kiss his cheek. "So finish telling me about Snorri. Knowing him, he's probably up to something that will get him into trouble."

"You don't need to worry about Snorri," he whispered, his voice husky with desire. "He's probably at this moment in the Hall of the Slain talking to Odin and my brother, Lor. If he hadn't let go of my mantle, I, too, would be there to warn my people—then I would have returned for you."

Jennifer smiled, relieved that the scientist had finally achieved his dream of going to Asgard. "Do you think he made it without any problems?" she asked as her hands burned a path down his stomach.

"I guarantee it."

Dar flipped her onto her back and pinned her there with his muscular frame. A callused hand caressed her body and made her hunger for more.

"Maybe we'll leave after dinner," he growled, trailing a finger down her stomach. "Right now I can think of something else I'd rather do."

The peal of the doorbell was soon followed by the roar of a dragon. Jennifer almost cried out with desire as Dar slid off the bed and reached for his pants and mantle.

"Don't move. I'll be back as quickly as I can."

Even with Killer behind bars, Dar always ran to answer the phone or the door before she did. Jennifer watched her warrior pad toward the stairs, his bare feet sticking out from beneath his amethyst cape. Jennifer threw on a sweat suit and an old pair of sneakers and hurried after him. If there was trouble, she wanted to be the first to know about it.

She reached the living room just as Dar threw open the door. The expression on his face was priceless as he hurried to put his sword behind his back before Mrs. Nordstrom could see it.

"Oh, there you are, dear. I almost gave up hope that you'd be home." Their elderly neighbor hugged a small wicker basket against her chest.

"Hi, Elvira," Jennifer said. "What can we do for you? Would you like to come in?

"No, dear. Much as I'd like to, I can't stay," Elvira said sadly. "Family matters take precedence over our weekly chats. Marcus has had a little accident. He's in the hospital. There was some kind of explosion in his lab. The scientist who called didn't give me all the details, but I'm sure Marcus will tell me all about it once I get there."

Her friend flipped open the lid of the basket and revealed her kitten. "Puddin' and I are going to nurse him back to full health. I just wanted to let you know that I may be gone for a couple of weeks. I didn't want you to worry about us."

The sound of sharp talons on carpeted stairs made Jennifer step closer to Dar. "Now that you mention trips, Dar and I are going to go visit his family. I'm not sure if—"

Dar put his arm around her and pulled her closer to his comforting warmth. "What Jennifer is trying to say is that she isn't sure when we will return. We may stay in Asgard for an indefinite amount of time."

"Why, that's wonderful, dear!" Elvira smiled. "If the people are half as nice as Dar, you'll love it there."

She should make arrangements just in case she decided not to return, Jennifer decided, wondering if fate had been telling her something by sending their neighbor over at just this moment in time.

"Elvira, would you mind taking care of my house for a while?"

"Of course, dear." Mrs. Nordstrom winked. "For however long you need me."

"There are people coming to fix it up," Jennifer continued, "but they've been paid. I don't know when we'll be back."

Beside her, Dar tensed. "Are you sure, sprite?"

Now was the time to show him how much she loved him. "I'm sure, Dar."

Making her decision, Jennifer found a piece of paper and quickly gave her friend power of attorney to make all decisions regarding her property and estate.

"There's a bag of gold underneath my bed," Jennifer told the older woman.

Dar put his arm around Jennifer's waist. "There is also a bag of jewels beside my spell bag on the bureau."

"Oh, my. I'll take care of everything," Elvira promised, putting down the basket so she could hug both Dar and Jennifer.

Firedrake padded closer. Before Jennifer could react, Puddin' jumped out of the basket and ran across the living room. As she watched, the kitten curled up into a tiny orange ball on her sofa.

"Oh, my God!"

His head down and his pointy tail in the air, Firedrake tiptoed toward the sofa. Dar raised his sword.

"Oh, isn't that cute," Mrs. Nordstrom cooed. "Your little bird is going to say hello to Puddin'."

It wouldn't be cute if the dragon ate the cat right before their neighbor's eyes. Jennifer decided to take drastic measures. Before the dragon could attack, she grabbed him by the scruff of his scaly neck and raised him to eye level.

"Firedrake, if you lay one talon on that kitten, you'll regret it." She shook him until his little green wings hung limp at his sides. "I'll buy a bushel of bird seed and feed it to you until you start chirping. Do you hear me?"

"Jennifer, stand back," Dar ordered, his sword gleaming in the bright sunlight. "I'll take care of the matter."

"No. That's okay. I think your *bird* and I have come to an understanding, haven't we, Firedrake?"

The dragon nodded. His translation crystal bobbed against his wide chest.

"Good. Now, if you know what's good for you, you will play nice with Mrs. Nordstrom's kitten."

Jennifer set the dragon down on the floor and, hands on hips, waited to see what he would do next.

"I don't think this is a good idea, sprite. Stand back, just in case."

She watched Firedrake stare longingly toward the cat, then turn back to look at her, a regretful expression on his face. "Oh, I don't think we have to worry, Dar. I think Firedrake has seen the light."

"Light?" Dar looked around the living room. "What light?"

Mrs. Nordstrom set the empty basket down on the floor. "Come on, Puddin'. It's time to go."

Jennifer gathered up the cat and put it into the basket, eternally grateful that Firedrake hated bird seed.

"Well, as much as I would like to stay and chat, I have to go." Elvira closed the lid of the basket. "Have a safe trip to Asgard."

"We will," Jennifer replied. "Good-bye, Elvira. Say hello to Marcus for me."

"Sure. Now that he's in bed, he might actually have time to listen to my stories about Dar. You know how famous scientists are; they never have any time for their mothers." She waved as she left. " 'Bye!"

Firedrake padded over to the door with a slipper between his two paws and stared forlornly after Mrs. Nordstrom. Jennifer ignored the dragon and urged Dar toward the stairs and their bed. "Forget about the slippers. I'll get a new pair when we get to Asgard. Come on. I think we have some unfinished business to discuss."

"Were any of your ancestors sorcerers?"

It was an odd question, but he sounded serious, so she answered truthfully. "There were a couple of sea captains, a few merchants, and a pirate, but no sorcerers that I know of." She smiled.

"Amazing. I never expected to love a woman who could charm demons and command dragons to do their will." He pulled her into his arms. "I haven't forgotten my promise. Once we reach Asgard we will be married according to your customs."

Jennifer could just see it now. She would walk down a long aisle of Valhalla in a white lace gown. Fierce warriors would be sitting at the long tables with their swords raised in a salute. Dar would wear his ceremonial costume, complete with mantle and no underwear.

Desire surged through Jennifer as she stared at Dar's naked torso. She licked her lips. "I just had the wildest fantasy. How about if we leave for Asgard now, find a nice pile of hay, and continue our lessons of love there, right behind the Hall of the Slain?"

Dar lowered his head until his lips hovered over

her mouth. Her heart soared as his roaming hands and hard body promised her delights beyond her imagination and limitless nights spent within the circle of his loving arms.

"Far be it for a mere sorcerer to deny a sprite her desires," he whispered between long, passionate kisses. "Do you need to gather your belongings?"

Jennifer realized she had everything she needed right there in front of her. "No. I'm ready when you are."

"Good. Then I can begin the incantation."

She looked down at his bare feet. "Don't you want to put on your boots?"

"*Nei.* It would take too long. I have a strange compulsion to find a pile of hay as quickly as I can."

She felt the same way. A smile on her lips, she kissed the base of his neck. "Then what are we waiting for? Let's go."

With one arm around her waist, Dar used his free hand to reach into his mantle and pull out his crystal ball. "Firedrake, leave the slipper. You will have tastier things to nibble on when we arrive in Asgard."

The dragon spread his wings and soared gracefully into the air. He landed on Dar's shoulder and stared at Jennifer from his lofty perch. She could have sworn the dragon winked.

Dar tightened his grip around her waist. Jennifer took one last look around her house, then closed her eyes and prepared herself for the journey.

"From Asgard I have arrived, and to Asgard I will return . . ."

She pressed her head against his chest and listened to the steady beat of his heart.

". . . we stand in this house, the sun of Midgard above us . . ."

The lights around them brightened and began to pulse in time to his words. "... thousands of brave warriors from Midgard, the world of Earth, at the tables of Valhalla ..."

"I love you," she whispered. "With all my heart."

"I love you, too, sprite. I promise that I will protect you always and love you with all my heart," he replied, his lips near her ear.

Her fierce protector. Her tender lover. What more could a woman ask for?

"... we warriors practice daily to hone the skills of warfare so we may be sure to win the battle of Ragnarok, the Twilight of the Gods ..."

Jennifer held tight to her soul mate's mantle as she felt herself being hurled toward a black void. The exhilaration of the moment far exceeded the discomfort as the transportation began.

Then Dar said the words that would change their lives forever. "I, Dar, sorcerer of Asgard, do hereby send us to another time, another place ..."

As she started to dematerialize, Jennifer knew a moment of fear. Then she felt his arms tighten around her and knew everything would be all right. Dar had said they would be together, and she knew in her heart that he always kept his promises.

Firedrake's roar echoed off the walls of the room.

Dar's mantle swirled around them as a strong wind whipped through their hair. Jennifer leaned her head against Dar's chest and held on tightly to his hand as a loud clap of thunder sent them to another time, another place.

"Valhalla!"

THE RELUCTANT VIKING
SANDRA HILL

The Key
Lynsay Sands